Bright
Morning

Kate Roberts

One Bright Morning

Translated by

Gillian Clarke

Gomer

Published in 2008 by
Gomer Press, Llandysul, Ceredigion, SA44 4JL

ISBN 978 1 84323 959 8

A CIP record for this title is available from the British Library.

The original Welsh-language version was first published in instalments
in 1957-8 in *Y Faner ac Amserau Cymru* under the title *Tegwch y Bore*.

This book is published with the financial support of the
Welsh Books Council.

Printed and bound in Wales at
Gomer Press, Llandysul, Ceredigion

1

'Something's burning.' Dilys Roberts came into the common room, closing the door behind her.

'Take the saucepan off the stove, someone!' Betty Jones waved the spoon wildly in the air, where she stood stirring cocoa into cold milk in a row of cups on a tray.

Ann Owen snatched the saucepan from the gas stove as the milk began to rise, and she bore it swiftly to the tray, the milk subsiding.

'Did you burn yourself, Ann?' voices called.

'No. I'm thick-skinned.'

Everyone laughed.

'Just a little in each cup,' said Betty. 'Oh, the milk has curdled.'

'I'll get some more,' said Dilys, setting off at once.

That was just like Dilys. Willing, reliable, serious Dilys, slenderest of all the girls. Her eyes were large and round, giving her thin face the expression of an owl. The others had the rich-fleshed, round-faced look of youth.

'Dora! Dora!' they cried as Dora Lewis followed Dilys into the room. In their excitement to welcome Dora, no-one remembered to thank Dilys for fetching the milk. Small Dora with her round body, clear amber eyes, russet hair, wide smile, and the sweetest nature of them all.

'Bring it here, Dilys. We can top it up with cold. It doesn't matter if it's not boiling. It's only a farewell do, not a welcome party.' Betty stood possessively over the cups.

'I shouldn't be here,' said Dora, 'not being a member of the senior common room.'

'So what?' said Maggie Bevan. 'We can't do without you. You practically live here anyway.'

'I have spent a lot of my time with you,' Dora admitted. 'I'd rather your company than my room-mate's.'

They sat about anywhere, on chairs, on the arms of chairs, on the floor. Dilys passed the cakes.

'I want a cream one,' said Jennie Davies.

'You're fat enough already. Griffith won't like it if you get any fatter,' said Betty.

The others laughed. Jennie blushed and looked pleased. She was dark and plump. If anyone teased her about Griffith her short neck completely disappeared into her shoulders. Her cheeks nestled in the frills of her lace-trimmed collar, worn a shade too high for her round face. She was in love with Griffith, a brilliant chemistry student, and she never stopped talking about him, night or day, to anyone willing to lend a ear. Most of them listened generously because they were fond of her.

Gwyneth Hughes leaned thoughtfully against the fender. She was as different from Jennie as it was possible to be. Bosomy, with smooth light-brown hair brushed and coiled into a fashionable chignon halfway between her nape and the crown of her head, she would never dream of choosing a collar that did not suit her. It was Llew Vincent, the handsomest man in college, whom she loved.

'Penny for your thoughts, Gwyneth,' said Jennie, hoping to share some talk of love.

'They're not worth a penny.'

'No?' said Dora. 'That's no way to talk about the best-looking, most charming, if not the cleverest man in college.'

Gwyneth kept her silence. She smiled with eyes so luminous they seemed wet with tears. Her love was not for student gossip. She was a diligent student, and the strain of revising for exams had left shadows under her eyes. The only time Gwyneth squandered were those moments spent in conversation with Llew as they strolled the college corridors. Unlike Jennie, she faced with a clear mind one truth about her love for Llew: that it was not reciprocated. Gwyneth returned her attention to the chattering company.

'There's someone who'll be sorry to leave tomorrow,' said Maggie Bevan. 'Ann there.'

There followed a chorus of cries. Ann flushed. 'She's a dark horse, but she has plenty to say to Richard Edmund.'

Dora winked at Ann.

A stranger entering the room would not have looked twice at Ann. Of average height, oval-faced, with good teeth, rather dark hair and grey eyes, she was a girl whose beauty seemed a matter of chance. Her clothes were the cast-offs of a well-heeled cousin of similar build. But it was no chance that her blouse was perfectly pressed, nor that the embroidered double collar, worn not a whit too high, was finished neatly with the tie favoured by most of the girls. Her hair was coiled fastidiously into a roll at the back of her head and finished with the ribbon of black velvet fashionable in 1913. It was only when you spoke directly to her that you really noticed Ann Owen's face, expressive, changing from moment to moment, from sentence to sentence. Now her look of yearning turned to anger at being teased about Richard Edmund.

'You can't tell us it's nothing,' said Mattie Lloyd, who had been listening in silence. Her honey-coloured hair, dark-blue eyes and dark brows against a honey and roses complexion drew everyone's gaze, whatever she wore. Her face was expressionless.

'I've told you it's nothing,' said Ann, her face burning.

Their laughter mocked her fierce denial.

Suddenly a grey head appeared round the common-room door. It was the warden.

'Oh! The Welsh girls!' she said, in English, then disappeared.

'Who did she expect?' said Maggie Bevan. 'Japanese?'

Everyone burst out laughing. When they finished, a silence fell over the room like the silence in the dinner hour in summer. Small sighs arose from various corners. 'This time next year where will we be?' Dora wondered aloud. She was the only one who was not leaving college.

'*Where will I be in a hundred years*? as the old tramp used to sing round the streets of Treorchy in the old days. *You won't even get to Tonypandy if you don't get your daps on*, said the passing collier.'

This time no-one laughed with Maggie. South Wales was a foreign country, and they didn't get the joke.

'Where will we be tomorrow, come to that?' asked Ann.

'I'll be home in the Rhondda eating a hearty supper,' said Maggie.

The conversation, like their college days, had dwindled, and one by one they rose and quietly left the room.

Dora linked arms with Ann and led her upstairs to the room she shared with another second-year student.

'Let's have a cup of tea. That cocoa was horrible. We'll cut some bread and butter.'

She walked along the landing to put the kettle on the gas ring. They ate without speaking for a long while.

'You're lucky to have another year', said Ann, 'though I'll be glad to earn some money. Three happy years, gone like a dream.'

'And ending with even more promise than they began,' said Dora. 'Come on, you can tell me. How much do you like Richard? Are you "keen", as the girls say?'

'It's the truth. He's just a friend. I've only known him a month.'

'A lot can happen in a month.'

'Nothing very exciting to me. I like the boy, but I'm not in love with him.'

'It's a shame you're leaving. It'll be strange for me. I'm going to try for a room of my own next year. I'd prefer that to sharing. I'm sick and tired of Rachel.'

'Dora! I've never heard you speak a bad word about anyone before. I'm shocked.'

'She's so mean. If she came in now she'd want to share our tea. She never buys anything herself. When she wants something she takes it.'

'A shame we didn't meet sooner, then we could have shared a room. Here we are, the pleasures of friendship only just beginning, and it's goodbye.'

'Yes, but we can write to each other, and, who knows, maybe we can share a place one day.'

'It won't be the same. Time will change us. The atmosphere in the common room tonight could never be recreated. If we met in a year, wore the same clothes, made ourselves the same awful cocoa, it would be different.'

'Oh, Ann, you do sound low. Look forward! Think of the future!'

'To what?'

'It's pointless to look back. Lay your college days by in a treasure chest, and open it from time to time.'

'I'm on my own from now on.'

'What a wonderful chance for someone as special as you. You can work miracles.'

'With sixty children in a class?'

'Good experience. It'll help you get a better job in the future.'

'You are a ray of sunlight, Dora.'

They kissed each other goodnight.

They could hear the distant sounds of young men going their different ways after their own farewell parties.

As she walked along the corridor on her way to bed, Ann met Rachel. They passed like strangers with a brief 'Goodnight'.

In bed Ann found herself weeping silently. They were not tears of regret for her college days. She'd told Dora she was afraid of her new life alone, but it wasn't strictly true. She looked forward to independence. Had she been forced to stay another year, she would have been disappointed. What hurt was to hear Dora speak ill of Rachel. Perfection was spoilt. Dora, the friend without fault, who saw the best in everyone. To Dora everyone was nice. The minister was nice. His wife was nice. His congregation were nice. Few of the students were Baptists, so Dora often found herself invited to tea at the minister's house, where, of course, everyone was nice. Yet Dora had found a flaw in her room-mate's character. Would she soon also find fault with Ann? Dora had fallen from grace, and despite the cocoa, the banter, the comradeship, the evening was spoilt. By tomorrow night they would all have scattered far and wide, but it should have been an evening for the treasure chest, as Dora put it. She and Dora had been so close, two in one, the perfect friendship. Tonight a hairline crack had appeared, not enough to shatter, but a flaw in what had been immaculate. Oh, Dora, Dora! The unchangeable had changed.

Ann turned away from the sight of girls chattering their way down the path from the hall to the road, to look back at the ugly, red-brick building, with its regular rows of rectangular windows, where she had felt so much at home for the past three years of her life. It looked as strange and as unwelcoming as it had on her first day. Except for the porch. The curve of the porch was beautiful, with its pair of white clematis meeting over the arch. At first, even the porch had looked dark and unfriendly, but for her it had changed when, coming out of lectures, she was welcomed inside by young voices and the aromas of cooking, and the hall table where, every morning, letters lay waiting. To a country girl the porch seemed grand and elegant. To leave this building with its clematis-clad porch for a smallholding with monkshood and wolfbane at the gate was like leaving the elegance of Paris for an old-fashioned, homespun country village. For three months the great door would remain closed, the building empty and silent, until new voices came to wake it in the autumn.

The crowd at the station mingled, luggage wagons weaving among wicker baskets with hockey sticks and tennis racquets strapped to them. An outburst of cheering greeted each favourite coming down the steps onto the platform. Laughter dominated the sound of the crowd. A few couples stood apart from the throng, whispering or looking into each other's eyes, as they had also stood apart in the college lobby. As Dora had not yet arrived, for a moment Ann belonged among the crowd, with no-one special to talk to. Richard Edmund came down the stairs unnoticed. He looked scholarly, tall and thin with mouse-brown hair and deep-set eyes whose colour you could not name. Suddenly shy, Ann turned her head as if to study the rails. Richard approached her.

'Mind the truck,' he said, catching her arm. She moved awkwardly in his grip. She looked down a moment, then ventured a question.

'Have you come to join the fun?'

A stupid question, she thought. She knew he'd be leaving at the weekend.

'I wouldn't call it fun. It's sad to watch friends go. I'll be seeing a lot of them next year, but it won't be the same.'

'When are you going home?'

'Early next week. I'm in no hurry. I can't call anywhere home.'

'Oh?' said Ann abruptly as though she had received a shock.

'I'm an only child. My parents died when I was young. I'm going to my elderly uncle, but there's no hurry. I'm glad of an excuse to see the Professor about my dissertation.'

She could think of nothing to say.

'Where's your green cap? You look beautiful in it,' said Richard.

'In my bag. It's easier to pack than this one.'

She knew her green cap was prettier than the black parson's hat she was wearing. She'd bought it last year in Wrexham when she was on teaching practice. It was made of six triangular sections sewn in a circle, with a double row of top-stitching at the rim. Just a hint of curly hair showed beneath it. She didn't think a man would notice. His compliment melted her reserve.

'May I visit you sometimes at Blaen Ddôl?'

'Of course,' she said. 'It'll be a nice change from reading all the time.'

'I hadn't thought of it quite like that,' he replied.

At that moment Dora came towards them down the station steps. She smiled at them curiously. The train drew in before another word could be spoken. Dora said 'Goodbye' quickly, and crossed the bridge to the other platform to wait for her own train. Richard waited at the carriage door until the very last moment, then, just as the train began to move, he caught hold of her hand. He took off his cap, and stood waving on the platform until the train was swallowed by the tunnel.

As the train drew into the station at Caer Sant, Ann looked up from checking her luggage to see two eyes looking at her between the bars of the gate, like the sad eyes of a monkey in a cage. Her brother Bobi was the last person she expected to see. Bobi and home were far from her thoughts. On the journey in the train only two things had swum round and round in her mind like fish gleaming in a lake: the green cap, and that small squeeze of her hand. Student days were over. Something new had begun.

Of course, it was Bobi's dinner hour from the shop. He ran to her and picked up her bag.

'What's the matter?' she asked, seeing his pale face.

'I'm hungry,' he said. 'The stingy housekeeper gives us disgusting rancid sausages and keeps the best food for herself and her cronies and the boss doesn't know.'

'Here,' said Ann, handing him sixpence. 'Go and buy yourself something to eat. I mustn't miss the brake.'

'Oh, Nani! Can you spare it?'

'I think so. I sold some of my books.'

'Not all of them, I hope.'

'No. I kept the Black Book, and a few others.'

'Is that an interesting book?'

She tried not to laugh at his eager innocence.

'No, but I thought I should keep it. What do you want for supper tonight?'

'Have you any money left?'

'Yes, I have.'

'How much?'

'I can spare half a crown.'

'Oh, Nani, a tin of tongue. We can get one for two and fourpence, enough for five.'

'All right.'

'And Nani, it's my first communion tomorrow night and I'm scared.'

'It's nothing to worry about. We can talk about it tomorrow. Goodbye Bobi bach, and stop worrying.'

The brake was full of women sitting close together, their knees touching to make a table where they rested their baskets, just as a few hours earlier they had set out their butter on the tables in the market hall.

'Well, Ann. Have you finished in College?' asked one.

'Yes.'

'How nice to have finished your studies,' said another woman with heartfelt warmth.

Some of them gazed on her fondly, while others stared as if in their opinion she had no business going to college at all. Ann turned her head away and said nothing. The fish glimmering in her mind were joined by another. Bobi's innocence. Had it been a mistake to send him to work in a draper's shop, instead of the quarry?

As she reached the door of her home she breathed the aroma of coffee. A brimming jug covered with a saucer steamed on the hob, and a plate of bacon and eggs was keeping hot on the stand that clung to the grate with iron claws like a bird to its roost.

'I couldn't think of anything else,' said her mother. 'Your father won't think of lifting potatoes before the hay is in.'

'Oh, this will be lovely.'

'I must get back to my butter. We have a two-week old calf, and the cow is giving so much milk, or I wouldn't be churning today.'

'Where's the calf?'

'Gone to the Foty to be reared. A very pretty heifer calf, black and white.'

'Oh! What a pity. I'd love to see it.' Her childhood had not quite deserted her.

She went into the dairy where her mother was slapping a pat of butter into shape on the slate slab.

'It's too warm. It's soft as a pancake,' said her mother.

'It looks fine. There's not a crack in it. I saw Bobi in town. He doesn't look well.'

'I know. That old housekeeper who works for the boss doesn't feed the lads properly.'

'I bought a tin of tongue for supper.'

Her mother said nothing. She bent her head over the churn and put her finger into the hole in the handle to clear the cream, then she pulled a scalding dishcloth through it. Ann felt a pang of disappointment.

'Well,' said her mother lifting her head again, 'no need to beg money off anyone to send you to college any more.'

Ann knew it was true, all too uncomfortably true. Why did her mother have to bring it up now? She gritted her teeth like stones on slate, and thought of the surprise she had brought for supper. Her mother looked tired. Already her cheeks had begun to fall in like the cheeks of old women. In the glow of the skylight her skin was sallow. Tenderness welled up in Ann, and she held her tongue.

'I'll clean the house for you. It won't take long. But I'll go and see Dad first.'

'He's in the stackyard,' said her mother. She looked suddenly happy. 'Look, I won't stay long over at Mam's tonight. I'll come home as soon as I can and make us a bit of supper with the tin of tongue. There's lettuce in the field. We'll have a real feast.'

Her father was in the stackyard trampling heather for the foundations of the haystack, sometimes treading on the spot, gazing out over the fields instead of down at his feet. Like a horse stamping, Ann thought to herself, in her college Welsh.

'Hi!'

'Hi!'

Her father walked towards her, pushing his cap far back on his head and resting his arms on the gatepost. Sweat stood in the creases of his forehead and he looked into her face like some trusting old dog, as the quarrymen look when they are together.

'And when do you start at Blaen Ddôl?'

'Tuesday.'

'You've got the whole world in front of you now.'

How good it was to hear someone talk of beginnings instead of endings. She saw herself on a white cloud swimming in the air, the world before her, and not a single footprint on the snow. She returned to the present.

'I've brought us a tin of tongue for supper.'

Her father smiled. He was fond of his food.

2

They did not have the tin of tongue for supper that night after all. As they finished tea Huw walked in, shaking water-drops from his hair and radiating pride. He held fifteen trout laid out on a bed of grass and wrapped in a cotton handkerchief. His bearing demanded applause. This was his first big catch. He tossed the fish onto the table among the tea things, where they gleamed, silver and starry.

At first Ann gasped to see the result of his new-found skill, such a great haul landed with his bare hands. Then she felt hurt. She could have saved her half-crown. Disappointment sharpened into pain, as if she'd let a gold sovereign slip through a hole in her pocket. Fate always brought a famine or a feast. In Fate's place stood Huw. She kept her admiration to herself. Some of the trout were scarcely bigger than minnows and Huw should have followed the old song's advice, and cast them back to the cold waters of the river.

'But I thought . . .' began Bobi as he came in and sat down at the supper table, before he was silenced by a look from Ann.

'Look, Bobi. Aren't they good?' said Huw.

'Easy to know who paid for these,' said Bobi.

'Not you, boy,' said Huw.

'They *are* good,' said Ann fervently, stressing the word to show her victory over the meanness which had overwhelmed her momentarily at teatime. Her mother fried the trout in butter, for once forbearing to say, 'It'll all be the same in a hundred years.' And indeed they were good, their silver turned to gold.

His mother answered Bobi's unspoken question. 'The tongue will keep. The trout won't.'

'Is there tongue?' asked Huw.

'Yes,' said Bobi proudly, 'Ann bought it for supper.'

'Oh, we can have it in the week.'

'No you won't,' said Bobi fiercely, 'we'll eat it when Ann and I are here, won't we Mam?'

'Yes. It's a big tin.'

'It's only fair,' said Ann, to herself.

Sunday dinner was over. Ann and Bobi washed up in the dairy while their mother had a nap in her chair by the fire and their father went off to bed. Huw was reading a Scriptural commentary on the sofa. Ann threw the red chenille cloth over the kitchen table and tidied the room. As she set off for her walk in the fields she sensed peace settle on the kitchen like heavy velvet. She walked through the potato fields to her stone, the special stone where she'd played house on a thousand childhood days, and where, when she was too grown-up to play, she went to dream.

The stone was her castle, a great boulder half-moated by the shallow ditch, half-resting against the bank where the hedge leaned over to make a natural cupboard where she'd hidden her things. This had always been a place for her alone. It was hers, her private place to stow away treasures and the secrets of the heart. She'd guarded her den fiercely against all intruders, every horde of blackberry-gatherers. 'It's *my* den, mine!' Once such a place has been so possessed and loved, it never loses its place in the heart.

Today the ditch was dry and shady, hidden by long summer grasses, the stone solitary beyond its curve. She too loved solitude, not all the time of course, but she had always needed time to be alone, time for her own thoughts. So often, since she was old enough to think, she found herself at odds with people.

But this was no time to hide herself away. Bobi needed her. She remembered how nervous he was about his first communion and her promise to talk to him about it. She must return at once.

'I'm scared about tonight,' he said.

'What about? About holding your own cup?'

'No. It'll be easier than passing the big one. But I don't know what I'm supposed to think about.'

They'd never talked about religion. It was private, and difficult.

'You're supposed to think about the sufferings of Christ.'

'All the time? I can't. It's an awful long time to be thinking about something like that. I know I'll start thinking about that horrible old housekeeper.'

'Oh, Bobi! Don't think about angry things. Think of Mam and Dad.'

'I'll think about you giving me sixpence. What a shame we couldn't have the tongue for dinner.'

'It'll all be one in a hundred years. Are you feeling better now?'

'I'll think about nice things. They only taught us the catechism. They never told us how to think.'

Reason told her that meditation on suffering was appropriate for such an occasion, but her heart said Bobi was too young to understand. The sermon was long and tedious. The preacher was American and he quoted verses in a monotonous voice, wandering about aimlessly from Calvary to the Garden of Eden. Ann wandered too. She was with Richard, talking on the station platform. She went over the conversation again and again. Had she read too much into it? Maybe he'd forgotten all about it already. As her father had said, her whole life lay before her. She tried not to think about Bobi, but he kept coming back into her mind. She could see his back as he sat in the front pew. She looked at the place below her bowed head, and there she saw his initials, R.O., carved with a knife. She hadn't noticed them last time she was home. A heaviness lay on her heart. She'd felt spiteful towards Huw over the trout yesterday afternoon and wished she'd kept her half-crown. Petty thoughts that cried out for forgiveness. People troubled her. She was forever raging at some injustice or other. It hadn't occurred to her mother that the tin of tongue should be kept until she and Bobi were home to share it. Nothing mattered to Mam except thrift. A tin of tongue would serve five so she wouldn't waste it on three. Such meanness of spirit troubled Ann deeply. Was this what religion was about? Was Christ's greatest ordeal having to put up with people?

The service was dignified enough, the readings fitting. Ann felt sorry for the row of children in the front pew. There was more to first communion than becoming members of the chapel. They were putting childhood behind them. They were adults now. She thought of her stone and of all the times she'd sat there when Bobi was just a baby in a shawl in her arms, her face against the soft hair which grew close to his head like the unopened bowl of a buttercup, she full of her own thoughts, Bobi pointing at everything with his fat little fingers, saying 'Ooh! Ooh!'

Children, preacher and deacons shimmered before her eyes as if sunlight were playing on creatures in a cage of latticed wires. She realised she was watching them through tears. Her heart was a fool to feel so tender. They were fine, strong children, fit for life.

'He that was rich became poor for our sakes,' said the preacher. Sacrifice! They were always going on about sacrifice. Parents' sacrifice to put the likes of her through College. What sort of sacrifice was that when you had to pay it all back one day anyway? It was a struggle, certainly, but she was tired of hearing about sacrifice. It was a misuse of language, in her opinion. She was at it again, raging away in the midst of Bobi's first communion. The family had never wanted for anything. There was meat for dinner, cake for tea, trout for supper. Bobi ought to be ashamed of himself telling her he was starving. None of them had ever starved, had ever endured real want, or cold, or nakedness, or war.

The service and Ann's raging drew to a close, and everyone walked out quietly. She waited outside for Bobi, and they walked home together in silence.

3

On Monday morning two letters arrived, an unusual event in the country. One bore Dora's handwriting. The other had a Bangor postmark, though Ann did not recognise the hand. Maybe it was from Richard Edmund. She flushed at the thought. As it was only hours since she had spoken to both of them, the contents must be important. She opened Dora's letter first.

> ... I've been worrying ever since we parted on Saturday. I wanted to cross the bridge to say goodbye, but you were talking to you-know-who. I was in a quandary. Should I say goodbye or keep my distance? In the end I felt I just had to speak to you. I was drawn as by a magnet, although my head warned me I shouldn't. Now I'm worried I may have blighted your life like blind fate. Maybe R.E. was about to say something important and I blundered in and the chance has gone forever. These things happen ...

What a worrier Dora was! It was typical of her to fret about being tactless. Ann opened the other letter.

> Dear Miss Owen,
> Were I not such a lazy fellow I would have arrived at the station in time for a proper talk to you on Saturday morning, though our brief time together ought to have been enough for what I wanted to say. When you want to say something really important you don't need much time. But I didn't say it, and I find it even more difficult in a letter. However, as you've given me permission, I will come to see you in Blaen Ddôl.
> > Sincerely,
> > Richard Edmund

> Dear Dora,
> Thank you for your letter received this morning. A letter from you and one from RE, so soon after saying goodbye, made me think something dreadful must have happened.

No, you have not blighted my life. RE had nothing to say to me on Saturday morning, nor in his letter today. He seems to have something on his mind, but his letter is extremely prosaic. The prosaic is difficult to interpret. One can search the forest of the poetic for metaphors in the undergrowth, meanings stirring the trees, and still find nothing, but in a garden of flowery words there is at least the chance that the writer has hidden a message of admiration. However, when someone like RE tells me in a roundabout prosaic way that he wants to see me in my new surroundings, I can't tell if he wants to bring me a message of great importance, or just come to tea.

Had you not interrupted us he would not have written. His mind is set deep as his eyes inside that head of his. I think he may improve on further acquaintance.

You'd think I'd be feeling on top of the world. But I'm not. The prospect of starting her first job terrifies this 22-year-old girl. I know nothing about Blaen Ddôl, or the school, or the landlady. I only know she is a widow, and the place is clean. Before I went to College at least I knew we'd all be in the same boat, that we were in it together. Remember how Prof used to sing, 'Oh, Lord, let them teach me well, and let me learn slowly'?

There I go again! Nostalgia! However, hope springs eternal. I could do without a trauma with Richard just now. I need to concentrate on my new career. Maybe if he never does manage to speak his mind, it'll be for the best. Had I met him sooner I'm sure my degree would have suffered, and it was hardly brilliant anyway.

The past three days at home I've felt so restless. I just can't settle at all. On Saturday I tried to get rid of my energy and stop myself thinking by cleaning the house top to bottom. I just wanted to run in the fields like a pig in the wind. I couldn't even sit still in chapel, and as I could hardly run up and down the pews, my mind went racing instead.

I wonder what sort of place Blaen Ddôl will turn out to be? When I put up my hair and wore my first long skirt (and that was a real change for a schoolgirl) my ankles felt hot but my neck felt cold. I'll be cold all over out there in the world earning my living. In college we were all piled up like a cairn and treated as one. From now on we are each on our own.

I must admit I was shocked on Friday night to hear you run Rachel down, yet only yesterday I found myself feeling critical of my own mother. Twice in one afternoon I was blaming her for being unfair. At communion I felt guilty about it. She's gone to look so old and worn.

I have to wear my old clothes to go to Blaen Ddôl. Mam says I can have new things after the summer holidays. She's seen some nice material in the shop in Pentre Isa, charcoal wool with a fine green stripe. One of my relatives is an excellent dressmaker. I'll take her a picture of one of the new narrow skirts to copy.

I went to visit Nain yesterday. As usual she had the Bible open and her reading glasses beside her. She was sitting in her chair waiting for me. She made me a lovely tea, a loaf she'd baked herself and the best butter you've ever tasted and some red-crusted cheese. As I left she gave me five shillings. 'For passing your exams.' A whole week's pension!

In the morning Mam and I did the washing and ironing and we packed my luggage. It was a lovely drying day, and we pegged out with the sun in our eyes. Mam wrapped some butter in rhubarb leaves for me, and enough bacon, eggs and bara brith to last the week. I'll be setting off like a quarryman for the barracks on a Monday morning. By Friday next I'll have devoured all the food and a week of my new life as a teacher.

Dear Dora, if you could only be with me hidden behind the blackboard when I'm giving my lessons next week.

Affectionately,

Ann

PS I have talked of nothing but myself. Letters can be self-centred things.

4

One day after school Ann hurried home, looking forward to her tea in Mrs Evans's cosy parlour. It was the only meal of the day she ate alone and she relished the privacy, the chance to be herself. As she was the only lodger meals were quiet times, but tea on her own in the parlour seemed as luxurious as a visit to the hairdresser. She could stretch out and indulge in a lovely long think. Today she was more than usually happy. She'd prepared her lessons well and the hours flew by so fast she hadn't looked at the clock once. The children had enjoyed using clay and old tea-trays to make castles like those built by Edward I.

She put the day aside, as full of hope as a woman setting a crock of yeast-dough close to the fire to rise under a clean cloth. The evenings were drawing in. She looked forward to the fireside, and a book.

Mrs Evans was in the hall to meet her. 'Miss Owen. You've run out of bread.'

Ann had just remembered she needed bread. She walked to the shop to buy a loaf and two small cakes for her tea. She took them into the kitchen to cut her bread and butter. Mrs Evans put a doily on the plate, and placed the two little cakes on it as if she were performing a sacred rite. Despite her efforts she could not make the arrangement pleasing.

She looked up, scrutinising Ann from head to toe. 'You have chalk on your skirt and in your hair,' she said, as if Ann were a child getting ready for school in the morning.

'Could be worse,' said Ann. 'Better than head-lice.'

'For shame!'

'Teachers often catch head-lice from the children.'

'Not in Blaen Ddôl!'

'Good heavens! Even lords and ladies catch germs at gooseberry time.'

'Gooseberry-time has been and gone.'

'Not in the hills.'

'You talk like a book.'

'That's how one should talk.'

Mrs Evans laughed . 'I certainly could not talk like that,' she said.

'Of course you could. You know your Bible?' she said.

Mrs Evans sat on a chair and bent her head, laughing.

'What's wrong?'

'I can just hear myself saying, *"and Job answered and said".'*

Ann began to laugh. 'No. It wouldn't do at all.'

She carried the plates to the parlour and Mrs Evans brought in the teapot, and left, closing the door behind her. Alone in the room Ann felt like purring. The two cakes looked less forlorn now and the buttered bread was ribbed like sand left by an ebbing tide. Mrs Evans had put jam in a clean dish, with a silver spoon beside it. The cloth on which they stood was spotlessly white and starched.

Ann paused, teapot poised between table and cup, and listened. She could hear someone talking. Mrs Evans came into the parlour and said, 'There's a young man to see you, Miss Owen.' Someone was standing behind her in the passage. It was Richard Edmund.

'Oh!' said Ann, standing awkwardly over the poised teapot like a housewife caught wearing a grubby apron by unexpected visitors. Then she straightened up, recovering her dignity.

'Mrs Evans, I'd like you to meet Mr Richard Edmund from Bangor College. He is reading for his master's degree, and has come to Blaen Ddôl to research Roman remains.'

Richard looked taken aback for a moment, before he took the hint.

'Yes. I really ought to have warned Miss Owen that I would be coming today, so that she could make enquiries for me.'

'Well!' said Mrs Evans, 'I have lived here in Blaen Ddôl for more than half a century and never till this moment heard of any Roman remains.'

'People forget about things. Interest in history comes and goes.'

Mrs Evans's gaze was expressionless, as it had been in the kitchen.

'I'll fetch another cup and saucer,' she said.

As Mrs Evans left the room, Ann put a finger on her lips and grimaced at Richard. Mrs Evans returned with the china and a slice of rhubarb tart on a plate. The door closed and the two were silent for a moment before Ann burst out laughing.

'What's funny?'

'The rhubarb tart.'

'What about it?'

'Too much for one, not enough for two. Are you good at Maths? Can you divide it.'

'Half a helping each!'

'No, but I can cut it in two.'

'And make it three quarters each.'

They laughed together. 'It's for you,' Ann said. 'It wasn't on the menu before you arrived.'

'Don't be silly.' And the portion was cut into two.

They pulled their chairs towards the fire. Ann eyed his cycle-clips. No matter how attractive a man might be, cycle clips could put a girl off. Richard, as if reading her mind, bent down and took off the clips.

'Did you cycle all the way from Anglesey?'

'Not all in one day. I stayed in Bangor last night, and I'm returning to Bangor tonight.'

'Are you working?'

'Yes. Though not on Roman remains. That was a good one. I'd never have thought of such a good story.'

'Well the story worked. It produced rhubarb tart.'

'How are things going?'

'It's too soon to say. It's hard work.'

'You should be teaching in a Grammar School, with small classes.'

''I'd miss something about this place.'

'You're worth more than sixty pounds a year.'

'It seems like a fortune to me. Because I started before the summer break I get holiday pay too.'

Richard gazed at her. She looked beautiful in her white blouse with green spots and a green skirt, loose tendrils of hair curling against her neck. She was still no more than a girl herself, and it was wrong that she had to teach such a big class. He saw it wearing her down in a few years, the roundness of her face giving way to lines. The fire had flushed her cheeks, and she stared into the flames, smiling.

'What are you thinking about, Miss Owen?' he said.

'Oh, Ann, please.'

'Ann, then.'

'I was just thinking how lovely it is to be sitting here quietly together by the fire.'

'You have a good place here.'

'Yes. Mrs Evans is not the usual sort of landlady.'

'Like the ones in Bangor.'

'Maybe. I don't know any Bangor landladies, but this one is an interesting person.'

'In what way?'

'Well, she's a bit pious, but she has a sense of humour.'

'That's an odd mixture!'

'She can be sharp, she can be charming.'

'A natural combination.'

At that moment there was a tap at the door, and Mrs Evans came into the room.

'Aren't you coming to chapel, Miss Owen?'

'Not tonight, Mrs Evans.'

'Don't let me stop you,' said Richard. 'I must be going soon if I'm to get to Bangor before dark.'

At the mention of chapel Ann felt the spell break. Richard tucked his trousers into the cycle-clips and at once became a rather ordinary, not particularly appealing young man. He paused, full of something he wanted to say, but could not speak.

'May I come and see you again?'

'Of course you can, though I don't know what Mrs Evans will think.'

'Could we meet somewhere else?'

She bit her lip and thought about it. 'We'll see,' she said.

Once he had gone she couldn't settle down to read. She sat staring into the flames. A chance had been lost, and it was her own fault. She thought of Richard cycling all the way from Bangor just to see her. He must be attracted to her, and yet he had said nothing of his feelings. They planned to meet again. That was something.

Ann turned from the fire at last and began to clear the table. She walked back and fore between the parlour and the scullery, carrying the dishes, thinking about the rhubarb tart. Mrs Evans had hidden it from her but had produced it when Richard arrived. Was that a sign of meanness? Or had she thought the table looked rather bare, and brought the tart to give it a more abundant air? In the end she gave Mrs Evans the benefit of the doubt. After all Richard got his portion. She washed up and began to prepare supper as a nice surprise for her landlady. They could have boiled eggs, she decided. She had more than enough to spare. The water was already simmering when Mrs Evans came back from chapel.

'You missed a good prayer meeting at the *seiat* tonight, Miss Owen,' she said.

'Really? Would you like a boiled egg for your supper?'

'That's very kind of you.'

'I have plenty of eggs.'

'There were quite a few in chapel, considering it's the first night after the holidays. Will you come with me next week, Miss Owen?'

'Thank you. I'd rather not, if you don't mind.'

Mrs Evans stared at her as if she'd refused a hundred pounds. 'You won't?'

'I don't like the *seiat*. I never went in college.'

Neither spoke a word during supper. The older woman looked sullen. The younger half-smiled, not smugly, but because she felt she had offended her landlady and she was trying very hard to look pleasant. When supper was over they turned to the fire. Mrs Evans sat on the three-legged stool and stared in front of her.

'Tell me, Miss Owen, if you don't mind my asking, what have you got against the *seiat*?'

'Well, I think that kind of prayer meeting might have been appropriate long ago, when people felt the need to confess their sins in public. But who wants to make such an exhibition of oneself today?'

'It's not just a public confession. It's sharing your religious experience.'

'No, of course it isn't,' said Ann impatiently. 'People say the first thing that comes into their heads. If they dared to confess their true feelings the chapel would be emptied in a moment, or it would be packed full.'

'What do you mean?'

'The thoughts that pass through the mind, even in chapel, can be horrifying. You surely don't believe that the nice little verses of scripture and what they say about them are their true inner thoughts?'

'You never know. Maybe people are recalling powerful spiritual experiences from their past. Perhaps the feelings come back to them.'

'I can imagine such memories coming back as you fall asleep at night, but not to order in chapel.'

'You've picked up some odd ideas in college.'

'I didn't learn such ideas there. College doesn't give you ideas. When I lived at home, going to the *seiat* used to drive me crazy. Seeing some man, or often a woman, crying as she recited a verse from the Bible, knowing she was too mean to put a coin in the hand of a hungry child.'

'Maybe that's why she was crying.'

At that they both managed to laugh. But Mrs Evans had not yet got everything off her chest.

'Do your parents go to the *seiat*?'

'Not regularly. They are thoughtful people, but not pious. They'd die on the spot if someone asked them to express spontaneous religious experience.'

'Do they attend chapel on Sunday?'

'Of course. I'd like to see someone in Wales today try to miss chapel. They'd be chased with a pitchfork.'

'But you like going to Sunday chapel?'

'Yes, I do, and to the meeting after. People are more honest there.'

'The minister will be calling on you soon.'

'Oh, I hope not.'

'Why? He thinks he's caught a big fish, having you as a member. He'll give you plenty to do.'

'Oh, dear. It's peace and quiet I want,' said Ann. She remembered the kind of evening she'd looked forward to as she walked home from school. There always seemed to be something to shatter her peace. She was ready for bed, but Mrs Evans hadn't finished with her.

'Mr Edmund must be a clever young man to be doing his MA so early.'

'Yes. And he works hard.'

'Are you courting?'

'Not yet.'

Mrs Evans looked hard at Ann as if she were mad, and as if her parents must be crazy to let her out of their sight for five minutes.

'Will you be courting one day?'

'I don't know. All I am certain of is that we are not courting now. I may still be saying so when I'm eighty.'

'I don't believe he came to research Roman remains.'

'Time and his thesis will tell. A man may kill two birds with one stone.'

Ann took her candle and went to bed. Her head was splitting and she was relieved to rest it on her pillow. She felt as though she'd been cross-examined in court. Had she been able to answer her interrogator with a clear yes or no there'd still be no peace. Word would spread that she was a strange girl. Despite her denial she had no doubt that tongues would wag and people would say she was courting. She went over the evening's events from the moment she got home from school. Would things have turned out differently had she expected Richard? She could have warned Mrs Evans. She would have prepared more food. She would have rehearsed the visit over and over again. Maybe that's how the chapel folk prepared themselves for the *seiat*, rehearsing their emotions over and over until they believed they were real. She had handed the seed of doubt to Mrs Evans, and now she regretted her words. Mrs Evans was a sincere woman and Ann had sown unease in her mind instead of letting her keep her illusions about the *seiat* people. What was the use of poking a dead fire? It wouldn't quieten her own mind. Nothing could banish her own doubts.

And there was Richard. His visit troubled her. She had felt awkward. It had been like acting in a play and he could not find the words to say what was on his mind. It wasn't her own home, everything around her was rented, and even her words had seemed borrowed. Richard was such a laconic man. 'You can't converse with a mute,' as the saying goes, even with a flood of borrowed words. Yet she mulled over his brief visit with pleasure, like rereading a treasured letter, remembering an exchanged glance, a gesture, a smile. She turned the hours over in her mind and school was forgotten. Teaching was just a job that had to be faced. The other was something for slow savouring. Mrs Evans's interrogation was an irritation to be endured. Where would it all lead? Out of the mists sweeping her mind one clear fact emerged: an event might last a moment, analysing it could last a lifetime.

5

Ann made her way home from school one afternoon, her head down against the wind, mulling over her day. Nothing out of the ordinary had happened, yet everything seemed to conspire to frustrate her teaching. The days raced past, but she felt she was getting nowhere, as a dog chained to a wheel runs to exhaustion without gaining ground. She was sure it was because the headmaster's desk was in her room, which meant he overheard most of her lessons. As she reached the front doorstep of her lodgings, she sensed rather than saw someone step from the doorway of the shop next door. It was Bobi. She was surprised to see him. It wasn't his half-day. Something must be wrong. He looked upset and he'd been crying.

'Bobi! What's wrong?'

'I'm in trouble.'

'That housekeeper again?'

'Yes. I've left the shop.'

'Come in. We'll talk in the house. Wait here a minute.'

She went into the shop to buy a tin of salmon.

'Whatever the problem is let's talk about it over a good tea.'

She took his hand and led him into the passage.

'Mrs Evans. This is my brother, Bobi, come from town to see me.'

'How are you, young man? You work in a shop don't you? You've finished early.'

'Yes,' Ann spoke quickly, realising Mrs Evans had also noticed it couldn't be Bobi's half-day. 'He's not well, and came to see me instead of going home, not to worry our parents.'

Bobi's appearance supported the lie.

'Well, come in and have a bit of food to warm you up, my boy.' And off she went to fetch more plates.

'Now, tell me what happened.'

'I can't stand it there another minute. That housekeeper is getting worse. We have less food every day, and I know it's not the boss's fault.'

'How do you know?'

'I can see what's in the pantry. The door's always open and there's plenty of food in there. She's always making supper for some old witch from the town, and it's our food she's using. I caught them red-handed last night.'

Bobi looked better already, from the relief of telling his story as much as from the good meal he was eating. Warmth flowed through Ann as she watched him, her tender sisterly feelings giving way to pride. Satisfaction too, at watching him enjoy the salmon and bread-and-butter. Mrs Evans brought in another full plate.

'I was famished,' he said, reaching for another slice.

'Eat as much as you want. Right?'

'I went to chapel last night, I was so miserable in the house. When the boys are in they won't let me read in peace. They don't like reading. All they want to do is walk round town whistling at girls. I've been with them sometimes, but I can't see the fun of it. I feel stupid walking the streets with them. If I stay in, the old witch wants to see the back of me. So I went to the fellowship meeting.'

'The *seiat*! Did you enjoy it?'

'It was all right. I don't like the rubbish in the cinema, and it costs money.'

His sister smiled but Bobi spoke in earnest.

'The minister thanked me. No-one has thanked me for anything for ages. In town they look at you as if you're dirt.'

'Good for him then.'

'I went back happy as a cuckoo, really looking forward to my supper. I could smell frying halfway down the street. But who was there when I reached the house but Lady Toffeenose with a frying pan full of chops. You should have seen her face. She thought she'd got rid of me for the night. She gave me bread and cheese, and tea, and I sat on the sofa reading while they wolfed down the chops.'

'Where were the boys?'

'Walking the streets till late, as usual. All they got was bread and cheese and the smell of chops, like me.'

'So what happened?'

'Nothing last night, but today we had corned beef for dinner. I wouldn't grumble if we had potatoes and butter with it, but one measly slice of corned beef! At a guess I think we were supposed to have the corned beef last night and the chops for our dinner today. I don't know what Mr Price had because he eats his dinner half an hour before us.'

'Why did you come here?'

'I've had enough. I told her my dinner was stingy, and I walked out. So here I am.'

'What did the others say?'

'Nothing. They do the grumbling and let me do the talking. Will B. has finished his apprenticeship so he ought to speak out.'

Bobi fell silent and Ann felt a rush of pity for him again. They were all in a trap. There was no future for a boy in the quarry and many young men were emigrating to America. Education was beyond the purse of most people, and shop work was miserable. They were slaves. She was a slave in school, and her father was a slave in the quarry.

'I'm afraid I've lost my job now,' said Bobi, and I don't know how to tell Mam and Dad. If only the buses came our way, I could live at home.' He began to shake.

'They probably will one day. Don't worry, I'll come with you to talk to Mr Price.'

'Will you, Nani? He'll listen to you. Thanks for a nice tea.'

30

'I'm going to town with my brother, Mrs Evans. I'll catch the eight o'clock bus back.'

On the bus Bobi grew depressed again. Ann would have done anything to make him happy. Had she a purse full of coins she would have handed it to him, just to hear him laugh. He was only a skinny boy in knee breeches. Even though she thoroughly disapproved of the *seiat* she was glad he had found refuge there. How shaky were her principles, approving for other people what wasn't good enough for her. She was no better than the gentry offering their cast-offs to the poor. One minute she despised herself, the next she was making excuses. She wasn't forced to walk the streets to avoid some bullying housekeeper. How pleased Mrs Evans would have been to hear Bobi say he'd enjoyed the fellowship meeting! She sought fresh reasons for her own hypocrisy: Bobi had, after all, chosen the lesser of two evils. He probably had not really understood the full significance of what went on at the *seiat*, and he didn't like the cinema. A job in town was a country boy's dream, yet the closer they got to the town the more they realised the dream was an illusion. As the town approached she felt Bobi trembling. His hands were pushed down hard into his pockets and his elbows hugged his sides. A few hours earlier he had been brave, rising boldly from the table and striding out. Ann too felt her legs shake at the thought of confronting the big man in his grand house, presenting her little brother's case before the judgment of the rich. They were afraid, not of standing up for justice, but of the consequences. They weren't cowards like Will B. No-one in her family was guilty of dodging the truth. The great dread was poverty. Her family had never been paupers, dependent on the parish. She had no choice, she must save Bobi's job and his lodgings. Away then, to face the lord in his court.

Ann told Bobi to wait at the end of the street while she went to talk to the boss.

'Here, a shilling to spend. Before I'm done that housekeeper's turned-up nose will be pointing at the floor.'

Bobi laughed aloud. She walked up the street, through the gate, and pressed the doorbell firmly. She imagined someone quaking already in the kitchen. In the seconds before the door opened she prayed for strength to say the right thing. She was taken aback when the door was opened by Mr Price himself.

'Mr Price?'

'Yes.'

'I'm Bobi's sister. Could I have a word with you please?'

'Come in.'

She followed him into the parlour where a glowing fire greeted them. The whole room was red. On the floor was a red carpet with green flowers, the sofa and chairs were of red plush, the wallpaper was red. Against one wall stood a mahogany chiffonier. The fireplace was made of marble and on the mantelpiece stood a black marble clock. The atmosphere was hot and heavy. A brass bracket on the wall over the fireplace held a gas lamp that sang ceaselessly.

'Do sit down.'

'I'm sorry to bother you, but Bobi is very unhappy.'

'He has brought his trouble on himself.'

'Not without good reason.'

'I hear that he complained that his food was not good enough, and that he walked out. I had returned to the shop when it happened.'

Ann looked at Mr Price, wondering how much she dared say. So far his response was discouraging. His face was expressionless as a shop's dummy, an assemblage of features, mouth, nose and eyes. His body seemed no more than a stuffed suit of good quality cloth, only a developing paunch making him more human than the figures in his shop windows.

'It's not as simple as that,' said Ann. 'It's not the first time the food has been poor.'

'The food is not poor. It's always those who eat worst at home who are the first to complain.'

Ann felt anger rise like bubbles fizzing in a siphon. She paused a moment for the turmoil to subside.

'That's not true. Did you notice my mother when she came with Bobi?'

'No, I did not.'

'My mother has only had new clothes once this century and that was because a bonnet and cape had gone out of fashion for middle-aged women. She had a new coat then.'

This gave her time to cool down.

'What has that to do with it?'

'Everything. My mother would rather do without new clothes to make sure her family is well-fed.'

She felt cool and controlled. Mr Price had been staring into the hearth as if talking to the fire. Now he turned to face her, frowning. Then he looked into the fire again, rubbing the red plush arms of the chair with his hands.

'The boys eat the same food as I do,' he said.

Ann's voice was innocent. 'Growing boys need more than one slice of corned beef for dinner.'

'Who gets one slice of corned beef for dinner?' said Mr Price, his voice raised.

'That's what Bobi told me. Have I misunderstood?'

'I had chops, and they should have had chops too. I will soon find out what they had for dinner.'

'There's nothing wrong with corned beef, as long as there's something to go with it.'

'But that was for supper last night.'

'Unless I am mistaken, they were given bread and cheese last night.'

He rose suddenly from his chair as if he had been struck.

'I'll look into it. Where is Bobi now?'

'I left him waiting at the end of the street.'

'Tell him to come to the house, to the front door so that I can have a word with him.'

'I hope he doesn't lose his place. I know he tries hard to please you, Mr Price.'

'Yes, he's a good lad, he works well and is polite to the customers.'

They reached the hallway and Ann burst into tears, gave one little sob and fell silent.

'Well, he has a first-class ally in his sister anyway. Goodnight, Miss Owen.'

'Goodnight.'

That last sentence revealed for the first time a sign of feeling in Mr Price.

It was dark outside and she could scarcely make out Bobi,

33

leaning against the wall, shivering with cold. She whistled and he came running to her.

'Well?'

'I think everything's alright. He wants you to go in through the front door so that he can talk to you. He's going to look into it. Don't worry.'

'Thank you Nani.'

'Be sensible. Not a word against the housekeeper. Just tell him about the food. I must go. Come and see me again in Blaen Ddôl to let me know what happens.Ta ta.'

'Ta ta.'

As she looked back she saw her brother walking away from her with his head held high, then she heard the gate click shut.

On the bus she curled, exhausted, inside her shell. She thought about her family at home, ignorant of all that had happened. That was just as well, as long as things turned out as she hoped for Bobi. She felt suddenly homesick. She couldn't have said why, but she longed for supper at home tonight. She'd have to tell Mrs Evans the whole story, if only to save being interrogated. 'He works well and is polite to customers.' Is that the limit of Bobi's talent? Or her own? Was that all there was to work, 'good at her job and kind to the children'? Bobi cutting calico and dressmaking material, putting the roll away tidily, making out a bill, giving change. Smiling when you felt like cursing a customer. Looking busy when the boss was looking in case he caught you idling. And nothing to show for it at the end of the week but profit for the boss. Her own life was not so different. At the end of each week she could point to neither profit nor achievement. But at least at the end of her day she could relax in her lodgings, plan her lessons, and read in peace. One could hardly meditate on the subject of cutting calico or buttering-up customers. Her face was flushed from the confrontation and the hot room and she raged once more at the injustice done to her defenceless young brother. The support of a whole tribe of relations would be powerless if Mr Price decided to sack him. How different was her own position! She thought of college days. To be sent down you had to commit a terrible offence. Would she have been expelled for a crime like Bobi's? She'd had no grievance at college, but if she'd had cause for complaint her fellow students would have rallied to her support. Bobi stood brave and alone because the other boys were intimidated by fear of unemployment. That's what being a wage-earner meant: to be terrified of losing one's place, right or wrong. In those happy student days she never spared a thought for such things, or for Bobi, who had no doubt been miserable then too. She was determined that he must never suffer again, even if she had to rescue him from the shop. Somebody had to stand up for the weak.

At home, supper was ready, her toast keeping warm on the stand by the fire.

'I thought toast would do as you had salmon for your tea.'

'Just what I need. I have such a headache.'

'I'm sorry. How is your brother now?'

Ann moved to the table, sat down and told Mrs Evans the whole story. She warmed to her theme as she talked, Bobi's cause growing stronger with her every word, and Mrs Evans's eyes growing wider by the minute. When she heard about the fellowship meeting and the chops she cried out, 'The poor dear boy, and that old skinflint. It's too good a name for her, and that other old woman, whoever she is.'

'He's so young,' said Ann.

'Indeed. Who would send a child to work in a shop?'

'We have no choice. They must work somewhere.'

'Yes. You're right. It's terrible, when you think about it. Something should be done. Things must be changed.'

'How much better off are we?'

'Not at all, really. We just plod blindly on like pit-ponies. Nowhere to turn.'

At this she shook the small curl that lay on her forehead, the little curl she pinned up every day, as she had been doing since about 1860, thought Ann. It might as well be 1860 for all of us. Neither the world nor Mrs Evans's little curl had changed one jot.

'Your brother must come to tea again and tell us all about it,' said the landlady.

'Thank you,' said Ann. 'And thank you for your kindness to him today.'

'Poor lamb, and him not having his chop after going to the fellowship meeting. He shall have chops for his tea when he comes here.'

Ann went to bed, and for the first time that day she thought about Richard. What would he think of Bobi's dilemma, she wondered. She'd heard nothing from him since his visit.

6

Dear Dora,

I can't sleep and my candle's still burning beside my bed, so I thought I'd write to you. I've nothing sad on my mind, but my thoughts are keeping me awake. They weave a web inside my head, no strand stronger than another. If you were here I might be able to express myself better, but even if not, two witches are better than one. Perhaps all this mental hyperactivity is because I have no-one to tell my secrets to. I am the only new member of staff at school this year, so the others have all made their friendships already. They are friendly enough at school, but at the end of the day we all go our separate ways like spokes of an umbrella.

Mrs Evans is very kind to me, gives me a comfortable home and good food. But I can't talk to her. I just answer her questions. She wants to know everything, not in order to listen to me, but because she is so inquisitive. She has a curious mind and I am the little flower where she finds her honey. (I'm not really calling myself a flower!) At least she doesn't carry tales out of school. She is lonely, and maybe my company stops her talking to herself. She's quite a character, and an intelligent woman I think. I suspect she'd like to take me in hand, like a child. She's been trying to get me to go with her to the *seiat*.

She does her hair in a most peculiar style. There's one little ringlet on her forehead, and her head runs in a horizontal line from the curl to the bun on the back of her head, like women in the 1860s. It wouldn't surprise me to see her come into the parlour in a crinoline one day. In spite of her nosiness I like her, but I couldn't share this tangled mesh of thoughts with her. I wonder if I can really talk to anyone but you.

Richard Edmund came here recently. He came without warning, and was given a nice tea and a warm welcome by Mrs Evans. I told her he was doing research round here but she was sharp enough to see through it. I still don't know why he came and haven't heard a word from him since. You'd have thought a journey all the way from Bangor on his bike would have heralded something. What on earth drove him to come all that way? I can't imagine anything but wildfire driving anyone to Blaen Ddôl just for a cup of tea. However, RE is no fire. Nor is he cold. There is something intimate in his expression. He's not inarticulate either, as some young men are, though he speaks hesitantly as if drawing his words from the very depths of his mind. He told me that morning on Bangor station that he has no family but the old uncle with whom he lives. Maybe there's tragedy in his family history. He doesn't talk about it. He works hard, and possibly doesn't want to be distracted from his work. But why did he come here? That and the farewell on Bangor railway station that morning have kept him in my mind.

You'll be wondering why I've said nothing about my job. To tell the truth, it's the last thing I want to talk about. I can't wait for four o'clock each day to come home to my digs for a cosy read by the fire, unless Mrs E tries to chat. I shouldn't feel like that after only a few months of teaching. Perhaps if I could concentrate on teaching my own subject it would be better, or if I and the children had our own classroom. Imagine, there are sixty children on a good day. And next door, through a thin partition, sixty more and two busy teachers. The head's desk is in my classroom, and he's rarely out except when he's teaching woodwork to the big boys. Four times a day the infants pass under my window ten minutes before the end of my lesson, and I can't hear the sound of my own voice.

The head suffers from extraordinary outbursts of rage and whatever is close at hand suffers. As the children in my class are closest to him, they suffer most from his tantrums. The Wednesday morning lesson needs a lot of preparation and, before the bell rang for the first class, two boys were helping me, the head busy at his desk. The boys had clogs on and they were trying to walk tip-toe not to make a noise. The more you try not to, the more noise you make, and the two boys kept kicking the iron feet of the desks with their clogs. They made a dreadful clatter. Eventually the head came out from behind his desk, caught the boy nearest to him by his jersey, lifted him into the air almost as high as the ceiling lamp, and suddenly dropped him. There was a deadly silence. The two teachers next door were watching through the glass partition, terrified. Something weird happened inside my head. I saw a hanged man dangling like a puppet on a string. I caught a glimpse of the boy's shirt between his jersey and his trousers. It was so clean! I suddenly began to weep and then to laugh. Hysteria, I suppose. It lasted a few moments and the headmaster glared at me, stupefied. The two boys sat down, the one who was dropped was white as a sheet, his eyes fixed on me. The head stood in the middle of the classroom staring at me, and he walked towards me looking not at me but through me, as though he could see somebody else's head beyond mine. I had to go to the cloakroom to recover.

The incident passed, and nothing like it has happened since. I forget such things when I witness the head take the class. He relieves me sometimes, especially for geography lessons. I suppose he can't resist taking over when he hears my clumsy efforts. He's a born teacher, and can make the children understand things without being too simple or too complicated. On those occasions I really admire him, and feel quite jealous of his skill.

Today Bobi came to see me, having walked out of his job at the shop. I went to town with him to reason with the boss. The poor food wasn't his fault, but the housekeeper's. It was a revelation to me. Three years at college were a life of luxury. I was well-fed, had no worries, and was quite shut away from other people's misery. All the time I was so enjoying my final year, poor Bobi, only a young boy, was working in a shop in town living a very different life from mine. Now I see how unfair it all is. The first injustice was that he wasn't given a chance to stay on in school, and maybe only a couple of marks robbed him of the opportunity. The very thought of it accuses me like an aching vein, throbbing ceaselessly. I want to cry every time I look at Bobi, and am so worried something bad will happen to him. I know this is foolish, but I can't get him out of my mind.

I've spent an hour writing about myself and I haven't said one cheerful thing. But I know you'd listen to all this without interruption if you were here. That's what I call a good friend.

I hope you're enjoying the end of your vacation and that you're looking forward to next term in college. I won't say you're lucky, despite this letter. I am being broken-in to life, and the experience awaits you. It's not easy, but it has to be faced.

Warm regards,
Ann

7

'What a pity you wouldn't let me cook him some chops,' said Mrs Evans, moving round one corner of the table, while Ann moved round the opposite corner as they laid the table together, like two people observing a game of cards.

'No, that would be too neat a solution,' said Ann.

'What do you mean?'

'Well, Bobi was upset because he didn't get chops for his supper, and if we gave him chops for tea today it would look as if we were trying to find the perfect answer.'

'But that's just what we are doing, isn't it? I'm sure you'd be happy if the children gave you perfect answers.'

'Not always or I'd be out of work and the lesson over before I corrected the children. Giving Bobi chops would be too symmetrical, like twin jugs on a dresser.'

Mrs Evans glanced at the china dogs on the mantelpiece.

'Oh, dear! I've put my foot in it again. Actually the dogs are just right. I don't like things to be a perfect match, and they are each other's opposite.'

'Well, your dress matches you. It looks very pretty.'

'It's made up from an old suit.'

It had been made in the latest style, with a narrow skirt and a short bodice. The skirt was joined to the bodice by a strip of green silk, a shade darker than the sage green of the dress. The neck was bound with the same silk, and a band of it ran down the front of the bodice. Mrs Evans wore a black skirt and blouse, with a white collar.

'Bobi did the right thing, walking out like that,' said Mrs Evans, her head on one side like a bird, as she arranged pastries on a plate.

'He did. They were lucky to be rid of the housekeeper so quickly. That's the power of money. Mr Price could afford to give her a month's wages instead of notice.'

'It's worth more than money. The boys were so unhappy.'

'What kind of a woman is the new housekeeper, I wonder?'

'We'll find out when Bobi arrives. It was thoughtful of him to write and tell us.'

Mrs Evans had clearly taken Bobi to heart.

'It was. Fair play to him.'

'The youngest, is he? And really spoilt?'

'Not a bit spoilt. My mother had no time to spoil us. She's sorry now.'

'Well, well!'

'She and my father worked so hard for us. There's no sense in it, trying to keep a two-cow smallholding going, and my father working in the quarry quite a distance from home.'

'No sense in it at all. But at least you must have enjoyed plenty of eggs and milk and butter.'

'That's true,' said Ann, thoughtfully. 'Are you ever afraid something is going to happen to someone, Mrs Evans?'

'To whom, for goodness' sake?'

'I mean, someone you're specially fond of. When I was about nine I used to be scared my father would get killed in the quarry.

Whenever someone called at the school door I thought it was someone come to say my father had been killed.'

'You grew out of it, didn't you?'

'Yes, quite suddenly. Now I've begun to worry about Bobi.'

'The thought of anything happening to my Robert never crossed my mind. But something did happen, and he was only a young man.'

It was Mrs Evans's turn to look thoughtful.

'Why are we talking of such things just before a party?'

'Why indeed?'

They heard a firm rap of the door knocker.

'Here he is!'

Ann ran to the door.

'We were just talking about you.'

'Come to the table, Bobi. You must be famished. Your sister insists that I join you for tea. I don't usually.'

'Of course you must,' said Ann. 'Most of this lovely food is yours.'

Mrs Evans ran to the scullery and filled the silver teapot with boiling water. Ann looked at Bobi. He had made a great effort to look clean and smart. His hair was oiled and his shoes shone. Mrs Evans came in bearing three steaming plates of haddock on a tray. She scurried back for the teapot. The haddock was a surprise to Ann.

'You're looking better, Bobi.'

'Yes. Old Ma Toffeenose had the sack straight away.'

'Tell us all about it.'

'Well, I told Mr Price as much as I could without letting him think I had a grudge against her. He asked the other lads too. I was sorry for them, especially Will B.'

'Why, for Heaven's sake?' asked Ann.

'He's unhappy at home. He's lost his mother, and his father has married again. His stepmother wouldn't understand him being out of work.. You can guess how scared he was.'

'Poor boy!' said Mrs Evans.

'But fair play to him he told Mr Price exactly what I'd told him in the parlour, and John, the other boy, mumbled the same story too.'

41

They all laughed.

'It wasn't funny at the time. My fate was in the balance. By then I felt I didn't care any more. It was the housekeeper's night off and our supper was ready before she went out. We went straight to bed and couldn't sleep a wink. Will was groaning as if he had a fever.'

'What a night!' said Ann.

'All because of an unprincipled old woman,' said Mrs Evans.

'We came down to breakfast so limp you'd think we'd slept on the clothes line, one after the other like a train, hiding behind each other, not wanting to go into the kitchen. I went in first, and one look at Madam was enough to tell us what had happened.'

'How was she?'

'She looked as if she hadn't slept a wink either, like she'd been through a threshing machine. But we had a marvellous big breakfast. By the night she'd gone, and next night another lady was there.'

'And what's she like?'

'So far so good. She's a new broom.'

'She can't be as bad as the last one,' said Ann.

'Mr Price must have been quick about it,' said Mrs Evans.

'That's how he is in the shop, eyes everywhere. What we can't understand is how he was so blind to what was going on.'

'Perhaps he lived in terror of her,' laughed Mrs Evans.

They sat round the fire, and although they tried to squeeze more out of the housekeeper story, they failed. The saga was done. At last Mrs Evans said, her hands linked behind her head, 'You attend the fellowship meetings, I'm told, Bobi.'

'Yes.'

Ann knew what was coming and she looked daggers at Mrs Evans.

'It's a pity you couldn't persuade your sister to go.'

At once Ann felt cast out from the warmth of the room into the middle of an icy pond. Sweet moments of sharing a fine tea and good talk, then a mouthful of wormwood. She flushed.

'Don't you go to the *seiat*, Nani?'

'No,' she answered, stubbornly.

She held nothing back in her explanation to Bobi.

'Mrs Evans and I disagree about the *seiat*, Bobi. In my opinion people who make an outburst of religious feelings in public are hypocrites. Remember that old woman, Suntur Coch, wailing her verses? And she one of the unkindest of women. There are too many like her.'

'Yes, I remember. There's no-one like that in the town. The people say a verse and the minister replies.'

'I suppose he might as well comment on that as on anything.'

'People shake, just saying the verses.'

'But at least they learn the scripture that way,' said Mrs Evans.

'All the scripture they ever learnt was when they were children.'

'Heaven forbid!' said Mrs Evans, getting up to clear the dishes.

When she and Bobi were alone Ann said, 'Take no notice of me. Don't stop going if you enjoy it.'

'I do enjoy it, but I wouldn't if it was like at home. The minister in town is worth hearing.'

'I can't explain to you, Bobi. I'm older than you. I'm sorry Mrs Evans mentioned it. We don't have to enjoy the same things.'

'No, of course. Don't worry, I wouldn't go only there's nowhere else,' said Bobi.

'I'm glad you like going.'

Ann could not explain why she felt glad, especially as she so disapproved of the *seiat* herself. Perhaps one day her brother would come to the same conclusion. If so, it was better he should find out for himself without her influence. If not, it was still better for him to do without her opinion.

She had put it right with Bobi, but there was still one bridge to be mended. Walking to the bus with Bobi she recalled the feast and the happy ending to the housekeeper affair, rather than the bucket of cold water Mrs Evans had thrown over the afternoon. Her landlady had built a beautiful castle, and had demolished it with one unexpected blow. Religion could be so divisive. She felt closer than ever to Bobi as he waved goodbye. He was so serious, so idealistic, for a fifteen-year-old boy.

8

As she turned away from the bus stop Ann found herself face to face with Bess Morris, one of the school teachers on her way to the pillar box to post a letter. They walked along the road together.

'Do you have to go straight home?' asked Bess. 'Why not come for a walk?'

'I'd love to. But I'd better call in to tell Mrs Evans, or she'll wonder where I've gone.'

Mrs Evans was sitting by the fire, looking thoughtful and despondent.

'I'm going for a walk, Mrs Evans, with Miss Morris from the school. I won't be long.'

'That's all right, Miss Owen,' she replied curtly.

They walked along the street towards the main road. It was quiet in those days. An occasional car went by but there was plenty of room to walk in the middle of the road. It was a lovely evening, daylight waning, the air dusky and clear. The same dusk veiled the mountains, blurring definition between the summits and the sky. After the heat of the day there was a healthy coolness in the air.

'I've just seen my brother off on the bus,' said Ann. 'He works at Price and Price, in town.'

Bess Morris stopped in her tracks, with the expression of one who's just solved a mystery.

'I was right. I was sure a relative of yours was working in Price's. He's so like you. He's a very pleasant boy.'

'Yes, he is.'

Bess linked arms with Ann and as she did so Ann felt the comfort of friendship flow through her. In the warmth of the moment, and still upset by Mrs Evans, she told Bess the whole story, including Mrs Evans's impetuous remarks about the *seiat*.

'It's a pity Mrs Evans worships that chapel so much. She lives too close to it.'

'Yes. It only encourages her fervour and prevents someone like me feeling close to her.'

'It's understandable. She became very pious after losing her husband.'

'Where do you go?'

'We are Church. The *seiat* doesn't bother us. Worship is what we do.'

Ann missed the little dig.

'I don't think I'd like church. I love a good sermon.'

'The trouble with good sermons is that you hunger for one every week, each one better than the last. The beauty of church is following the same ritual every time.'

'I can't understand that.'

'You would if you went. It's a beautiful service written by people of genius. You follow their thoughts and they become part of you.'

'Their experience becomes yours?'

'It's perfectly possible.'

'That's Mrs Evans's argument. I don't see how you can borrow other people's thoughts.'

Bess laughed. 'We won't argue tonight. I rather think you get too much argument about such things from Mrs Evans. Come home with me.'

They had reached the back of a terrace of houses where lights shone in the windows. Bess led the way through the gate. Someone was playing a harmonium.

'That's my father. We like singing.'

'I'm no singer.'

The music stopped.

'I've brought Miss Owen from school to meet you. I was right, Mam. That young boy in Price and Price is Miss Owen's brother.'

She threw her cap on the sofa.

'Come in, my dear. I'm delighted to meet you,' said Ellen Morris.

'You're welcome,' said her husband. 'Come by the fire.'

Ellen Morris had just finished her ironing. She took the ironing cloth and the blanket off the table, folded them and put them away in a drawer. A row of freshly pressed and folded linen shone on the brass rail under the mantel shelf.

'Don't let me interrupt you,' said Ann.

'I've just finished.'

She rattled the hot coals in the smoothing iron, opened the

little door in the front and emptied the contents onto the embers of the fire. She stood the iron on its end on the fender. Bess spread a cloth on the table.

'Do have a cup of tea with us,' said Bess's mother. 'We just have a bit of bread and cheese now. We had our meal when William came in from work.'

'Yes, thank you. I hope Mrs Evans won't think I've got lost.'

'You have nice lodgings,' said the father, 'but it's a pity Catrin Evans is so obsessed with the chapel. She never used to be.'

'Wasn't she?'

'No. It's since she lost her husband. Like some people turn to drink after a tragedy.'

'Shame on you, father.'

'Well, it was a terrible shock for her. And fair play, she's very sincere.'

'She should keep her religion to herself,' said Bess, 'and leave other people alone.'

'She's not all misery,' said Ann. 'And she is intelligent. It would be worse if I had to put up with interference from someone stupid.'

'How do you like Blaen Ddôl, and the school?' asked Ellen Morris.

'I like it well enough. The work is hard, but it would be just as bad anywhere.'

'I wonder,' said Bess. 'The rest of us feel very sorry for you, having to teach in front of the head every day. He should have his own room. But what can you do with an old school-building like that? The infants are a real nuisance.'

'That's true. But it's good experience for teaching smaller classes one day. The children in my class are lovely, and they come to school so clean, every one of them.'

'It's a credit to their mothers,' said Ellen Morris. 'They get by on such low wages.'

Ann was beginning to feel restless. She should be going. She hadn't liked the look Mrs Evans gave her when she called in at the house. Bess came to see her on her way.

'Come again,' she said. 'And don't keep to yourself at school either. Come and talk to the rest of us at break-time.'

'There's so much to do.'

'You can be too conscientious.'

'Thank you. I'm so glad we met today. Let's meet more often.'

'We'll go for a walk one Saturday.'

Ann knew she would have quarrelled with Mrs Evans had she gone straight home from the bus. She was glad she'd met Bess. It seemed more than an accident that their paths had crossed at that moment. Mrs Evans's mood had not changed when Ann reached the house. She was sitting in the same place, stiff as a statue. She lifted her head as Ann sat down beside the fire.

'I won't have any supper tonight. I had a bite with Bess Morris, and we had such a good tea today.'

Mrs Evans made no response.

'Thank you for making us such a lovely tea,' Ann continued. 'It was a treat for Bobi, and he wished me to thank you again.'

'Miss Owen.'

Ann knew something serious was coming. Her landlady did not move her head, but continued to stare into the fire.

'I'm so worried. I ought not to have mentioned to your brother that you don't attend the *seiat*.'

Ann fetched the stool and sat down beside her.

'Listen, Mrs Evans. You surely haven't been sitting here fretting all this time?'

'I have indeed,' she said, and began to sob.

'I'll make us a pot of tea,' said Ann, and off she went.

'Come on now, Mrs Evans. Drink it while it's hot. Here's bread and butter too.'

'Thank you. I'm glad you are not angry. I was worried that's why you went out.'

'Nonsense. Let's be honest with each other. I must go out more often if I'm to settle down here. You must expect to see me going out with Bess Morris, or other friends.'

'Bess is a nice girl. And your brother is a dear boy. He must come more often.'

'He is. And he's got too much sense to think I'll go to Hell if I don't attend the *seiat*.'

'You may be right. Forgive me. I've lived in too narrow a world.'

47

'I don't blame you. We have different ideas. I respect your opinion.'

Ann knew she was too young to be telling an older woman she respected her opinion. She went off to bed feeling depressed, although the day had ended better than she'd feared. As Bobi felt sorry for Will B, so she pitied Mrs Evans. Whatever had happened in Mrs Evans's life long before they met was a mystery to Ann. Yet those events influenced Mrs Evans's attitude to her, like someone walking towards her in the dark with a lamp. The beam moved on the ground ahead of its invisible bearer. The light dazzled her. There was dark ground between them. On unknown ground like the school it was all too easy to miss one's step. Bess had made it clear that the other teachers noticed that she did not join them for break, but didn't blame her for it. At first it was shyness that had kept her away, and she'd used her work as an excuse. She must overcome her reserve. Bess had given her a glimpse of what Church was like. She couldn't understand how anyone could enjoy the same service week in, week out but she wanted to understand her new friend's point of view. Her thoughts went back to teatime. In their exuberance they had forgotten someone. The old housekeeper. What was it like for her to be thrown out on the dole? It was easy to say she got what she deserved. If it comes to that, what does any of us deserve?

9

Well-being warmed the room. It rose from the hum of conversation on the first floor of the restaurant. It steamed from the aromas of meat and vegetables on the table between them. Ann forgot every pang of anxiety that had accompanied her journey on the train. There was not a doubt or a scruple left now as Richard Edmund's eyes gazed into hers with an admiration and love she had never known before. She was sure no-one had looked at her like this since she left her cradle. She arrived half an hour or so ago in a turmoil of emotions. It was good to see the faces of old friends from college, to be greeted like a child coming home. The old intimacy of friendship was mixed with nostalgia and pride in her independence and her own money in her pocket. It was a peat fire burning steadily under a griddle suspended on a tripod, where her own private loaf was baking beautifully.

She didn't mind now about student teasing. No-one could hear their conversation, and she didn't care if they could. At the still heart of the noise, the chatter, the scraping of chairs, the steam, she and Richard were alone.

In the train she'd worried about several things. The morning after her talk with Bess a letter came from Richard inviting her to meet him in Bangor. She had planned to go home on Friday after school, and return to Blaen Ddôl on Saturday evening. She went home once a month, and as the days grew shorter she would return by the last bus on Saturday rather than walk back on Sunday evenings as she had when the days were longer. When she read Richard's letter she was in a quandary. Should she postpone her visit home, or shorten it so as not to disappoint Richard? In the end she compromised, telling her mother she must be in Bangor by one o'clock. It was possible by brake and train, without cutting short her visit home by too many hours.

Home was so sweet she was almost sorry she'd promised to leave early for Bangor. The old quarry supper on Friday evening with all the family except Bobi, the good talk afterwards, and off to bed, tired and happy. Lingering over breakfast with her mother next morning, tea, home-baked bread, marmalade. Nothing more, but it was good, and her appetite was healthy. Her mother told her with warmth how she'd finished all her work on Friday afternoon so that there would be nothing to do on Saturday morning, no ironing, no baking, no churning, no cleaning the bedrooms, so that they could talk. Though rather tired, her mother's face wore the satisfied expression of one who has worked hard but is not worn-out like an old mare at the season's end, as she was wont to say. To crown this air of contentment, she had a new black suit. Ann's heart melted to hear such things. The world was getting better. In the narrow valley of her mountain home, the 'world' was the one they battled with every day. They knew there were other worlds far away from farm, chapel and quarry, but the only real world was the one they lived in.

'I can go out a bit now,' said Ann's mother.

Ann knew exactly what 'now' meant. There was no longer any need to scrape for money for her education. Ann's heart was so close to her mother this morning that she heard no reproach in the word. Her mind raced ahead.

'You must come to Blaen Ddôl one day.'

'I'm sure I will. I've ordered you a new winter coat.'

They talked about Bobi. Her mother was relieved that things had turned out well after all, but she did not thank Ann for her part in the outcome. Happy as she was from the sweetness of the visit and absorbed by the thought of meeting Richard, Ann noticed the remark without resentment. In fact it offered her conscience a little freedom from guilt about not quite telling her mother the truth about the visit to Bangor.

These things had returned to worry her in the train. Since leaving college it was as if she were walking over barbed-wire hedges. Suddenly her mind returned to the moment.

'Remember, I'm paying. I'm telling you now so there's no argument,' said Richard.

'That's not fair. I'm earning now.'

'Chickenfeed! Are you offended?'

'Of course not.'

'I just mean you deserve to earn more.'

'That's all right. My mother's had a new suit out of it. The first for ten years.'

Ann noticed something in Richard's eyes she had not seen before, something between sympathy and sadness. His eyes were a clear blue. He was quiet a moment then he said,

'It's wrong. Life's so unfair.'

'That's true,' she said.

'I've had good fortune too,' he said. 'I can't blame life too much.'

They rose and left the restaurant. Richard paid the bill, and bought her a quarter of chocolate. She felt close to tears.

Fallen leaves crunched underfoot as they walked up the hill.

There was a weak warmth in the sun and instinctively Ann turned her face towards it. The wind crept into the sleeves of her jacket.

'You're cold,' said Richard. 'You should be wearing an overcoat, though that suit looks lovely on you.'

'I love it. I'm reluctant to put it away for the season. My mother's ordered a winter coat for me. I never had one all the time I was in college, and never seemed to need one.'

He took her arm and drew her to him. Warmth surged through her body, quite different from the warmth she'd felt when Bess took her arm the other night. This was the heat of excitement, not the friendly warmth that makes you want to share your secrets. They reached the top of the hill.

'Shall we sit here, on this stone? Are you sure you won't get a chill?'

'I'm fine.'

She found herself talking nineteen to the dozen to hide her feelings. She talked for the sake of talking, about school, about Blaen Ddôl, about Mrs Evans, about Bobi, on and on without pausing to hear his response. At last she stopped talking. After a while he said,

'It's a fine thing you have a good home to go to.'

'It is indeed.'

'I wish I could say the same. I was eight and ten years old when my parents died, just old enough to know what I had lost. If I'd been five I'd have been too young to realise. At fifteen perhaps I wouldn't have felt it so much. My mother was brought up by her uncle, and when they married my parents went to live with him. It was a smallholding, and he just about managed to live off it. The place wasn't big enough to support a family so my father went to work in one of the quarries in your part of the country. He slept in the barracks all week. He caught a fever and died. My mother survived him by just two years. Looking back I realise she must have grieved too deeply and lost the will to live even for my sake. I missed my father of course, but at least I had my mother and I think I was happy enough. I never thought about whether I was happy or not. But after my mother died there was no refuge anywhere. I find it impossible to describe the pain of crying myself to sleep every night. Every morning I expected to see my mother at

51

the breakfast table and I'd run out to the shippon to find her. My uncle didn't really understand children, and when he hired a housekeeper things were even worse. I'd rather have seen my mother's empty chair than find a stranger sitting there. My uncle was nearly sixty then. The woman would send me on errands, often at night. I'd wander about the village in the cold not wanting to go home. I see now she had her eye on my uncle. In the end she left and things were better. My uncle's moved to a house now and he rents out the smallholding. I pay for my education, and uncle's generous to me. He pays me something from the rent every month. I had some today. I'm sorry. I must be depressing you.'

'It is a very sad story. It makes me ashamed of all my complaining.'

'Time heals and hardens the heart.'

'So they say. I don't know. I've no experience to go by. It seems wonderful that one can struggle and survive such tragedy.'

'In church one Sunday they were singing a psalm, and when they came to the words, *My tears were my food day and night,* a marvellous feeling came over me, like my mother putting her fingers through my hair to brush it away from my forehead. Then it happened again with *All thy billows have gone over me,* and *Thy song is with me through the night.* I was too young to understand but I was comforted.'

Ann was silent, thinking over what he had told her.

'I've made you sad.'

'A little.'

'Don't be sad. Let's talk of the future.'

'Are you Church?'

Ann blushed as if she'd said something out of place.

'Yes. Anything wrong with that?'

'No. But they say Anglesey is full of Methodists.'

They laughed together.

'Let's go. It's getting cold. I wanted to tell you my story. I've never needed to tell anyone before. I hope you're going to fill the void for me, because I think the world of you.'

He kissed her with great tenderness. Ann could think of nothing to say. They walked in silence towards the town and as they reached it Richard said,

'Have I offended you?'

'Not at all. I'm just too happy to speak.'

'That'll do for me,' said Richard.

10

The last train grunted and ground to a halt in the station. The streets were still. A little earlier you could hear the voices of the men coming out of the pubs and bars, arguing, debating, joking, laughing, a drop too much taken. Then 'Goodnight,' 'Goodnight,' 'Goodnight,' fading further and further away, the man next door shutting and bolting his door, and the long following silence. One lonely whistle, as if someone were calling somebody lost, and at last the cessation of all sound.

Ann sank into Mrs Evans's feather bed, not quite ready to be drowned in sleep nor nervously wakeful either. Her mind played hide-and-seek with images passing before her eyes. Preachers waiting on the station platform; preachers sitting in the compartments of the train; preachers everywhere, spotless and respectable in their silk hats and their tailcoats. They were remote beings, familiar yet alien. She was filled with awe at the vision.

Then the restaurant, and Richard's face. His voice telling his story. His arm in hers, his voice saying again, 'I think the world of you'. That was worth more than the kiss, and the inflexion in his voice worth more than the words. That tone of intimacy and the stress on the word 'world'. It was a world far from the one against which her family battled. It was not the world of the preacher either. She heard the preacher's voice, 'We love Him because He first loved us.' Fear touched her. That was chapel. It was not the world of lovers. A thought came to her. Who fell in love first, she or Richard? She pushed it away and lay tense with fear. His name beat like the tick of a clock in her ears and above it the monotonous choral speaking of preachers. 'I love the beauteous letters of His name.' Oh, God! She had profaned the holy words of Morgan Rhys, and for such an earthly meaning.

She brought herself back to earth. Richard was Church. Well, that wasn't a problem. She could leap that hurdle. Much more important, as it touched her family, was her job. If she and Richard loved each other it would lead some day to marriage. Yet she must work at her job to pay off the debt for her education. She would have to choose. A married woman could not be a teacher. Love that ignored duty could only lead to pain. She pushed the thought away. Sufficient unto the day. If she stayed with Mrs Evans she'd have to satisfy her curiosity too, though that was the least of her worries. It wouldn't hurt to share her secret with Mrs Evans if it gave her pleasure, though it certainly would not please her mother. What if Richard tired of her and fell for someone else? Foolish doubts. That was not Richard's way. Suddenly out of nowhere Bobi walked into her mind, his face gazing sadly through the station railings. What would he say? 'I'm happy for you Nani.' She dismissed everyone from her mind until there was nothing but one voice, Richard's voice unaccompanied. What was that hymn? Why did hymns keep breaking into her mind? *And the sweet low tone of thy voice.* What would Bess say? Love, so common a human experience. It was awful the way feelings swung between the world of faith and the world of the flesh and the heart. Sleep flowed closer, and sweetness with it. She saw her day draped over the back of a chair, a beautiful dress waiting to be worn for the first time.

The chapel was cold but the huddled congregation made a communal warmth. Ann had almost overslept, and daydreamed over her breakfast until Mrs Evans made her stir herself. 'You'll be late if you don't hurry, Miss Owen.' It didn't bother her. She would return to her daydream in chapel, as she always did. The preacher was not a compelling speaker though everyone appeared to be listening. It was not the traditional sermon praising God for arranging our salvation. Nor was it about the Cross, or atonement, or the rewards of faith, or sanctity, or the fall in Eden. Its theme was honesty in ordinary everyday human relationships, between master and servant, servant and master, between men and women in their daily lives. A sermon from the heart, without theology. Yes, things were changing, thought Ann, sermons like everything else. She might have enjoyed this sermon the week

Bobi was in trouble at work, but not today, somehow. It was too dutiful and narrow. What her heart craved now was something that expressed the spirit of a freedom heedless of tomorrow, like the poem 'A Hymn to Summer' that she'd copied into her autograph album, and into other people's albums too, when she was in college. Her duty, according to this preacher, was to deny that spirit. Her duty was to her parents, to keep her feet firmly on the ground and to serve others. Her soul rebelled. True, he urged them to love one another, to do everything with love. But how could she love people who didn't love her first? She couldn't accept such a doctrine. It took two to love. The poet understood. She stared at the preacher. He was smartly dressed, handsome, well-spoken, sincere, and, according to Mrs Evans, he practised what he preached. The good shepherd. He was everything, Ann thought, but a man you could fall in love with.

She slipped swiftly out of chapel intending to walk through the woods alone. She changed her mind. The woods would be dark. She didn't want darkness today. She took the mountain road, the weak sun on her face, and felt she was again on Bangor mountain. She climbed away from the road and sat on a stone by a little stream. It made a silky sound, soothing to the ears, far from the voices of people and chapel. Sheep grazed intently, ceaselessly, as though there were no tomorrow, monotonous as a life devoted to duty, without a moment for private joy. But there was another way to live. There was excitement, there was the joy of hearing a voice say, 'I think the *world* of you.' To be the only person in somebody's heart, instead of sharing attention with the crowd. She was happy sitting there among the reeds by the stream until a cold breath of air made her rise, thinking of her dinner. As the wind changed a foolish thought came to her. Yesterday had changed her life. Could her mind be changed again just as swiftly? She rejected the thought. Impossible. Her cup was full and running over.

'An excellent sermon, wasn't it?' said Mrs Evans, setting the meal on the table.

'Mm.'

'Didn't you enjoy it?'

'It was all right.'

'Mr Hughes is a good preacher, and such a nice man.'

'I don't know much about him.'

'You won't find a better man, or a better preacher.'

'He sounds too perfect to me.'

'It's impossible to be too perfect.'

'I find it easier to love imperfect people.'

'But you must have someone you can look up to in the pulpit.'

It wasn't worth arguing. Mrs Evans had her gods, and she, well – perhaps, had only one.

11

The bell rang for the end of afternoon play. 'I'll call for you tonight to come for a walk,' whispered Bess as she and Ann parted to go to their classrooms. 'And take no notice of Lyd Edwards.'

It wasn't Lyd or her manner that upset Ann in the staffroom at break. Had someone else spoken, less provocatively and with less sarcasm, Ann would still have been hurt. It was the fact that it had been mentioned at all that mattered. Lyd Edwards had smiled as she threaded a pencil through a curl on the nape of Ann's neck. 'I saw someone with her sweetheart in Bangor on Saturday. We're not the little innocent we appear to be.'

Ann forced a formal smile. Everyone laughed except Bess, whose face darkened as a frown passed across it. Ann said nothing, and all but Lyd Edwards realised that not everyone enjoys being teased about love. Lyd didn't give up.

'You make a lovely couple. We won't be able to keep you here much longer, Miss Owen.'

Still Ann said nothing, her lips pressed tightly together.

'Come, come!' said another. 'We all enjoy a little tease when we're in love.'

And with that the bell rang.

Ann was shaken. It was not as if she'd been caught doing anything wrong, but she wished she had not been seen or that they'd held their tongues. Lyd Edwards should know teasing can harm love in its early days. She tried to forget it, knowing Bess wanted to talk to her.

Bess called for her at seven o'clock and they set out for the mountain.

'I must tell you about Lyd Edwards,' she said as they left the main road. 'You must think she's very catty.'

'I can only judge by her behaviour.'

'Perhaps I shouldn't say so, but I must be frank. You hated being teased, didn't you?'

'Yes.'

'I thought so. You went very pale.'

'Oh?'

'Yes. And it's my fault for not warning Lyd. She said she'd seen you.'

'Did you wonder why I hadn't told you?'

'Of course not. The man she saw you with could have been a relative. But nothing stops Lyd. She'd taunt Lloyd George himself, to show off.'

'He'd be a match for her.'

'She goes too far. But that's not what's on my mind now. I want to talk about school.'

'Go on.'

'Do you ever find your opinions of people at odds with others?'

'Often, since I left college. Never before.'

'That's good,' said Bess with a sigh of relief, 'Well, I'm fed up with Lyd Edwards. She waltzes through life as if she were Lloyd George. She thinks that being so witty and attractive she can treat people as she likes.'

'She's quite attractive, but I haven't noticed her wit.'

'Wait till you've been with us a year and you've joined us for break more often. What annoys me is that her clever tongue deceives everyone into thinking she's intelligent. She even fools the inspectors.'

'Really?'

'Well, maybe not, but she certainly thinks she can. There's one person she can't fool.'

'Who's that?'

'The Head. No-one deceives him. You know him well enough by now.'

'I don't really know him. I can see he's hard-working, and a good teacher, but he has a terrible temper.'

'Yes, he has. He devotes his whole life to school, and does far too much. It's a shame he has such a bad temper – he's better than he used to be – because it gives Lyd an advantage over him. It's her excuse to find fault with him. She mimics him brilliantly, but she just doesn't know when to stop. I'm sorry. You must be tired of hearing me run her down.'

'Not at all. I'm rather enjoying it.'

'I want you to see how it affects me. Lyd makes herself popular by being witty and attractive. She gets away with doing as little work as possible because the Head is the way he is. She does nothing with the girls when the Head takes the boys for woodwork, and I have to teach that class the year after.'

'That's not right,' said Ann. 'Is she a good teacher? Some people make up for laziness by being gifted teachers.'

'That's what I'm trying to tell you,' said Bess. 'People think she's clever because she's witty. But she is *not* clever at all,' she added emphatically.

'Perhaps I owe you an explanation too. I just wasn't ready for teasing. I didn't know anyone had seen us on Saturday. It wasn't just being seen that I minded, but hearing her talk so frivolously about something that is serious for me. She walked all over my clean floor with her dirty boots. It wouldn't have mattered if it were just a flirtation. Or if I'd wanted the secret to come out then the teasing might have helped. It's hard to explain.'

'Don't try.'

'I've known Richard Edmund as a friend for quite a while. We used to talk sometimes, and I thought nothing of it. Saturday was the first time he told me how he felt. Being teased so soon really hurt.'

'Yes, I understand.'

'Maybe it wouldn't have hurt if we'd been going together for months.'

'I don't know. There are some things you should never tease people about. No-one knows what goes on between two people. It's nobody else's business.'

'No, but I'm glad we've talked tonight.'

58

'Me too. I'm afraid I may have said too much about school.'

'It's as well for me to know. Forewarned is forearmed. But it's strange.'

'What's strange?'

'How we learn, how different things always are from one's expectations. Did you imagine, Bess, leaving college, that it would be heaven on earth afterwards?'

'I did. I thought once I had a job it would be happiness ever after. I've found that earning a wage is the least of our worries.'

'I'm shocked that people can hurt me so much.'

'Mind you, there are two sides to that,' said Bess.

As the light of a window shone momentarily on Bess's face, Ann felt how good it was to have her friendship. Hers was such an honest face. Ann was glad she'd shared her secret love with her new friend.

'A talk like this does one good,' Ann said. 'We had to emerge from the glasshouse of college sooner or later, where all was perfection. Talking of Lyd reminds me of a girl who used to write verses in the girls' autograph books, and the lines always seemed to fit some little weakness in the album owner. We used to laugh at them. We thought she was clever. Now I can see she was making fun of people.'

'It's even worse. It's exploiting power over people. I'm not sure that Lyd is quite as bad as that. I think she's just showing off. I hope you won't hate Blaen Ddôl because of what I've told you. I'd like to keep you here a long time.'

'Trivial teasing wouldn't make me hate a place, unless it turned to bullying. Anyway, you and I are friends, I hope,' said Ann.

'That's for sure.'

'Mrs Evans is a bit of a nuisance,' Ann continued. 'She is beginning to annoy me, though she gives me a good home. It's as if she wants to possess me.'

'You must talk to her about it.'

'It's not easy with someone as kind as she is. She is not exactly devious, but she does seem to be trying to manipulate me, as if to replace something she has lost. Anyway, it's sweet of her to ask you in for a cup of tea.'

59

'Yes, and I'd like to come. It's hard to know how to deal with someone like her, so kind in some ways and so irritating in others.'

A little later Bess added,

'I'm beginning to think there is no such thing as freedom.'

When they arrived at the house and Ann saw the warmth of Mrs Evans's welcome, she was prepared to overlook all her faults.

When Bess had gone Ann forgot the day's hurt. She turned her thoughts with pleasure to the evening's conversation, warming herself at friendship's fire before going up to bed.

12

Blaen Ddôl, Monday, Thanksgiving Day, 1913

My Dear Richard,

I've just arrived back at Blaen Ddôl. I left home too early for evening chapel and got in too late for the service here. Mrs Evans left my supper on the table, but I won't eat before she returns. It's hard to think of eating alone after happy meals at home with the family. So here is a fine chance for something I've been longing to do for days – write a letter to you.

I've been full of longing since I got back. It was so good to be home. I was up before seven this morning to be at chapel for eight o'clock. I used to think washing in cold water and going to a cold chapel were part of the unavoidable sufferings of Sunday. I was almost eager to kneel on cold stone. A cup of tea, a sandwich, helping to lay the table for second breakfast. I'd make a point of getting up early to show my fervour.

A warm little prayer meeting, three people came for second breakfast, men who live too far away to go home between services. It happens every year like a ritual. Mam on her feet, waiting on us at the big table. She got some barley from somewhere and kneaded the dough in a huge crock. The slices of bread were so long and thick you could turn them over in your hands like whalebones without them breaking. Oh! But they were good with cheese, Mam cutting slices at the round side-table, us at the big table, her arm sweeping the loaf. There is always something sweeping about Mam, the way she cuts bread and the things she says.

It's the same every year. Old Siôn Tomos comes in first, stooping, and looking for somewhere to hang his hat – he's so bent he can't see the hooks on the back of the door. 'Give me your hat, Siôn Tomos,' says Bobi, and he tosses the hat onto a hook without even looking. Then the old man moves up close to the fire to have a warm, saying as always, 'Duw! It's bitter out there.' Mam sits him at the end of the table closest to the fire. He still wears velvet trousers for chapel like old people did years ago, and he wears them without apology as if they were the height of fashion. Griffith Roberts, one of the deacons, is next to arrive, a fine, sensible man. Last comes shy Robert Huws who likes his pint on a Saturday night. You should see how such different people mingle once the meal begins. It amazes and delights me. Griffith Roberts sits in the big pew in chapel where the important people sit, and it's no time for Robert Huws to play the fool when he's in the company of the deacon. Siôn Tomos has been the same ever since I've known him. A serious little man, he rarely laughs, and then only quietly to himself. Between these people and my father there is a deep empathy that is obvious on these occasions, though they are all so different. It's hard to say what it is, a kind of loyalty binding them together like a length of twine. They understand each other on everything that matters. Perhaps it's because all their lives they have worked together and faced danger together in the quarry. Sitting down to eat together like that is as much an act of celebration as all their singing and praying in chapel. They don't put it into words, but it's there. They never complain or mention their daily hardships.

As usual talk turned at last to the subject of Richard Williams, a neighbour of Siôn Tomos. He's an atheist who comes to chapel once a year, on Thanksgiving night. 'I wonder if he'll come this year?' is the annual question. 'He'll come,' said Siôn Tomos. 'He's been having doubts. He's called in there every day this week. He'll come, just in case.' 'Lots of people come just in case all the year round,' said Mam. This time nobody contradicted her. Old Siôn changed the subject by asking me, 'What part of the world are you living in now, Ann?' as if I were a sailor. When I told him he said, 'You're grazing new pastures now.' The whole time I was at college he asked me the same question every year. Then he'd say, 'Are you *still* there?' as if I ought to have been working long since, and was taking something I hadn't earned. These people understand each other but they don't understand other generations or other kinds of work.

There was the usual *hwyl* in the singing and the praying in chapel. Edmwnd Prys is very popular on Thanksgiving Day and ignored all the rest of the year. It's difficult to say which is better, the Welsh of the hymn book and the Bible, or the heartfelt prayers of the people. They've influenced each other. How many hundreds of times have I heard the words, *We beseech you, hear our prayers*, or *Admit us to Thy loving care*. I suddenly understand that last phrase, Thy loving care. And the hill of Zion. Such language flowed, and I felt glad to be alive in times like ours. How long, I wonder, will these people and their way of life survive?

Tomorrow I'll have to think about school, and work, though I haven't the heart for it. Joni Dafydd will be late as usual, and the Head will ask him what he was doing, and as usual Joni will reply, 'Coming, Sir.' The Head has given up replying 'So is Christmas,' and the children have given up laughing at the joke. But Joni has no new excuse for being late. Ponies are his passion. He doesn't care about bikes. He might as well stay home with the ponies for all the good education is doing him. He'll slip through school like oil over water, and he has more in common with old Siôn

62

Tomos than with boys of his own age. He and the old folk are legendary creatures, like characters in the Mabinogi.

I'm rambling on without a word about you and me, though what I really mean to write about is us. In writing about those other people I'm trying to show you how much you mean to me. In a way you are part of what they are part of, though you're not like them, because I'm so happy about this new experience that has entered my life.

I can hear Mrs Evans coming in. I must finish this tomorrow.

In her letter to Richard, Ann failed to mention the one thing that had spoilt the pleasure of being at home. She hadn't had a chance for a long talk with Bobi since he came to tea at Blaen Ddôl. The new housekeeper was a kind woman, and things had greatly improved at the boss's house. Yet Bobi still seemed unhappy with his life. In her love for Richard she could forget Bobi, just as she had forgotten him in her carefree college days. This Sunday her conscience had reproached her and she had felt overwhelmed by the old tenderness for him. He followed her about as if he wanted to talk, and when the family gathered round the fire he was pensive and did not join in the conversation. Finding herself and Bobi alone in the kitchen on Sunday evening, she took the chance to talk to him.

'Are things any better in the shop now, Bobi?'

'Yes. Things are better in the house now. The shop work is the same as usual, but I've lost interest in it.'

'Why, Bobi?'

'Oh, I don't know. It's the same old work day in, day out. Cutting calico for the same people at the same counter.'

'That's what work is like. That's how it is for me.'

'No. You are dealing with living things, and living things change.'

'Less than you'd think. We are all like bits of wood.'

'I want to go somewhere. I want to see the world.'

'The only people who can go off to see the world are those with enough money to travel. If you think life would be less monotonous if you moved to a big city, you're mistaken. It would be shop, house and bed there too. Maybe there'd be a few more evening entertainments, but you'd soon be sick of those too.'

'I don't know,' he said unhappily. 'I work and eat with John and Wil B, all day and every day, and they never say anything interesting.'

'Listen, Bobi,' said Ann. 'You need to educate yourself. Why don't you go to night school?'

As the term had only just begun, Bobi promised he would make enquiries about night school. After parting from him in town, Ann could not put him out of her mind. At heart she was sure he was lonely. She was glad she had a shilling to give him, and he was grateful to accept it. If only he could find a friend like himself. He had plenty of brains in his head if he'd only had the chance to use them. He had lost his chance. She could not bring herself to put these things into words in her letter to Richard. She shifted her anxiety for Bobi out of the room of her imagination, and thus she managed to write about the visit home as if she had no care in the world. Her imagination transformed the events of the day into a celebration of her feeling for Richard. She could not bring herself to express her love more directly.

13

Richard and Ann were strolling the streets of Bangor, sodden leaves underfoot, raindrops from a heavy shower shaking down on their heads from the trees. Ann wore her new coat, its collar turned up. A dark-blue, double-breasted coat, pleated into a band at the back with a pair of buttons. She wore a dark-blue velvet cap. Richard wore his dark grey overcoat and his cap was light grey. At his throat he had knotted a cravat. The sky cleared for a moment with great spaces of blue from which hung little white clouds like old men's beards.

'Why did you write me a letter like that, Ann?'

'Didn't you like it?'

'Of course, but.'

'But what?'

'It's not my idea of a love-letter.'

'Nor mine either.'

She paused teasingly for a moment, watching the smile on his face.

'But didn't you like hearing about those old people?'

'I did, but I'd rather hear about you.'

'It was about me.' She was still teasing, but she was serious too. 'I'm not sure I can put it into words, Richard. You see, Thanksgiving has happened to me every year of my life, the same people, the same talk, and because of you it was as if I were looking at them for the very first time.'

'Because of me?'

'I was so happy because of us. Somehow, they'd grown precious to me. Before, they were just the same old people coming for breakfast. I suddenly saw them as a little community of men who really understand each other. I thought, how long before such people have all gone.'

'Never, I hope. You're a strange girl, expecting me to read between the lines for my love letter.' He pressed her body against him. 'You're beautiful in your new clothes.'

'I made the cap from a few shillings worth of velvet, the same pattern as your favourite.'

'It sits well on that head of hair.'

'There was I thinking you were such a shy boy in college.'

'I am shy.'

'You have plenty to say for yourself today.'

They laughed warmly. Then she grew serious again at the thought that something else had prompted her to write as she had. Should she confess her worries about Bobi? Why should she spoil things? This was perfect. Might such a confession now cast a shadow on Richard's love just as Lyd's teasing had somehow wounded her love the other day? She was not sure. The provocation of a colleague was outside their love, but Bobi's happiness lay within its boundary. Gathering clouds consumed the blue of the sky.

'Let's go and have tea. It looks like rain,' Richard said. 'Let's go to that cosy little cafe by the clock tower.'

'Let's have a nice hot toasted teacake,' said Ann.

'With sugar melting on it,' said he.

'Jam on mine,' said she.

'Isn't this fine?'

'Perfect.'

They found a table for two in a corner behind the door.

'Nobody will see us here,' said Ann.

'What does it matter?'

'It matters to me.'

Richard looked hurt.

'Don't misunderstand me. If my mother knew I was with you she would not be pleased.'

'Is she so puritanical?'

'No, but she wouldn't like it if she knew I was courting so soon after leaving college.'

'You're old enough.'

'Dear Richard! My grandmother had children at my age, but granddaughters today are expected to work to pay for their education.'

'Yes, you're right. I haven't a family to think of,' he said thoughtfully.

'Let's forget about everybody and everything. This teacake is good.'

'All the more delicious for sharing it. How is Bobi? Is he happy now?'

'What made you think of him?'

'The tea.'

'To tell the truth, I need to talk about Bobi, but I've been avoiding it.'

'Why? Is something wrong?'

'In a way, no. Yet there's a lot wrong. The shop and his lodgings are as good as can be expected now, but he's dissatisfied. That's another reason I wrote about the old people.'

Ann waited for Richard to speak, but he didn't. He stirred his second cup of tea. She continued.

'He's bored doing the same work, day in, day out, and seeing the same lads, who according to Bobi are very dull company. I've tried telling him we all have tedious jobs to do, but he doesn't believe me.'

'Poor Bobi,' said Richard, sympathetically.

'He says he wants to go away, but how would that help?'

'Not much in that kind of work. He obviously needs something more demanding, more creative.'

'Yes. I have persuaded him to go to night school.'

'A good idea, especially if the others would go with him. He might be shy on his own.'

'I don't understand this anxiety over Bobi. I seem to worry about everything that happens to him. He earns a pittance, and I can't give him any money.'

'Of course you can't. It's a pity you couldn't get a Grammar School job.'

'I'm afraid I'd have to go far away to find a place. I don't want to go away now.'

Richard took her hand in his. 'Things aren't too good, are they? They'll get better.'

'I hope so.'

'Listen. We'll take Bobi out to tea in Bangor one day in the holidays.'

Her eyes shone. 'He'd like that.'

As they said goodbye at the station, Ann said hesitantly, 'Richard. I want to thank you.'

'What for? Not for a pot of tea?'

'For understanding about Bobi. I was afraid you'd think I was being foolish.'

'Listen, Ann, your pain is my pain.'

In the train it was not the agitation of love that filled her heart, but the peace that came from being understood. The sky was cloudless, and a clear moon shone over the Menai Straits.

When she arrived in Mrs Evans's kitchen she knew at once that something ominous had happened. Her landlady looked at her so accusingly that Ann wondered if her watch had stopped. Was it midnight? If it had been, Mrs Evans could not have looked more cross.

'Your mother has been here this afternoon.'

Ann collapsed into a chair. It was the last thing she expected to hear.

'Why on earth didn't she write and let me know?'

'That's between you and her. But I'm afraid I may have put my foot in it.'

Mrs Evans looked anxious.

'When I told her I thought you'd gone to Bangor to see your young man I thought she was going to have a heart attack.'

'You didn't tell her that?'

'I didn't think there was anything wrong with mentioning it. I thought she'd be pleased.'

'Oh, Mrs Evans,' said Ann, and she laid her head on the table and started to cry.

'What's wrong, Miss Owen? What was I to do?' said Mrs Evans as if she were acting a drama.

'Oh, Mrs Evans fach,' said Ann. She lifted her head. 'You don't understand. My mother wants me to keep working to pay her back for my education. Nobody's supposed to think about marriage after an expensive education, according to her.'

'You're going too far, Miss Owen. When I told her who the young man was, how clever he is, she recovered herself. Fair play, she never uttered another word, though I could see she was upset. We had a nice afternoon together.'

'Poor Mam. She's been promising to visit me one day. She has a new suit but hasn't been out anywhere for years. And I wasn't here to welcome her.'

'You weren't to know.'

'She must think she can't trust her own daughter out of her sight.'

'You're wrong there, Miss Owen. She's very proud of you and of all her children. She was telling me how glad she is that you are beginning to find your feet. We had a good chat. She is a lady, and a kind one. She brought me a pound of fresh butter and one for you, and a dozen eggs for us to share.'

'I'm sure you made her a nice tea.'

'Don't worry, my dear. Your mother will come to see us again.'

Ann went upstairs, limp as a rag. She was so sorry for her mother who'd looked forward to spending an afternoon with her daughter, but hadn't thought to let her know. Ann could imagine Mrs Evans's welcome would make her mother feel like a queen.

Maybe it was a good thing after all that Mrs Evans had given away her secret. She could not deceive her parents forever. It would suggest she wasn't proud of Richard. She was now forced to face reality. She was a fool to imagine she could keep her love balancing in the air like a balloon, an eternal romance hanging in the ether, never touching the earth.

She must face her mother. She had an idea. She would write to Bobi and ask him to talk to Mam about her and Richard. It would make him feel grown up to be trusted with something so important. It would give him the sense of responsibility he needed so much at the moment. She tried to banish the matter from her mind, and remember the brief, happy hours she had relished with Richard, and to ponder her heart before it grew cold with knowledge. She saw again the penetrating gaze in his eyes as she told him of Bobi, eyes that were wise and generous enough to include Bobi in their mutual love.

14

Sitting in her chair in front of the fire one cold November evening after tea, Ann faced the fact that duty is a stern mistress. She must rise and shake herself and leave this lovely fire because in half an hour she must take the children's service in the chapel at six o'clock. Life at Blaen Ddôl had settled itself into a pattern, one week like another. She decided long ago that she could only do her work in short periods separated by time spent on the needs of her own life. Time to think about yesterday, about tomorrow, about Richard, about Bobi and about home. To Ann it was just as important that her inner life should have a pattern as that the outward things of her life should be orderly. She must have time to read too. What use was education if it didn't teach you how and what to read?

There was little enough time for reading, between school work, chapel duties and tiredness. At least she now knew the best and the worst of Blaen Ddôl. She could fly away from it all when she was with Richard. Her mother had grown used to the idea that her daughter was courting. Bobi was happier since he began attending night school. He had managed to persuade John the apprentice to go with him, but not Will B. who still preferred the cinema. For all her reasons for contentment, Ann's restless mind wandered like the old hymn. *Where in this world will be my resting-place? Which will be my road?*

In this world. Although tonight the pattern seemed set, she could not imagine Blaen Ddôl being her world for long. One day she would rise and go. Mr Hughes, the minister, and his wife would be at the chapel before her for the children's service. He was tireless. He was everywhere. He worked at his own pace, arranging jobs for everyone. His chapel and its services ran like clockwork, with never a thing amiss. Ann hadn't the heart to refuse to help such an energetic man, though she felt no closer to him now than on the first day she met him. Oh, how sweet it would be to laze by the fire this evening.

'Do come home for supper,' said Mrs Hughes at the end of the service. 'It's going to be a cold night.'

There was warmth in her invitation and Ann accepted readily.

'We'll go straight home. Dan has a meeting with the deacons and he has to visit sick members afterwards. Hurry on ahead,' she told her children, 'Open the door and light the lamps.'

Supper was laid in the back parlour, a cosy little room with a fire that burned up as soon as the poker stirred it. Mrs Hughes gave her two shy children their supper first, with milk to drink instead of tea.

'Now then,' she said, 'off you go to your father's study to do your homework, then upstairs to bed. I like a little bit of peace from the children,' she said to Ann. 'That's one good thing about the manse. There's plenty of room to shoo them away when they get under your feet.'

She spoke tenderly, as though she were gathering them on her lap rather than sending them off to do their homework. She was a tall woman, lean but strong. Her flushed cheeks sharpened the blue of her eyes. Her light auburn hair hung untidily about her forehead, its disorder only enhancing her attractiveness. She showed two rows of good teeth when she smiled. Ann guessed she must be about forty years old.

'Have you settled down here now, Miss Owen?'

'Yes. I like it well enough, though it's not really my element.'

'We're none of us in our element. Only love can transform a place.'

Ann blushed, but Mrs Hughes seemed not to notice.

'An attractive girl like you should have a sweetheart, then the other boys would leave you in peace.'

Ann blushed more deeply and burst out laughing. 'That's the first time I ever heard love called useful.'

'Well, that's up to you. But it does make one happy whatever the place is like. Why am I talking like this? I don't like to become too complacent myself.'

'Really? My brother is far from complacent in his job in town.'

'There's hope for him then. He'll make something of himself.'

She rose and went to the kitchen to cut bread and butter, singing as she went.

'I'm sick and tired of Blaen Ddôl,' she said, taking up the conversation where she had left it. 'We've been here six years, and I never see anything but chapel, shops and street. Town sometimes on Saturday afternoon.'

'Everyone lives like that, as I try to tell Bobi.'

'Bobi?'

'My brother who works in town.'

'I see. But I can't imagine a worse world than the chapel to try and make a life. Piety is a dreadful thing to live with day after day.'

Ann wasn't sure if she meant her husband's or the congregation's piety.

'You see, godly people are so dull once they've given up sin. They take up quarrelling on committees where everyone wants to be number one, and Dan has to pacify them all. It's far easier to handle the sinners.'

Ann's laughter filled the room.

'It's the truth,' said Mrs Hughes, cutting a slice off the ham and laying it on a plate. 'Look at old John, Pen y Bigyn. Drunk and disorderly on Saturday nights, and like a lamb when he's caught. His contrition is easy to deal with.' Suddenly she said, 'Do you ever visit the cinema, Miss Owen?'

'Not often. It's a bit expensive in town.'

'Go when you can. It'll do you good to see other people's lives. It's a chance to see a species other than chapel people. The trouble is in the cinema the virtuous always seem to win.'

'Don't you like seeing the virtuous win?'

'My dear. I see and hear nothing but the triumph of virtue. It would be a nice change to see them lose once in a while. And there's poor Dan, working like a dog on a wheel, all day long turning and churning.'

'Well, at least there's butter in the churn at the end of the day.'

'You've got me now,' said Mrs Hughes, leaning back in her chair to laugh.

'I lived in London for a year once, with an aunt of mine. She was a good sort. We used to go to the theatre together, and that was the best time of my life, something to remember always. It's time those children were in bed.' She went to the study.

Her husband came into the room and sat down at the table.

'Come on, Miss Owen,' he said, 'I am hungry.'

'And how were the sick?' asked his wife as if she were asking the price of pigs at the mart.

'All better, thank God,' he said, passing the beetroot to Ann. 'How are you settling down in Blaen Ddôl, Miss Owen?'

'I've just asked her that. Ask her something else, Dan. Has she got a sweetheart, or something.'

'Well, have you?' he asked.

'Yes,' she replied without hesitation.

Mrs Hughes put her knife and fork down suddenly, opening her eyes wider to stare at Ann.

'And I've just spoken so frivolously about love,' she said.

'Don't worry,' said Ann. 'We all put our foot in it sometimes,' at once regretting her childish observation. Mrs Hughes laughed merrily, but there was no smile on the face of her husband as he remarked, 'He is a Methodist of course?'

'Indeed no, he's Church.'

The minister's face dropped.

72

'What difference does it make? Catholic, Agnostic, Methodist,' said his wife. 'I can't understand the fuss about which denomination people belong to. Come, Miss Owen, help yourself. Take no notice of your minister.'

It was obvious who was the boss in the house.

The mood of the evening might have shattered but Mrs Hughes went on.

'Dan is so loyal to everyone and to his denomination in particular that he just can't imagine anyone belonging to another one.'

'It's a problem,' Ann began. Before she could say more, Mrs Hughes placed her husband's slippers in front of the fire.

'Come on, Dan. Have a smoke.'

He mellowed at once and was cheerful for the rest of the evening. But it was his wife who began every conversation and it became obvious he was not a natural talker. The real pleasure of the evening ended with his arrival. Ann found him difficult to like, and as she watched him, a handsome man, exhausted tonight in his chair, she wondered whether they were a well-matched couple. She was so amusing and restless, he so hard-working and, in Ann's eyes, dull. Yet his wife laughed tenderly at his weaknesses. She understood him thoroughly. Ann looked forward to knowing Mrs Hughes better.

15

Ann soon learnt that the pattern of her life in Blaen Ddôl was not as fixed as she had thought it was. The corners stretched and the middle sagged. Soon after the evening in the minister's house she began to notice flaws, weaknesses in the weave of it. Maybe it was about to fall apart and she would soon have to leave the place. The weakest part of the pattern was her commitment to the school, though it was there that she worked her hardest.

Duty. The necessity to earn money. That's what drove her life at Blaen Ddôl. After today's events she saw how easily it could all cave in like a cake baked in a luke-warm oven. She had been the cause of one of the Head's violent outbursts. She had left the classroom with a child who felt sick. The Head was out of the room. When he returned he found the class in uproar and their teacher absent. She got back just after him, and before she could explain, before he saw the pale child beside her, he began to rant and roar, denouncing her in front of the children. He watched the child return to its place, then, without withdrawing his words, he sat in his desk with his back to the class.

After the first moment, Ann did not worry much about it, because she had witnessed such injustices many times before, and the Headmaster must have seen that he'd made a mistake, though he would not admit it. If he were a real man he would have apologised.

She did not join the other teachers at break today, aware that their gatherings in the staffroom made his temper worse. She knew that some of the teachers, including Lyd Edwards, had heard the row through the thin partition wall. At the end of the afternoon Lyd approached Ann with a wide smile. 'You've had a taste of his tongue. You're not the favourite you thought you were. Don't worry. He was only taking it out on you instead of his wife.'

No doubt she expected Ann to laugh. The word 'favourite' hurt. Lyd saw that her flippant wit was not appreciated and she returned to her room.

Ann did not see Bess after school, but hurried home, brooding on Lyd Edwards's sarcasm. Surely Bess would call and see her if she knew what had happened, so when Ann heard a knock on the front door and footsteps in the hall outside the sitting room door she thought it was Bess. Instead, it was Mrs Hughes who appeared behind Mrs Evans at the door. The landlady withdrew, and Mrs Hughes came into the room.

'Forgive me for calling on you without warning.'

'That's all right, Mrs Hughes. I'm glad to see you. Do sit down.'

'I'm been worried about speaking so frivolously last night.'

'I enjoyed the evening immensely.'

That was not quite true about the latter part of the visit. A doubtful smile lit Mrs Hughes's face and she untied the veil over her hat and put it on the table.

'I'm glad. I'm thoughtless with people I don't know very well, I speak before I think.'

'You weren't thoughtless with me. It's rare for me to have the pleasure of such lively conversation.'

'I've been worrying all day that you might think I meant Dan when I said it was hard to live with piety.'

'If I had thought so, once Mr Hughes arrived I had plenty of opportunity to realise you were not referring to him.'

'It's not Dan, but the chapel people, and not all of them either.'

Ann recalled a talk she'd had with Mrs Evans in the lunch hour. She had not mentioned her visit to the manse to her landlady, but all the birds of the air carried her news and she knew Mrs Evans's pointed question was a bait.

'A nice meeting last night, was it?'

'Very good.' (Curtly).

'Were there many there?'

'The usual.' (Even more curtly).

'The minister's wife is good with children.'

'Yes?' (innocently ignorant).

'Yes. Better with the children than she is on committees. She has a hasty tongue and says the silliest things.'

Ann was silent.

'She is sorry afterwards, of course,' said Mrs Evans, 'when the damage is done.'

Ann offered no hint that she'd met Mrs Hughes last night. There was something in the character of the minister's wife that made her feel she'd make a better friend than anyone else in the chapel.

'I'm glad you understand, Miss Owen,' Mrs Hughes continued. 'It's because I know Dan's godliness is sincere that I can live so happily with him. The piety of many of the chapel people is nothing more than hypocrisy.'

She's being rash again, thought Ann, looking towards the door. She was afraid Mrs Evans might have heard. Mrs Hughes looked in the same direction.

'I must talk quietly,' she said, laughing.

'I said the wrong thing mentioning your sweetheart. I wouldn't have said a word if I'd known. It's insensitive to tease people in love. It's for them and no-one else.'

'That's all right. You didn't know.'

'You've a nice place here,' said Mrs Hughes. 'But I imagine it's a bit of a cage, with somebody watching your every breath.' She nodded at the door.

Ann felt uneasy while at the same time relishing the secret manna of gossip. She could see how Mrs Hughes might turn a committee into a cabaret for some people, into a nightmare for others.

'I must go, or Mrs Evans will throw me out. You must come and see us again. Something tells me we could be friends. You're not like the rest of them.'

At that moment they heard someone else arrive, and there stood Bess.

'There you are then, Miss Owen, here's company for you. Good evening Miss Morris.'

'Good evening Mrs Hughes.'

When Bess sat down Ann began to laugh.

'What are you laughing at?' she asked.

Ann told her.

'She gets a rough deal,' said Bess. 'I don't think people here understand her at all. I won't say just chapel people, because there are others who find fault with her too.'

'Why?'

'She can be impetuous. She speaks in haste sometimes. The faithful support her just because she's the minister's wife. Jane Jones, our next door neighbour, cleans for her, and she thinks very highly of her. She's kind to Jane, and she's a good wife to her husband.'

'It's a funny thing, Bess, but outspoken people who speak from the heart are less admired than those calculating people who sharpen their knives before piercing the flesh. They are called sensible people.'

'Wise people,' her friend corrected her. 'Sensible people are of this world. The wise are on another plane, whether they're church or chapel.'

'Lyd had sharpened her knife this afternoon,' said Ann, 'but she didn't get her pound of flesh.'

'So I heard.'

'Who told you?'

'Lyd herself. I thought it outrageous that she called you the Head's favourite. That's Lyd for you. Stabbing straight for the heart. She was most disappointed that you didn't answer back. Had you done so she could have stabbed you again. All the better had there been an audience. Audiences fire her.'

'Hurting people is her spur, and she's applauded while poor Mrs Hughes is denounced for not thinking before she speaks.'

'You aren't worried about what Lyd said, are you Ann?'

'I was, at teatime. I'm all right now. You help me see things in perspective.'

'There's only one perspective for her and that's hurting people.'

'I could have walked right away from Blaen Ddôl this afternoon.'

'Don't talk of leaving. The Head will be fine tomorrow, and you can show Lyd you're not on her side. She's dying to get you to run him down.'

'I find it easier to forgive him than her. He's just foolish, and sick too.'

At that moment Mrs Evans came in with a tray of tea and sandwiches for them both. Later, when she was alone again, Ann's spirits were high. It was clear Bess had come especially to comfort her, and that was at least as important as the words she had spoken. Mrs Hughes had called in search of comfort for pain she'd brought on herself. Ann thought of Dora. The more friendship she found in Blaen Ddôl the less she felt the need to write to Dora. Dora was outside her life here, and her interest could only be that of a spectator of the drama. That was fair enough. Ann was no more than a spectator of Dora's life now, though only a year ago she had been part of it. And what of Richard? There seemed little point in telling him these troubles either. She didn't want to turn him into a mere spectator. Already she had shared her fears for Bobi with him, and he had understood and shared them. Their love must not be used as a chalice of tears. Mrs Hughes managed to attend to all her husband's needs and to live a happy life with him. How pitiably blind people were, people like Lyd Edwards and the others who stood in judgment of the minister's wife. Yet she had to live amongst them. If Mrs Hughes could do it, she too could manage to endure the taunting tongue of Lyd Edwards.

Mrs Evans did not bring up the subject of the minister's wife again that evening. Ann's silence paid off. Bess could have told her if it was a sensible silence, or a wise one.

16

Ann was in thrall to the minister's wife. She couldn't explain it. Charm was an enigma. She was attractive certainly, but there were women who possessed greater beauty. Her impetuosity was at times akin to folly, yet there could sometimes be more wisdom in the things that rushed suddenly into her head than in all the clichés of her husband's congregation put together. Perhaps it was because she was different, an outsider, that Ann was drawn to her. Ann had often met non-conformists in her college days but she had been unimpressed by them because their ideas and personalities were unlike her own. In Mrs Hughes she had encountered a rebel in a kindred spirit who expressed her own subconscious mind.

Ann didn't pursue her company, but neither did she reject the slightest hint of an invitation to the manse. At home Mrs Hughes was herself. She, her husband, her children were a part of each other. On committees and at meetings she was the odd one out. Her mind could not adjust to the mentality of a committee so her views were ignored. At home her eccentricities were understood, her strange sayings normal. Ann was not surprised when Mr Hughes stopped her in the street one day to say how glad he was that she and his wife had become such good friends. She saw from the look in his eyes how much he loved his wife, and she suddenly liked him. Good for him, thought Ann. He must be aware of the opinion which the members held of his wife, but it did not affect his deep esteem of her.

Ann noticed that when all three of them were together in the manse her friend did not express her real opinions. She did not fear her husband, of course, but it seemed she could deal with only one close friend at a time. She danced on the surface of things when the three of them were together, reserving her most original ideas for when just the two of them were together.

One Thursday evening when the minister was away preaching, Ann was invited to the manse. They were friends enough by now for Ann to help with the washing up after supper, and the children, Gwen and Emyr, had lost their shyness of her. By the time the children had gone to bed and the dishes were washed it was half past eight. They were just sitting down for a leisurely talk by the fire when there came a knock at the door. Ann felt resentful, as though it was her own privacy that had been invaded.

'Oh dear. Who's this interrupting our chat,' said Mrs Hughes, rising to answer the door. She was smiling when she returned.

'A lad with a note for Dan,' she said, putting the note on the dresser. 'You'd never believe the things that disturb the life of a minister. Some weeks I don't know how he finds time to write his sermon.'

'Some of us are lucky enough never to be disturbed,' said Ann.

'How long do you think you'll stay in Blaen Ddôl?'

'I haven't thought about it. It wouldn't be easy for me to get away, even if I wanted to. There are not many jobs about.'

'You don't intend to stay here forever, surely?'

'Certainly not. I hope to teach my own subject, Welsh, some day, but that looks hopeless at the moment. There's no pleasure in teaching subjects for which you have neither the enthusiasm nor the aptitude.'

'It's not a very good school to teach in.'

Something told Ann she should be wary of being drawn into talking about the school.

'Don't be afraid to speak. It's common knowledge that it's a bad school, and specially difficult for you, coming from outside. Too many of the teachers were brought up here.'

'I don't know about that, but if I did move it would be to teach my own subject.'

79

Mrs Hughes would not leave the subject alone. 'I have a hunch – no proof mind – that Lyd Edwards is a mischief-maker. I've never liked her. She tries to be funny on committees and at meetings, but I don't find her amusing. I've never heard her utter a single profound thought. People hereabouts regard her as some sort of goddess.'

In her heart Ann agreed, but she said only, 'I don't know her very well.'

'It's not in my own interests to advise you to leave Blaen Ddôl. I'd like to keep you here. I'd love fresh pastures myself. It's not good for the mind to stay in one place too long. You get too used to the same people and the same work, the mind loses stimulus. A quiet life breeds complacency.'

'I haven't had time to get too used to Blaen Ddôl.'

'Of course you haven't. Perhaps you'll get married.'

'Not yet. I have to pay for my education. And another thing, we must not assume that love always leads to marriage.'

'Don't leave it too late, education or no. I'd love to move but where could we go? Life with Dan and the children would be the same wherever we lived. There is a life beyond work and home, and maybe that's the way to stimulate the mind. We have the occasional lecture here but I don't count those. Nothing ever happens. People accept low wages, they take injustice as their due. No-one gets outraged. I'd like to walk down the road one day and see someone stand on a wall ripping his hair and his clothes to shreds in protest against injustice.' She looked at Ann. 'You're saying nothing,' she said.

'I'm listening and I completely agree with you. Carry on talking!'

'Wouldn't it be great if you leapt up on a chair in that school and spat scorn on those who force you to teach things you hate to a class that is far too big? It is cruelly wrong.'

'That would be the end of my career. I'd never get a job again.'

'There you are. The end of the story. Pounds, shillings and pence. I'm at the end of my tether sometimes in that chapel and feel like screaming the house down. But that would finish poor Dan's preaching. I wouldn't want him to leave the ministry. It's his life. There's no point in my wishing he'd chosen a different profession. He wouldn't be Dan, and then I wouldn't be me, because he's the man I know and love. So I must put up with the chapel. There's no escape.'

'There are worse ways to live.'

'You're right. And Dan earns more than many of his parishioners. I sometimes think complacency can't last. There'll be trouble. The people will rise up again.'

Ann had much to think about before she went to sleep that night. Her mind was in a state of excitement after listening to Mrs Hughes. How different were her two friends! Bess calmed her with her earthy wisdom, her kindness and honesty. She seemed quite content to live at home with her parents in Blaen Ddôl. Perhaps that was why the injustices of the world passed her by. Apart from her annoyance at the behaviour of Lyd Edwards she expressed no anger at the way things were. It was odd that Ann's two friends, though so different from each other, shared in common their judgment of the teacher. But at that moment Lyd Edwards didn't bother her at all. Saturday was coming, and her meeting with Richard. Life was good. Why fret about low wages, about a better world? Yet it was Mrs Hughes who saw the danger in such complacency.

17

'You know,' said Ann to the minister's wife one Thursday evening in the vestry when the children had gone home, 'I don't understand why we have debates about temperance at the children's service.'

They were discussing the special Christmas session.

'Neither do I. I can't think of anything to say on the subject. It ought to be possible to have a debate without mentioning temperance.'

'I wasn't just thinking of the subject, but the form of the debate. People taking up opposing positions. Soon they're at each other's throats. That's not the way to present the issues.'

'What would you put in place of the debate?'

'I thought we could use a story that the children could act.'

Mrs Hughes was standing on the library ladder replacing books in the book cupboard when she turned and looked directly at Ann.

'A brilliant idea. You've hit the nail on the head. Why didn't I think of it? Quite a few of the children could be involved in a play. I've been wondering how I could find things for them to do. Look, come to supper. I can only offer you pickled herring, but a pickled herring could lead to great things. Dan won't be back from his meeting in town till nine.'

'And what did you have in mind for the children to act?' said Mrs Hughes later, at home in the manse.

'We could turn a Bible story into a play, but we'd need Eastern costumes and that would take time and money. Or maybe we could use part of *Those Two Boys* from *Children's Wales*. It's a very funny story, and it would be easy to adapt.'

'One chapter wouldn't be long enough, would it?'

'We could put several chapters together. There's no need to keep every detail of the story, and we could write extra dialogue as long as we follow the story and the characters.'

'You decide. You understand these things better than I do. Why are you looking sad?'

'Was I looking sad?'

'You do sometimes. A look passes over your face, a sort of shiver like when somebody walks on your grave. Are you worrying about school?'

'I don't think so. I'm not worried about anything.'

'Your talent is wasted here.'

'You can't waste what you don't have.'

Ann was impatient to get home and begin working on her idea.

'Remember, the committee will have to agree to it first,' said Mrs Hughes.

'Surely they won't refuse an innocent little idea like this?'

'You never know. We'll have to use the vestry, and that's next door to the chapel, and there are those who say no play should be performed this side of Hell.'

Ann sighed.

'Oh, we'll win the day somehow. These things come to try us if we want to do anything connected with the chapel. It's a wonder I have a scrap of energy left by now.'

It was not, after all, an objection to putting on a play that came to try Mrs Hughes's patience when she put the idea to the committee. When she had explained the project, the Sunday School superintendent called the first question. 'Who,' he said, 'will prepare the children?'

'Well, it was Miss Owen's idea, so she should do it.'

'But the committee has not yet decided.'

'No. The committee has not decided. It was Miss Owen's idea that we could put on a play here with the children.'

'And therefore she thinks she should produce it?'

'Naturally, since it was her idea,' said Mrs Hughes.

'I don't see why we should pander to every stranger who comes into our community,' said another. 'Why can't we invite one of our own young people to do it? What about Lyd Edwards, for example?'

Mrs Hughes was about to say something hasty when she caught her husband's eye, and that silenced her.

'I'll tell you why, Edward Jones,' said the minister calmly, 'because your young people don't support the children's prayer meeting, and Miss Owen has done so faithfully, week after week, even though she's not on the committee.'

'I'd like to know who your local people are,' said his wife. 'Everyone came here from somewhere. We were none of us here a hundred years ago.'

Someone chuckled, hiding behind his neighbour's shoulder.

'If Edward Jones objects to a newcomer producing the play, then we can easily ask a local person,' said Mr Hughes. 'But I'm afraid that would mean writing a new play too. We can hardly ask Miss Owen to hand over her script. She has taken the trouble to adapt one of Winnie Parry's stories, not an easy task. Therefore we will have to ask someone to write a play and to produce it, or forget the whole idea. Remember,' he added, 'we might make a bit of money selling tickets for the performance.'

His wife was impatient for her husband to sit down so that she could add one more dig, in the hope of hitting the spot.

'There's nothing to stop Miss Owen producing it for one of the other chapels, or for the school, come to that.'

'I propose we ask Miss Owen to do it for us,' said someone who spoke for the first time. 'I've only been here a year myself.'

Not everyone laughed. Mrs Hughes went home boiling like a pan of potatoes, but she was glad Ann was not on the committee and full of admiration for Dan's tactful wisdom. His face was expressionless and his voice betrayed no hint of emotion, so no member could have accused him of anything worse than innocence.

Just before Christmas, after many a trial and tribulation, the children were ready to perform their play. As she was to find out over and over again, Ann discovered that it was not the final performance that was important, but the process of making it. She learned the true worth of Mrs Hughes, who gave her time selflessly. She would not let her own children take part. She'd been the minister's wife long enough to know the risks of gossip if her own children were in the play. The shy Gwen and Emyr were very happy to leave it to others. The two smallest children had the biggest parts and the most lines to memorise. They had to play the Two Lads, and Ann had extended the story of the clock so that it would last twenty minutes. She might have made things easier for herself had she cast two brothers for the parts, but tact demanded she shared the important roles among more than one family. Mrs Evans let her bring the children home to rehearse. Despite her tuition, the children kept falling into the old habit of recitation, speaking the lines with their eyes fixed on a spot on the parlour wall. The only child with a natural talent for acting was the girl who played the part of Kate. Mrs Hughes had to remind Ann that she was not working with a sophisticated college drama group now, but with country children who had never seen a play in their lives.

Bess and Mrs Evans helped to make the costumes, adapting old clothes and cutting them down to size. Something must be found for the children playing the two old women. Ann remembered her mother's old bonnet and cape, and Mrs Evans still had some too. The chapel promised to loan them an old grandfather clock from the chapel house.

Mrs Evans rose to the occasion. Such events brought out the best in her. When the costumes were mentioned she said, 'Why don't you invite your mother to come for the play, and she can stay here the night with us.'

'Good heavens! Mam never leaves home.'

'There's a first time for everything. Invite her. She hasn't been to see us since the Saturday you were away.'

Ann felt touched. Mrs Evans was right, despite her sly little dig. Ann had not asked her mother to come since that day.

On the night of the play nothing disastrous happened. Ann's mind was torn between anxiety for the performance and pleasure at the thought of her mother staying the night with them. When her mother arrived in the afternoon there was nothing left to do. Part of the vestry was curtained off to make a stage. Ann had a few anxious moments behind those curtains during the evening. One second before the house-lights were dimmed, when the boy playing Bobby tightened his braces a button burst off his trousers. Bess had warned her of such last minute disasters, and had advised her to pin a row of safety pins to her coat. Then, as the curtain rose, for a few breathless moments Bobby and Willie stood staring wordlessly at the audience before gazing back at Ann who was standing in the wings. Once they began they were away. Another heart-stopping moment came when Elen held the candle dangerously close to Miss Jones's hair as they looked at the clock.

The vestry was full. Everyone was happy. Ann sensed the amazement of the audience to see the children acting so well. Nobody in that audience minded little lapses in the smooth running of the performance, so much did they dote on the 'little ones'. 'Aren't they beautiful?' could be heard between the laughter. At the final curtain the applause was long and heart-warming. People thronged about Ann to congratulate her. The look on Mrs Hughes's face reassured her that things had gone well.

Ann turned down the invitation to supper at the manse. It would have seemed ungrateful to Mrs Evans, and she was glad to unwind after the performance with her mother at home in her digs. Mam and Mrs Evans enjoyed each other's company, and they loved seeing their old-fashioned clothes worn on stage. How beautiful the old styles were, they said.

To Ann there was something poignant in seeing her mother enjoy herself so much. Children nowadays had so many things she had lacked, and she was happy to see it. She had relished every word the children had spoken, and recalled every detail over supper. It was a great event for her mother, not only because it was Ann who had coached the children, but because of the stage, the clothes, the words, the spectacle. The thrill of the evening captured her heart and mind. What had been achieved by those children was more important to her than the evening's fun and laughter. How different her mother looked dressed in her best. Ann was so used to seeing her in working clothes. Yet, despite the finery, nothing removed that fleeting expression Ann sometimes caught passing over her face. It was not sadness, exactly. It was sweeter than that, though not really sweet either. It was the look of someone who had defeated a great sorrow but could not quite conceal its traces. She felt suddenly flat. The play was over. She would no longer be rehearsing the children night after night, and the pleasures of working together as a company were over. But Christmas was coming. Seeing her mother so contented by the fire made her begin to look forward to it.

'I hope they'll manage the milking tomorrow morning. Elin Jones has promised to help.'

'Forget about the milking,' said Mrs Evans.

'Quite right,' said Ann. 'For once in your life you don't have to feed man or beast.'

18

It was a silent, windless Christmas morning. The mountains loomed in the frozen dark of December. A grey stillness lay on the countryside. Nobody was expecting the postman, except Ann. In those days there was a delivery on Christmas morning. The children were too grown-up now to have gifts of oranges and handkerchiefs, and adults could not afford to exchange presents.

The Christmas parcel from the shop had arrived and been unpacked days ago. The pudding was simmering on the fire, the calendar announcing the new year soon to arrive was hanging on the wall. Embers glowed red-hot under the oven. The crackle of roasting beef was music to the ears and its aroma sharpened the appetite. Bobi and Ann, and Roland back for Christmas from working away, were watching the pigs feeding in the sty, lifting their heads now and then to listen to the human beings who gazed down on them.

'They should be glad to be alive,' said Roland.

'And those too,' said Bobi, watching hens scratching about in the dung heap.

'Pity one of them's not in the oven,' said Roland.

'Oh, no!' said Ann. 'I couldn't eat one of our own hens.'

'You can eat someone else's cow,' said Bobi.

'I can indeed,' said Ann. 'Can't you just smell that roast, coming from the kitchen.'

With that she ran to meet the postman. There were letters for her from Richard and Mrs Hughes, and a few Christmas cards. Inside Richard's letter was a linen handkerchief edged with lace. She blushed with pleasure and embarrassment. She had sent Richard nothing but a letter and a card, being uncertain if it was appropriate for new lovers to exchange gifts. True, she had been short of money, as she had bought little presents for Gwen and Emyr Hughes and had given something extra to Mrs Evans on top of the rent. All that, and the money she paid to her mother, left little over from five pounds a month. But since she had received a full month's salary before school broke up, she had a little more than usual this time. She could give half a crown to Bobi. His need was greater than anybody's, and he would enjoy the money more than anyone in the family. He had the intelligence to value the gift too. Richard's letter overflowed with love. He apologised for sending such a small present. And she had sent him nothing. What sort of Christmas would he have with only his old uncle and the housekeeper? Would she ever be free to bring him the love and fulfilment for which he yearned?

She opened the envelope from Mrs Hughes. It contained a long letter, but no card. Mr Hughes was ill. The night after the play he had collapsed and she'd had to send for the doctor who had prescribed a good rest. Her tone was depressed as is often the way with usually high-spirited people. She mentioned the play, how much her husband had enjoyed it, and how he had been too tired that evening to remember to thank Ann properly. He sent her his thanks for taking so much responsibility from his shoulders and for giving them all so much pleasure. Perhaps she had misjudged Mr Hughes, and might after all grow fond of him one day. Mrs Hughes wrote that Ann herself should write a play next time.

The strange thing was that the idea had crossed Ann's mind too, and Mrs Hughes had thought the very same thing. In fact, it was not the performance that had given her most pleasure, but the process of adapting the story. Of course, it was only a small achievement, but she had successfully taken a story and shaped it to fit the discipline of the stage. It was even more satisfying than getting the children to speak their lines fluently. The night she had gone home from the manse to begin the task she felt such a strong urge to write that, for a few days, the obsession displaced even Richard from the forefront of her mind. Now she was taken by a fresh creative impulse to write a play, this time not based on someone else's story but on an original idea of her own.

There were cards from Dora, Bess and Mrs Evans. Dora's card contained a note promising to write soon. Time and place had distanced her and Dora, but not their hearts. Would their friendship survive their parting? And poor Mrs Evans. She had to spend Christmas with her brother and a sister-in-law with whom she did not get on.

The family round the table this Christmas Day was complete. Huw was grown-up now, but they all still sat in the places they had occupied since they were children. They went as instinctively to their own seats as each cow takes its stall in the shippon. To change old habits now would be to tempt providence, like walking under a ladder. The smell of roast beef filled the room, steaming-hot, tender meat ready to be carried from oven to table, the potatoes roasted to a crisp brown, white and floury inside, the sauce red as oak from the juices of the meat, a creamy white cauliflower anointed with butter, the pudding gleaming with sweet butter sauce. A world of plenty. Bobi and Roland insisted on having some sweet butter on its own, just like when they were children. Everyone talked and Roland grew gradually closer to them again as if he had never been away. It was his first visit since the summer, and he wouldn't be home again until next summer, because the journey cost more than he could afford. Each time he left he wept till his eyes were swollen. Ann could not stop herself weeping with him. It was one of those facts of life that had to be endured. When he got back he would write home without ever a mention of his feelings. Bobi could learn some of Roland's stoicism, thought Ann. Her father said what he always said, year after year. 'Well, here we are, a whole family again.' This time it struck Ann as strange. He was not usually short of original things to say. Did his habitual little sayings conceal things too powerful to speak? Did that really define his idea of a family? They were whole in more ways than one. Familiar love needs no words. It sang beneath the natural rhythms of their conversation, as when you take aim at something and touch something else. Each one of them knew their own private joy at coming home. Ann thought of the supper last summer when Bobi was disappointed about the tin of tongue, and at once banished the thought lest it spoil the happiness of the moment. She thought of Richard. Whatever was set on the table for him that day, she knew there would not be the warmth of a family life like hers. Again she grieved that she had not sent him a present. She'd know better next time and would send her explanation in a letter. She would write this very night. She couldn't imagine what it was like not to have a family. He would never write of his sense of loss in a letter. What sort of loneliness was it to be without father and mother, without brother or sister? Did the old emptiness come back to him at Christmas time?

Ann's mind often meditated on such things lately, things she had never considered before. She had been content to live for today and for tomorrow without ever a backward glance. These were new thoughts. She weighed and measured people and things and sorted them into their order. She saw them as beings shoved from behind and threatened by perils that lurked ahead. One day perhaps she would shape these ideas and write them down, just as she adapted that story for the stage.

For today she must put aside all but the pleasures of the moment, feasting, going to the chapel Christmas eisteddfod, just being home without thinking about teaching the children, reading and writing to Richard.

She shook herself and began to clear the table. She and Bobi went into the dairy to wash the dishes. Bobi took off his jacket and put on his mother's apron. He scraped the saucepans with a knife and scoured them with a handful of grit in an old cloth. Ann began to wash the dishes in a pan of hot water.

'Don't rush. I'll dry them when I've done this,' said Bobi.

So the work was done, cheerfully and noisily.

'Are you going out to tea, Nani?' asked Bobi, knowing it was a long way to the next village for the chapel eisteddfod.

'No, no-one's invited me. Are you?'

'No, and I'll refuse if I'm asked. I'd rather come home for tea.'

'Me too. It's great to be home.'

'It is.'

Ann did not want to mention the shop. Today must be perfect. She had lost interest in the eisteddfod meeting since she had given up competing in it, and she would have been glad to give it a miss this year. But to stay away from the eisteddfod on Christmas day would be like eating a jam sandwich for dinner. It was an annual event. She and Bobi went together with Huw and his friend, though nothing would stir Roland from the house. He had no intention of moving until he had to catch his train back to work.

The Christmas day eisteddfod had not changed at all. The same competitions, the same competitors, the usual debate, though not on temperance this time but on books, a short performance by the poets (very amusing), the five-minute speech (not so amusing), the choirs (neither as numerous nor as eager as they used to be). Ann longed for it to be over, and Bobi said so too as they walked home. It was they who had changed, not the eisteddfod. There came to Ann's mind the sight of Mrs Hughes standing on the library ladder in the vestry the night she'd suggested doing a play instead of holding a debate, and saw again the joy in her eyes at the thought of something new. Nothing revolutionary, just new. Would there ever be innovation in the chapel eisteddfod? A single new idea? Yet it was for the old ways that she yearned tonight as she hurried home with her brother: Christmas supper, cold meat, fried potatoes, a slice of cold pudding, this time without sweet butter, sitting round the fire talking about the eisteddfod, and reading Daniel Owen.

No, Ann would break the habit tonight. She would write to Richard. She must. She must tell him every thought that had passed through her mind that Christmas day.

19

The first page of the new calendar, January 1914, looked strangely unfamiliar on the classroom wall. The days crept by, the new year as thin and bony as a freshly-shorn ewe after the rich feast of Christmas. Early one cold day, a bitter wind piercing the cracks in the window frames, the children sniffed and sneezed without handkerchiefs, and Ann wore her outdoor jacket over her winter dress. The headmaster was busy with figures at his table near the stove. The children's hands were blue, their knuckles white as new potatoes from pressing down their pens as they tried to write. Occasionally a child stopped writing to blow a mouthful of warm breath into frozen cupped hands. Those furthest from the stove and closest to the windows turned up the collars of their jackets to cover their ears. The sky was dark and Ann feared another storm was brewing. If she or a child sneezed the headmaster winced as though he had been bitten by a fly. Each time a child blew on frozen fingers he turned to identify the perpetrator of the noise, but the importance of the figures he was working on subdued his rising rage. This continued all afternoon until the last lesson. Ann prayed the day would end without an outburst.

A quarter of an hour before the end of the day the headmaster rose suddenly to his feet and dismissed the class. He left the room to tell the other classes they could go home. For a moment they did not realise their good luck, then the children smiled at

Ann as if she were responsible. 'Thanks Miss,' came from here and there in the room, then the sound of desks closing, and the chatter of jubilation, until the room was silent and the cheerful chattering had moved on to the cloakroom.

Ann rejoiced too. Fifteen minutes was a tiny scrap of the new year, *bychwing*, as her father would call it, but at the end of such a miserable day it was a mouthful of time to relish. Like a child with a halfpenny, she could not decide how to spend it. No doubt she would squander it at Mrs Evans's fireside after all. Bess had been full of cold at lunchtime, and declared she was off to bed straight after tea.

On the first night back after the Christmas holidays Ann had called at the manse, so she did not feel she could visit the Hughes family again so soon. As a child she had been told often enough, never wear out your welcome. The manse had seemed less cheerful than usual that Monday. Mrs Hughes was distant, though glad to see her. Instead of bubbling over with words she had little to say. She asked after Ann's family, and about Christmas, the sort of formal enquiry she might have forgotten to ask in the full spate of her usual flood of conversation. When Ann asked after Mr Hughes, she understood the reason for her friend's low spirits. Her mouth trembled and she turned her head away. Then the dam burst.

'Oh, Ann. I'm afraid Dan's worse than I told you in my letter. It's not just exhaustion. He's got a weak heart.'

'Well,' said Ann. 'It can be helped with care and good nursing. We shouldn't give up hope about heart disease, or tuberculosis. Plenty can be done.'

'That's what the doctor told me, but he's supposed to rest and I know he won't. He insisted on going to all the services today instead of just one of them. and he can't afford to rest. The chapel can't carry an idle minister.'

'I'm sure they'll be tolerant for a while because Mr Hughes has worked twice as hard as he needed to for so long.'

'Oh, Ann. You're such a comfort. I haven't talked to any of the members about it, and I don't want any of them to know yet. I had to talk to you tonight. I feel upset because he insisted on going to chapel at 6 o'clock.'

'I won't mention it to anyone. I'm sure he must have been feeling better or he wouldn't have gone.'

'Yes, he's better than he was. But he should rest more, especially in this cold weather. He's too conscientious by far. Let me make you a cup of tea. I feel better after talking to you.'

'No thank you. I've had tea. I just wanted to see you. It's horrible being back.'

'Yes, and the beginning of a new year is like a kitchen without a fire. Listen,' she said as she opened a drawer and took out a box of chocolates, 'this is for you. I was too depressed to post it in time for Christmas.'

So it's home to Mrs Evans for me tonight, Ann thought, unless she too could take an early night, like Bess. No, not with only a candle to read by. Tonight was the *seiat*, so Mrs Evans would be out at the chapel and Ann could read and write her letters.

To her great surprise, there, leaning against the wall beside the door, was Richard's bicycle, and inside sitting by Mrs Evans's fire was Richard.

'I found Mr Edmund waiting in the cold when I came back from the shop,' said Mrs Evans, 'and I made him come inside. He was going to wait outside for you.'

'I went to the library in Bangor and it was closed,' said Richard, 'so I thought I'd cycle over to see you.'

Ann could not hide her pleasure, even from Mrs Evans.

'It's a very lucky day today, Mrs Evans. They let us out of school fifteen minutes early.'

'What was the matter?'

'Runny noses. Sneezing. Sickly faces. It's an ill wind that blows nobody any good.'

'That's a misleading proverb, don't you think, Mr Edmund?'

'We'll take it as the truth today,' he replied. 'Next time it may prove false.'

At such times Ann felt fond of Mrs Evans. No matter at how inconvenient a time they might arrive, she always had a welcome for visitors. Ann did not want to take advantage of her welcome tonight. If she did, Mrs Evans might feel she must keep out of the way, and stay in her small kitchen.

'Let's go for a walk to warm up,' she suggested.

93

'Don't feel you must go out on my account,' said Mrs Evans. 'You're both welcome to stay here.'

'Thank you, Mrs Evans,' said Richard. 'I need to stretch my legs after peddling all this way. Thank you for my tea.'

'You're welcome. Come whenever you like, my boy.'

'I'm so happy to see you,' said Richard taking Ann's arm.

'Me too. I was thinking how I'd give the world to see you as I left school today. Bess has gone home with a bad cold, and I don't like to trouble Mrs Hughes too often. How was your Christmas?'

'Same as usual. Three of us at table and not much to say to each other. Elin Roberts cooked a good dinner, but the three diners were miles apart. Not like a family at all. The conversation was amiable enough, and there are plenty of things happening in a village to talk about. But a real family would have something warmer.'

'Did you go to church?'

'I did, before breakfast. I felt refreshed after going, like when there's been a shower. I enjoyed my afternoon.'

'Yes?'

'We had an early dinner. Elin Roberts went home to her family for the rest of the day and my uncle went off to bed. I sat by the fire reading. At least you can be sure no-one will disturb you on Christmas day. They all went to chapel to the eisteddfod meeting, but I didn't feel like it.'

'You're not used to it, I suppose.'

'No, I'm not. The competitions are for regular chapel-goers. I was suddenly overwhelmed by warmth because of you. This time last year we weren't courting,' he said suddenly, and stopped. 'I laid the table for tea with the best tablecloth and my mother's best china. My uncle was astonished when he saw the table.'

'What did he say?'

'Are we having visitors? I hope not, I told him. Then I thought how nice it would be to drink tea from a delicate cup without any strangers around.'

'Giving yourself a treat.'

'Indeed. And thinking of you.'

'So that was your Christmas?'

'With your letter as well it was good enough.'

'I felt bad that I had not sent you a present, but I wasn't sure if I should. I didn't want to seem forward.'

'I know. That's why I like you.'

They hardly noticed that they had walked nearly two miles out of the village, the road growing steeper all the way. The wind buffeted them in gusts, piercing their clothes, but they were too absorbed in their talk to feel it.

'Tell me about your Christmas, Ann.'

'As I told you in my letter, it was exactly the same as always, and yet different.'

'Yes. Things do change, however slowly.'

'I wonder if that's why my father says every year, well, here we are a whole family again?'

'I expect so. He can see the day coming when some of you will get married.' He pressed her close to him.

'I never thought of that. I suppose I thought he was just grateful we'd all survived another year.'

'Yes. But why? You're all young and healthy. I suppose all families do suffer bereavement, but I have no-one to lose now but my uncle. You're only afraid to lose someone you love.'

'Don't be gloomy.'

'It's my way of telling you how much you mean to me. Look. We've arrived somewhere.'

'Yes. Pen Ddôl.'

'A pub. Let's go in for a warming drink, shall we?'

'No, I don't think so, I've never been in a pub.'

'Come on. You won't go to hell.' And he pushed her in front of him before she could resist.

'Give this young lady a drink, please. She's perished with cold.'

'A glass of rum?'

'Fine.'

'Not much warmth in your love!' said someone standing at the bar. Richard took no notice. He escorted Ann to the fire and carried the small glass of rum to where she sat.

'I will have bread and cheese, and a glass of beer please,' he said to the landlord. 'I have a long cycle ride in front of me.'

'With the cold wind ahead or behind you?' the landlord asked. But Richard did not tell him where he was going.

'Talk about a new year,' said someone. 'I'd already like to see the back of it.'

Richard took a crown piece from his pocket to pay for the drinks and the food, and told Ann it was a Christmas gift from his uncle, as he sat down beside her at the fireside with his beer and bread and cheese. Ann said nothing. This was a new aspect of Richard and of life. She looked about her. The pub was like a widow's kitchen turned into a small shop, the counter acting as the bar, and the fire close enough to warm them all. Instead of the rowdy people she'd been brought up to expect in a pub, there were half a dozen men sitting quietly staring at each other as though there was nobody else in the world. An oil-lamp hung from the ceiling and shed a clean light into the corners of the room and onto the wrinkles of the customers' faces. When she got used to the light, Ann noticed a man she knew, a member of her chapel. She broke into a sweat. By tomorrow all Blaen Ddôl would know that she had been to the pub, and that she had been the only woman there.

'Drink up,' said Richard.

She did, and as the warmth filled her it lifted her spirits and cleared her reason. Of course, the man would say nothing. It would be so easy for her to tell his story too. She began to laugh as she saw the funny side of the situation. The *seiat* in the chapel. The *seiat* in the pub. Mrs Evans in the chapel. A *seiat* of some half a dozen in the pub, and she with them. If they only knew how much experience and talk there was in common between drinkers and other people. The truth would out all right if the drink did the talking.

'Richard, is this is all right?'

'It's wonderful.'

'I want to break from the *seiat*, but not from the rest.'

'Nothing will come of it.'

'I could always come to Church with you,' she said laughing, realising that her head was spinning. 'I'm drunk aren't I?'

'Not at all. You're happy, that's all.'

'I don't need rum to make me happy tonight.'

'No, but I did need to prevent you from catching cold. You know it's a lot colder than when we left Blaen Ddôl.'

'Impossible. I was freezing in school.'

'I thought we could walk here without realising it would get so cold.'

'I hope it'll be like this every January of our lives. I'll remember January 1914.'

Her head began to steady, and she glanced at her fellow member of the chapel. He smiled at her, a smile from the heart, lighting up his face conspiratorially. It was good to meet a fellow sinner, Ann thought.

As they walked home she was perfectly sober and quite unrepentant. They walked briskly down hill with the wind behind them, their feet warming up as they trod the hard road. What would Mrs Evans say if she knew Ann had been to the pub? And Mrs Hughes? And Bess? Who cared! In this free spirit she kissed Richard, thanking him for being different from everyone else.

20

Ann was sitting by the fire after setting the table for supper when Mrs Evans returned from chapel. She had been musing on the strange events of the evening. She felt as she used to when she was a child sitting on the swing, being pushed as far as the ropes could reach, trying to touch the gable-end of the haystack with the tip of her toe. It was a thrilling sensation, and only when it was over did she feel scared by her own daring. Tonight she was delighted with her own boldness: she had visited a pub, and it had been pure pleasure.

'Oh, you're back then,' said Mrs Evans, sounding surprised, 'but it was very cold for you to be out so long. Weren't you frozen?'

'Not at all. We walked as far as Pen Ddôl and Mr Edmund took me into the pub for a drink to warm up.'

'Where?' asked Mrs Evans, sitting down in her chair as though she had heard bad news.

'To the pub for a tot of rum. It was even colder on Pen Ddôl than down here.'

'You went into a public house, Miss Owen?'

'Yes. What's wrong with that?'

'Were you never taught in the Band of Hope that it's a sin to drink alcohol?'

'There's nothing wrong with a warming drink to keep out the cold.'

'What would your mother and father say?'

'Nothing. Mam would certainly understand, and my father has an occasional drink.'

Mrs Evans turned her head to stare into the fire, a favourite posture when she was offended. Ann thought the inquisition was concluded, but Mrs Evans began again.

'Does your family truly believe in such things?'

'What things?'

'Going into public houses.'

'If you are asking if my family approve of drunkenness, they certainly do not, but they wouldn't see anything wrong in my having a tot of rum in an inn on a cold evening. I've told you before, they are chapel-goers, but they aren't pious or narrow-minded. Good God, where would they have got the money to go to a pub?'

'Shame on you Miss Owen, using such language. I'm shocked at Mr Edmund enticing you into a public house.'

'Look, Mrs Evans. Don't you make insinuations about my *cariad*.' She managed to bite her tongue on the word *evil*. 'Accuse me if you like, but leave Richard out of it.'

Ann was really angry now, and when Mrs Evans turned from the fire to look at her the floodgates opened.

'It's nobody's business what I do. You live your narrow little lives in this village as if chapel were the beginning and end of the world. You don't even understand your Bible. You'd give Paul a telling off for offering Timothy a sip of wine. You'd censor the psalms. You've forgotten what it's like to be young.'

At that she rose suddenly, rushed out to the hall, put on her coat and went out. By now she was in tears but she swallowed them as she saw she was walking straight into Lei Pritchard, one of the teachers at the school. There was no way of avoiding him.

'Hello, Miss Owen. Where are you off to this cold night?'

'Oh, Mr Pritchard. Nowhere. Nowhere. Out for some air.'

'There's enough air creeping under the doors tonight.'

'Out to look for some peace. There's none of that indoors.'

'Would you like me to come with you?'

'No, thank you. I need to be alone to find some privacy.'

She whirled away. There was something odd about Lei Pritchard tonight. He was a quiet little man who listened amiably as they talked at break at school, keeping his counsel, but taking in every word. His eyes were even bluer tonight than usual, as if he'd been drinking. Ann was glad to get away from him. She remembered Mrs Hughes's advice that having a sweetheart kept other fellows away. She walked fast, not knowing where she was going. She thought of Richard cycling to Anglesey, the wind of the dead against him. A strange peace possessed her at the thought of him. In speaking out she had rid herself of everything and everyone but Richard. She regretted nothing she had said, only what she had forgotten to say. She remembered how her mother enjoyed a glass of stout in the tavern with the other women, when they took a pig to market. What was wrong with that? Heavens, the women worked hard enough with never a penny to squander, and Mrs Evans would deny them a glass of stout. What did she know about fattening pigs or mucking out a shippon or feeding mash to calves or washing the threshings? As for her father, he loved company and a good story. He enjoyed these things over a cup of tea at home, and about twice a year he would enjoy them over a beer in town. It was like a Sunday School treat to a child. Why should they be denied the small comforts they so richly deserved, just because fate had decreed they live their lives on the blue slate slopes of the mountains and had appointed people like Mrs Evans to be the guardians of their souls?

She turned back abruptly, hoping Lei Pritchard had gone home. She would have to face Mrs Evans or stay out all night. She went through the house like a whirlwind, telling her landlady she wouldn't be wanting any supper tonight, and she was half-way up the stairs before Mrs Evans could say a word. There was no hot water bottle in her bed tonight, and she didn't need one.

Once under the bedclothes her mind began to work more calmly. She would have to face the consequences of the evening's events. The man in the pub might gossip. On the other hand, he might keep silent. But if he talked, the minister and the headmaster might get to hear about it. She did not know how the head might react, but she had a good idea what the minister would think. She couldn't be certain about Mrs Hughes. It was one thing for Mrs Hughes to say she had no room for the temperance movement, quite another to act upon her opinion. Ann would tell Bess everything if she was well enough to come to school tomorrow. She was sure Bess would take a sensible view. But Mrs Hughes was the minister's wife, and she revered her husband. If it came to the crunch no doubt she must side with him. Ann realised that if she married Richard she would join the church without regret, because there she could worship God without fear of an interfering congregation. Or was leaving a religion as difficult as leaving a family? She knew her days were numbered in Blaen Ddôl, though it seemed pointless to seek new lodgings now, if Mrs Evans was willing for her to stay. She would look for another job. That wouldn't be easy, especially doing the kind of teaching she really wanted. If no job could be found she would have to stay, working harder than ever in Blaen Ddôl. Oh, the tedium of hard work. Out of the turmoil one thought was clear. Richard must not know about tonight, for he would blame himself for getting her into trouble. Her ideals about people, so bright and held so dearly in her college days, were being trodden down one by one. People were made of clay. Her relationship with Richard must remain perfect, the one unspoilt thing.

Her mind returned to the walk to Pen Ddôl and the happy talk they had had. She thought of the tea Richard had prepared on Christmas afternoon. How strange that he had set the table with his mother's best china. What grief must be in him! She realised that it was not only for the pleasure of sipping tea from fine porcelain, but for the sense of communion with his mother that he had used her fine china things. She knew nothing of such a longing. She fell asleep thinking of him, his company, his long journey home.

Mrs Evans had recovered herself by the next morning, and neither she nor Ann mentioned what had happened. Ann was more stubborn. She couldn't forget it, and she was as determined to leave Blaen Ddôl as she had been before she fell asleep. She didn't mind about Mrs Evans now. She didn't mind about anyone except the headmaster, for he alone had the power to frustrate her future. Even that prospect troubled her only inasmuch as it would affect her parents. They would be hurt if she lost her job.

She was glad to see Bess in school, but there was no chance to talk before 4 o'clock, on the way home from school. When she had heard the whole story, Bess laughed.

'To think of you in all that trouble, and I was in bed sipping a tot of rum as a medicine to cure my cold,' she said.

'Really?'

'Really. My mother's favourite remedy every time. She went out to fetch it last night.'

'So I wasn't the only woman to go to the pub yesterday evening.'

'No. But your real sin in Mrs Evans's eyes was to sit down in the pub, knocking it back like a man.'

'Knocking it back indeed! I drank it at one gulp. Richard took his time over his beer and bread and cheese. Mrs Evans doesn't know that.'

'She ought to know there's other nourishment in the world than tea and scones.'

'What shall I say if the story gets out?'

'Don't worry about it, Ann. Let things take their course. Perhaps that man will keep his mouth shut. It sounds like Lyd Edwards's uncle. He lives with them.'

'Oh no!'

'What does it matter? They can't kill you.'

'The school managers could sack me.'

'Not without the head's agreement, and knowing him I don't think he'll take any notice even if he hears about it.'

'Tell me, Bess, does Lei Pritchard drink?'

'He goes out for a drink every night, and no-one says a word about it.'

'How old is he?'

''Goodness knows. He could be anything between twenty and forty.'

21

A small tot of rum in a pub grew into a big story. One wee tot became a quart of wormwood for Ann, and the trouble it caused her did not die away. Not all her acquaintances were like Bess Morris. Lyd Edwards found out about it, and it was far too great a temptation for her to keep her mouth shut. Days later, when Ann thought the fuss was over, Lyd raised it again in the staffroom at school.

'You'd never guess where some people spend their evenings,' she said.

Ann knew what was coming and it gave her a moment to think.

'The Pen Ddôl pub is perfect for young couples to go out drinking.'

Ann flushed but kept her temper.

'Yes it is,' she said. 'And it's very handy for other people too, people who don't want to be caught drinking down in Blaen Ddôl. Little do they know who might have seen them. Maybe I saw someone. But I don't give a damn who sees me taking a tot to ward off a cold.'

She needed all her courage to tell the truth. She felt like a suffragette leading the women's movement, determined to brazen it out with an air of couldn't-care-less.

'It's lucky someone was kind enough to buy me that tot of rum,' she added, 'or I'd have been home in bed next day and you would have had to take my class, Miss Edwards. Think of the trouble I saved you.'

Everyone but Bess stared in amazement because they had not understood Lyd's malicious remark. After a pause Lei Pritchard laughed as though he had solved a mystery, and he nervously entered the discussion.

'That was a nasty dig you had there, Lyd. You'd better watch it. You won't have the last word in this school.'

'No, I suppose not,' she replied, 'but some people attend chapel or pub as if they were one and the same place.'

'If a pub is a hostelry I fail to see what's wrong with it', said Ann. 'The ale-house was as hospitable and close to the chapel as the chapel-house itself years ago, and the preacher preached all the more eloquently after a tankard.'

'Did you preach the better for it?' asked Lei.

'Ask Mrs Evans,' said Ann, realising as she spoke that Lei understood her. She had an idea he knew she was piling word upon word without conviction, whistling in the dark to keep her courage up. If she said any more she might begin to believe it herself.

Bess was silent no longer. 'It's nobody's business where we go after four o'clock,' she said, 'as long as it doesn't stop us doing our job in school the next day.'

'Here's to that!' said Lei.

'You've found your tongue today,' said Lyd.

'I find it every night,' he replied, 'and lose it next morning at school, according to Bess's rule.'

Ann felt depressed by this argument and decided, without consulting Bess, that she must speak to the head. Wise Bess would no doubt have advised her to leave well alone, but Ann needed to be unwise for once for the sake of her own peace of mind. Once she knew his reaction she would know what to do. She asked the head if she could talk to him at his home that evening, to avoid staying behind after school and arousing suspicions. He agreed readily.

At home the headmaster was a different man. He cast off his authoritarian air. He was no longer the watchman with eyes everywhere, seeing that work was done, seeing that there was order, discipline and silence. At home he was easy and relaxed. He could smoke, and speak in Welsh. Ann noticed that even the colour of his eyes seemed to have changed. She had thought them steel-blue, but now they were nut-gold. She told her story, stumbling over her explanation of who Richard was. The more she talked the weaker her case sounded in her own mind, but she brought her story to a confident conclusion.

'Miss Owen, why are you telling me this?'

'Because people are talking, and I was afraid you would hear a false version of it.'

'In principle I have no right to interfere with what you do outside school hours. If parents complained I would be obliged to listen and act accordingly, but this is nothing.'

Ann felt calmer and began to talk more fluently.

'Mrs Evans made a fuss.'

'Yes, she would. If it weren't so cold in the chapel she would move her bed in there. I don't know what has come over the woman. People like her are good at looking after people's creature comforts, but they can't leave it there. She must be caring for your soul too. Look for another place.'

'It would be difficult to find better lodgings.'

'No, I mean look for another school, and leave a hole like this.'

'But . . . but . . .'

'I don't want to lose you, but you deserve a better job. Blaen Ddôl is like a mask over a face. The world changes but Blaen Ddôl is frozen. I'd leave tomorrow if I could.'

'But surely a headmaster is happy wherever he is?'

'My dear Miss Owen, the same people who trouble you trouble me too. A headmaster must abide by the rules of his community and must go to chapel like everyone else. You are fresh from college. You will soon discover that nobody is free but those rich enough to snap their fingers at work. Go home, tell Mrs Evans to mind her own business, and enjoy yourself while you're young enough to have no responsibilities.'

Ann went home feeling much better, wondering at the secrets of the human heart. Now school seemed the bright and hospitable place while her lodgings were dark and cold, for Mrs Evans would never again be as she was before their quarrel. She was brisk and cool, though she did nothing to neglect Ann's physical comfort. Ann no longer felt able to invite Bobi to tea in case he was not made welcome, and she hoped Richard would not turn up unannounced, as he must know nothing of the quarrel. She did not want to feel indebted to her landlady for anything.

As she entered the house that night she knew her days at Blaen Ddôl were numbered. The headmaster had described it well. It was like a mask over a face, stiff and unchanging. Its inhabitants knew neither spur nor ambition. She was, as Mrs Hughes had once described her husband, the wheel of a butter-churn going nowhere. After the elation that followed her talk with the headmaster, Ann's spirits sank again as she walked into the dark passage of her lodging-house. Each time she entered the house now she dreaded that her landlady's mood might be darker than ever. But tonight Mrs Evans was eager to speak to her.

'Mrs Hughes called. She would like you to have supper at the manse tonight.'

She sounded more friendly than she had for days, and there was a note of apprehension in her voice, as though she had guessed Ann might look for other lodgings. Ann hesitated. She had not spoken alone to Mrs Hughes for a while, and now evidently she wanted to talk to her alone. Or would her husband be there too? What if she had heard the gossip? If so, Ann must tell her the truth. She put on her coat and set out, though not with the same eagerness as when she had gone to the manse before Christmas.

'Oh, Ann, it's good to see you. Such a long time since we had a good chat.'

'How is Mr Hughes?'

'Much better. He's away tonight.'

Ann breathed more easily. The old brightness had returned to Mrs Hughes's eyes. Her voice was lively, and a strand of hair fell over her forehead. She was so warm that Ann was tempted to tell her the story before she was asked, but she held back. It was best forgotten. Mrs Hughes brought to the table a succulent piece of boiled ham, and gave the children their supper first. Ann recalled the first time she had come here to supper. They had shared the same feast that happy evening which now seemed so long ago. When the children had gone to bed they drew the table closer to the fire, and sat down to supper together.

'Tell me, Ann, has anything upset you recently? Don't tell me unless you want to.'

Ann trembled. 'What have you heard?'

'That you and your boyfriend were seen drinking in a pub and you got into trouble with the headmaster.'

The half-lie forced Ann to tell her story again. She was weary of it and had begun to forget the exact sequence of events. It sounded like somebody else's story.

'As for the last part, it's a downright lie. When you called tonight I was over at the headmaster's house. I told him the story myself before anyone else could speak to him, because Lyd was taunting me in school today.'

'I'm glad I asked you. I know the truth now. I was in two minds about raising it, but between friends there should be no secrets.'

'Yes, I agree. Perhaps you think I should have come to tell you sooner. But I thought nothing of it before Mrs Evans showed her teeth. Even that didn't really count. But once Lyd began to talk I knew her version of the story would be all round the village and the head would hear of it. May I ask who told you? Don't tell me if you don't want to, but was it Lyd, or Mrs Evans?'

''Not Mrs Evans, fair play to her.'

'It's good to hear that, or I'd have to look for another place. Does Mr Hughes know?'

'It was he who heard about it.'

'And of course he was offended.'

'I must admit he was at first, until I said there would be an explanation. No use condemning someone without hearing their side of the story.'

Ann put down her knife and fork.

'I'm sorry to say this, sitting here sharing your supper, but I must be frank. I don't need an excuse to go to the pub. If I'd gone there for fun to enjoy a drink with Richard, it's nobody else's business. I know things go on in pubs that shouldn't, but that's the fault of the people not the pub. I can't for the life of me see why someone shouldn't occasionally drink something stronger than coffee or tea if you can afford it, without people interfering. It's high time to stop connecting the temperance movement and the chapel. It breeds hypocrisy.'

'I agree with you, Ann, that's just what I was thinking. I can't understand why we argue over a few sins (if they are sins) or why we're obsessed by it. But I'm married to Dan and daren't voice my opinions around Blaen Ddôl or he'd lose his ministry. He doesn't agree with me, but as I never feel the urge to go to the pub we don't argue about it. I have my views, Dan has his, and we live together happily because I never put my convictions into practice.'

'I'm horrified to think that I live in a place where such a trivial thing could cause such a commotion.'

'Yes, the chains of a society like this lock round us, and the only way to be happy is to submit to the fetters.'

'Well, I'm not accepting it. I will rebel, not by going to the pub, but by leaving Blaen Ddôl.'

'Surely not?'

'Yes, I've made up my mind. Chapel people are not going to tell me how to live.'

'You accepted the rules when you joined the chapel.'

'I was too young to know what I was doing.'

'You'll find the same troubles wherever you go.'

'Maybe, but I will have made my protest. I can never feel happy here again.'

'I'm sorry, Ann, but you see how I'm trapped. I can't rebel, because I love my husband and children. Maybe you won't notice the chains once you're married.'

'Perhaps not. At least if I marry Richard I'll start with a great advantage in the matters we've talked of tonight.'

'There may be other fetters.'

Ann did not reply. Her last remark had been sharper than she'd meant. As she left Mrs Hughes said,

'Believe me, I'm on your side. I was born too soon to be a rebel. I hope you won't stay away from here. Look,' she said, and her eyes filled with tears, 'we'll plan to meet after the next children's service.'

'We will,' said Ann. 'That will be a great pleasure.'

Mrs Hughes did not mention how she had spoken to her husband on Ann's behalf. He had planned to give her a piece of his mind on the subject of alcohol. He had even called her 'a real little hussy', and pronounced her unsuitable to the job of teaching children. His wife persuaded him to say nothing. She knew Ann better than that, she had said. As always she managed to calm him without raising her voice. She would have a more encouraging story to tell him on his return.

22

The winter of 1914 melted, like many another winter, as lightly as the cold mists rising from the mountain tops. For Ann it was a long and bitter time. She could not share her troubles with Richard, the one person who could have comforted her. Nor did she wish to tell her family, even Bobi. He was too young to understand either side of the question. She was disappointed in Mrs Hughes, though Ann guessed it was hard for her friend to be torn between her husband's faith and her own convictions. Only Bess truly sympathised. Mr Hughes avoided her when he could, and when they met he was cool and distant.

She decided not to remain in Blaen Ddôl beyond the end of the school year. She bought newspapers that advertised teaching posts. The papers brought a new excitement into her life. There was never a vacancy for a post to teach Welsh, but she enjoyed reading the notices anyway, and maybe there would soon be a post teaching her second subject. She did not apply for any of the jobs. She knew she had no chance. Some were in places she had never heard of, other names were familiar, their location vague. She imagined herself taking a train to these places. In her daydreams she was appointed to one of these jobs, and she moved to live there. She imagined wonderful schools, easy, eager children, exciting work, a good salary. Half the evening musing by the fire, and the dream would dwindle. When the newspaper came the following week she looked forward to browsing again all night at the fireside weaving a romance about some new place. Although she had never been there, she pictured the houses, the school, the people. She dreamed of new friends, a flood of invitations to tea or supper. More than anything she imagined her new lodgings with a sitting-room of her own, paid for with the extra money she would earn. Without the prying eyes of a landlady she could invite her friends in for the evening. She folded the newspaper and looked up, dazed to see Mrs Evans sitting opposite her. All the power of her imagination failed to dissolve that lady into the mountain mist.

She mused on her friends, and decided Bess had one shortcoming. She was warm, loyal and kind, a good judge of character, but she suffered from complacency. She was intelligent but her mind was not enquiring. She was in the same condition today as Ann had been when she was a student. She disapproved of things without wanting to change them. She never questioned her beliefs. She could not see that something was wrong with the educational system, and with the capitalist system. To Bess the systems could not be questioned, but people were to blame. She blamed managers for low wages in the quarry, and head teachers and teachers for the poor quality of schools.

As soon as Ann had left college she knew something was gravely amiss with a system that allowed injustice to continue unchanged. It was not the difference between one shopkeeper and another that accounted for Bobi's poor wages. Long apprenticeships, poor food, low pay were the same everywhere. It was the same for teachers. And there was something wrong somewhere when teachers could not teach Welsh to young people when they were trained to do so.

She had to admit that, even if the system were reformed, difficult pupils and overbearing colleagues would still try an idealistic young teacher's enthusiasm. Bess was no reader. She read only in order to prepare her lessons. The local and the chapel libraries were poorly stocked, but it was possible for the determined reader to beg or borrow good books. Alas, Bess lacked the kind of mind that could stimulate Ann and give her the spur that would help her to live in Blaen Ddôl.

At first she thought she had found such a friend in Mrs Hughes, only to discover that her mind was original but undisciplined. Ann had noticed that Mrs Hughes's ideas were uttered as a kind of reaction to her husband's views, and once uttered they dispersed under the power of her loyalty to him. Ann knew that for these reasons they would never become really close friends, and no doubt Mrs Hughes knew this too. She visited the manse less often and missed the warm welcome she had known there. Even when the minister was away she felt reluctant to visit, as if she only called at his house as soon as his back was turned. Ann was in no doubt Mrs Hughes felt this too. She was all too aware of her husband's attitude to Ann, though not how cold he was towards her when they met.

Mrs Evans regained her composure. Now it was Ann who was cold, refusing to respond to Mrs Evans's attempts to be friendly. Neither Richard nor Bobi had visited since the quarrel. Ann led them to believe Mrs Evans was not well and she did not want to impose on her. Mrs Evans mentioned how disappointed she was that neither had called to see them recently, and Ann could not refrain from telling Mrs Evans why she had asked them to keep away. She had intended inviting Dora for a weekend, but abandoned the idea, and wrote to Dora to explain. Dora would understand.

When Mrs Evans heard why Richard and Bobi had not come she was distressed. Her welcome was warm and genuine, and she could not understand Ann's stubbornness, and she told her so. Ann's reply shocked her.

'I could forget, Mrs Evans, but what happened that night follows me everywhere and has depressed me so much that I hate Blaen Ddôl. It is not so easily over and done with.'

'But Miss Owen, I never breathed a word to a soul, and you told me about it yourself.'

'More fool me. I acted in innocence.'

'Well, I would love to see Bobi, and Mr Edmund, for all that.'

'So would I, but the welcome would not be the same. The old joy has gone.'

'Really, Miss Owen, how can you take it so hard? I was only thinking of your own good.'

'That's the worst part about it. I don't want other people's beliefs forced down my throat.'

One night, after the children's meeting, Mrs Hughes suggested they thought about the play to end the term. Ann told her firmly that she did not want to be involved. Mrs Hughes was taken aback for a moment, then she asked why, and reminded her how they had promised to write another play, and how they had looked forward to it.

'I'm sorry, Mrs Hughes. I can't.'

'Will you tell me why?'

'I don't enjoy doing anything for the chapel any more.'

'Tut! Put the past behind you.'

'People won't let me forget.'

'Take no notice of them.'

'How can I? They turn away when they see me.'

'Those people are nothing to do with the children's meeting.'

'Unfortunately they are everything to do with it, and they probably would not want me anyway.'

Later that evening in the manse, it dawned on Mrs Hughes whom Ann meant. That same night for once Ann was glad to go home to Mrs Evans, who had cooked her a tasty supper. She had some stale cheese which needed using, and she toasted it by the fire on buttered bread. As though reading her thoughts Mrs Evans asked, 'Will you be doing an Easter play with the children?'

'Not as far as I know. Maybe someone else will.'

'Aren't you going to do one?'

'No.'

'That's a pity. You did so well last time.'

Ann sighed. 'This is a good supper. It was cold in the vestry.'

As she enjoyed the feast she could not help wishing she were in the manse, planning the play with Mrs Hughes. But she had no intention of giving in.

She and Richard rarely saw each other now. He was busy working to complete his thesis in time for its submission. Ann retreated deep into herself until she felt locked in. She could hardly summon the will to get out of bed in the morning to go to school. She began to fear all her parents' sacrifice had been wasted. Better had she stayed home on the farm to help her mother with the milking, the churning, the baking and the washing. Her depression would not lift, and she knew this was not how a young girl should feel. She gave up dreaming of another job, or another place. She could not even imagine a future life with Richard. Half of her mind told her she should stick to teaching, and the other half told her to marry Richard. All her anxiety would melt if she could talk to Richard, but this she could not do without revealing that he had been the unwitting cause of her pain.

She avoided people. When she saw Mr Hughes in the street it was now she who crossed the road. She rushed away from the children's meeting as soon as it was over without stopping for a word with Mrs Hughes. No plans were made for a concert.

One thing cheered her. The headmaster announced a rise in her salary. The rule was that a young graduate with no teaching experience should receive sixty pounds for the first year, instead of seventy five pounds. The head had succeeded in his battle to change the rule, and the probationary period was reduced from a year to six months. Ann had worked for more than half a year at Blaen Ddôl School, so there was back-pay due to her as well. She wept to hear the news, but even this joy did not make her eager to write to Richard or her parents. She waited a few days before writing. When she heard from Richard and her mother she wept upon reading her mother's letter. 'The wheel of fate is turning for us' wrote her mother. 'Once Bobi has finished his apprenticeship, your father and I can feel easier, and can go out a bit instead of being forever chained to the farm.'

Her mother had described her own mood perfectly. She was chained, not by her work, but by the narrowness and prejudice of the people.

23

Ann's comment that people were avoiding her lingered in Mrs Hughes's mind. She guessed it referred to her husband because Ann had said those who shunned her had everything to do with the children's meeting. Dan was fanatical about temperance, no more, perhaps, than many other ministers, but his mind was unyielding on just about anything. He had not changed his mind about his wife since the day he had fallen in love with her, nor had he changed his mind about his vocation to the ministry. Once he had formed an opinion, nothing could change it by a whisker. Daniel Hughes knew no flexibility.

His wife was quite the opposite. Though neat and tidy about the house, intellectually she was a will-o'-the-wisp. She had an opinion on every subject and her mind could be altered, not completely, but by a little here, a little there, to include in her tolerance all that her husband shut out from his. She was adaptable. Her beliefs fitted no corner. They melted into each other. They overflowed.

She was unhappy about Ann Owen. The trouble had upset her, and she was sadder than ever since Ann had refused to help with the children's end-of-term concert. She'd noticed the grave expression on Ann's face, and the sudden changes of mood reflected there. Ann never called at the manse as she used to. She still listened solemnly to the sermons on Sundays but there was no expression on her face of their effect on her. Things had gone too far and lasted too long. Mrs Hughes would speak to her husband. She was fond of Ann and knew how hurt she was. One Thursday evening at their fireside after supper, Mrs Hughes broached the matter. Like Mr Hughes's habits of thought, his daily routine was fixed. He rarely went to his study after getting home from chapel, making sure every task was done before leaving. He relished the hour after supper as a glass of wine might be enjoyed by other men. He did not allow himself the pleasure of looking forward to it lest it take his mind off his work at the chapel.

'Have you seen Miss Owen lately, Dan?'

'Which Miss Owen?'

'Miss Ann Owen.'

'Only in the distance. Why?'

'I am worried about her.'

'Why?'

'Such unhappiness in her face.'

'I haven't noticed.'

'Have you been close enough to notice, Dan?'

'What do you mean, Alice?'

'Have you been avoiding her?'

'I can't say I'd cross the road to talk to her.'

'Answer me, Dan, are you avoiding her?'

'Has anyone said so?'

'She tells me people are avoiding her, though she didn't say who. I can't believe you are one of those people.'

'Perhaps I am. To be honest I have nothing to say to her. I don't like her. I know you do.'

'Very much, and I can't understand what you have against her.'

'I'm not against her. I just can't take to her. There's no need for her to stop coming here on my account.'

'You talk like a child. Do you think she'd want to come here if you are avoiding her?'

'I can't see that she's worth all this attention, or that she should be allowed to ruin my evening. She's just one member of the congregation, that's all.'

'Shame on you, Dan. You who preach about the lost sheep. If Miss Owen did something foolish, *if,* I say, then surely you are the one who ought to cross the road to seek her. She's a young girl in her first job away from home.'

'She's not far from home.'

'You would not like me to describe you as an unimaginative man, would you Dan?'

'No, I wouldn't.'

'Well you are. You're a very unimaginative man.'

'How?'

'Think of this girl. Her first job out of college, in a school she was not trained to teach in. Her qualifications are for a quite different sort of school. And fair play to her, she has done everything possible to adapt herself. It's been delightful to work with her on the children's services.'

'I hadn't thought of it like that. I expect people to be willing to come to chapel without me running after them.'

'You don't have to run after people, and you don't have to avoid them either.'

'You're right, Alice. Invite Miss Owen for an evening, and I'll be as nice as I can.'

'The question is, will she come?'

They felt no anger with each other.

At that very moment the subject of their conversation was making her way home from town, happier than she had been for a long time. She had decided to give Bobi a treat on the strength of her rise in salary, and rather than ask Mrs Evans if he could come to tea, she decided to go to town on Thursday afternoon, Bobi's half-day. On the way to the bus she felt she had something to look forward to, not with quite the same anticipation as before meeting Richard, but it was a fine feeling nonetheless. She was going to give Bobi something, happiness, perhaps, and she felt some of that happiness herself. She knew nobody with a greater ability to enjoy himself without the means to do so. A frail-looking boy, he had a hearty appetite and was ready to swallow life whole.

The evenings were lengthening. The countryside was shaking itself from its long sleep though its eyes were not yet wide open. The waters of the lakes and ponds gleamed cold and clear. Spring was in the air with its joys and its restless longing, a *hiraeth* which lingered even in the empty city streets of a Thursday evening. Ann would have preferred to go out with Bobi on an evening when the streets were alive with the bustle of people, an atmosphere Ann had always loved when she had been at school in the town. Tonight you could fire a gun and be sure no-one would get shot. But tonight it had to be, as this was Bobi's afternoon off.

Only one rather old-fashioned cafe was open, in a rather gloomy side street between two lamps. But once the gas-lamp was lit the tables shone in their white cloths. Bobi and Ann ordered cold meat, pickles, bread-and-butter and bara brith. There was no choice, except on market day. They were hungry and the meat was tasty, the bread good and spread with farm butter. They were celebrating. They could not have said quite what they celebrated, but it was not just the little rise in Ann's salary. They were celebrating the giving and receiving of pleasure. The meal cost only one shilling and sixpence each, but was worth its weight in gold for its meaning.

Ann looked at Bobi's face from time to time, a pale face, his eyes almost colourless against the pallor. His strong teeth gleamed white as he smiled. She remembered her grandfather's face from when she was five years old, a quiet, serious face that she had not forgotten. Bobi was the living image of the portrait of her grandfather on the wall at home. She remembered Mrs Hughes once told her she had a sad face. She and Bobi were alike except that her hair was dark. Had Mrs Hughes seen that same quiet seriousness in her face? Their mother's face had the same gravity, except when she laughed.

'How's life, Bobi?'

'Fine. Not much happening.'

'There's not much happening anywhere.' She would not mention the tot of rum.

'Things are much better at the house now. The new housekeeper is a nice woman.'

'Good.'

'We have a better life but I still get bored with the dull routine of it. It's different at home. If things are the same every day at home I don't mind.'

'Yes, it's strange isn't it? Feelings and conversation make the difference.'

'No-one in the house talks at the table.'

'How's night school going?'

'Pretty good. We learn a lot. Most of the subjects are interesting. John the apprentice is brighter than you'd think. He says nothing at table, but he talks to me on the way home about all the books he's reading.'

'He reads a lot?'

'Yes, and he remembers it all. I've started going to the library with him.'

'That's very good.'

'Nani, Mam's not well.'

Ann stopped eating, unable to speak.

'Don't worry. I don't think it's serious. She has a pain in the stomach and she vomits a lot.'

'Has she been to the doctor?'

'No, she won't go.'

'I had quite a cheerful letter from her only a few days ago.'

'Oh, yes, she's cheerful enough. She has good days. Don't let's talk about it now.'

Ann could not stop thinking about it. She must go home soon. She told Bobi so.

'There's no hurry, but she'd love to see you. Do you still see Richard?'

'Yes, but he's been very busy lately. His thesis has to be finished.'

'He'll get a good job one day.'

Bobi's face glowed with pleasure as he said this, then darkened again with something that looked like sadness.

'Never mind, Bobi, once your apprenticeship is over you'll get a good job too.'

'I hope so. There are some jobs going in shops for someone who knows it's not just about cutting calico and being polite to customers.'

'That's the way to talk.'

Time to catch her bus came much too soon. Ann hated parting from him. She gave him a shilling and he returned her his usual warm, innocent smile.

On the bus, thoughts of her mother overwhelmed her. Her heart was happy as she thought of Bobi, and then the thought of her mother pierced her. What if something terrible was wrong ? It was so like her to refuse to see the doctor. She was stoical and stubborn and would drop rather than give in. What if she should die? No-one in her family had died, and death was such a stranger she could not imagine it entering their house. She would go home at the weekend to see for herself, and, like so many times before, making the decision banished her fears.

The lights of the village came into sight. She remembered, with pain, that it was Thursday, and how every Thursday she used to go to the manse after the children's meeting. The session would be over by now. She had absolutely no excuse to go there. Had it not been for Mr Hughes she might have called in. Sometimes she felt a powerful urge to go to see him and to speak her mind, to demand an explanation of his attitude. But although there was no pious talk at home, she had been brought up to respect a man of the cloth. She sighed as she opened the front door of her digs, recalling Mrs Hughes's friendly face. She'd have given a great deal at that moment to be able to tell her friend about supper with Bobi, and to share her anxiety for her mother.

24

Ann was sitting at the edge of a path, little more than a sheep track, halfway between Blaen Ddôl and home, the second Friday evening after seeing Bobi. The village houses had disappeared below the brow of the hill as though they had turned their backs on her and taken one step closer to the valley floor. There was not a house in sight. All about her was the bare mountainside, the grass cropped and pale, an occasional sheep grazing intently without lifting its head. A lamb tugged at the udder of its patient mother. The mountain wall bulged and caved as it meandered the slope, rusty barbed wire connecting its iron pillars. The stones of the wall were rounded and whole, free and loose in the wall, yet they stood sound as they had for generations, blunting the teeth of the wind for man and beast.

Ann was considering fear and cowardice. She was afraid to arrive home tonight, fearing to find her mother worse than Bobi had told her. She was too scared to go home at all the previous Friday without warning her mother first. She recalled the many kinds of fear: the fear that had possessed her as a small child when she could not sleep, darkness like a black curtain between her and the familiar furniture in the room; the fear of standing up to recite her verses in chapel even though she knew the words perfectly well; fear of punishment when she had done wrong; fear of loneliness as she set out for home after tea today. The other evening at the manse she had experienced for the first time a fear that was like awe. She got to her feet to continue walking, her mind set on that last kind of fear to offset the greater fear of being overwhelmed by darkness before she reached home. Mrs Hughes had invited her to supper and she had accepted gladly, anxious at the thought of meeting Mr Hughes face to face, but eager for the company of his wife. She'd worried about his opening remarks, in case she felt cornered in some way. Before supper he had asked,

'And what do you think of Blaen Ddôl now, Miss Owen?'

His wife flushed.

'The place or the people?' Ann asked, playing for time.

'People make the place,' he replied, stressing each word. No imagination, thought his wife.

'It reminds me of a dress I had when my grandfather died. It was white, trimmed with black.'

Mrs Hughes laughed.

'They are like people everywhere,' Ann explained. 'Good, bad and indifferent. I don't completely love Blaen Ddôl as you'd love a plate of your favourite dinner. Maybe my taste is at fault. I can't pursue my own subject at school.'

'You ought to apply for a post where you have that opportunity,' said the minister.

'I would if there were such a job to be had. Staying here doesn't help me.'

'Why is that?'

'One learns a few tricks teaching children of this age, but they don't help with older children. I'm afraid I must give it up even though there is no other job in sight.'

Even as she spoke she knew she could do it. She could give up her job.

'And I'd looked forward to another play from you,' said the minister without the least trace of disappointment in his voice. It was his wife who looked disappointed.

After supper Mr Hughes went out to visit one of his congregation. At least, that was his excuse. Ann had the feeling he was tired of being courteous.

'You didn't mean it?' said Mrs Hughes when he had gone.

'Of course I did,' said Ann as though the conviction had been with her for months rather than minutes.

'It'll be strange for me, Ann. I have no-one else to talk to except you. When I talk to Dan he just laughs at me as though my ideas were foolish notions. But I do think seriously. The best thing that could happen in this village is for someone to stand up in the middle of the sermon to debate the issues. Anything to break the monotony. I can put up with the unavoidable monotony of housework, but the monotony of minds that never change is unendurable. People like your Mrs Evans.'

'Yes,' replied Ann. 'I feel the same, except when I go home. I love home because it never changes.'

'I wonder why?'

'I don't know. They are all individuals. They all speak their minds without bowing to the opinions of others.'

'I wish I could persuade you to stay. I'd looked forward to having your friendship for much longer. You take me seriously.'

'I'll miss some things about the place, especially coming here. But I have to overcome those feelings.'

Ann considered this conversation as she walked, remembering also the talk she'd had with Richard after seeing Bobi. She had gone to see him fearlessly, her heart beating as excitedly as when she had gone to meet him for the first time. It was he who suggested that she could leave her job without having another post to go to. He knew people who had stayed so long in a job that they never found the post they really wanted. Talking to him made her feel quite different from the way she had felt in the minister's house the other evening. With him she'd felt a need to leave Blaen Ddôl, but not the school.

'Apart from your own happiness you must think about earning a better salary,' he said, 'and the chance to teach the subject you've specialised in.'

'You are right, Richard. There is no conviction for me in what I'm doing. I'm clumsy and the children know it.'

'What we need is a good job each.'

'It'll be easy for you, Richard. Welsh isn't your subject.'

'But we haven't met today to talk about things like that.'

Walking the paths, and over tea, they had talked of a future that lay beyond a mere teaching appointment. Farewell after hours of talking, and anxiety for her mother quite swept away.

After walking for an hour over the hills towards her home, another fear overtook Ann. This time it wasn't fear of seeing her mother ill, but of telling her she was giving up her job. It was her family who would suffer the effects of her decision. They would miss the money, and be disappointed that their daughter was out of work. Their neighbours' opinion would matter to them, though they didn't care much what people thought about other things. People would say, without understanding, that she had been a failure in Blaen Ddôl.

She sat down at the edge of the stony path and gazed out to sea. It was nearly dark now, and the lights of the town flickered on one by one. Bobi was somewhere down there. He too would be better off if she had a better job. A lapwing whistled over the bog and she was suddenly cold. There was melancholy in the dark blue of the sky over the sea in the country of the Mabinogi. She thought of Gwydion's magic, and wished a magician could charm a job for her, a place to make her happy and her loved ones proud. She thought of Mrs Hughes, and the look of disappointment on her face. She was a discontented woman, intellectually frustrated, with not a sympathetic friend to talk to. She should write a book, pour all her thoughts into it, and publish it without telling anyone. That would stir her husband's complacent mind and burst his foolish balloon.

Thinking these thoughts set her blood racing. She spoke aloud, 'I'm alive. I feel it in my heart.' She would leave Blaen Ddôl and face the world. There would be no turning back. She would leave her home too, if necessary, travelling light without luggage or fear of anything except dishonest thinking. Many an unemployed quarryman had set out for the south with less than she had.

Now, as home drew near, she was fearless. She could even face finding her mother gravely ill, an unlikely event or she would have heard about it. The first thing she saw as she entered the kitchen was the lamp's bright glass set ready on the table. Her mother was pale, smiling cheerfully with a white shawl about her shoulders. Her father looked up from his newspaper and smiled, asking his wife, 'Has the kettle boiled?'

Huw, reading a book on the sofa, offered his help. 'There's a little quarry-supper in the oven for Ann,' said his mother, and Huw got up and brought it to the table.

'Let me take off my coat!' said Ann, seeing how everybody was waiting on her.

It was her favourite supper of mashed swede, liver, onions and gravy.

'I could eat a second helping,' said her father.

'What about you, Mam?' asked Ann.

'No, indeed, in case it repeats on me tonight. I enjoyed it, but without the onions, and I kept it down too.'

'Good.'

Ann gave a silent sigh. Things were not as bad as she had feared. They all enjoyed oatcake and tea to follow, and her mother had some bread-and-butter.

On Saturday morning Ann was up early. After her long walk she slept well, and by morning her young limbs were refreshed. Seeing her roll up her sleeves to begin the housework her mother said, 'I wish Bobi had been a girl.'

'Why?'

'To help me in the house. The work is getting too much for me.'

'Have you seen the doctor?'

'Bobi told him and he called to see me.'

'What did he say?'

'That I have too much work, and the smell of the butter and the milk in the churn isn't good for me. Nothing wrong with my stomach, he said. Your father and I are thinking of leaving the farm and moving to a cottage.'

'Good.'

'But there's nothing to rent or buy at the moment.'

'Would you like me to give up work for a while?'

Her mother wouldn't hear of it. 'Don't waste your life.'

Hopeless to mention it now, thought Ann. She remembered the decision she had made on the mountain the night before and she was even more certain of it now. They sat at the fireside together, and Ann made a rice pudding, which they ate with buttermilk halfway through the morning. She talked of her problems at school, and the difficulty of finding a better post while she was employed in Blaen Ddôl. She exaggerated a little, stressing each detail, while her mother listened in sympathy.

'I can see,' said Ann, reaching the end of the story, 'I could kill two birds with one stone. The doctor is right. You need to rest. The neighbours will think I left work to look after you.'

'It would be lovely to have you home for a while,' said her mother. 'Children leave home and they never come back. It would be wonderful to have you helping me. But do you know what I'd like even better?'

'No.'

'For you to find a post that suits you, for me to get well again, and for us to find a little house without any land. I'd be sad to lose the animals, mind.'

'Yes. It's a shame we can't have everything.'

With that nod of understanding from her mother, Ann had overcome the first big hurdle.

PART TWO

1

One cold evening in November 1915 Ann Owen was sitting in her room in the lodging house at Ynys-y-Grug. It was over a year since she had come to Ynys-y-Grug, and Blaen Ddôl now seemed very far away. She seemed to have been hurled here. She had made her decision to give in her notice, though she had no job to go to. She was short-listed for a job at the County School, but was not appointed because Welsh was her special subject, and the County School needed someone qualified to teach both Welsh and Latin. She followed her old headmaster's advice and handed in her notice.

She little thought then that it was to be the war which would offer her the first chance to teach her own subject. Barely had the summer vacation passed without a job to look forward to when she found herself at Ynys-y-Grug, standing in for a man who had enlisted. Until that moment she had never even heard of Ynys-y-Grug.

So here she was with a room of her own, having gained a measure of independence, though she had lost some things too. She had just finished her supper, a slice of her landlady's home-made bara brith, and a cup of Cafe au lait, sweet milky coffee to which one need add only hot water. She was still hungry though she had only just finished her meal. The scrape of butter was so poor that she preferred to eat the bara brith dry. Her landlady had baked it for her son in France. Baking the weekly fruit loaf for her son was her sacrifice on the altar of anxiety. The only time Ann ever saw her smile was when she brought her gift of a slice of bara brith, saying, as she always did, that she had baked it to send to Morgan.

It was the last evening of the half-term break, and Ann had stayed in Ynys-y-Grug to enjoy the rest from work, because it was too far and too expensive to go home. She and one of her colleagues, Miss Williams, had been walking in the hills, and the exercise had given her an appetite, too much of an appetite. Now she must spend an hour writing her letters. Writing and receiving letters had become her life. Her salary was now a hundred and ten pounds a year, but she was no better off because of the difficulty of her parents' situation. The quarry where her father worked had been closed down at the outbreak of war. She had bought nothing new to wear since leaving Blaen Ddôl, except for underwear needed as winter arrived, and to buy those she'd borrowed money from the wife of a colleague. Miss Williams had invited her to go into town one Saturday afternoon, so the loan meant she could make one journey instead of two.

Her life was more confined than it had been in Blaen Ddôl, because of the travel difficulties. On the other hand there was more to do here. There were drama groups, and literary societies where excellent lectures could be heard. The chapel in Ynys-y-Grug was smaller and drew fewer famous preachers, so it was a more congenial place to worship. It was warm round the stove in the vestry on a Sunday morning, and the sufferings of the war brought people closer, to pray, not to listen to sermons.

Here in the evenings she saw more of her fellow-teachers than in Blaen Ddôl, because like her most of them were in lodgings. They would tap on her window and come in for a chat. They never talked about the war, but of village life, books, sometimes about school work. If the war was mentioned there were too many points of view, so they avoided the subject.

After a year of uncertainty and insecurity, Ann knew only too well that the nations had lost sight of the war's original purpose, the defence of small nations, and that now it was about other things, about power, and the loss of power. God alone knew. In the first months of the war, seeing 'United We Stand' on the poster outside the paper shop in Blaen Ddôl on her way to school every morning in July 1914, she had not known what to think. At first she had believed the newspapers, but shapeless clouds soon overwhelmed her mind and she saw no meaning anywhere. She became filled with scepticism. There was only one certainty, that she was Welsh and it was not Wales's war. She wasn't sure what would happen to Wales if England lost the war, but she hated to hear talk of 'dying for your country', and mothers saying they would willingly sacrifice their own sons. One could have understood had they said, 'That's it, we can't stop the war, we can only suffer and hope it's soon over.' One such was her landlady, and Ann felt moved hearing her sigh as she went about her household tasks.

Richard found a job teaching in England, then joined the Medical Corps. It was the first time a hint of criticism of him had crossed Ann's mind. In her opinion he could have waited until he was forced to go, and it may never have come to it. Yet she could see his point. He was not a pacifist, but he did not support this war. He had joined out of a feeling of comradeship with his friends. Many had enlisted, some had been killed, and he felt he could no longer live in comfort while his friends were in danger. He explained that he had no home or family or anyone who would suffer for him. She was on the point of writing to tell him he was wrong, that he might have no family, but that she would suffer for him. Then she stopped herself, remembering that, aware of how deeply she would be affected by the news, it was to her he had first written of his enlistment. As she suppressed that hasty letter she realised her own doubts were no excuse to stand in judgment against him for doing what he believed to be right. He wrote often, and warmly.

There was worse news. Returning one dark evening from a walk she found a letter from home awaiting her. Her brother Huw had written to say Bobi had joined up. Reading this news she felt as much pain as if Bobi had been killed already. Pain was soon replaced by fury that Bobi had done something so unnecessary, only seventeen-and-a-half years old and hurting their parents so much. Huw wrote that they were heartbroken. Ann's heart was broken too, though she knew, however much it hurt, it was worse for her parents. Nor could she say why she suffered so much more now than when she heard Richard had enlisted, except that Richard was older and had some experience behind him to face the world. Also, she could understand why he had joined up. Then she realised, without being told, why Bobi had done so. Bored with the monotony of his life he was seizing the chance to see the world. If he regretted it, as surely he would, he had no experience to lean on. She wasn't afraid he would turn out badly, but that he would lose his innocence, and would experience things a young boy should not know. One thing was certain, if he came back alive, his attitude to home would be quite changed.

She thought of running down to Miss Williams's lodgings to share her troubles, but she was not sure how much sympathy she could expect. Miss Williams was Welsh, but had lost her roots and language, and her attitude to the war was like that of an English patriot. Ann avoided talking to her about the war, or things to do with home that Miss Williams would not understand. Judging by her clothes Ann did not think her friend would know what it meant to live hand to mouth. Their affinity was deepest when they talked about books, especially when Ann spoke of Welsh literature, and there had been intimacy between them that afternoon as they walked on the moors. Indeed, Ann liked her very much and admired her cultured ways. Thinking about such things Ann saw one thing clearly, that the war would mean most to those with strong family ties. It would speak most profoundly to those whose roots were deep in Welsh soil, and who had only the vaguest understanding of what this war was about. She could not expect a girl like Miss Williams to see her point of view. Best not to mention it at all.

There was a tap at the window and in came Miss Williams carrying a paper bag with something inside.

'There was a parcel waiting for me when I got in,' she said, 'from Mam. She's managed to get some butter from somewhere, packed it with some buns and sent them to me. So I've brought them to share with you.'

'I'll see how much tea is left,' said Ann, going to the cupboard. 'Ah! Enough for a pot.'

She went to the kitchen to ask for hot water, the teapot and tea things.

'Have you had bad news, Miss Owen? You look upset.'

'Yes, but let's enjoy the treat. The buns look delicious.'

'I brought some for Mrs Beddoe too.'

'I'm sure she'd love them now with a cup of tea. Her husband is on nights, and the children are out.'

She took them to the kitchen, and was rewarded with a warm smile of gratitude.

Awkwardly, controlling her emotions, Ann told her news. Miss Williams gazed into the fire for a long time before speaking.

'I'm so sorry,' she said at last. 'I lost my only brother when he was five years old, and now I can't help thinking perhaps it was all for the best.'

Ann said nothing. In her heart she knew it was better for Bobi to be in his present plight than to die at five years of age. At least she had enjoyed seeing him grow from childhood to youth, and she still hoped he would come home safe. She'd been able to spoil him a little. It was now her turn to sympathise with Miss Williams.

'Of course, time eases the pain,' she said, 'but we talk more about Edgar since the war than we have for ages, with Mam thinking how she'd rather still have him today, never mind the worry, than lose him as we did.'

Ann felt closer to her friend now than at any time since she'd known her.

'But do cheer up. He won't have to leave the country yet a while, and maybe the War will be over before then. How are you enjoying *Tess*?'

She had lent Hardy's novel to Ann.

'I'm enjoying it very much, though it's so sad.'

'Wait till you get to the end,' said Miss Williams, and away she whirled before Ann could thank her properly.

The visit gave Ann the heart she needed to face the difficult task of writing home. She had a deeper insight now into the character of her friend, of whom she had been rather in awe. It was in that grateful mood that she went to bed, thinking of hearth and home. With thoughts of such things, and of school work next day, where at last she was teaching bright children with conviction, she felt spurred to face the future.

2

'And everyone says she is bound to become quite unbalanced, because it was he who supported her and saved her from her own foolishness. I can't comment, not being a member of the chapel.' The letter was from Bess Morris, and Ann stared at it, unable to believe the news it brought her – that Mr Hughes, her old minister, had died of a heart attack.

Her next ordeal was to write to Mrs Hughes. She had never before needed to write a letter of condolence. Her family always visited the bereaved, but she had never entered a house of grief. It was difficult to know what to write because she could hardly describe Mr Hughes as a friend. Had it been her friend who had died there would have been no such problem. So Mrs Hughes was right to worry when her husband was unwell two years ago. Ann had not liked him, but then, he wasn't her husband. She disagreed with the local gossip reported in Bess's letter. Dan Hughes had not saved his wife from folly in meetings and committees. He was stuck in a rut with the people he served, and took their side, while she saw the narrowness of their ways, and would prod them in the ribs from time to time to wake them up.

After all, it was not the chapel or the parish Mrs Hughes had married, but the love of her youth, and she had refused to let trivia spoil their life together. Knowing this, and that it was usual to praise the dead, Ann could not for the life of her think what to say to her friend. She would write tomorrow. Maybe by then the right words would come. The scandal of the tot of rum would seem as nothing by now, and it certainly meant nothing to Mrs Hughes. Ann felt the calm water-meadow of her life turn into a torrential waterfall.

Then there was Bobi's letter, expressing not a hint of self-doubt. She did not expect him to say sorry, but she thought he might at least say he hoped he had not caused too much pain. Not a word. It was a letter brimming with excitement, full of his new open-air life in the company of boys his own age. His excuse for enlisting was that it gave him a chance to leave the shop. Wil B had joined up, and no-one had replaced him but a young apprentice. Work was harder than ever, and the boss more vigilant. To conclude he wrote that as he had joined the guards it was unlikely his battalion would be sent abroad.

Ann's heart told her she should write and point out to him how thoughtless he had been. From Mam there was just a note, but all her feelings were in it. 'I never thought Bobi would do such a thing,' she said. Ann drank the full draught of her mother's sorrow to the dregs. She wrote that her father was thinking of following the example of some of the other quarrymen, and going to Liverpool to find work. Huw had already gone.

Ann's thoughts returned to Blaen Ddôl and the not entirely

unhappy year she had spent there. She knew she could never return or take up where she had left off. The break was complete and could not be mended. Poor Mrs Evans, Bess Morris said in her letter that she had been obliged to take in soldiers, and that the comfort of her home was spoiled. Her floors were bare, her furnishings gone, and the rent no consolation to her.

Ann came home from school that afternoon to face all this. She was already upset because she had offended one of the teachers. Today was one of the days when teachers had their dinner in the school kitchen, the day of the girls' cookery class. They usually had a cup of tea after dinner. Ann was not aware that making tea was the job of anyone in particular, and intending to be helpful she got up to make it. As soon as she touched the teapot Mr Lewis, who was standing beside her, took hold of the pot saying, 'That's my job.' 'Oh.' said Ann. 'Can I help you?' 'No,' he said, 'nobody makes it properly except me.' His tone was genial, but Ann could see that she had really annoyed him. Miss Williams explained on the way home that Mr Lewis was just a bachelor set in his funny ways, that he truly believed only he could make the tea, and that he always made it. Ann considered apologising to him, but she didn't. It seemed too silly. Yet it niggled all afternoon. Ever since coming to Ynys-y-Grug she had thought Mr Lewis rather strange, a merry bird trotting from classroom to classroom, never walking, always with a friendly word as he passed her. Soon after she came to the school he remarked that the graph of female beauty had not decreased one jot since her arrival. It was a while before Ann understood the remark. Today she knew she had upset him. But Mr Lewis's reaction was as nothing and not worth a thought compared with the letters waiting by her plate. She hoped that he would never have anything worse to worry about in wartime than getting to the teapot first.

She decided against writing letters tonight. It was Bobi she was really worried about. How different he was in his letter from that time they had dined together in town. Perhaps by tomorrow she might begin to see his point of view a little. It was so difficult to enter the minds and hearts of others. Mrs Hughes, going to bed alone tonight, how could her feelings be imagined? Ann knew nothing of grief. And Mam. How was it possible to guess at her despair, or was that a little easier to understand since Bobi had hurt her too? She could not fathom Bobi's heart nor the adventurous spirit of a boy. She would settle down to read *Tess*, where clouds were also gathering. She must face her life and get on with it. Maybe tomorrow there'd be a letter from Richard.

At noon next day Ann was surprised by a letter from Mrs Hughes herself, telling of her husband's death. It had not been as great a shock to her as people thought, since she had heeded those early warnings and noticed other more recent signs of his declining health. He had worked without stint since the outbreak of war, writing letters to all the boys from the chapel who had enlisted, writing letters on behalf of parents to their children, and filling in endless forms. People were kind, she said, but she'd give a lot to see Ann just now. People sympathised with her about the loss of their chapel minister, but Ann would understand it was her husband she had lost. 'I know,' she wrote, 'people here thought Dan did not have the right sort of wife to support him in the chapel, but I know I didn't marry the minister. I married the man. He knew that too and always left the chapel behind when he came home. That's why he never went to his study when he came home from chapel. No husband ever understood his wife better, and in his conscious moments before he died he never once mentioned the chapel. He talked only of the happy times we had shared. I often spoke of leaving Blaen Ddôl but never thought I would be leaving without Dan. I must keep going, and care for the children to stop myself pining away. I'll take it one day at a time. The worst is yet to come.'

Ann knew now how to write her letter of condolence. There was a brief note from Richard to say he would soon be going overseas, and that he must see her before he left.

Suddenly she heard again the laughter of girls in the common room the night before leaving College, and recalled how she had turned to look back at the white clematis growing over the porch. Twenty-six months ago. Tomorrow once more Mr Lewis would trot over to the stove with the teapot to make the tea. A week from now where would Richard be?

3

The train shuddered forward again. The journey was endless and Ann so impatient that she found herself holding her breath when the train stopped too long at a station. And there were so many stations, and she was longing to reach her journey's end. She had suddenly heard from Richard that he was going abroad, and as time was so short they had arranged to meet in Shrewsbury. She told herself it was just a meeting. She tried to think of it as just like all their other meetings, important but not exceptionally significant. But another thought thrust itself into her mind: maybe she would never see him again.

As her journey progressed the thought receded. To meet was enough. To look neither before nor behind, just to see him, to hear his voice express the way he felt about her. Everything else receded, like being scared to ask the head for time off that afternoon to catch the train. It meant gaining hours of Richard's company, as they would have the whole of tomorrow together. She'd had to explain why it was so important for her to catch the train, and the headmaster's knowing smile had set her teeth on edge. All that was far away now. Richard's letter had caught her without any money, but Miss Williams had come to her rescue, offering to lend her the money before she was even asked. With the passing of time she liked her colleague more and more, and she was less shy in her company.

The train screeched again as it started out of a station, a momentary burst of noise and then silence before a second explosion of steam, and the few people on the platform slowly disappeared from view like travellers through a dark doorway. There were a great many soldiers on the train. More than half the passengers in her compartment were soldiers. Some were playing cards using a newspaper for a table. One slept, his face slack, innocent. She was reminded of Bobi, though she hadn't really thought about him since Richard's letter came. The compartment was a self-contained world travelling somewhere without any connection with the darkness outside, a cocoon of warmth. Ann wore a warm, dark-blue coat buttoned to the throat, made for her by the tailor at home before she left Blaen Ddôl, and her feet felt cosy in spite of the little shoes she had chosen to wear instead of her old-fashioned high-laced boots. Her hands were snug in white woollen gloves.

At last the world of the compartment stirred into life, everyone lifting cases and kitbags and moving into the corridor before the train stopped.

There was Richard, looking strange in his uniform, tanned and thinner than before. She felt shy and awkward. It was he who spoke first, and with joy.

'I don't know what sort of place I've booked us into. I didn't have a choice.'

'It doesn't matter, as long as it's somewhere to lay my head.'

She was filled with the thrill of anticipation, and nothing in the world mattered but to be together in that precious moment. People darting past them along the twilit street were unreal, the streets themselves were unreal, and so was the war.

But the world returned when they arrived at the hotel with its grey face, its poor food, its shabby carpets, and people who glared at them, hearing them speak a strange language. Richard was driven to ask, in his strong Welsh accent, whether he looked like a German or something, then they were left in peace. But, thought Ann, he is different, his eyes set deeper than ever in his head, his hair blacker.

'How is everything, Ann?'

'School is fine. The work suits me perfectly, and the children are bright. But . . .'

'Yes, but the war. Messing up our lives. But we can't stop it. I don't know what on earth we are fighting for, if we are fighting. I'm not fighting anyway.'

Ann wanted to ask him, 'What are you going for then?'

He went on. 'I have never done anything so purposeless. My thesis had a purpose. But there is no purpose whatsoever in what I am doing now.'

'You can help relieve the suffering.'

'I can, but why, in the end?'

'Well, the poor lads can't help it. It's the men in power who are to blame.'

'Yes, but they say they know what the war's about and that

those obeying orders ought to know why too. Mind you I'd fight as hard as the next man if the cause were one I could believe in.'

'Would you, Richard?'

'Yes, I would, but what you really believe in is always something close. You can't believe in something remote. Wales is close to me and in me. I'd fight for Wales.'

'I've never thought of it like that.'

'No, Ann, and you don't need to. You're a woman and it's you who'll suffer, it's you who must stay home.'

'But Richard, you're not going to face the heart of the danger.'

'Not if I'm feeling too cowardly. But this sort of thing whips up daredevil passions. I must stop depressing you.'

'No, you're not. It's so good to be with you.'

'Oh, yes.' He spoke warmly. 'Times like these make one think there are no feelings any more, no tenderness, only cold, hard existence. I'll be giving help to the wounded, but it's a very hard way to learn how to do it.'

'Yes, I suppose so. Or war wouldn't be war.'

'How is Bobi?'

'His letters are cheerful. He's in his element. I hope they won't send him overseas.'

'Not with that battalion, unless he volunteers to go.'

'That's what I'm afraid of. I know Bobi, if the other boys go he'll want to go. But it seems he has a displaced bone in his sternum.'

'If that's so he won't have to fight even if he goes overseas. He'll just do guard duty.'

'That's dangerous enough.'

'Of course, everything is dangerous in a war. But here we are talking about the war again.'

*   *   *

Next day was fine but misty, and the sun rose into the morning mist like an orange sphere. They could find nowhere comfortable to sit down, and tired of window shopping they stopped for lunch. Ann was just beginning to think that they could not spend the whole day like this, that they wouldn't have anything to talk about, just moving from shop to shop, when Richard suggested they should walk into the country. The air was like spring, and although it was damp with sodden leaves underfoot, the early sun touched their faces, lifting their spirits. The landscape was flat and wooded against a backdrop of low hills, with clusters of ochre-washed cottages. It was a strange, silent countryside. They walked unaware that they were walking, only that their bodies burned with energy and that they could not stop walking to face the truth. Neither spoke of what was foremost in their minds.

At last they reached a little village with a church and an inn. They went inside the church. It was small and ancient, with that musty smell of old churches everywhere. After looking round the church for a while Richard stepped into a pew and knelt down with his head bowed. Ann, Nonconformist as she was, felt awkward and strange, as if Richard were someone she didn't know. Then in a moment she followed suit, and instantly felt at one with him. She prayed that he would come home safe, then at once was struck with guilt that it was he for whom she had chosen to pray, that she had put him before Bobi. How could she have forgotten Bobi? Vulnerable Bobi. She rose, accusing herself of thoughtlessness. They walked out arm-in-arm, and went into the pub to ask for tea. The moment they set foot in the little parlour with its low ceiling they felt they were back in Bangor. A bright log fire was spitting in the grate. A small table with a white cloth was set before them, and tea was brought, home-made jam, bread-and-butter, yes, butter, and some simple cakes. They could have purred.

'I went to Anglesey,' said Richard.

'And how is your uncle?'

'He's aged a lot, and he's more forgetful than when I last saw him. I didn't know whether to tell him I was going overseas or not. But I did tell him.'

'How did he take it?'

'He didn't really take it in, which was all for the best really. I've a feeling he won't live long.'

'Does that make you sad, Richard?'

'Yes and no. He's had a good life, but a lonely one in recent years. I hate to think of the old home broken up.'

Ann thought of Mrs Hughes. The manse would soon be empty.

'Do you know what I'd like, Ann, if anything happened to my uncle?'

'No, I don't know.'

'To keep the old house, and for you and me to live there.'

Ann blushed. It was the first hint he had given that he wished to marry her.

'But you have no idea where you'll get a job.'

'We can keep it for holidays.'

'That would be wonderful. But what are we doing, spinning dreams? So much could happen before then.'

'Whatever happens, there's no harm in dreaming.'

They hated leaving the cosy room, grown shadowy with firelight flickering on the walls.

'I'll remember this afternoon for a long time,' he said.

'Me too,' she said.

'Not because I have to leave, but because I'm so proud of you, Ann.'

Now her conscience pricked her again, this time for not worrying about Bobi as she knelt in the church, but she said,

'I'm proud of you too.'

'There'll be better times ahead.'

'I hope so.'

The hotel seemed miserable after the little country inn. The fire burning in the hearth was the only comfort. All the other guests were out except one, and he sat reading. They did the same. There was nothing else to do. What a pity, thought Ann, they had not said their goodbyes straight after tea. There was something distasteful about the room. The clock ticked the minutes slowly by, and suddenly, into the silence of the fender, a mouse came scurrying. Then another, picking crumbs, flicking up their heads repeatedly. Ann could have sworn one of them winked at her, its ears pricked. They glided smoothly, their tails sliding far behind them like the trains of wedding gowns. Richard and Ann watched, mesmerised. The creatures looked about them, quite tame, until the other guest sensed a presence apart from theirs in the room. He lifted his foot, intending to stamp on one of the mice, but they vanished as quietly as they had come, like little grey ghosts. Ann laughed aloud, and their fellow guest threw her a black look.

Next morning there was no time to think about anything except catching the train. It was standing at the platform, the symbol of all meeting and all parting, significant to everyone, meaningless to no-one, like a great heartless horse, as if it said, 'Do as you like, I'm off.' Ann's train left first, and she was restless to be gone and to be done with the bitter moment of parting. They talked to fill the moment, small talk to hide their feelings. 'I hope you have a good journey.' 'I hope Bobi will be fine.' 'I hope you'll get leave soon.' 'I hope, I hope, I hope,' and the whistle blowing, a hurried kiss, and the train shunting loudly out puffing steam into the air. Richard receded further and further from her on the platform, waving. She sat in the compartment facing strangers, choking back tears. She closed her eyes.

4

When Ann opened her eyes she saw a pair of blue eyes shining at her out of a friendly face. It was a young soldier with fair hair and a ruddy complexion. Ann sensed he had been staring at her for some time, and she turned her head to gaze out of the window. He took a packet of sweets from his pocket and offered her one.

'Come on,' he said, 'this will cheer you up. There's nothing like eating to stop it hurting.'

'Thank you,' she said, smiling.

'That's better. Those teeth are too good to hide. Go on, smile again.'

This time she laughed.

'There you are. You'll feel better now. Parting is terrible.'

'Yes,' she said, choking a sigh.

'Is he going to the Front?'

'Yes.'

'Keep your spirits up. He'll be back.'

'I hope so.'

'Don't let yourself think anything different. Hope brings a man home from war. That's what my Nain says, and she's never wrong.'

This time Ann laughed at his naivety. But there was something charming about him. He talked incessantly and Ann was forced to respond. The sun rose shining into the mist just as it had yesterday, and she recalled with a pang their walk in the country. How far away it was! Yet Richard seemed so close, in spite of her conversation with this lad. Richard would be in his train by now, hurtling away in the opposite direction. They were travelling farther and farther away from each other. In a few days there would be a sea between them.

'I'm going overseas soon.'

'Are you really?'

'The sooner the better. I'm tired of being in this country. Nothing but drill and marching, and the cinema every night.'

'But you're away from the danger here.'

'Danger? Danger is all in the mind. Once you're in the midst of it you don't think about it.'

That's Bobi talking, she thought.

'You see, all we've got while we're kept in this country is anticipation, like waiting to go to the dentist, and too much waiting makes you weary. Once you see the dentist you forget to be scared.'

Ann did not understand soldiers, but arriving at the station where she must change trains she felt as if she'd been sheltered from the rain and must once again face the weather. The soldier leaned his head out of the window as she crossed the platform. She realised, for an awful moment, that it was possible to find someone else attractive apart from Richard.

She went straight to the waiting room and there in the cold and the gloom she began to write a letter to Richard, to keep the Devil at bay. She was ashamed of having spent an hour enjoying someone else's company. But the closeness to Richard which she had known for a moment on the train was lost. The smile of the talkative soldier faded too, and the icy waiting-room quickly filled with people staring in disappointment at the ashes in the cold grate. She gave up trying to write, and she went out and began to pace the platform like a caged animal.

Darkness was falling as she reached her lodgings, and as soon as she set foot in the parlour she knew something was wrong. She could hear murmuring from the kitchen, and above it a high-pitched sound of wailing. As she lit the lamp a woman she did not know came in, closing the door between her and the kitchen. She looked back to make sure it was shut, and said quietly,

'They've heard their son is lost in France. Word came this afternoon.'

Ann slumped into her chair. For something to say, she asked,

'Are they sure?'

'As sure as the word of a boy from the village who was with him.'

Ann went straight to the kitchen where people were sitting about on chairs, and her landlady sat by the fire, her face as white as her apron and marked by bitter weeping. Her husband sat opposite her, his eyes dry, his expression shocked. The children were not there.

'I'm so sorry, Mrs Beddoe.'

There was nothing more to say in front of all those people.

'But do take heart. Let's hope it's not true.'

Mrs Beddoe began to weep again. She raised her head to look at Ann, as if she could see that she too was troubled. Her gaze pierced Ann, as if she knew. It was a look too penetrating to bear, so Ann returned to her room. The neighbour brought her some food. As soon as she finished her supper she returned to the letter she had failed to write in the station waiting-room. Now her feelings overflowed. This was the meaning of war. War was in the next room, now. She could feel Richard close to her. She was kneeling beside him in the church, breathing his uniform, touching his arm, his hand on her hand as they drank their tea, watching his back as he walked away from her along the platform. She wrote all this in her letter, and as she wrote the voices in the neighbouring room dwindled one by one until there were only the sounds of a man and wife trying to comfort each other at the news which had reached them. The face of the soldier in the train had disappeared without trace. She could no longer even hear his voice.

Next day she had a letter from Richard, written on the train on his way back to camp. It was clear nothing had distracted him from her. 'I am writing this so as to lose none of yesterday's joy, because I want to cherish it and take it with me when I go overseas. It proved the strength of the bond between us. The world is cruel to part us, and so many others like us, at the very moment of the blossoming of our love. We can only wait for the war to end, without letting ourselves think too much about our daily duties. Yesterday really happened. Remember, the mice got away before the Englishman could crush them.'

Far away as he was, there was something tangible and real about Richard. She felt no doubts about him, just fear for his safety.

Next day in school she heard that Morgan Beddoe had indeed fallen in battle. The boy who sent the news had said he was lost. The family, clinging to that frail ambiguity of language, would hold on to their hope till the death was confirmed by the War Office. Seeing her landlady drag herself about the house with never a smile on her face, Ann felt it would be better for her to know the truth at once. What were a few days of false hope worth? Only Mrs Beddoe could answer that. Ann had never known such loss. Yet she knew at any time the sword could fall on her. It struck Mrs Beddoe hard a few days later, and her grief raised more than a stone wall between them. It was an impenetrable barrier. Between them words had collapsed.

Then silence. It was odd receiving Richard's first letter from France saying he had arrived safely, and nothing more, no hint of warmth behind the news. It was like a signpost on a lonely road showing the way, leaving the traveller to make the best of the journey. Bobi was still in his posting, though Ann sensed he was restless. The other boys often went to the cinema. He was sending half his wages home to Mam. The food was not very good. She sent him stamps, and sometimes half a crown. She knew his complaints were fair, and that one so young should not be in the army. But he was a soldier now, and she couldn't read his mind any more. Her mother's letters were more cheerful. Her health had improved. There was no talk of Roland going overseas yet, and her view of Bobi's situation agreed with Ann's. It looked as though life went on as usual.

A letter came from Mrs Hughes from Blaen Ddôl, a letter that showed life did not go on as usual for her. She had done nothing about looking for work. Her only comfort was to be at home where she could feel her husband's presence. Although he was no longer there, coming and going, only home made her grief bearable. Worst of all was going to chapel and coming home without him. And now the officials of the chapel had written to her, kindly enough, to ask if she could vacate the house in the New Year. She asked Ann to visit her during the Christmas holidays. It was odd to be so reminded that Christmas was not far away. It would be a strange Christmas.

She gave herself wholeheartedly to reading, and in spite of the terrible ending of *Tess*, she resolved to read more of the work of Thomas Hardy. He drew her on, and every chapter encouraged her and gave her strength. The suffering of the characters was so real. They went from one discouragement to the next, and she felt she was walking beside them sharing their lives and their pain. Her thoughts returned to Blaen Ddôl and a conversation she'd had with Bess Morris many months ago, about entering the experience of others through the Book of Common Prayer, and turning them into one's own. She could not in the least understand why she found experiences in a novel easier to share than the feelings of Mrs Beddoe or her friend Mrs Hughes. These were enigmas she could not solve, and many years would have to pass before literature could shine its light fully into her own life.

5

Waiting and waiting, Christmas Eve, and past nine o'clock. As promised, Roland and Huw arrived at nightfall. Nobody was sure if Bobi would come. In his last letter he had not been certain of being granted leave. They waited for him anyway, hoping he would reach town on the eight o'clock train and get a lift from there. Ann kept busy all day, baking, steaming the pudding, cleaning, her thoughts with Richard in France, flitting occasionally to Bobi stationed in the North of England, and her thoughts gave fire to her hands and feet as she sped through her work. Now they sat round the fire after a supper of bread and cheese, the cheese like limp leather, but the bread-and-butter good. The boys talked, comparing their experiences, while their father listened with a smile on his face. Their mother gazed into the fire saying nothing. Ann well knew where her thoughts were.

'Did he say anything in his letter to you, Ann?'

'No, nothing. He wasn't expecting home leave, certainly, or he'd have said something about it.'

Her mother turned her face again to the fire.

'He won't come now,' said her father.

'No, I'm afraid he won't,' said her mother.

'How do you know?' said Ann. 'There are all sorts of late trains on nights like this.'

'Not in wartime,' said Roland.

But they waited a little longer, until their father said he was going to bed.

'Would you like me to stay up for a bit,' asked Ann, 'and you all go to bed?'

'No, I'll wait up with you,' said her mother firmly.

So they did. Her mother nodded off once the others had gone to bed, and Ann picked up her book. She found herself watching the clock, and staring into the fire. She was glad now that Mrs Hughes had declined her offer to keep her company over Christmas. Knowing how hard it would be for her friend to spend Christmas without her husband, Ann had offered to stay with her. But Mrs Hughes had refused, wanting to face the worst and find her courage from the start. Now, as she watched her mother dozing dejectedly, Ann wondered how she could have thought of being away from home at such a time.

'Come on, Mam, let's go to bed. He won't come now.'

'No, he won't,' she said sadly, 'we'd best go.'

Ann carried the cat to its box of straw in the shippon. The sky over the sea was dark blue, and lights gleamed fitfully from far away across the county and the town. She could not see where the sea met the land, only a formless world. It was utterly silent, and across that silence came the harsh cry of a bird. She noticed her father had forgotten to feed the cattle, a most unusual lapse.

She brought fodder, and the two cows leaned their necks expectantly towards her on the manger. She closed the shippon door on their munching and blowing. She heard again the hoarse croak of a bird. She opened the gate and stepped out into the lane, hoping for the sound of footsteps on the road. Soon, indeed, she heard a great many footsteps, people on their way home from chapel. She turned back to the house and went to bed.

She dreamed she was still on the train like two days ago, the train stopping at every house, and the doors slamming incessantly. Then someone began to rattle the doors, banging and shouting, 'Hullo there!' like the sound of someone trying to wake the house. She woke up, and knew at once that someone really was knocking on the door and shouting 'Hello!' She got up at once, put on an old coat and was down in the kitchen in a moment, but her mother was there before her, and she had already opened the door for Bobi.

'I'm starving,' were his first words.

'Get some heather from the back, Ann, pack it between the cinders, and fill the kettle.'

The heather blazed and clouds of white smoke rose into the chimney, the kettle began to sing and dishes rang between scullery and kitchen. The kitchen hummed, the heather spat red, and sparks leapt in the grate.

'I've only got boiled eggs for you,' said Mam, 'you can't have a feast.'

'Wonderful,' said Bobi. 'At least I'm sure they're fresh, and not addled.'

Ann noticed there was not a sound from her father, and she went to his room. He was lighting the candle with a trembling hand. In the pale circle of candlelight Ann saw that his face was ashen.

'What's the matter, Dad?'

'It's just the shock,' he said.

She ran downstairs, took a teacup from the table and fetched water from the dairy.

Bobi went into the bedroom to find his father lying with his head in his hands, unable to speak.

'There you are, Dad.' Ann had returned with the cold water.

'I'm fine now. Something came over me. How are you, Bobi? How did you get here?'

'I arrived in Bangor at eleven o'clock, and walked. There was nothing else I could do.'

'Out with you, I'm getting up,' said his father.

Ann went to the door to fetch the coat he wore sometimes at night, and she put it round his shoulders.

Half past one in the morning and the kitchen was crowded and noisy, her other brothers awake and down from the attic. There they still were until three, when their father said, 'To bed with us or morning will be here.'

Ann's cup was only half full. Richard was not home. She was pleased Bobi looked so well, grown taller, and his face glowing with health instead of the old, pale look. What had come over her father tonight? Overcome by the excitement of having Bobi home, no doubt. He was no longer in regular work, only helping out here and there, a humiliating situation, she thought, for one skilled in the cutting and dressing of slate. She began to wonder if he was eating properly. As well as anyone else these days, she supposed. At least tonight the door was locked and bolted, and the family safe home.

Her mother was already up, the milking done and the fire lit under the oven when Ann got up on Christmas morning. They ate a simple breakfast together, and Ann took ·the others their breakfast in bed. Her father was better, but looking old, Ann thought. Well, she looked older and thinner herself. There would come a day when she would look like her father, but she pushed the thought away. There were years of youth ahead of her, years of happy life. She hoped there would be a letter from Richard today. That would be something.

Running back and fore between the well and the house, she discovered her brothers talking secretively together, pretending they were looking at the pigs or the hens. They fell silent as she approached them. If they but knew she did not want to hear their secrets. She would prefer not to know if their departure overseas was imminent. Today she would rather live in hope.

There was no word in the post from Richard. She knew anything could happen between writing and posting a letter, so

145

she was not too worried. Two or three letters might well arrive together.

Once again the family around the dinner table was complete, but this time her father did not comment on it. When you most expect things, they do not happen. Either her father's memory was going, or he had stopped himself deliberately. To Ann the dinner did not seem as good as two years ago, though, judging by the way the boys devoured it, it ought to be ten times as good.

'You're not eating, Ann,' said her father.

'Yes I am. I was just daydreaming.'

Bobi looked at her, and it was the first time he had paid her a second's attention since his arrival in the night. They all talked at once and to everyone, and Bobi made no attempt to speak to her directly. Was it, she wondered, a natural distance arising from his move away from home, or was he avoiding her? Fortunately in her letters she had never expressed her opinion that he was too young to enlist, but now she knew she must tell him in case he was thinking of going overseas. She knew Roland would have no choice in the matter. She did not mention the Christmas afternoon eisteddfod at chapel. She would wait and see if Bobi suggested it first.

She expected Bobi to help her with the dishes as usual, but he did not. He went for a walk with Huw. It was Roland who dried the dishes for her.

'Where has Bobi gone?'

'To see the lads in the neighbourhood. Why?'

'Nothing. I was just wondering.'

'He shouldn't be in the army. He's too young. I hope he won't regret it.'

It did Ann good to hear someone echo her own thoughts. She could not say much to Roland here, with her mother and father still in the kitchen. When the dishes were done she persuaded her father to go to bed for a little sleep and her mother to rest in the armchair. She placed a cushion behind her head to help her to relax, then she raked the ashes from the oven and tidied the hearth. She filled the iron kettle with water ready for tea, and put it on the hob by the fire. Then she went to have a wash. She undressed and got into bed, something she had never done

146

before. She had never missed the Christmas eisteddfod at the chapel. If it came to that, there had never been a war before. Tradition was beginning to break down, and she did not like it. Nothing was right somehow, and yet it was more in rage than sorrow that she took to her bed. Tranquillity overcame her once she was tucked under the sheet. Bodily tiredness was good, and sleep banished care for a while. When she rose at three she was ready for work again. She put on a warm grey dress with a clean pinafore over it. She took the best dishes out of the glass cupboard, and recalled Richard telling her how he had done the same thing two years ago in his home. She polished the dust away, and as she looked at them gleaming on the table, it gave her more pleasure than anything that day. They had to begin tea without Bobi, and Ann could have strangled him when he came in halfway through the meal. He did not seem to care about anyone any more.

After tea, before he could avoid her again, she spoke to him under her breath.

'Come out with me, I want to talk to you.'

He looked surly, but he came.

'Now Bobi, why are you avoiding me?'

'I'm not.'

'Yes you are. I've had hardly a word with you since you came home.'

'I've only been home a few hours.'

'Never mind. There was a time when you wanted us to talk.'

He did not answer. Ann continued. She tried to explain her feelings. 'I hope you are not going to tell the authorities you want to go overseas.'

He did not answer.

'I don't know if you realise that Mam and Dad are worried sick that you are in the army at all.'

'I don't doubt it, but what could I do, I was so unhappy in town, and all the other boys were leaving one after the other.'

'All right. What's done is done. The best thing you can do now is to stay in this country. Did you see Dad last night? It wasn't waking too suddenly that upset him, but being overwhelmed with joy that you had come home when he'd given

147

up expecting you. It's a pity you couldn't have taken a peep through the window last night to see the sorrow on this hearth.'

'Well I did my best to get home, and it was only after I'd begged and begged that they let me come.'

'I'm not complaining about that. I'm trying to get you to see what things are like here. Remember, Mam and Dad are not so young any more.'

'No they aren't, but I'm young, Ann, and I don't see why I can't enjoy myself just because they're old.'

Ann saw his point. She also noticed the 'Ann', instead of the familiar 'Nani'.

'Of course, but you should try to spare them unnecessary pain. They have known nothing but hard work all their lives.'

'All the more reason for their children to know a different life.'

Then he suddenly changed the subject.

'How's Richard?'

'I'm glad you've asked at last. He was all right when I last heard. That was a week ago. I heard nothing today, but maybe the letter has gone to Ynys-y-Grug.'

'Bad luck, Nani. I'm sorry. I'm afraid it's you who must put up with the worst of it.'

'Oh, no, no, no,' she said bursting into tears.

Bobi put his arm round her neck. It calmed her.

'Bobi, come with me to the eisteddfod tonight?'

'Of course.'

'Oh, I'm so pleased. I felt like a murderer going to bed after dinner. It's the first time I've ever missed it.'

'We haven't missed much, for sure.'

'No, but we've broken a tradition.'

In chapel Ann knew Bobi had spoken true. They hadn't missed much. Yet she was happy to be there with Bobi beside her. There was a sprinkling of military uniforms in the audience, and one of them was Bobi's. Ann noticed he had not been able to change his clothes all day. Before enlisting he had worn knee breeches. It gave her a shock. The boy had become a young man. That was why there was difference and tension between them. She wanted him to be a boy still, a boy in knee breeches. She tried to listen to the competition, but there was nothing to interest her there. The programme was cobbled together, and many whose names were down to compete were absent. For some it was impossible to attend, since they had been posted overseas. She was glad when it was over.

'Let's hurry home to supper,' she said to Bobi.

Either he did not hear her, or he slipped out to see someone, but there was not a glimpse of him when she reached the chapel porch. The crowd was so large and the road so dark that she did not try to search for him. She waited at the edge of the crowd, but there was no sign of him so she decided to go home.

'Where's Bobi?' were her mother's first words.

'I don't know, I lost him among the crowd coming out. I thought he'd be here before me, because I waited there for a while.'

'Let's start,' said Roland. 'I'm hungry.'

'So am I,' said Ann.

Ann felt angry with Bobi again. She had hoped their talk had made him see a little sense, and she knew how her father enjoyed nothing more than seeing the whole family round the table. This was not only a matter of feelings. He was a fastidious man, and to him it seemed as discourteous to come in late for a meal as to arrive late for chapel or the quarry.

Before they had finished Bobi arrived, soaked with sweat as if he had been dragged through the river. Wherever he had been, at least he had run all the way. Ann did not question him. She was glad to see him no later than this.

6

Ann approached Blaen Ddôl with mixed feelings. It was no longer her village. Neither had she put down roots in Ynys-y-Grug, since her job was temporary, and she was well aware that the sooner the war was over and the absent teacher back in his place the better for everyone. Nor were her feet on firm ground at home. Everyone had gone but her mother and father. She felt like an umbrella snatched by the wind, hovering in the air with nowhere to settle.

Her journey was pleasant despite those early January days, days thin as a sheared sheep, comfortless days, especially now. She knew there would be a welcome from Bess Morris, Mrs Hughes and Mrs Evans. And Mrs Hughes would be happy to see her now that Christmas was over, in spite of her grief. It still left a bitter taste in Ann's mouth. Such things might be easier to bear in the spring. In only a few days she would be off again to Ynys-y-Grug, leaving her parents to endure the emptiness. A bundle of letters had come from Richard after Christmas. She had learned not to take it for granted that he was still safe by the time she received them.

Mrs Evans had prepared her a dinner as fine as it was possible to expect. A portion of fish, potatoes and cabbage, rice pudding with apples, not too sweet. The house looked starker than it had, with her floors stripped of their rugs and her dresser of dishes. Her hearth was as warm as ever, and she in the same clothes, her hair done in the same late nineteenth-century style. She looked less sure of herself, crestfallen somehow.

'You're staying the night here, aren't you Miss Owen?'

'Well, thank you. I wasn't thinking of staying the night. I thought Mrs Hughes would be glad of my company.'

'Do come back here,' pleaded Mrs Evans, 'I'd be glad of your company too.'

'All right. I'll explain to Mrs Hughes. She'll understand.'

'Of course. And come in as late as you like.'

'That's fine. And how *is* Mrs Hughes?' Ann asked hesitantly, remembering that Mrs Hughes was not held as highly in Mrs Evans's esteem as her late husband the minister had been.

'Well, to tell the truth she is bearing up well, though it has taken its toll. Everyone is very sorry for her. And how are your mother and father?'

'As well as can be expected, worried about the boys of course.'

'Yes indeed. This old war. I had a very bad time when the soldiers were billeted here. Coming home drunk every night dragging the rugs with their feet, and awful language. One of the last things poor Mr Hughes did was to write a letter on my behalf to have them moved out. Oh dear, we shall miss him.'

Ann wanted to smile as she thought how the wheel of Providence, in which Mrs Evans so fervently believed, had turned full circle. Only justice, after all the fuss she had made about one tot of rum. Ann would have laughed had it happened at the time, but today it gave her no pleasure to hear how Mrs Evans had suffered. She had been punished too severely, and her air of disapproval had quite vanished.

'I had a Christmas card from Bobi,' she said proudly.

'Oh, really?'

'Yes. How is he looking?'

'Oh, very well. He's grown taller and stronger, and he looks really happy.'

She stifled a sigh, remembering the tea party and Bobi sitting here, at the table.

Bess Morris was out when she called, and Mrs Morris began by complaining about how her daughter was working like a fool for the soldiers.

'I rarely see her once she's swallowed her tea,' she said. 'She's out every minute helping to send parcels and so on. There's no sense in it. I warned her to be home in time to see you.'

At that moment Bess came running down the stone steps and appeared, breathless, at the back door.

'I'm sorry Ann. How are things?'

'Oh, not bad considering.'

'Considering what?'

'Well, all my loved ones have joined the army.'

'Good. It's a pity not everyone is like them, then the war could be ended all the sooner.'

'Don't talk nonsense,' said her mother, 'it's not good for families that the men must go.'

'No, it's not,' said Ann.

'Oh, we won't quarrel about it,' said Bess, 'but that's how I think the war will be brought to an end.'

She spoke with the austerity of one who believed in taking the medicine, however bitter, as long the desired end was achieved. She changed the subject.

'Things have changed a lot at school. Everyone is glad to have the soldiers here. Lyd Edwards has fallen in love.'

Ann felt no more interest in the affairs of Lyd Edwards than if she lived on the moon.

'She is so happy now that she has given up trying to be witty. She's completely changed her ways. She'll be her old self again once her sweetheart goes to France.'

Bess did not ask about Richard, so Ann said nothing either. She realised how completely she had left Blaen Ddôl behind.

'Make a cup of tea,' said Mrs Morris, 'Miss Owen won't want to hear nonsense like that.'

'Don't you, Ann?'

'Well, it's strange how things that could once sting don't hurt any more.'

'Sting?'

'Well, yes. Lyd Edwards was once a thorn in my flesh. It seems so trivial now that there are greater things to worry about.'

Bess did not fall for the lure. As she carried the dishes to the table she moved as one who was driven. She was not making tea for a friend. She was getting a job over and done with.

'I suppose you're staying with Mrs Hughes tonight?'

'No, I've promised to go back to Mrs Evans.'

Bess raised her eyebrows.

'The cat and the pigeon are friends again?'

'She was good to Bobi, and she wants me to stay with her. Mrs Hughes will be more understanding about it than Mrs Evans would be if I stayed with Mrs Hughes.'

'Mrs Hughes has had a terrible shock and it's told on her,' said Mrs Morris.

'Tut! She'll marry again,' said Bess. 'It'll have to be someone who'll keep her. She hasn't lifted a finger to try and get work.'

'As she'll have to leave the house there's no point in her seeking work here,' said Ann, 'and she needs time to recover from her terrible loss. I can't imagine how I would manage in her place.'

'She feels it deeply, Miss Owen, but Bess thinks we must all put our feelings under lock and key for the sake of the war,' said Mrs Morris.

Bess made no move to see her friend out, and Ann had nothing to say to her either, since all efforts at conversation in the house had failed. She set off to Mrs Hughes's house unhindered by the fear of wearing out her welcome that she used to feel when she lived in her old lodgings.

'Ann. It's good to see you. Come in by the fire.'

'I'll hang up my coat in the lobby.'

'Yes, do. Come on in,' and Mrs Hughes took her into the back parlour.

'Will you have a cup of tea?'

'No, thank you. I've just had one in Bess Morris's house.'

'She spared time for you? She's obsessed by the war.'

Ann said nothing. She could not get over the change in Bess Morris, and the change in Mrs Hughes too. Instead of the familiar sturdy figure, her body now seemed slack as a flour-sack from which a good deal of flour had been taken. But she was as warm as ever.

'How are things with you, Ann?'

'I'm fine. But how are you?'

'Well, I'm bearing up quite well. I must, for the sake of the children. They've gone to friends up the hill this afternoon. I gave them as good a Christmas here as I could manage, in spite of all the shortages, and we invited some of their friends in. I bottled up my feelings, and so did they. When you're bereaved you keep close to the wall. You never tell anyone how you really feel.'

'I suppose not.'

'How is your family? And Mr Edmund?'

'As you can imagine, tense and worried and hoping for the best. Bobi came home for Christmas, and we were all together again. Richard is in France, of course. It's odd how accustomed one gets to confusion and change these days.'

'Yes, we have to accept things, don't we? We have no choice.'

At that moment the children arrived and ran to their mother.

'You remember Miss Owen, don't you?'

'Yes, very well.'

'But they've grown, haven't they, Miss Owen?'

'They have. I'd hardly know them.'

'There's a fire in the study, so you can go and read in there.'

'All right. We'll go in there after we've played for a bit.'

And off they went.

'I want them to get used to going into the study from the start, as though it's the most natural thing in the world, and they talk about their father as if he had never left the house.'

At this Mrs Hughes's voice choked.

After a delicious supper of baked potatoes, onions and cheese, when the children had gone to bed the two women turned to the fire and Mrs Hughes launched her thunderbolt.

'Tell me Ann, you didn't like Dan, did you?'

As she was wondering how to reply, Ann caught a glimpse of the woman who shocked the chapel committees, the woman who would blurt out the most startling things.

'Well,' said Ann slowly, 'you see, I was a young girl straight out of college, and a bit scared of preachers, out of awe of course, and somehow I never got close to Mr Hughes. I don't know why because I had a great respect for him. Once or twice I thought I might get to know him, but then came the fuss about the rum, and you know what happened next. The young always react against what they think is unfair, and I'm afraid that was the mood I was in when I left Blaen Ddôl.'

'Thank you for your honesty, Ann. Dan was a hard worker, and methodical too. You know, he may have looked as if he could stand on his own two feet, but he needed someone behind him. He never showed that side of himself in chapel, but at home he was as dependent on me as the children. Only I knew that side of him, and that's why I loved him so much. You remember I once told you how difficult it was to live with piety? Dan found that with the chapel people. I could take his sort of godliness, but I had a pretty good idea the trouble he had with the godliness of some of his congregation. He didn't think I talked nonsense.'

'I understand that.'

Somehow Ann thought it was another man who had died and not her old minister, yet if he came back now her relationship with him would not really have changed. It was Mrs Hughes alone who knew the man, and it had been impossible for her to convey that knowledge while he was alive.

'I've been thinking about you a lot, Ann.'

'Have you? Why?'

'I was very sorry for you when you came here, a place that didn't suit you somehow, and it took something like a war for you to find somewhere more congenial. And now the very thing that gave you that place has broken your home, driven your sweetheart away and brought you such sorrow. Has it spoilt everything for you, Ann?'

'It depends what lies ahead in the future, Mrs Hughes. I'm hoping for the best.'

'And your father and mother have so looked forward to seeing all of you get on in the world.'

'Yes. It's hard for them. They're no longer young.'

And there, in front of the fire, they shared confidences. Ann told her story about Christmas Eve, and Mrs Hughes listened as intently as if they were her own family's worries, easing some of her own grief by sharing another's worries. Ann could not help feeling glad Mr Hughes was not there, and the next moment she felt sorry for admitting such a thought. She ventured to ask her friend her plans for the future.

'I have to leave this house, and Blaen Ddôl,' she said, 'I couldn't live in another house in Blaen Ddôl, and I don't want to live with one of my two sisters. They think I am a fool. I was thinking of finding a place as a housekeeper, where I could keep the children with me.'

As Ann rose to leave, Mrs Hughes spoke,

'Writing a letter for Mrs Evans about moving the soldiers out was one of the last things Dan did. He worked much too hard, letters every week for all the boys in the chapel who were in the army, filling in forms for everyone. Very few knew how much he did.'

Walking back to her old lodgings, Ann thought of all she had seen after spending only half a day in two houses, how much friends had changed, and how much her opinion of friends had changed, including her opinion of the dead. She thought the change in Bess was the saddest thing. It was she who had lost her balance. Mrs Hughes, whom people thought unstable, had come through the storm.

Mrs Evans had placed her slippers on the fender in front of the fire, which was burning low and red. She went through to the back kitchen and returned bearing a tray with two glasses.

'There,' she said, 'I've made us a hot drink of whisky, lemon and honey.'

Ann nearly had a fit. And yet, in spite of the apparent inconsistency, she realised that this was Mrs Evans's way of saying sorry about the fuss over the tot of rum.

7

Ann was sitting by the fire in her room reading her letters, after eating a frugal meal. The post more than made up for it. Two letters from Richard, one from Bobi, one from home, and one from Mrs Hughes. A feast of letters. By now receiving and writing letters was as much a part of her life as marking her pupils' work. Pleasant work when the letters were like today's. Usually she scanned them quickly first, and then, when she was sure there was no bad news, she read them all over again slowly, relishing every word. Naturally Mrs Hughes's letters no longer bubbled over with wit, but neither were they depressing. It was six weeks since Ann's visit and she was still in Blaen Ddôl. She said the deacons were pressing her to leave the house, but she felt too low-spirited to search for a house or a job.

'I've complained enough about Blaen Ddôl,' she said, 'but now that I have to leave I want to stay. Dan is buried here, though I know it's sentimental to say so. However, for now it's something to cling to. If you weren't so far away I'd come and live near you.'

Her mother sounded in better spirits, her health improved, and Ann knew it was because the boys were still this side of the sea. Her father felt better, she wrote, for seeing the boys over Christmas, and he had not suffered another funny turn since then. She said she was very busy sending parcels to the boys every week, some butter, and little loaves. Ann had told her mother about Miss Williams sending things, and her mother was a good one for picking up tips.

Bobi seemed in his element, and there was no hint of bad feeling in his letter about the straight talking between them over Christmas. Short rations were his chief grouse, her own problem too, but it was the endless marching that made him so hungry. She must send him some money, she thought.

Richard's letters were necessarily very brief, self-censored, both short. One sentence was broken off as if he had been interrupted. Cut short before he had finished. But there was still the same shared feeling, the same concern, the same longing for the war to be over. She crossed her legs contentedly before the fire, warming herself once more before setting out for school.

At that moment she saw the telegraph boy walking up the path from the street to the front door, and without wondering whether it was to her or her landlady that he brought a telegram, she ran to answer the door. She was shocked to see it was addressed to her, but when she saw it was from London she recovered herself. Richard on his way home, his uncle seriously ill, letter to follow. At that moment she realised how little she had thought about Richard's uncle since he had gone to France. He was Richard's only relative, and as far as she knew Richard was all the family the old man had, his next of kin. What Richard's departure overseas must have meant to the old man suddenly dawned on her. She could have visited him over the Christmas holiday. His illness was serious enough for Richard to ask for home leave. And she, who was so close, had not given him a thought, had not considered going to see him. She consoled herself by thinking that Richard could have asked her to go if he had wanted. Maybe the old man was shy. Maybe he would resent her as someone who might take Richard away from him. Her sweetheart had never told her much about him, only that he had been kind to him since he lost his parents. Her conscience calmed and her spirits lifted on her way to school. There was hope she might see Richard again soon.

Two days later he sent word from Anglesey that his uncle had suffered a stroke, that there was no hope for him, and next day a letter came to say he had died, and that Richard would try to see her before returning to France.

Luckily it was Saturday. There would be no need to beg a

favour of the headmaster. Richard was to travel to Cardiff late on Friday evening, and she would go there to see him early on Saturday morning. He would take the overnight train to London.

Cardiff station was so crowded when Ann stepped down from the train that looking for Richard felt like looking for a needle in a haystack. However, she spotted his head above the crowd before he saw her, and never had she seen an expression so bleak with anxiety. When he saw her his face was suddenly transformed. He caught her in his arms and lifted her from the ground.

'Oh, Ann, I'm so happy to see you. I've been on fire with longing ever since I woke up, and it seemed such a long wait for your train to come in.'

'I'm so sorry about your uncle, even though it was his death that gave us this chance to meet.'

'Yes, indeed. Come on, Ann. Let's go out for a really good meal. I'm hungry now.'

And they pushed through the crowd, hurried along the street, and shouldered their way through the restaurant into the farthest corner.

'Let's have a good dinner, Ann.'

'Yes, if we can get one.'

They were not sure what they were eating. It was a mixture of minced meat, rice and other things, but it was hot and delicious and they were happy to be together.

'I was sure I wouldn't be able to see you, Ann, because I have to make the crossing to France tonight. I had the funeral to arrange, and only yesterday to do everything else. The housekeeper went home to her sister's the night before last, straight after the funeral, or I could have given her some of the jobs to do.'

'Poor you! And you do look tired.'

'I can sleep on the train tonight. I've been feeling lost for days. I never thought it would hurt so much to lose the old man.'

'You've lost everyone now, haven't you?'

'Everyone except you, Ann. It would have been terrible to return to France without seeing you. Ann, look at me. Don't ever leave me, will you?'

This was quite different from the cautious Richard she knew. She looked into his eyes.

'No, of course I won't.'

'Forgive me, Ann. Yesterday in that empty house I realised what my uncle meant to me. He never showed me much feeling though he was always kind, gave me money every time he collected the rent for the fields, things like that. And he was always there. I never went home to an empty house. He showed he cared by staying home, and the housekeeper told me he felt quite lost when I went to France.'

Ann listened attentively.

'You know, Richard, when I had your telegram I felt terrible that I hadn't been to visit him over Christmas.'

'He wouldn't have appreciated your kindness, I'm afraid. He had become very strange towards the end, so I understand.'

'He obviously worried a lot about you.'

'He did. And the poor old man has left everything to me. The house and the fields. That touched me keenly.'

'He had no-one else, did he?'

'No, but I have seen old people leave everything to the housekeeper. He left her twenty pounds.'

He fell silent.

'Listen Ann,' he said, 'will you be offended if I give you a little present?'

'Richard, you mustn't. Spend it on yourself in France, to buy food.'

'I get plenty of food, luckily. No really, it would make me happy to give you something. You don't get many luxuries.'

And he pushed five pounds into her hand.

'No, Richard.'

'I insist. Buy yourself a warm coat.'

'I suppose this one is rather shabby. It's served me well, Sundays, holidays and work.'

'I didn't mean that. I'd just like you to have a coat with a warm collar.'

'Let's go and buy it now.'

Without further ado they bought a pale blue coat with a narrow fur collar. Ann wore it at once, and carried the other over her arm. Time did not dawdle that day. Though the air was cold there was warmth in the streets crowded with strollers, warmth in the shops, and warmth at the tea table. They talked of their everyday lives. Ann told him about Christmas and her visit to Blaen Ddôl. It was the first time she had mentioned the fuss over the tot of rum. She had kept quiet about the upset, but as it had ended so happily with the fall of Mrs Evans it was easy to tell him now. It was the first time Richard had laughed all day.

'Better late than never for Mrs Evans to see sense. It's a pity we can't arrange for people like her to spend three days at the Front. Then she'd see what a trivial matter a little drink is.'

'Listen,' he said after a moment, 'I wonder if Mrs Hughes would like to stay in our house for a while until she finds a place. She could put her furniture into storage.'

'Oh, Richard! You are kind. It would be such a comfort for her to know she had somewhere to go.'

'No, it's not kind at all. It would help me. I wouldn't have to worry about the house getting damp, and I don't want any rent.'

'She'd be thrilled.'

'And Ann, I want to give you the front door key. The back door key is with the next door neighbour, and I'd like you to be able to go there during the Easter holidays, that is, if Mrs Hughes has not moved in.'

Ann was silent after she took the key from his hand. This was trust indeed. He could not trust her more if she were his wife.

'Penny for your thoughts, Ann?'

'I was thinking I'm not half good enough for you.'

'Nonsense!'

There they were, sipping tea, eating bread and margarine, talking. He saying the things he'd left out of his letters from France.

'Life has become so strange. I can't believe I was tending the wounded in France only nine days ago, and here I am with you and so much has happened between then and now.'

She fell silent, not knowing how much she dare ask him. Her face flushed with heat.

'And it's odd how one comes to accept it all. To see a soldier in pain made me flinch at first, but now I can even watch them die.'

160

Ann shivered.

'At first I was passionate about easing their suffering, but the work has become as much of a routine as my work as a teacher was. Teaching the children, taking their work home to mark, going to bed. Now, tending the wounded, sometimes with no time to show proper compassion. Now and then, when there's time to think, you see the pointlessness of war and wonder how it will end. Where I'm working now there's a doctor from Bolton, a bachelor who lives with his mother, and they made a pact that he would never write home once he came to France, except for a formal card once a week just to confirm that he is well, and she would only write to him if she were ill. He's devoted himself utterly to the lads. He'll sit for hours at the bedside of the dying, staying with them right to the end.'

'Fair play to him.'

'I could never cut myself off from the outside world like that. I don't know how I'd survive without your letters, and an occasional book. Thank you for sending me *The Critic*. But you know, reading those articles about the war gives me a very strange feeling that we're in different worlds. They're talking about something I'm in the middle of, and I'm not thinking of the war as a war, only as a job to finish so that I can go home. You know, reading the story of Mari Lewis writing a letter to Bob in prison is more real to me than reading the editorial on the war in *The Critic*.'

'That's difficult to imagine,' she said.

'Ask anyone and they'd tell you the same. Nowadays writing to the parents of one of the boys to tell them he's getting better is as natural as dressing myself. To me it's not a favour, it's a job. Like cradling their heads when they're in pain. Now I must go. I'm much better for seeing you, Ann.'

'I hope you'll come again before long, and that the war will soon be over.'

He said nothing, but took her arm firmly in his, and they walked back to the station through the crowds. He turned to her in the middle of the street.

'Ann, you do look beautiful in that coat.'

'I can't thank you enough.'

'I hope one day I will make you very happy.'

'And me you. Remember, we've stolen a lot of happiness today from under the nose of Fate.'

As the train drew out the last thing she heard him say was, 'I hope Bobi will have the sense to stay this side of the Channel.'

8

The holidays came and Ann was home again. The war grew closer month by month, with news of a neighbour's son killed in France, another wounded. Sorrow spread throughout the neighbourhood when such news came, but most people accepted it without complaint, just as they had accepted news of a man killed in the quarry before the war. There were those who were bitter about the war, but they were powerless to do anything but talk of their bitterness. There was more anti-war talk since the conscription law came in.

Ann was thinking about these things on the train as she travelled to Richard's house. Only yesterday she had heard of the death in France of a widow's son. He'd enlisted in haste and regretted it a thousand times, so they said. He was her only son. Ann brooded on the woman twice bereaved, and the tragedy of the son who had enlisted unnecessarily and had been killed. She tried to imagine the woman's feelings, but found she could not cross the boundary where all that suffering lay. Furthermore, matters of the heart were private. There was something sacred about people's feelings for their loved ones. She looked out of the window and saw soldiers being drilled in a field, marching up and down, endlessly marching and an officer shouting at them as if they were dogs.

Some of them would soon be in the midst of the massacre, more than likely, and somewhere far away Bobi and Roland were going through the same drill. To watch them was to be amused by the madness.

The train pulled into the little country station and she set off on the two mile walk to Richard's home. She was glad to think of nothing but the moment. If the war should end today she would have got through it without loss, but it would be tough on those like the widow alone in her house weeping that it had not ended just a few days sooner. There was however no end in sight, and the war dragged itself onwards.

All about her there were signs of new life. Lambs in daisy-bright fields. Clear blue air, the sound of a train sharp and emphatic piercing the distance, warmth rising from the earth. The far mountains of Arfon were splendid under their snowy summits. She was on a strange errand, visiting her lover's home, an empty house, and she was going there for the first time without anyone to welcome her. She felt as if she were married to him, so much trust had he placed in her. She seemed to be walking a road where there could be no turning back. What if she changed her mind about Richard? Or, more possible, what if she had a change of heart when she had come so far with the key to his house in her pocket? She banished the thought as an absurdity. When they met in Cardiff during the term her feelings for him had been warmer than ever. Though his leave was so brief he had insisted on seeing her. He had been generous towards her, and to Mrs Hughes. It was with more passion than ever before that he'd told her how much he needed her support and her help.

Walking along with the sun warm on the nape of her neck she was happy in the knowledge that Mrs Hughes would have somewhere to lay her head, and that no doubt it was here she would visit her friend in the summer holidays, and not Blaen Ddôl. She'd had another piece of news to cheer her since coming home: Dora had been appointed to a teaching post in Bont Wen, only twelve miles from Ynys-y-Grug. She was sure to see a lot of Dora now. The walk passed happily in the company of these not unpleasant thoughts.

The first thing that struck her as she opened the door was the smell, a musty smell as if the door had not been opened since the day Richard left. Damp ran down the walls, and the sight of it sent a shiver through her body. Richard had told her that Mrs Pritchard, the woman next door, would light the fire once a week, but it was difficult to believe that a fire had ever been lit there.

He had told her there would be plenty of coal in the shed, but when she went to look she found only a little small coal and some slack. There was no firewood. The ashes in the grate might have lain there since the last day Richard was home. While she was wondering what to do, she heard footsteps approaching the door, and a woman walked straight in without knocking.

'Why didn't you send to say you were coming?' were her first words.

Ann assumed this must be Mrs Pritchard.

'As I don't know your address how could I?' said Ann.

'If I'd known you were coming I'd have lit the fire today instead of in a day or two, as I do every week.'

Ann looked at her, and she blushed. Mrs Pritchard was about thirty-five, pretty enough to look at, with red-brown hair and eyes of the same colour. Her upper lip was a perfect bow. As Ann looked at her, she stared back as if challenging her to say she had told a lie. Ann realised that it was best to keep her silence in this place, so far from anywhere.

'It's a damp old house,' said Mrs Pritchard at last, 'no matter how often you light a fire.'

'Right then, I'd better make a fire at once,' said Ann, 'I need firewood from somewhere.'

Mrs Pritchard sat down in a chair and made no move to rise, her eyes fixed on Ann as if relishing her predicament. She did not offer to fetch wood. Ann's dilemma was not so much getting wood for the fire – she was sure to find some at one of the neighbouring houses – but knowing how to deal with this woman. She could hardly tell her to go, since she too had a key, and in a way had as much right as Ann to be in the house. Her attitude was entirely hostile. So Ann said simply,

'I'm going to find some kindling.'

She did not know where to go, but she had noticed a shop on her way here, about five minutes walk away. If she were unlucky there she could try one of the houses. She explained her need to the shopkeeper, and in a moment she was given an old box already broken into sticks. She must hurry if she was going to clean the whole house before she left. She hoped Mrs Pritchard would have gone away. She couldn't clean the house under someone else's eye, especially such an unfriendly eye. When she got back to the house she found the neighbour gone. She put on a coarse apron over her pinafore, and began to lay the fire with the little coal there was. She filled the big iron kettle from the spring that flowed in the lane. She put it on the fire, and as she waited for it to boil she ate some of the sandwiches she had brought with her and drank her milk.

She washed the floors of the back kitchen and the best kitchen, and while they were drying she went upstairs to do the dusting. It certainly needed it. She stood on a chair to wipe the top of a clothes press and was overwhelmed by a strange sensation. She had no idea what was in the cupboards. She supposed many belonged to the dead man, and some to Richard, but even if she opened a cupboard and saw something of Richard's, it would be like looking at dead things. Wearing clothes gave them life. There were mould-speckled photographs on the wall, which she guessed must be pictures of his uncle, his father and mother, and Richard as a small boy. His father wore a gentle expression and his mother looked defiant. They might have been quite different in reality. Richard with an innocent look aged about nine or ten. It made her fearful, as if the room were full of ghosts. They had all been here, but she could not say, 'I remember when that was taken.' Yet one of these people was now part of her own life.

She hurried so that she could dust downstairs. She was less nervous there, and the fire looked cheerful and companionable. Indeed, the room now looked as cosy as if someone still lived there, and she almost expected to see somebody sitting in the armchair. She imagined herself and Richard sitting together in the kitchen some day, the summer holidays, friends and family coming to visit them. She could see her father and mother, Bobi, Mrs Hughes, Dora, and Richard's friends round the table, talking and laughing, and Richard happy to be in his old home. No, she thought, this was her vision. It was not Richard's. He would see his own father and mother there, especially his mother, and might feel that strangers should not be in her place. She could not believe any mortal man could love a girl enough to see her family where his family should be, especially when they were dead. This was a shrine.

She looked at the dishes in the glass-fronted dresser. There was the tea set Richard had taken out on Christmas Day two years ago. She looked more closely at it, then thought that dishes were not like clothes. She wanted to hold them in her hands, and she opened the door. They were decorated with little blue flowers and a gold rim. She thought she would polish them, and she went into the back kitchen for a cloth she remembered seeing hanging on the back of the door. She began to wipe them one by one. She did not dare take them all out at once and place them on the table. Suddenly she heard someone at her side and in her fright she dropped the cup. It shattered. Mrs Pritchard had come in wearing slippers. She smiled with satisfaction to see Ann jump.

'Richard will never forgive you for breaking one of his mother's cups,' she said, 'he thought the world of her. And you'll have bad luck after smashing a cup.'

Ann could not speak, only gaze at the fine fragments on the floor, shards too small to consider repairing it. She knew the news would hurt Richard, but she also knew he would forgive her. She went out to the back to fetch a coal shovel and brush, and she swept up the pieces and cast them onto the garden. Then, as if the woman were not there, she took her fountain pen from her bag and opened the drawer of the dresser to look for a piece of writing paper there, just as she would have done at home. Then she sat down at the table to write to Richard and tell him the whole story. But the woman was not going to give her any peace.

'Richard's very hard,' she said, 'he has no feeling at all, and his uncle was the same. They wasted no time on emotions in this house when his mother died. That's when Richard hardened his heart. He was like a lost dog about the place waiting for a pat on the head, but his uncle wasn't a man to spoil dogs.'

'I'm sorry, Mrs Pritchard, but I must write this letter in time to catch the post on my way home.'

'When will you be back?'

'I can't tell you that.'

'So the house won't want cleaning for a bit.'

'Possibly.'

'Oh, well, I'm off then.'

Ann told Richard all about the day. At first her only thought was to tell him about the cup, but as Mrs Hughes would be coming to live here she thought she ought to mention the empty coal house. Maybe things had also disappeared from the house. She waited for the fire to die down, then she doused it with water. She wiped the dust from the mantelshelf. On her way to the station she ate the last of her sandwiches. She thought she should visit the house once more before going back to school, bringing her father and mother and Mrs Hughes with her. But her day had been so unhappy that she gave up the idea. At that moment she felt only hatred for the place. It had disclosed none of its secrets to her, nor had she felt Richard's presence there, except for a moment as she looked at his books upstairs. Maybe the house had meant less to Richard after his mother's death. But she knew he valued the tea set, and she had spoilt its wholeness. Something came slowly into her mind. There were two or three cups and saucers of the same pattern at home, the remains of a set. It was a common design. She would ask her mother for a cup. Still, the tea set which had belonged to Richard's mother was no longer whole, and it was she who had broken it. The woman had been like a witch bringing a curse into the house to do her harm.

* * *

'I don't know what's wrong with this house, but there's something odd about it,' said Mrs Hughes to Ann as they sat by the fire in the living room in Richard's house.

Ann decided she had better visit the house once more before the end of the holidays, and Mrs Hughes came too in case she did decide to live there. They swept the floors and dusted, then they cooked themselves some eggs and sat down to eat. Ann felt as Mrs Hughes did about the house. In fact, after the experience of her first visit she was glad of company this time.

'It's hard to say what it is about this place,' said Mrs Hughes, 'it's tidy enough, and as clean as you could expect an empty house to be, but there's an odour here, not a stench really, but the odour of death.'

'Don't frighten me, please.'

'To me it feels as though nobody has loved it for years.'

'How can you say that?'

'Oh, I don't know. When someone loves a house, they buy something new now and then, a cushion cover or a rug or something. Look at how the cover has been patched on this chair, even the binding of the mat has been mended.'

'The housekeeper's handiwork, no doubt.'

'Yes, but surely she wouldn't have patched things up like that if she'd had the money to buy new ones.'

'Likely enough the old man didn't have much to spare.'

'Maybe. Did you see the little cloth on the table upstairs, under Mr Edmund's books? Quite threadbare, though clean enough.'

'Yes, I noticed that, but maybe it belonged to Richard's mother and he wanted to keep it under his books. His mother meant a lot to him.'

'It must have been miserable for him in the holidays.'

Ann sighed. She knew the things Mrs Hughes said were all too true, but they were truths she did not want to hear, truths that her friend should have kept to herself. Still, looking into the fire and at the dresser full of pretty china, she thought the kitchen cheerful enough. Mrs Hughes noticed her staring into the fire.

'You're dejected, Ann.'

'No, just thinking you're right. When I came here before I felt there was something wrong with the house, but I couldn't have said why, as you have.'

Her mind filled again with what the woman next door had said on her first visit. Richard was hard. She had taken no notice, the words of a spiteful woman. Now she could not avoid connecting that word "hardness" with the miserly things she saw about her.

'Look at the dresser,' she said. 'That's lovely. I don't know why but it's there I see Richard.'

At that moment the woman next door arrived, starting at the sight of Mrs Hughes. In a moment she had recovered her composure.

'Oh,' said she, 'I see you found a cup to match the one you broke.'

'Yes,' said Ann, 'and this is Mrs Hughes, my friend.'

She did not explain further and Mrs Pritchard's inquisitive eyes showed her disappointment.

'Oh. Where are you from then?' was the woman's next question.

'From London,' was the reply before anyone else could say a word.

'Oh, Miss Owen, I bought a hundredweight of coal since you were here last, I don't know who's going to pay for it.'

'I'll pay for it,' said Ann, 'but there is no need for you to buy any more. Summer is coming and the weather will warm the house.'

'A very small hundredweight of coal,' remarked Mrs Hughes. 'Tell me, do they give full measure in Anglesey?'

Mrs Pritchard flushed and went out.

When she had gone the two women burst out laughing.

'Let's cheer ourselves up,'' said Mrs Hughes, 'no use being miserable. I'll go and see what we can have for tea.'

She went into the back kitchen and came back with a pot of home-made plum jam. The kettle was singing on the hob. She moved it onto the fire. She ran to the shop to buy some biscuits.

'Dishes on the table, Ann. We'll have a cup of tea, and some of this jam.'

Ann took a tablecloth from the drawer in the glass cupboard, and she laid the table with the everyday dishes kept in a round basket on the big table in the back kitchen.

'This is what I call a good tea,' said Mrs Hughes. 'Your mother's butter's delicious and this jam is really good. It was at the back of the cupboard under the big table.'

A lump came into Ann's throat when she saw the pot of jam. It restored life to the house. It was something home-made some time in the past. Richard had tasted jam from the same batch last year or the year before. It was indeed a lovely tea.

'I must take the tablecloth home to wash,' said Ann.

'No, I'll take it, it's more than likely I'll be back.'

'To a house you don't like?'

'You can drive away the odour of death bringing children to a house.'

And as she looked at her Ann felt that if anyone could bring warmth to drab surroundings it was Mrs Hughes. Despite her slack body there was something steely in her bearing, and wherever she was there was comfort.

'The biggest problem is how to deal with Mrs Pritchard,' she said.

'Bolt the door,' said Ann.

As they walked to the station Ann said,

'Did you know, my brother Roland has gone to France.'

Mrs Hughes stopped walking.

'You've kept that to yourself all day, and I've been piling on the misery with talk of odours of death and such things.'

'I didn't want to talk about it. I was hoping a day in Richard's house would console me and in the end it did. And at least Roland is alive.'

'Yes, and there's hope,' said Mrs Hughes seriously.

'I'm sorry I mentioned it now,' said Ann.

'Not at all. These are the things we must bear.'

As she said farewell to her friend at the station, Ann wished she could have accompanied her to Blaen Ddôl. The attraction was still there. But home was where she must go. That's where anxiety was. Her mother had pickled some herrings after the baking was done, and the three of them enjoyed their supper without talking about what was uppermost in their minds, but without being able to forget.

*   *   *

Ann's thoughts returned to the day when she and Dora walked down from the mountain into Ynys-y-Grug one fine Saturday evening in May. Her friend had just told her she was courting Harri Roberts, one of the college boys Ann had most disliked. She managed to smother her 'Oh!' of disappointment before it could escape her lips. But she could not express any pleasure. Harri Roberts's face was the nearest thing to a bulldog's Ann had ever seen, and she could not imagine a more ill-matched pair. Dora was everyone's favourite in Hall at college. It was amazing how much assertiveness Dora had gained since those days three

170

years ago, when she was a shy violet who wouldn't say boo to a goose.

Ann's landlady had cooked them a tasty supper of onions simmered in a sauce, and Ann had some of her mother's butter, brought with her at the beginning of term. Ann thought her landlady a magician, always conjuring something delicious for her meal though she was still grieving for her son. She even suggested baking a loaf of bara brith to send to Roland. Maybe such kindness gave her the strength to get through the dark days.

'Perhaps,' said Dora as she ate her slice of bara brith, 'it might surprise you to know that Harri is a conscientious objector.'

'Is he?' said Ann. 'He's the last person I'd have thought would be against the war.'

She recalled his rude and pugnacious opposition to every proposal that came from somebody else in the college Welsh Society. Peace had been the last thing on his mind. Perhaps this was his latest way of opposing things, fighting something most people supported.

'I'm surprised you support the war, Ann.'

'I don't support it. I don't understand enough to be against it. I wouldn't be against war if I knew what we were fighting for.'

'Then why don't you at least oppose this war?'

'I don't know. I don't know anything, only that those I love are in the middle of it, and I won't say anything against them.'

'You've got no backbone, or you wouldn't help the war in other ways.'

'How am I helping the war?'

'Well, you belong to a drama group which goes round raising money for the soldiers.'

'Listen, Dora, it's what keeps me going. I work hard at teaching, I enjoy congenial company, and I can't see that it's helping the war to give a bit of comfort to the boys in the trenches. I'm not saying they ought to die for us, but they are there, and a pair of socks or a few cigarettes helps them a little.'

'But you're helping the war to last longer.'

'That's what Harri says, isn't it? You have no brothers, Dora. I think you'd change your tune if you had. No one's holding your family to ransom. I don't know why Roland and Bobi enlisted, but they did, and I can't turn against them, although I can see what a stupid thing this war is. I don't see anything stupid in what's happening in Ireland. The Irish know what they are dying for.'

'Those are Richard Edmund's ideas aren't they?'

'Possibly. But he's never mentioned such things in his letters to me. He dare not. But I know if I were in Ireland I'd be fighting oppression.'

'The English will never give in to a handful of Irishmen.'

'No, they won't. They are too stupid to see that Ireland is a small country just like the other small countries whose freedom they're supposed to be fighting for in France.'

'You have some strange ideas in your head, Ann.'

'No stranger than those in Harri's head. Suffering helps you understand a lot of things.'

'You're taking this war much too seriously.'

'Perhaps you think the war is a bit of a joke.'

'No, but there are many people with more to worry about than you. Your two brothers are alive and one hasn't gone to France.'

'We only feel our own pain, Dora. Many people are ready to sacrifice their own families and other people's families. But let's not spoil our Sunday talking about the war.'

And they both laughed, but not as heartily as they had laughed together on Ann's last Friday evening at college.

9

Ann was perplexed about Dora. She had thought having her nearby would bring the company and comfort of a friend who was sympathetic to all her worries and her fears. After Dora's visit she knew that she would be no comfort, rather a thorn in her flesh every time they met. Had it been anyone but Dora she would have quarrelled with her that Saturday. Thinking over their talk later she realised Dora had said some very cruel things. She must be crazy about Harri to have swallowed his ideas whole without so much as a pinch of salt. She felt like telling Dora what she and all their college friends thought of Harri, but maybe that would make her cling to him all the more with crab-like tenacity. Dora had certainly changed. Lines were already appearing about the mouth in her round, plump face, and Ann could imagine her becoming a quarrelsome, cross old lady.

However, Harri was not *her* lover. She could not imagine change ever touching his face. She had never seen a smile on that surly countenance. He looked as if he had a grudge against the world, and everyone was out of step except him. She remembered how rude he could be in company, and what a bad loser he was. Once he had marched out of the Welsh Society after being defeated in a debate. But there must be another side to him, and maybe Dora was the only person who had seen it. Yet Ann could not just put her out of mind. Dora meant something to her. She couldn't give her up as she had given up Bess Morris. She had not written to her since returning to Ynys-y-Grug because she was sure Dora's mind was unbalanced. That's how it seemed to her, and she thought it best not to write since it was quite impossible to keep the war out of her letters.

Then one morning word came from Dora inviting Ann to spend the weekend with her; she was very upset, Harri had suddenly changed his mind about pacifism and had joined up. The facts were simply told, keeping Ann guessing all week about the details. She assumed there would be only two choices for Dora. She must change her mind about the war, or she must change her mind about Harri. She could not imagine Harri could go on loving someone who disagreed with him on any subject. What would she say if Dora asked her opinion? Well, she had learned never to put her thumb into a lovers' pie, and she also knew it was in the nature of love to go against the advice it sought.

On Friday morning Ann had worries enough of her own, and Dora's problem seemed trivial. Her mother had written to say that Bobi was on his way to France. She could not hide her regret and pain. 'He's so young,' she wrote. It was true. Not yet eighteen, he was sixteen-and-a-half months too young to be called-up to serve in a war. Ann felt as if she had been thrown to the ground. Her mind struggled between two thoughts, the pain of knowing Bobi was now in danger, and hurt at his disregard for the feelings of others. Her mother had enclosed his letter. He assured them he would be in no danger, that he would be on watch duty, but her mother knew as well as she that nowhere was safe in a war.

Because of the food shortages, she decided to go on Saturday morning and to keep Friday evening for correspondence. Writing letters was by now an important part of her life, though it was not always the pleasure it had been in Blaen Ddôl. She almost felt that in Ynys-y-Grug she lived through her letters. She longed for letters more than the drama group, the literary society, and other associations. She could neither loosen her grip on her old life, nor fully grasp the new. She belonged nowhere. Without knowing why, she found herself weeping over the letters she had written. Mrs Beddoe came in with a glass of rhubarb wine.

'Have this, Miss Owen, it will do you good. I know you have your troubles.'

She was gone before Ann could thank her. It warmed her heart to think of such kindness from one who could so easily have been preoccupied with her own grief. The letter to her parents was the hardest to write. How to give them heart, when her own heart was so heavy. Her tears for Bobi were knives. She remembered the night of his first communion. These were like those tears, shed for his lost youth and his blind inexperience. Then her letter to Richard. A letter that made her whole disposition grateful that she had him to turn to. He had taken the broken cup calmly, nothing to fuss about, and how happy he was to know that her mother's cup was now part of his own mother's set. She foolishly imagined he and Bobi might bump into each other sometime. But no-one knew yet where Bobi had been posted. She decided to write to Mrs Hughes. She could pour out her heart without fear of boring her. And a letter to Roland, with nothing in it to worry him.

The bus journey down the Cwm excited her. She was thrilled at the life she saw. As the bus wended its lumbering top-heavy way down past hundreds of houses she felt such seething vitality could never end. The odour of death was not here. It made her feel heedless, heedless of life's frailty, heedless of money, heedless of everything. Still, there were enough lonely places up above the houses on the bare mountain, and the slag-heaps on the slopes weren't half as friendly as the cairns of rubble in the quarries of the north.

Dora was waiting at the bus stop with a friendly smile on her face.

'Let's have dinner,' she said, 'and go down to the Docks this afternoon.'

'Fine,' said Ann, who rarely visited a town. She could lose herself among the bustling crowds. As they moved from shop window to shop window like bees from flower to flower, there was no chance for Dora to talk, even if she wanted to. Ann yearned for the fine things on display, but she well knew that more money than ever would be needed now to send parcels overseas. Dora said not a word about Harri over the tea table in the restaurant, and Ann wondered if she'd had second thoughts on the subject and had decided not to talk about it. She was glad to go back to Dora's lodgings. She was no town girl, and she grew weary walking the hard surface of the streets. Although it was early summer, there was a fire lit in the small room. The landlady was pleasant, and she had cooked some faggots for their supper. Ann felt completely refreshed stretched out in the chair, her slippered feet on the fender. She almost hoped Dora would not talk about her trouble so that she need not think about anything but taking a little nap. But there was no avoiding problems.

'What do you think of Harri?' was Dora's question.

'I don't know. That's a question for you Dora.'

'Did the news surprise you?'

'Not really. What about you?'

'More than surprised. Shocked, and I don't know what on earth to do.'

Ann ventured to speak.

'About which do you feel more strongly, Dora? The war, or Harri?'

'That's what I can't decide. I was hoping you'd throw some light on it for me.'

'Listen, Dora, don't expect anyone to advise you on the subject of love. If I advised you to change your mind about the war and stand by Harri, you'd stick to your pacifism. If I said keep to your principles and give up Harri, more than likely you'd stand by Harri.'

'Why do you say that?'

'Because love is stubborn and opposes interference. It's a matter for two people, not three.'

'Of course,' Ann added, 'I don't see that it's impossible for you to go on loving each other, in spite of your difference of opinion about the war.'

'I'm afraid that would be impossible for Harri.'

'Naturally you know him.'

'Yes I do, and we argued ourselves breathless on the subject before he enlisted.'

'Don't you think he could let you keep your own opinion about it?'

'I don't know. It's not that which is worrying me.'

'What then?'

'Well, I don't know how to say this, Ann. But I've been having some awful thoughts.'

Ann held her tongue and showed no wish to know more, lounging lazily in her chair, not looking at Dora.

'I've wondered if Harri is a coward,' said Dora, 'seeing how the conscientious objectors are sent to prison for refusing to enlist.'

'It's quite natural.'

'What? Natural for me to think like this, or natural for him to jib at prison?'

'It's natural for anyone to jib.'

'I see. But then, you're not against the war.'

'That's not why I say it's natural. I'm a coward myself, and I know what it is to be afraid. I can't blame anyone for doing what I'd probably do myself.'

Ann was beginning to feel some sympathy for Harri.

'I don't care about that,' said Dora, 'I believe war is wrong, any war, and there's no such thing as a just war.'

'Have you tried to imagine yourself in the lads' place, Dora?'

'No, I haven't.'

'Perhaps you'd feel different if you did. You don't have to go to war or prison, and it could be that it makes you feel quite secure on the subject of war. But say you were a young man, and your best friends had gone to war, it would be very hard for you to stay home, you'd be feeling so much for your friends. But because you will never have to go, you're completely confident about your stand.'

'I'd be just as adamant if I were a man.'

'Let's drop the subject, Dora, and go to bed. We can't resolve it. All I can say is the old saying is true, that men must fight and women must weep. Bobi has gone to France.'

Dora was about to say something.

'No, say nothing Dora. If you're so against war, try to understand my feelings tonight. You'll never see your family torn apart by war.'

'I'm sorry,' said Dora, 'that's all I was going to say. But I might yet see my own life in shreds too.'

It was impossible to guess the effect of this conversation on Dora. Ann was inclined to think she would stick to her beliefs and give up Harri. And if compromise could not be reached, then there was truth in Dora's final remark. For the first time Ann felt sorry for Harri.

10

'She behaves as if she's the only one with a brother in the war.'

'She's the only one on the girls' side of the school with a brother in the army, and she's very fond of her family,' spoke a kinder voice.

'She looks as if she comes from the back of beyond,' said the spiteful voice.

It was the tail-end of a conversation Ann overheard as she went into the staffroom at the end of a school morning. It gave her quite a shock. She knew they were talking about her, she knew it was Miss Williams who had spoken kindly, and she knew it was only a fragment of the gossip that she'd heard. We are so snugly tucked into our shells that we go through life imagining nobody talks about us, though we gossip about other people. Ann did not show she had overheard anything as she came into the room, and Miss Williams winked at her. An uncomfortable silence lasted until the group dispersed and hurried away to lunch. Neither Ann nor Miss Williams mentioned it as they walked together to their lodgings.

So that's what they thought of her in the women's staffroom, Ann thought as she ate her dinner. People had noticed how worried she was. She knew there was malice in the voice which made the last remark. Ann understood only too well. To them she was a peasant. She knew the others came from families who could afford to pay for their children's education, and that some of them were all too conscious of it. Still, she could not completely discount their remarks. She must behave differently, that's all, and completely hide her feelings. To be honest, wasn't Dora's pain worse? Her pain was the result of circumstance. She had no choice about what happened. Dora would have to decide one way or the other about Harri, and the whole course of her future life would depend on it. No such question had arisen between her and Richard, and it was most unlikely it ever would, unless one of them changed utterly.

Was she too much of a home bird? Thinking it over and over she knew she could not help it. It was inevitable in a cautious family who had never seen the world and never wanted more than they could see from their own doorstep. The bond that united them so closely was unspoken but as real as the mist which often divided theirs from the other smallholdings. Ann sought an explanation, but the only light she could cast was that the struggle to survive on those bare hills was so hard that they expected nothing beyond the family. Times were even harder in her Nain and Taid's day, and there had been bad times for her mother and father, and just as it looked as if things were getting better for them there came the outbreak of war. War was a new thing, a strange thing to those used to tilling the poor land of the hill farm, or splitting slate in the quarry. They knew about struggle, the struggle against the landowner to carve out a place for their smallholdings from common land, but her people had understood what that battle had been about, and blood had not been shed. They did not understand what this struggle was about. They were the blind feeling their way along the wall of the world. If something should happen to their children, they would be left with nothing to rejoice about in the better world which was promised, if it ever came. She and her family were on a single emotional wavelength along which they transmitted their anxiety one to the other.

That night the drama company were winding up work for the season with a cup of tea and cakes in the vestry where they had rehearsed all winter. The companionship was always exhilarating, and they spent their time talking about things that were nothing to do with work. All winter the stove in the vestry never went out, and whenever she went in, the room and the company were warm. There she would forget all about school and enjoy a respite from the noisy energy of the children. Ann was looking forward to tonight. She would forget about the silly incident in school, an incident which grew bigger the more she brooded on it. When she opened the vestry door the others were sitting round the stove just as if it were still burning as it had been throughout the winter. As she came in they stopped talking suddenly and the women went out to make the tea. She greeted the men then went to join the women. They chatted for two hours before someone said, 'We're foolish to stay inside missing the fresh air when it's so lovely outside.'

They meandered in a leisurely way along the street, chatting and fooling about as if they were the first words they had exchanged that evening. People stood in little groups here and there in the street, smoking and talking happily. Branches of lilac hung over garden walls and the scent of wallflowers reached them. They climbed slowly up the hill, stopping now and then to emphasise a conversational point, nodding to people standing on the doorsteps of their houses. The houses were clean in the midst of the grime. There was more money about now. There were plenty of young people around too. One by one the company left for their homes and lodgings until no-one was left but Ann and Ben Phillips.

'Tell me, Miss Owen,' he said at last, 'are you happy here in Ynys-y-Grug?'

179

'Why do you ask, Mr Phillips?'

'Well, to be honest, it was about you we were talking when you came into the vestry tonight. Some of us are concerned about you.'

'Do I look unhappy?'

'No, not exactly. But you don't look as if you're happy either. And remember, it's concern for you we feel, not criticism.'

'I'm happy enough at school. I love the work. But it's the war.'

'Is anyone belonging to you in the army?'

'Well, two of my brothers have gone to France, and I have a friend in France. But I don't think he is in danger because he's with the Medical Corps.'

'I'm sorry. I didn't know. Try not to worry.'

'I'm not so anxious for myself, but I'm thinking of my parents. I know how they worry.'

'There are people in school who support the war so passionately that they haven't given a thought to someone like you.'

'I don't know about that but perhaps I worry too much.'

'Not at all, it's only natural. Try not to worry for all that. Forgive me for talking about it.'

She went home greatly cheered. There were those who thought differently from the female teaching staff. And then she remembered that Miss Williams was great friends with Ben Phillips's family. Her friend had turned up trumps. She had never before felt so much at home in Ynys-y-Grug, and she looked forward confidently to seeing Dora tomorrow. They had arranged to meet halfway between Ynys-y-Grug and Bont Wen, and she walked through the woods along the river bank. She had no idea what news Dora would bring her, but now she felt she could face her no matter what decision she had reached about Harri.

They walked on through the woods together, and the sun was shining on the waters of the river. It was a beautiful sight, in spite of the traces of rusty iron that ran through it. Today it was gentle and quiet as a stream running through fields. There was a clean greenness about the trees, and the young leaves trembled slightly in the air.

'You're looking better, Dora.'

'I feel better. I had a long letter from Harri today.'

'Oh,' said Ann with surprise. So they still wrote to each other then.

'You're surprised.'

'Well, I don't know. You sounded as if you were about to give each other up.'

'That night I had made up my mind it was impossible to go on, but I decided I mustn't act hastily. I didn't write to him. I just couldn't.'

'How did you feel, Dora?'

'Awful. Living in wait for a letter though it was my turn to write.'

'Let me say what I think, though I said I wouldn't. I believe that's the best thing you could have done.'

'Why, Ann?'

'Well, it gave you time to think about your feelings. Once you had written, you couldn't have taken it back without feeling humiliated. There's nothing worse than regret for making you feel small, in your own eyes anyway.'

'I can see now, after having this letter, that I would have regretted it.'

Ann didn't ask why, but she said,

'Remember. Dora, a difference of opinion in times like these is not the same as in peace-time.'

'How is that?'

'Because things happen so suddenly. What if you'd finished with Harri, completely convinced you were right that you'd never be happy with him. And say he was killed in action. How would you feel?'

'It would hurt.'

'It would, if I know you. He would have proved he was no coward, and you believing he was, and I can't imagine a more bitter regret than that, repenting too late, and knowing you had misjudged him.'

'I already regret mentioning my doubts about Harri. I ought to have kept them to myself. It wasn't a decent thing to say, even to a friend.'

'Look Dora, you can sometimes entrust more to your friends than to your lover.'

'It did me good to talk to you anyway. You could see Harri's point of view.'

'Because I am a coward myself.'

'No, indeed, because you have family in the war. I know you didn't think much of Harri in college.'

Ann said nothing.

'But I had a letter today from Harri which has made me decide to stand by him.'

'I'm delighted to hear it.'

Ann spoke sincerely despite thinking they were an ill-matched couple. She had seen enough while talking to Dora today to know it was her heart and not her opinion that ruled her, and that Harri the man was more important to her than his strange arguments.

'I had pages and pages from him', Dora went on, 'telling me his life history, and he's explained to me why he reacts against everyone. I'm not going to tell you the story. It wouldn't be right today. You can hear it another time. All I can say is he can't live without me.'

'That's fine, Dora *bach*. The story belongs to you.'

A cuckoo called and they stood still to listen. Ann could not move.

'What's the matter, Ann?'

She looked bewitched.

'Where are they now, I wonder? Richard, and Roland, and Bobi. Pity we can't see them. And Harri,' she said with warmth.

Dora turned her head away and looked at the river. She was crying.

'I know where Dad and Mam are,' said Ann, 'they're having tea together, and I bet you anything their thoughts are with the boys.' A picture flashed before her eyes. She saw herself in a pinafore, her coat cast off, looking for primroses in the school dinner-hour by a quiet stream in a field, clusters and clusters of them growing close together.

'Dora,' she said, 'have you ever seen such a place? There are no primroses here.'

'Well, come to think of it, there aren't. Come on. Let's have tea. Mrs Jones, who looks after the Working Men's Institute, makes a lovely tea in one of the rooms. The committee gave her permission.'

They were nearly there. They had the place to themselves, and had a delicious tea with their first gooseberry tart of the year. They had walked a long way from Dora's lodgings, so Ann decided to catch a bus straight home. They had enjoyed a beautiful afternoon, and everything had been smoothed out between them. Mr Beddoe was working the night shift, and Ann decided to keep Mrs Beddoe company in the kitchen. It was a fine end to the day.

11

At last Ann had a letter from Bobi, and no wonder she'd had to wait so long. It came from the Middle East. It was a shock. She had never thought he might be posted further than France. In her naivety she had connected distance with age, believing it to be impossible that someone so young would be sent so far away. Now she felt as if the distance had driven her brother from her forever and all those miles only added to the danger. The letter was distant too. He said nothing of his feelings, only that he had chosen to go overseas of his own free will, as he was in a non-combatant unit. He hoped she and their parents were not worried about him. Some hope, she thought.

As far as it was in her power she wanted to hide her anxiety from everyone. What she had overheard still stung, and she vowed not to mention her brothers unless someone raised the subject. She would hide in her shell and make herself shrivel. Only in her lodgings did she feel free to speak. Mrs Beddoe could not forget her grief. When the door was closed between Ann and the kitchen she often heard her crying to herself when everyone else was out. On these occasions Ann thought of going into the kitchen to comfort her, but she held back. Later, she would go in for a chat, and Ann knew that even that small act made Mrs Beddoe forget about her sorrow for a while.

Sometimes her landlady talked of her yearning, and Ann knew it comforted her at least as long as their talk lasted.

She also decided not to mention Bobi too often when she wrote home, in case they took her words as a sign of her anxiety. One thing she could do was to write often to her brothers, and send them parcels. She managed to convince herself that Richard was not in danger. Once again it was her guileless ignorance which made her focus on the wrong thing. She was shaken out of this one day when she had a letter from Richard telling her he was now very close to the firing line. Despite this news it was Bobi who filled her thoughts, and she found something else to worry about. She fretted that when he was in Britain she had not given him money and little comforts more often. She blamed herself for failing to do the impossible. She convinced herself she could have done it if she had tried harder. His full address was enclosed with his letter, so she would send him a postal order at once.

Mrs Hughes was now living in Richard's old house in Anglesey, and her first letter to Ann from her new home was a treasure, full of her life since leaving Blaen Ddôl. The church had put pressure on her to move out of the house now that they were looking for a new minister. 'It turned my stomach,' she wrote, 'to think of anyone taking Dan's place, yes, that someone *could* take his place, was too much for me, and I made my mind up at once that I would never try to find another house in Blaen Ddôl. It was such a piece of luck that Mr Edmund offered me this house.

'I couldn't describe the days spent preparing to leave, gathering things together for storage. You can imagine how hard it was moving things out of the study, his books, his papers, his sermons. But that did not touch me as much as other things. I felt those were church matters, but when I came upon his old gloves in his overcoat pocket, with the prints of his fingers inside them, it was almost too much for me. And worse, putting his slippers in a box, the slippers he had worn on the hearth the last night he was well, talking so happily with me in front of the fire. There was life in those things. I felt he hadn't finished with his gloves or his slippers. They were waiting for him to come home from an appointment. And it was a terrible thing to lock the door for the last time, and take the key to Tŷ Capel, and hear that woman say so coldly, 'I hope you'll be happy in Anglesey.' It wasn't so hard to visit his grave for the last time. There is nothing of our relationship in that place.

'The children were very quiet. Indeed, they managed to hide their feelings better than I did, unless looking forward to a new life made them happy, like moving to a new house used to excite me long ago. They stayed up late last night, and the three of us stared into the fire before going to bed. And Gwen said, 'It's a pity we can't take Dada's grave with us, isn't it?' I managed to get over it by saying we would often come to Blaen Ddôl to see the grave.

'A new minister and a new life will take the house over. I hope sermons and laughter will be made there again. But there will never be more happiness than Dan and I felt in that house. Leaving was a bitter, barren experience. There was an awful moment when I said, I'm going, I'll never return to this house. An experience to get through quickly, covering up all my feelings in the hope that I would never to have to go through such a thing again.

'In the train I realised that leaving Blaen Ddôl was no outing for the children either. They showed no interest in the places we passed through. They sat, one each side of me, their arms clasping my arms tightly. The wife of the minister here took it upon herself to arrange that there was a fire and the kettle singing by the time we arrived, and she sat at the head of the table. She had aired the beds too. She invited us to supper, and I came home with a happy feeling in my heart that I could not explain. We went straight to bed without giving ourselves time to think. I fell asleep grateful that I had a grave to visit in Caernarfonshire, and thinking how much more fortunate I was than those who've lost husbands and sons in the war, with no hope of ever finding their graves.

'The house is much more comfortable now. I've put some of my rugs on the floors, and a few of my ornaments here and there. It will be cosy in the winter. I wonder if Mr Edmund would like to come and stay when he comes home on leave from France, unless it would be too painful for him. We would arrange somewhere for him to sleep. I very much look forward to getting to know him. The children are settling into their new school and making new friends. Time will pass and we will get used to things. That's life. Forgive me, Ann, for tiring you. I know you have your own troubles. But I can't talk to my sister like this. She would think I was indulging myself.'

In a post-script she said that Bess Morris's health had broken down, she had been home from work for weeks, and hadn't the will to see anyone. It was hoped that she would not have to be committed to the asylum.

Apart from the news about Bess Morris, this letter gave Ann optimism and strength, to see how her friend had found a way to deal with her grief. It was as if she had mined a little joy from her sorrow. Her experience had drawn out something Ann did not know she had in her. It was the news about Bess Morris that upset her most. Her conscience accused her for not having written to Bess. She wondered if Bess thought she had forgotten her? On the other hand, her attitude to the war had made it very difficult for Ann to know what to say to her. She would write to her mother.

And there was Mrs Hughes's idea, a thought that had never occurred to Ann, to invite Richard to his old home. It had not occurred to her to wonder where Richard would go on his next home leave from France. Like Bess Morris she had become so obsessed with things that she'd forgotten about the comfort of those he loved most. She hoped Richard would go to his old home, to enjoy a little comfort there.

A letter came from Mrs Evans in her clear old-fashioned longhand. She complained that her life was comfortless, everything changing, the war long, food scarce and poor. The chapel was miserable too without a minister, and she hoped they would find a man as good as Mr Hughes. She did not mention Mrs Hughes or the children, but she talked of Bess Morris. She'd been working too hard on comforts for the soldiers, and she'd believed the war would never end, and some of the women on the committee had turned against her because she had accused them of not working hard enough. Mrs Evans asked about Bobi.

Ann's thoughts returned to the time three years ago, and the fun and joy of the leaving party in college. She felt she had grown more than three years older.

186

12

Ann knew something was amiss when she saw the letter from home on the dinner table, before she had even replied to her mother's last letter. She opened it swiftly, her eyes falling at once on the enclosed letter from the War Office, 'Robert Owen seriously wounded and dangerously ill.' There was nothing in her mother's letter but the fact that they had received this bad news, not a word about her own feelings. After reading it Ann felt frozen to the roots of her hair, and the coldness moved down over her face, and the next thing she knew her body had crumpled to the floor and she could not speak. At that moment Mrs Beddoe came in with her dinner, and found her lying on the floor. She set down the tray, helped her to a chair, and ran to fetch some cold water.

'What's wrong, Miss Owen?'

'I've had bad news. It's Bobi.'

'He hasn't been ?' She could not speak the word.

'No, he's been seriously injured.'

'Oh, come on now, he'll get better. There's hope yet.'

'Of course. It's my fault, taking the news so badly.'

'You couldn't help it. Come on, eat a bit of dinner.'

'I couldn't.'

'Come on. It'll do you good.'

Ann went to the table and tried to eat, but every mouthful stuck in her throat, and would not be swallowed.

'Stay at home this afternoon, Miss Owen. I'll send word to the school.'

'Thank you, Mrs Beddoe, but I must go back to work. I'm better now.'

She tried to swallow her dinner, and it sat like a lump in her chest. She walked to school without knowing she was walking. She passed people on the road without knowing they were there. When one of the teachers spoke to her she could not answer. She knew that the words would not come. She knew she was being unreasonable since Bobi was still alive. He must have been wounded as soon as he landed or very soon afterwards. It was the words 'seriously' and 'dangerously' that frightened her, and her mother's silence. After collapsing to the ground she had pulled herself together. She knew she ought to be hopeful, but she could not be. Reading the novels of Thomas Hardy had not prepared her for hope. It was upon people such as her that Fate descended. And he was so far away, the perils of the sea so great, should they send him home.

She went into her class, but she could say nothing to them. She tried to speak, but the words came out like someone mumbling. The children's eyes were on her. At last she managed to tell them to get on with some writing, and she stood close to her desk without moving. She felt it eased her pain to stay close to her desk, and she was not allowed to sit down. The headmaster came past and opened the door, looked at her, and went out again. He did this three times in an hour, but he did not come in and ask her what was wrong. Next lesson was a free period for her and another teacher, who asked if she was feeling ill. Ann told her the news as briefly as she could. The teacher expressed sympathy, and Ann turned to her marking. She saw the work in front of her as she had seen people on her way to school, without knowing who they were. But she continued marking without lifting her head. The last lesson of the afternoon arrived and she managed to teach the children as usual.

She was last to arrive in the women's staffroom at the end of the afternoon, and the others came up to say how sorry they were to hear the news. She was about to go home alone when Miss Williams asked her to wait.

'I'm truly sorry about everything,' she said. 'We all understand it's easier for us than for you. Perhaps you heard what Miss Jones said the other day. Now she bitterly regrets what she said.'

'Tut, it doesn't matter,' said Ann. 'It hurt me at the time. But now it seems nothing.'

'Let's hope for the best,' said Miss Williams, 'doctors today can perform miracles. And you will feel better if you let yourself hope.'

There was little comfort for Ann in her words. But as she climbed the hill she remembered Mrs Hughes and her letter, and how she had steeled herself to leave Blaen Ddôl, and she turned her heart to God to beg help for Bobi. Mrs Beddoe had made her a special tea, a lovely cake from her scarce ingredients, and egg on toasted bread. Ann smiled in gratitude.

'Are you feeling better now?'

'Oh, much better, thank you. I am going to enjoy this.'

She settled down to her letters at once. First the most difficult one to her parents. It was impossible for her to go home before Sunday. Then she thought of asking Huw to go, and he could let her know how things were. Surely he would do that for her. Then she wrote to Mrs Hughes and to Richard. Writing letters was her only way to pass time and ease anxiety. Miss Williams called in with a message from Mrs Ben Phillips inviting them both to her house for coffee.

They drank coffee, nibbled dry biscuits and made conversation. Ann knew very well why she had been invited, but no-one mentioned it. Thank goodness, Ann thought. It was no subject for strangers. She enjoyed the talk, and Ben Phillips was a splendid mimic. As she was leaving, Mrs Phillips asked Ann to call in any time she felt like it. She went home feeling like a stream with a skin of ice on its face. It would not take much to crack the ice either.

The news of Bobi was the same week after week. There was some comfort in this. He was tough and holding his ground. Then one day the chaplain wrote to say that they were afraid they might have to amputate Bobi's leg, though there was a slim hope that it would not be necessary. Almost at once a letter arrived for her at Ynys-y-Grug from the hospital administrator to say that they had amputated the leg, that he was as well as could be expected, and that they hoped they would save his arm, that Bobi had asked that his sister be informed so that she could break the news to his parents.

Ann knew she was stronger than her father and mother, and that she could bear this news, but she wished she could keep it to herself. It was the day before school broke up for the summer holidays. She had managed to convince herself that Bobi was strong enough to endure the operation. It would be difficult to convince anyone else.

*　　　*　　　*

Ann was on her way to Anglesey, this time to meet Richard who was home on leave. She saw his eager face before her train drew in at the station. He was looking much happier than the last time they met.

'And how are you, Ann?'

'I'm all right. You're looking much better.'

'Yes. But how is Bobi?'

'We get the same news every time, that he is seriously ill, and still in danger.'

'Yes, that's the War Office formula. How long is it since his operation?'

'It's hard to be sure. I think it happened before they let us know.'

'Yes, probably. But it's sure to be three weeks now.'

'I'm sure it is.'

'He should pull through after all this time, you'll see.'

'I hope you're right.'

She began to cry.

'Oh, Richard. I'll never forget the night I went home and tried to break the news. I completely failed, and there was Mam saying she wouldn't know what to do if they amputated his leg, and I had to use that chance to say it was done already.'

'Poor Ann!'

'I felt as if a terrible door had slammed behind me and I was twenty years older than before I had the news. The worst thing was that Mam went straight to bed without a word, leaving me alone to eat the supper she'd cooked for me. I'll never forget it. It's the worst homecoming I've ever had. But Mam was better next morning.'

'Try and forget about it, Ann. Let's be happy for today.'

'Of course I'll try, but it keeps coming back to me.'

'It'll go away when you hear Bobi is better. You love him, don't you Ann?'

'Well, he's the youngest, and I'm the eldest, and when I was in Blaen Ddôl and saw more of him I began to understand his problems. He should never have been sent to work in a shop. It bored him and he grew restless. I can see why he joined the army. And the poor lad never had any money.'

'No. We live under a cruel system. Some have too much, and the rest too little.'

'He moves me so much. The feeling runs like thread twisting through my whole family and ending with him. It closes with him. But let's not talk about it today. It's you I've come to talk to.'

'And that is so beautiful still in the midst of trouble. I can't live without you any more.'

'Listen, Richard!'

She stood still.

'What is it?'

'Listen to that sound.'

One element in the sound was the snap of the gorse seed, and another was the rhythmic sound of rakes turning over the hay, a regular, tick-tock sound, but silky too. Behind those other sounds ran the undertone of people talking, scarcely more than whispering.

'That's one thing that's changed since the war. The sound of conversation. Before the war it was louder.'

'How is Mrs Hughes?'

'I think she's quite happy. I'm glad, anyway. She's worried about hurting you, being in your old home when you come.'

'It would hurt a lot more to come home and find it empty. I haven't felt so happy for ages. To tell you the truth there hasn't been much joy in the house for a long time. My uncle was a quiet man, and his housekeeper a dull woman. And the old man had aged so much recently that he hardly knew I belonged there when I came home for the holidays. He'd lose interest in me in a day or two, the housekeeper had nothing to say once she'd cleaned and cooked for me. She had no idea how to make a house into a home.'

'It wasn't her house.'

'No. But the house is cosier now.'

They were almost there. Before they went in he held her tightly and kissed her.

'Ann,' he said, 'we'll have our own house one day. The war will end, and we'll take up our lives again, and Bobi and Roland will come home.'

'They will. I'm not worried about Bobi's leg. Just to have him home is the important thing.'

'I'm sure he'll be home. You deserve a better life, Ann, and I'll do my best to give it to you.'

Her eyes shone.

Mrs Hughes was on the doorstep, with the same welcome on her face as when Ann first saw her in the manse in Blaen Ddôl. She looked more like her old self in face and figure, her body beginning to become sturdier, her expression less sad, though she lacked her old glow. The room was hot from the sun and the fire, like baking day in summer. The table was laid for tea with a square white cloth, crocheted with a wide border of lace, and Mrs Hughes's best china. Often on summer Sundays before the war, Ann felt as she approached the tea-table at home the same languorous sensation overcome her as she felt now, watching the stream of hot tea poured into the cups.

'These sandwiches are good,' she said. 'What's in them?'

'Rhubarb chutney. I had to use something to disguise the poor butter we get from the shop. But there's real butter in the others.'

'Oh, they're good.'

Ann was suddenly overcome with shyness. She realised it was the first time she had been in Richard's company with a third person present. She could not speak directly to him. It was like being in a play. She could not talk directly to Mrs Hughes either. She was playing two parts. Talk for talk's sake, and she was afraid of betraying her feelings for Richard in front of her friend because one minute before coming into the house, when Richard had shown how much he loved her, she had not been able to speak. It was a moment like that other moment on Bangor mountain when he told her for the first time that he loved her. That time she had replied, but today she was overwhelmed, and forgot everything in that moment before they entered the house. And now she was in Richard's old home, and he was with her, not alone as she would have wished, but in the warmth of a good friend.

'Where are the children?'

'Out haymaking. It's impossible to get them to come in these days. They're in their element.'

'Yes, I'm sure. It's a lovely time.'

She thought of Bobi again and fell to musing. She saw again the row of earthenware dishes full of rice pudding on the dairy table, and she and Bobi slavering at the sight, hoping the harvesters would not gobble the lot. Today she did not feel such hunger, in spite of Mrs Hughes's lovely tea.

'Have you heard from Bess Morris?' was Richard's next question.

'Me, or Ann?'

'Well, both of you.'

Ann wondered why Richard was suddenly interested in Bess Morris.

'I've had a letter,' she said, 'at last.'

'And how is she?'

'Worried now about being so unfeeling towards me.'

'Just like she was worried before about wanting to bring the war to an end,' said Mrs Hughes.

'Poor Bess!' said Ann. 'I've never seen such a change in anyone. She used to be such a wise girl, but I believe she's basically very religious.'

'Then why did she want to support the war so fanatically?' was Mrs Hughes's question. 'She didn't have much sympathy for you.'

'No, that's true. But I now believe the war was a terrible shock to her, as if an evil had befallen the world, and she thought the best way to end it was to hasten it, to make it come to a head. I have another friend who believes all war is wrong, and that you should not help the war in any way. You see, both have firm beliefs and they stick to them. Whereas I'm no better than a boat without an anchor not knowing what I believe, seeing nothing in the world but blind Fate.'

Richard watched her proudly.

'I really don't understand you,' said Mrs Hughes.

'I don't understand myself,' said Ann, 'that's the trouble.'

'I can sympathise with Ann,' said Richard, 'trying to see both sides.'

'Not quite. Seeing it's always the bully on the sound side of the hedge, I'm with the suffering innocent.'

'Whose side are you on, Richard?' asked Mrs Hughes.

'He's for helping the innocent,' Ann answered for him.

'The innocent can be ungrateful too,' he said, turning his cup in the saucer.

So the conversation dwindled. For a moment three wasn't company.

When she had Ann to herself for a moment Mrs Hughes spoke with feeling, 'I'm so sorry to hear about Bobi. I hope he'll come through all right.'

'Yes, he's so young, so far away, so innocent.'

'And so loveable, though I've never met him.'

'It's the right word to describe him anyway. He wasn't loveable to the woman who kept house for the boss in town, when he challenged her about the bad food.'

'He showed courage then, and he'll be brave again, you'll see.'

'Are you happy, Mrs Hughes?'

'As happy as I can be,' she said. 'Make the most of Richard, Ann.'

The advice irritated her, but she said nothing. She knew it was her friend's impulsiveness, not interference. But she alone knew Richard's worth. It was no-one else's business.

It was cooler as they walked to the station, and the peace of a summer evening hung over the countryside. Men were going home, their hats tipped back on their heads, their shirts open, their skin sunburnt and gleaming with sweat. Some leaned against the banks looking over the clean fields with the satisfaction of those who knew the hay was dry and gathered in. The mountains of Snowdonia looked distant in the haze, the Menai Straits almost invisible between two lands of a single hue.

'That was a general sort of chat over the tea-table,' remarked Ann, 'not really talking to each other.'

'Yes. And Mrs Hughes is still not herself. You came out of it well, Ann.'

'I said more than I meant to. But you see I was very fond of Bess Morris.'

'People mean more to you than ideas, don't they, Ann?'

'I don't know. I've never thought about it, except that I like

194

some people and I don't like others. I like Mrs Hughes, but I didn't like her husband. But they liked each other.'

They both burst out laughing in the silence.

'Isn't the silence wonderful,' he said.

'Yes. The whole countryside at peace. It's hard to believe there's a war somewhere.'

'Yes, and in a few days' time I'll be back in the middle of the groans of young men.'

'And Bobi's somewhere in the terrible heat, and in pain. And if I know him he'll be suffering mental anguish too by now, if he's conscious.'

'He'll have the best chance, Ann.'

'Do you think so?'

'Yes. You see, no doctor would go out there into the firing line except to do their very best.'

'What a wasteful sacrifice, isn't it?'

'Yes, but it's an inspiration for life too. I have one horrible job to do before I go. I must burn my uncle's clothes.'

'Burn them?'

'Yes. There's only one suit and an overcoat worth saving, and I wouldn't like to see them worn by anyone else. The clothes belong to the dead man.'

A shiver ran through Ann.

'What is it, Ann?'

'I was just thinking about something.'

'What?'

'What has Mrs Hughes done with her husband's clothes?'

That wasn't quite what she was thinking about, but how hard it would be to burn a dead man's clothes, to see things that had been so close to his body and flesh going up in flames. It would be like burning the man himself.

They arranged to meet again before he returned to France, and as they said their goodbyes at the station Ann felt she had not cherished him as she should, nor savoured the day enough. She had let it slip from her as if she could take it for granted that she would have him for years and years. What if she never saw him again? It was odd how sanguine she felt about Richard, even carelessly trusting sometimes. Yet from the day she heard Bobi had volunteered for the War she despaired for him. In the train she thought about how unnatural the day had been, she enjoying herself, Rowland fighting in France, and Richard had said that despite the fury of the battle they were gaining hardly any ground. Bobi thousands of miles from home lying sick in hospital, if he were still alive. Huw in England. The family scattered. Though Bobi was so far away she felt closer to him than to Roland. It was to her that he'd asked the hospital to write, and he'd chosen her to break the news to their parents. It had been his way of communicating with her. As she walked home she was consoled by one thing, there would be neither good nor bad news awaiting her. The post had arrived that morning before she left, and there was only one delivery a day in the quiet country village.

13

Her mother was sitting in the rocking-chair by the fire, the palm of her left hand resting on her knee, the palm of her right hand rhythmically rubbing her knuckles. She looked straight ahead, and her profile was a graven image. This was how she looked when she was in pain. She had just told Ann that a letter had come from the War Office, and she sat waiting by the fire for Ann to open it.

'Oh!' cried Ann. 'He's better.'

Her mother was motionless. She stared straight ahead. But in a moment a sound broke from her throat, the cry she had kept stifled there. Now the floodgates burst open in a torrent of joyful tears. Ann went to her and cradled her head.

'There, there. There, there.'

She closed her eyes. She couldn't cry or speak. The news was unbelievable after waiting so long for it.

'Go and tell your father.'

She found him in the rickyard tidying the stack. He stood looking proudly up at the hay. He turned his head when he saw her, and Ann's expression was enough to make her father smile.

'You've got good news about Bobi.'

'Yes, he's better. Come to the house and leave the hay.'

He went to the sawhorse to fetch his hat. He looked back at the stack.

'That's it. I'm done for today. I'll get on better when I come back to it. The job has no savour when you're just killing time.'

She looked back at the haystack, and seeing the upper part so tidy and the lower half all higgledy-piggledy she began to laugh.

'What's wrong?' he asked, because he was proud of his skill at stack building.

'It's exactly like an old man's head with a beard all the way round his face.'

She took his arm and led him to the house as if she led a horse in a ploughing match. Her mother was busy preparing something to eat, although it wasn't long since they'd had breakfast.

'What can we have to celebrate?' asked Ann

'We can feast on bread-and-butter,' said her father.

'That old bacon is so awful,' said her mother, 'otherwise I'd fry some bacon and eggs.'

'We two can have an egg each,' teased Ann, winking at her mother.

'Oh, no!' said her father, 'I want one too.'

And the three of them began to laugh. They had emerged from a long dark tunnel, and they were like children laughing at nothing.

'This is the best egg I have ever had,' said her father.

And they all laughed again.

'True. There are eggs and eggs,' said her mother.

At that moment a neighbour rushed in, agitated.

'Have you heard the news?' she asked.

Their own good news had possessed them so completely that they could not imagine any other news could have arrived.

'Jane Davies's Guto has been killed in France. Just now the news came.'

The three of them looked stunned. They could not speak.

'Have you had bad news?' the neighbour asked.

'Sit you down Mary Evans,' said her mother. 'I'll make you a cup of tea. No, it's good news we've had, but we can't speak a word of it after hearing this. Poor Jane Davies!'

197

When the neighbour had gone, Ann's mother went to visit Jane Davies, and although he had promised his work was done for the day, her father returned to the stack. They could not rejoice now. Guto was the only son of his widowed mother, and he was her only support. He was over thirty, and a boyhood hero of Bobi's. He came to supper only weeks ago before he returned to France. He wasn't cut out to be a soldier. All he could say over and over again that night was, 'Nothing can be done. Just face it, and don't think.' That, and asking about Bobi.

When her mother returned she asked Ann to visit Jane Davies, in case there were letters to be written. Ann did not want to go. She had never looked grief in the face, and she felt afraid to do so now. Her own joy stood in her way. Yesterday she might have been able to face Jane Davies more easily. She was afraid as she walked the path to the house, afraid of the unknown. Afraid of failing to say the right thing, afraid of Jane Davies's feelings, afraid of the terrible thing that had befallen this widowed mother and which stood between her and other people, an experience which had singled her out and made her special. She was glad no-one else was there. Few had heard the news yet, of course.

Jane Davies sat by the fire, a little bundle of an old lady. Come to think of it, she was old. Guto was her youngest child. Ann stood by the table.

'I'm very sorry, Jane Davies.'

She could think of nothing else to say.

The widow inclined her head.

'Oh, it's you Ann. Come, my girl.'

This without looking at her. Ann went to sit in the chair opposite hers.

'Can I make you a cup of tea? It would do you good.'

'Thank you. I haven't had a bite to eat all day. I can never eat before the post comes. I eat heartily, or I used to, once a letter from Guto arrived. And even if there wasn't a letter I could still eat a little.'

Ann ran to the back kitchen eager to do anything but look into the old woman's face.

'And I'd put the kettle on to boil ready, when this old letter came.'

'There you are,' said Ann, 'try and drink it while it's hot, and eat a little bit of bread-and-butter. I've cut it thin for you.'

'Thank you. I was just beginning to feel faint when you came.'

Then, 'How's Bobi?' she asked.

Ann couldn't tell her the good news.

'About the same,' she replied.

'He'll be all right now, you'll see. He's over the worst. Let's hope they send him home soon.'

And she wept again.

'Bobi and Guto were great friends,' said Ann, 'even though Guto was older. Guto was a god to Bobi.'

'Yes, Guto enjoyed coming over for a romp with Bobi.'

'Yes, I can see Guto now carrying Bobi piggy-back, and Bobi crying out to him to do it again and again.'

Jane Davies smiled through the shining windows of her eyes.

'Those days will not come back,' she said.

'No they won't. Remember, Jane Davies, they wouldn't come back anyway. We all grow older, and we can't ever be children again. For you Guto will always be young, and nobody can take that from you.'

'That's quite true, my girl, but there was no reason for something like war to take him from me.'

'Do you need to write to anyone? I've brought some writing paper with me.'

'I'd like you to write and break the news to my two daughters, if you would.'

'Do you want me to tell them the truth straight out, or to say he's been seriously wounded?'

'The truth. That's how they told me. It won't make much difference to them. They don't worry about me. It was Guto who was my succour.'

Writing the letters reminded Ann that she had come out without opening the post which had arrived for her that morning. The news of Bobi had obliterated everything. She didn't like leaving Jane Davies on her own, but no doubt others would soon call. She might need to be alone for a while. Ann remembered the day the news came that Bobi had been wounded. She alone knew

199

what it meant. And today's good news was not something she wanted to share either.

It was selfish. Here she was, and her parents too for sure, lost in their own good fortune, forgetting Roland who was in just as much danger. Nor had she spared a thought for Richard. He was the last one on her mind, obliterated by the one who was foremost in her thoughts.

As she walked home, she recalled her last day with Richard before he returned to France. It was a pity he couldn't have heard today's news before he left. Could a single day ever shatter their love? Her heart was divided. Yet his was full of one thing, of her and the pain of leaving her. The ties between her and her family could not be loosened. He had no family to think of. Her thoughts must be shared among her loved ones, but for him there was only one. Was her love for Richard big enough to surmount all other loves? If a great storm broke, if it shattered her, not just her mind but her heart too, would she be able to give Richard all he wanted of her? Could she set aside love of kin for the sake of the greater, less self-indulgent love she knew was Richard's due? She knew she loved him. Life without him would be empty. But would it be totally empty? The day they met she could not talk to him. It had been like trying to reach a high shelf standing tip-toe, and failing to touch it. Until the time came to part. Then her heart brimmed with what she longed to say and she saw she had wasted their day. She hadn't said half of it. Overwhelmed with emotion she remembered something he had said to her, 'Remember, I too am going into danger.' He had stressed the 'I'. Was there perhaps the slightest hint of pain that she worried more about her brothers than about him? 'And don't forget,' he said then, 'I have nobody else to worry about me.' It was knowing about the danger which had thrown her into this quandary. She found it easier to express herself in her letters. The coward's way, she thought.

She went into the house to read the letter she hadn't opened that morning. A letter from Dora. She was upset, very upset for Dora. Harri refused to touch his cap to the officers and was in trouble every day in his new life. When he wasn't confined to barracks on short rations he wandered aimlessly about the camp. Some of the officers let him pass without comment. Other officers, twenty year-old former public schoolboys, gave him a tongue lashing. He was deaf to it all. Ann laughed after reading the letter, it was so like Harri to refuse to touch his cap to anyone, and so like Dora to worry about it. She was frightened they would put Harri against a wall and shoot him. Indeed, Ann's estimation of Harri grew.

Her thoughts turned again to Jane Davies. Ann could not forget her face. The little smile as she recalled some happy moment from Guto's life, the shadow that darkened it at the mention of her daughters, and the letter from the War Office. The sorrow of despair when she knew Guto would never come back. Was their happiness at the news about Bobi too fragile a thing for rejoicing?

14

Ann and Roland were sitting in the middle of a field in the second cut of hay. Roland was home on leave from France. Beside them was a quarryman's can half full of blackberries, sweet juicy fruit they had found hiding under the brambles which leaned over the stream. For a few days after he arrived home Roland had behaved very strangely. He would not talk to anyone, and as he lifted his cup to his mouth his hands trembled. He seemed deep in thought all the time, but his expression was not thoughtful, it was wild. Then he suddenly suggested to Ann that they went blackberrying. As his mood was so strange Ann had not dared question him. Had Bobi behaved so oddly she would have asked what was wrong.

There was a distance between her and Roland. She did not know him as well as Huw or Bobi. He had gone away to England to serve his apprenticeship while she was in college, and he only came home twice a year. He never talked about his work, but he relished being home, never went out, and broke his heart every time he had to leave. When they were children there was great enmity between her and the two younger brothers next to her in age, because she was a girl, and they would not let her join their games. She did not want to play with them when they captured wild birds with a riddle because in her opinion it was a cruel game, and she would spite them by knocking the riddle to the ground as they lay waiting for a bird to come along. At other times her way of getting back at them was to tease them with rhymes. They responded by pelting her with clods of turf. By the time Bobi was born she was old enough to carry him in a shawl, and even when he grew he was too small and his legs too short to follow his brothers, and they never let him play with them. So companionship and understanding grew between Ann and Bobi, an understanding that deepened during the college vacations when she came home to Blaen Ddôl.

'It's good to be home,' said Roland.

This was precisely what Ann was thinking at that moment as she looked at the view that stretched from Yr Eifl to Llanfair-Pwll, a view they had seen all their childhood without really looking at it, any more than they noticed their feet as they walked.

'Yes, it is,' she replied, unable to say any more.

The events of the past few days had been so kind to them that there was nothing to say but that it was good.

'Wouldn't it be nice if the war ended before I have to go back.'

'It would.'

'But it's too much to hope.' She didn't dare ask him about it. Anyway, it was politicians, not soldiers, who would decide when the war would end.

'I don't know why I ever left home.'

She couldn't answer. She knew one reason well enough, the quarryman's pittance, but as she doubted whether Roland understood that when he left home, maybe his remark was ambiguous.

'People here think it's paradise away from home. Families send their children away and everyone else thinks they have gone to a place flowing with milk and honey. "Away" is an imagined country, where everyone lives like a gentleman.'

'But you only left home to get on in the world, because there's no life for a boy here. You know what it's like in the quarry. It's all there is. So what's the point of sending boys there to work?'

'I'm sure I could have found something nearer home. If only to come home for Sundays. I could have made the same money round here selling herrings.'

'I'm not sure. Old Wil Herrings looked pretty poor to me.'

'Yes. Do you know why?'

'No, I don't.'

'If you give a herring a bad name you'll be giving Wil and the whole industry a bad name. He doesn't think it worth looking anything but poor.'

'Well, if he hasn't any money to buy better clothes he's bound to look poor.'

'It's not a question of money. Wil has decided that it's how a herring man looks. His ears hold his hat up, and you could skate on the herring scales stuck all over his suit.'

They both laughed.

'And he wears a coat with tails,' said Ann as she burst out laughing again.

'One of Squire the Faenol's, I'm quite sure.'

'No,' said Roland more seriously. 'It's never crossed Wil Herrings's mind to be anything but a chap who sells herrings, or to keep his clothes clean by wearing an overall, and something better than a hat from Noah's Ark on his head. Or to sell anything but herrings. Just think what the women here would like to buy for their cooking if they could get them. Other kinds of fish, fruit, plums, everything you can't buy from the shop here. It's never occurred to Wil Herrings to sell anything else.'

'You have to have money to start something like that, and you know how many bad payers there are round here.'

'Yes, but it shows how much business sense we have. That's the challenge. The first sign of hard times and we leave home for somewhere else, and expect someone else to give us work, instead of making work for ourselves on our own doorstep. It's high time someone thought of something useful to make out of the slate tips on the mountain.'

'I've never thought about it before now,' said Ann. 'I've taken it for granted that leaving home was the only way to find work.'

'If they only knew how much their children suffer far from home. You know what they say. 'At least he's working somewhere dry.' As if it was so terrible to get your feet wet, or your head. Yes, we work in the dry, but at the end of the day you don't have the comfort of your own hearth. You sit at table to eat like a row of cattle in the byre, and walk the streets afterwards until you come back to face the same company, the same lads, a cold room in winter with its gloomy old furniture, a freezing attic to sleep in, and tasteless monotonous food. Never a glimpse of the sea, or a field, a pig, a hen, except for dead ones hanging in shop windows. Oh, God, and Sundays. I hear a bit of Welsh on those days, and the women make tea in the vestry, but think of sitting in the vestry waiting for the sermon instead of sitting by the fire at home. Wil Herrings's life is better than that. And the worst thing about it is that our families think we're quite happy.'

Ann was sobered to hear the truth, and to hear the outpouring of words from her previously silent brother.

'I was glad to leave it all for the army,' he added, 'to breathe fresh air. And ladies of leisure were handing us white feathers in the streets of Liverpool.'

'You were longing for a change, like Bobi.'

'It wasn't so bad for him. Town is a thousand times better than Liverpool, and at least he could get home for Sunday. And he didn't have to go abroad.'

Ann winced at this criticism of Bobi.

'He never thought he'd have to face danger.'

'He's been sent further and further away from home. He ought to have been satisfied where he was.'

'Poor Bobi, he's been through enough now, and realised his folly.'

'I hope so.'

'No, don't say that. I don't like to think of him going through all that mental torture. He's in enough physical pain.'

Roland did not reply. Ann felt strange. She had never really known him, although he was her brother. All these years he had suffered away from home, and he had no sympathy for Bobi who had chosen to do the same thing. Roland didn't know Bobi either, not the way she knew him. A wave of sympathy for Roland swept over her at the thought of him enduring such a life for nearly five years, a life he loathed, and just one week in the summer had to be enough to compensate for it. It looked as if he did not have a girlfriend in Liverpool either.

'Well,' said Ann, lifting the can of blackberries by its handle, 'I hope Huw won't have to go. I don't suppose he will as his eyesight is poor.'

'They'll be calling up the blind and the one-eyed soon. They are making no advance in France.'

Ann's heart sank, thinking of Richard.

'Come and see Mrs Hughes with me in Anglesey one day, will you?'

'I don't want to move a step from here. If I go to Anglesey I'll have less time at home.'

'Will you come to Coedcyll to gather blackberries one morning?'

'Yes, I'll go there with you. I'm looking forward to having a tart for tea with these.'

Ann went back to work two days before Roland's return to France, and she wasn't sorry, as she did not want to watch him go. She knew it was something she could not bear to see, and she was sorry for her father and mother. The day after she arrived a letter came from Bobi. She was overjoyed to see his handwriting on the envelope. It was only a note, but he was looking forward to coming home. He was now longing for home, he said. He had written to their mother and father the same day, no strength to write more, but he had managed these few words.

Less than a week later she had a note from home enclosing a letter from a London hospital. On his way back on the train Roland had suffered something like a fit and had been taken to hospital. The letter said simply that he was ill and that he was now better than he had been. It was a nurse who had written to tell them the news. When Roland regained consciousness he had asked her to write on his behalf. Her mother said in her letter she would never forget the day he left. He was worse than ever and she was not at all surprised to hear that he had been taken ill. Her mother sounded very calm. Perhaps this was better than being sent into the firing line. Ann felt the same. But there was one thing Ann did not like: the strange look in his eyes, as if he had seen things he could never forget. She had heard he was a peerless marksman.

15

It would have been thrilling to be whirled to London by train across the flat English landscape, were it not for the war, and were it not for the fact that Ann was going to visit Roland in hospital. Miss Williams sat opposite her in the railway carriage, having volunteered out of the kindness of her heart, because Ann had never been to London before, and she had even offered, as she had once before, to lend Ann the money for the journey. They both wore warm tweed coats and skirts and white blouses. Miss Williams's suit was grey wool with a black velvet collar, and Ann's was light brown, with a collar of dark brown velvet. Miss Williams wore a black felt hat with its brim turned up at the back and down at the front, and Ann wore a similar one in brown. Their stockings and shoes were black. On the previous Sunday Miss Williams had worn purple silk stockings with her black silk dress, the first time Ynys-y-Grug had seen anything like it. But the big difference between their clothes was that Miss Williams's suit was of a much better quality than Ann's, though the style was similar.

Ann had accepted her colleague's offer with grateful warmth. She was invited to stay the night at Miss Williams's home, returning home on Sunday. However, now that they were on the train Ann wished she were alone. It was not ingratitude but a feeling of unease in her company. She felt Miss Williams was someone superior to herself, brought up differently, a few years older than her and a far more experienced teacher. Ann guessed she must be about thirty, and talent and professionalism showed in her bearing and her speech. Still, there was nothing patronising in her attitude to Ann. It was clear she wanted to help, and she sympathised with Ann's situation. But the differences between them that lay mainly in their background troubled Ann, hindered her, enslaved her. In Ann's opinion the most important thing in a conversation between friends was to feel free. Had Miss Williams not offered to accompany her, Ann would have asked Dora. Dora's heart was all in her voice.

Ann's only glimpse of London from the top of a bus was of endless noisy traffic. The hospital was set apart in wooded grounds, away from the noise of trams and crowds. The trees were beginning to turn. It was a fine place for Roland to recover.

Walking up the wide, quiet drive to the mansion house, the fear of looking pain in the face returned, of seeing change in people's faces. She clung to the certainties of childhood, and she could not admit the changes happening to people and to the world.

Thoughtfully she asked a nurse to warn her brother she was there before she went in. She was pleasantly surprised when she saw him, if surprise it was, since she had not the least idea what to expect. But he looked quite cheerful and eager to talk. As she looked at him the fear which had hung on her skin like a damp cloth evaporated.

'Are you better?'

'Oh, much better.'

'You're in a lovely place.'

'It's very good. It's quiet here, and everyone is kind. How is Bobi?'

'I had a letter from him the other day – just a short one. I'm sure there's one on its way to you.'

'I've been thinking a lot about him since I've been here. He'll have nobody to visit him.'

He began to sob.

'Now, don't you worry about it. Bobi's not thinking about things like that, I'm sure, but about getting better and coming home, and his mind is too full of that to feel lonely.'

'No. And when I'm better they'll send me back to France.'

'We'll try and stop that too.'

'It would be easier to melt Spanish iron.'

The fear returned to his eyes. In a flash Ann remembered the nightmares he had suffered in childhood. When they managed to wake him the look of terror would remain in his eyes for a long time.

'I've made too good a soldier for them.'

His sister could not see the connection.

'It's men like me who must face the danger, while others get the fame and the credit.'

'I'm sure you wouldn't want a commission.'

'Oh, no, but all they give to the likes of me is even greater danger and no safe haven.'

She did not encourage him to go on. She did not want to

know. She did not want to face the facts of his life in France. Ignorance was a softer cushion. But he continued.

'You forget about the danger when you're with your friends in the trenches, with the enemy out of sight, even if one of the lads is wounded right beside you, but when you are alone, and firing at what you can see . . .'

'That's enough. Try and forget about it.'

'That's the trouble. I can't forget.'

'Yes,' said Ann , 'we remember too much as a family. But we must forget about it now. We'll talk about other things.'

'Oh, Ann,' he said then, 'I don't really know you. You worry about us all. Bobi and I have been very thoughtless.'

'Don't talk nonsense. You'd have had to go by now. We'll all soon be home again together.'

A nurse brought them both some tea, and under its sweet influence their talk turned to happier things.

'I'm going to try and see the doctor,' said Ann moving away from the bed.

'Why?'

'I intend leaving no stone unturned to keep you from going back to France. Cheer up.'

'Oh, it is so good to see you Ann, and that's enough for me today. Good luck with the doctor.'

Fortunately she had no trouble getting the doctor to talk to her alone. A short, portly man between forty and fifty years old, beginning to lose his hair. A man who would have looked far less impressive in civilian clothes, but the broad shoulders and good cloth of his military uniform lent him an air of distinction. That, and the clean, comfortable room where he sat.

'It is very difficult to diagnose what is wrong with your brother. When he first came here his nerves were in a bad state, but he's much better now.'

'I'm glad to hear it.'

'I'm afraid he has no guts. He's very timid.'

'I don't think so.'

'Of course. You are his sister.'

'That's not why I say so. He would not have volunteered for the war had he been a coward.'

'Well, you know what boys are – following their mates, and other reasons.'

'Was there any evidence that he was a coward when he was in France?'

'No, that's the strange thing about it, his record is good, a skilled marksman, good enough to be a sniper.'

'Maybe that is the cause of his illness.'

'Tut! A soldier never thinks about danger, and every man like him ought to think of his country and doing his best for it. The sooner the war will be over.'

'Yes, but my brother is not fighting for his own country.'

The doctor looked at her for the first time. Till that moment he had been examining his papers. He took his time before speaking.

'Who is he fighting for?'

'Not for his country. Wales is our country.'

The doctor stared at her now as if he saw a relic from a museum sitting in the chair. He ran his eyes over her face as though he were examining her.

'I do not understand you.'

'No, an Englishman would not understand.'

('I've done it now,' Ann thought to herself.)

'Are you able to *make* me understand?' asked the doctor, with something like a mocking smile in his eyes.

Ann did not know whether it was mockery, or the curiosity of a man who had come across a person unlike anyone he had ever met before. She ventured warily to explain.

'The English know what they are fighting for, but the Welsh do not, because we are a separate nation.'

'Well I'm sure you are part of Britain, and you speak English.'

'Oh, somehow, but I never thought of myself as part of Britain, and there are many more like me.'

'Where on earth were you brought up?'

'In the mountains of Caernarfonshire, in the most beautiful place on earth.'

The doctor laughed.

'You are a strange girl. Have you anyone else in the war?'

'Yes,' and her eyes filled with tears.

'Where is he?'

'In hospital somewhere beyond the Dardanelles.'

'Is it serious?'

'He's lost a leg.'

'How old is he?'

'He's only nineteen.'

'I'm sorry. He's been very brave.'

'He was too young to think about it. Just an adventurous boy. My brother here is old enough to understand.'

'What's your father's work?'

'Quarryman, but he's out of work now.'

The doctor looked on her more kindly as he rose. She rose too.

'What is your work?'

'I'm a teacher.'

'Do you have a good salary?'

She shook her head.

'I'll see what I can do to get your expenses for coming here today.'

'Thank you very much, and thank you for sparing the time to talk to me.'

The doctor shook her hand warmly as she left, and told her to cheer up.

Facing Miss Williams's family at home would be easy after this. It was not far from the hospital and in a similar setting. Large houses surrounded by lawns and trees. When she first saw Mrs Williams Ann was struck by her beauty. A woman of perhaps sixty or more, dark hair speckled with grey, violet eyes, fine skin with a touch of colour in her cheeks. She was not as tall as she looked, but her straight posture gave the impression of height. When she spoke Ann was entranced. Her voice was low, soft and monotone. The monotone was almost its greatest attraction. There was neither laughter nor gravity in it.

Mr Williams was quite tall, a retired lawyer, a Welshman with a face full of humour. He looked as if nothing ever worried him, and war were a normal part of life. He wore a grey beard.

Miss Williams had a sister still at home, older than her, rather like her to look at but less distant. It was clear it was she who was in charge of food and household matters. The meal was splendid and it showed great ingenuity with scarce wartime rations.

During supper the mother talked, mostly to the table rather than to anyone in particular. Her voice ran softly on, neither lifting nor falling, and everybody listened respectfully. It became plain that she was working hard for the soldiers' comforts fund.

'I understand your brother is better,' she said to Ann.

'Yes, but not completely.''

'He's lucky to be where he is.'

'Yes.'

'It will come to an end now that Lloyd George has taken over.'

'Maybe, but recklessly,' said Ann.

'He is the cleverest man we have,' said the mother, this time to the table and not to Ann, and in a way that might have dismissed her from her presence forever. Before Ann could wish herself under the table, Miss Williams winked, and her sister helped her to more fish.

'Come, Miss Owen, you must be hungry.'

'I am of Miss Owen's opinion,' said Mr Williams, 'it will be recklessly done. But perhaps that's better than wait and see.'

'That is what I am trying to tell you,' said Mrs Williams.

'And let's hope it will sweep away those women who think they can win the war by wearing white caps and bandaging the wounded.'

'They are necessary,' said his wife to her teacup.

'The bandages, but not the caps.'

'Oh, there are plenty of silly women about,' said his wife, 'but they are not all like that.'

Ann did not know who was teasing whom, and she did not care. She went to bed and slept soundly.

In the morning the sister brought her breakfast in bed.

'I hope you slept well, Miss Owen, and that mother didn't upset you last night. We take no notice of her. It's Lloyd George she's mad about, not the war. She thinks there's no one like him. It's her way of showing she's Welsh.'

Ann laughed and said nothing, though she thought a good deal about the variousness of people.

16

'Don't you sometimes think we're very ignorant, Dora?' asked Ann.

'Who are "we"?' asked Dora without stirring, flat on her back in the bracken where they lay gazing up at the sky.

'Us, and people like us just out of college.'

'I've never thought about it. Do you think we're more ignorant than anyone else?'

'Considering we've had so much education I think we are very stupid.'

'In what way?'

'In our knowledge of things outside college, of people, of places and such things. There was I just now thinking, I'm not sure if that's Carmarthenshire over there, and I had no idea what the county was like before we climbed to the top of this ridge.'

They lay on the mountain summit facing Carmarthenshire, having walked from Ynys-y-Grug with a picnic lunch in their bags. They were resting now that they could see what lay on the far side of the hill. It was a warm late September day, the heat almost as fierce as summer as they climbed. They met nobody on their way, and saw no living thing but the sheep. Carmarthenshire lay stretched out before them like a vast meadow, and the low, far hills stood like ramparts in the distant haze. At their feet the great stacks of the furnaces were small as house chimneys, their smoke indolently rising. They could just make out the fine thread of a river running through the heart of it, the sun striking it here and there so that it looked like a chain of beads.

'Yes, about such matters we are very stupid indeed.'

'It's Williams Pantycelyn country, and nobody ever attempted to show us the county where he lived, or what kind of family he was from, or why he composed his hymns.'

'No, never, and we wouldn't know about him at all if it weren't for the chapel.'

'No, but I wasn't thinking of things like that, but of how ignorant we are of the things of the world. Take Miss Williams, she knows so much more than her school work. She knows about literature, and what is going on today in other countries, and she still wants to learn more and more.'

'Don't forget she was brought up in London, and that's an education in itself.'

'Yes, it's one kind of education. We've lived in the country, and that ought to be an education too. We should know about birds and flowers and trees and rural history and such things, or at least we should ask about them. But our education has not taught us to enquire about things.'

'No,' said Dora, 'just to read a book in college, and to close it when we left.'

'Yes, quite. Tell me, Dora, what were you looking forward to after leaving college? Tell me honestly?'

'I looked forward to getting a good job, to a good enough salary to live a comfortable life, enjoy myself a bit, put a bit by for the future, and perhaps to getting married one day.'

'Didn't you ever feel like doing something for humanity, teaching the children of Wales, like a mission?'

'No, never. But I never thought of neglecting them either.'

'Only of doing an honest day's work and hoping for the best?'

'Yes.'

'Well, I'm glad to hear you say so, Dora. I had nothing in mind except earning a salary, with something over to pay back my parents and enjoy myself a little. I believe I can say I do work conscientiously for the children, but that just makes the days pass more quickly. I am not making them civilised, just showing them how to follow me, and earn a living one day.'

'There's a lot of satisfaction in that too.'

'Yes, it's satisfying in a way. But I have never felt I was helping their minds to grow. Would it have been any different, do you think, if the war had not happened?'

'I don't know.'

'You know, Dora, I'd looked forward to travelling one day. Getting to London, seeing Europe with money in my pocket, just looking and looking. I managed to reach London without a penny to see how my brother was and get to know him a little better. I caught a glimpse of his state of mind. That's all I saw of the country.'

'That's life,' said Dora.

'No, Dora. We're too young to see it like that.'

'The war is responsible for that.'

'Yes, but if it weren't the war it would be something else. But, I don't know how to say this. We aren't prepared for a crisis. People just looking forward to an end to poverty, that's us.'

'That's quite natural for children of the war against poverty. That's the difference between us and Miss Williams. Her mind is sharp because the lack of money has never worried her.'

'Yes. Our reason for being against the war is that it spoils our plans,' said Ann. 'We're not worried if it kills thousands of brilliant young men.'

'We can't worry about them all,' said Dora. 'Pain is personal. We'd never stop if we worried about the whole world.'

'And we don't know the whys and wherefores, or we could do something to end it, or to hasten its end. You're right, the book closed when we left college. Here am I, happy today because I've heard they won't be sending Roland abroad again, and because Bobi's better and he wrote me a cheerful letter, and Richard will be in England for a while. And your worry, that Harri's on his way to France, does not hurt me.'

'Of course it doesn't, any more than your worries can really touch me.'

'What, I wonder, if the war had not come?'

'An impossible question to answer. It did come, and that's that.'

A cold shiver passed over Ann. Dora's answer was like the voice of fate. She gazed once more over Carmarthenshire spread out in its tranquillity. She had been looking forward to today's walk, a new journey of the mind to see a new land, a journey talking to Dora. She knew that if she had given her half a chance, Miss Williams would have jumped at the chance to come with them. She would have asked about their backgrounds, listened to their stories of childhood, loved the scenery, enjoyed every step she placed on the ground, and declared in the end that Wales was a fascinating country. She would have distracted Ann and Dora from their own lives, and for a while she would have made them think there was no such thing as a personal problem. But for Ann it was talking rather than walking she had most looked forward to, and the beautiful day and splendid scenery made a fine accompaniment to conversation. At the moment she couldn't say if their talk had been for the good or not. They had tried to open doors to dark rooms that were new to them, and had closed them without discovering their contents, but at least they had opened the door. Dora's last remark seemed to turn the key in the lock.

They walked home by a different path. Ann's eyes lingered on the landscape. She did not want to leave. It seemed to draw the sting from Dora's words. It lay stretched out in light like the promised land, and a feeling of peace came over her, like the peace she had found the morning the letter came with Roland's good news.

'We'll have tea before it gets dark, Dora, with the old lady where Miss Williams and I had tea once in the summer.'

The house stood in a lonely spot, and they found the old woman dreamily feeding the hens, as a woman does, enjoying the decline of a beautiful day watching her hens. She watched the hens as if she were thinking of something else.

'So you've come again.'

'Yes. Can you make us a cup of tea?'

'You're welcome, my dear girl, but you have a different friend with you today. What's happened to the other one?'

'Oh, she's fine. I've brought another friend to see the countryside.'

Like the last time, they drank their tea from old porcelain, perhaps a hundred years old. They had good bread-and-butter and Welsh cakes. They admired the beautiful oak furniture and the handsome face of the old woman. It was almost like a man's face, with its strong cheekbones.

'How long has the family lived here?' asked Ann.

'Longer than I know. Centuries at least.'

'It must be lonely living here.'

'Well, people from the farms walk this way. It's worse at night. If this old war ends soon, the boy will be back.'

'You have a son in the war?'

'I brought him up. He's like a son to me. He's in France at the moment. I had a letter this morning.'

'That's good.'

'It seems a long time, waiting and waiting, for a letter, and for him.'

'Has he been home at all?'

'No, and I just hope he'll come home once and for all. I couldn't bear seeing him go back again. Have you someone out there?'

'Yes. We must be going before it gets dark.'

They gave her half a crown, and thanked the old woman warmly.

'Come back soon. I'll be glad of your company.'

'Thank you very much.'

'You'd never think the war would have reached a place like this,' said Dora.

'No, you wouldn't. The poor old creature. But do you know, I couldn't bear to hear another word about the war. I was having my tea hundreds of years ago in that kitchen. The smell of the butter was enough, and the flavour was even better. The twentieth century had not happened as I sipped my tea. I could almost see you in your old flannel dress and petticoat. I hope her boy comes home.'

They were walking on a cart-track now, and it was getting dark. Twists of mist were rising from the bogs, and they turned up their collars and walked in silence. The morning had been so beautiful, but day was turning to night. The lights of Ynys-y-Grug came into view with its cluster of houses.

17

Bobi's letters were a joy to read. He was on the mend and would soon be on his way home. Ann guessed they had sent him to convalesce in a nursing home on a Mediterranean island to strengthen him for the long journey home, and the perils of the sea. The weather there was like late spring. Bobi revelled in it. He was now able to go out a bit in a wheelchair, and when it was fine enough he sat out in the gardens where the birds sang all day long. He described it simply in vivid but unflowery language. Vivid as one getting better, as one who was coming home. He had a good ear for voices, and, like many boys of his time, for the different songs of birds. His ear had much to listen to on the shores of the Mediterranean. His appetite had returned, and he had made friends among the other wounded soldiers. Sometimes he showed how he could not forget his long suffering, and in a tone older than his years told her that the thought of home had kept him alive. He did not elaborate on this: as children they had never elaborated anything. Yet Ann read in his simple sentences through what dark shadows he had passed. She shuddered to think how close he had been to death. 'Touch and go' was a phrase much used at home, and it gave her an image of a man clinging to a quarry face by his fingertips. She was glad they'd moved him from the hospital where he had suffered so much.

Roland was home on leave, and the authorities suggested he might be put to work on the land. He could practise by helping his mother at home, as their father had gone to work in Liverpool, lodging with Huw, and sorry he had not gone sooner. Her mother's letters were cheerful. Ann felt she had much to be thankful for. The war had struck so many without warning, young men she knew, the brothers of friends, young men from Ynys-y-Grug, brothers of pupils in her school. In some families it had struck twice. Her family had been luckier than most. She tried to put herself in their place, to enter their feelings like going into a cave, and then turning back from the darkness, from the dark border between one person and another. Then back to everyday life, looking forward with trepidation like someone in love to the day Bobi came home.

And Richard. With one thing and another Richard had been pushed into a corner. Fears for her brothers hovered in the air between them like gnat-clouds on a warm summer day. Their exchange of letters had become almost a formality. She loved him still, but she had lost the fire in her heart. No doubt the endless letter-writing was to blame. It was hard to keep the flame of love alive in mountains of letters. His last letter brought news which disturbed her like a cold breeze blowing the gnats away. He was to be given a long period of leave in Britain. Was he ill?

He gave no explanation. But if he came home well, and Bobi came home too, then her joy would overflow.

Suddenly Bobi's letters stopped coming, either to her or the family. For days she assumed he must have set off on the final stage of his journey home, and she wrote to her mother to say so. Then came a letter from the War Office with news that Bobi had been moved to a fever hospital seriously ill with dysentery. The moment she read it Ann felt it was the end. She tried to believe he was strong enough to recover once more, but it was a frail hope. A miracle was needed this time, and she must behave as if a miracle were possible. When miracles fail, our fellow human beings see us fail to live naturally or do our work.

A formal letter bearing the same news arrived every other day. And then, a fortnight later when the headmaster came to her room with a telegram in his hand, she knew the end had come. She could not speak, her mind was frozen. Miss Williams came to take her to her lodgings, and as they passed the post office she suggested Ann ought to send a telegram home to say what time she would be arriving that evening. Ann had not been able to think about going home. They walked together up the hill without speaking. Her friend had no words to say since she had offered her sympathy in school. Mrs Beddoe took Ann into the kitchen and sat her down by the fire, and as she prepared some food she wept her heart out. Ann's brother was her own boy.

'Try and eat,' she said, placing a brimming bowl of hot soup before her, 'You've a long journey ahead of you.'

Ann ate the soup without tasting it, and she went upstairs to pack her bag. 'I'm so sorry,' said Mrs Beddoe as she walked Ann to the station, 'and that's all I can say. That's all anyone could say to me. What else is there to say?'

'Yes,' said Ann, 'no one can say more, it's too much for anyone to understand. We can only accept it and try to let it sink in. Later it will be hard.'

'Yes, you're right, and it almost gets worse with time.'

Miss Williams was at the station on her way home to lunch, and this time she spoke quickly.

'I'm very sorry, and so are all the staff, and here are some chocolates for you,' and she handed Ann a box. 'Try and keep your spirits up. It's easy for me to say, but you have to go on living, and your brother wouldn't want you to break your heart.'

Miss Williams's words meant nothing to Ann, but the fact that she and Mrs Beddoe were standing on the station touched her. They were there, and they were alive, trying to console her. She felt almost sorry for them.

'Thank you so much. Thank you so much.'

She collapsed weeping out loud into her seat on the train. Then she remembered Richard. She had spared him only a fleeting thought since last night. Bobi had obsessed her night and day for the past two weeks. There was room for nothing else, and now he more than filled her mind. Now that he was dead, she died herself in body, mind and spirit, shrouded in vast tragedy. It was inconceivable for her to stand outside herself, to think of Bobi as he was, gone from life. A great curtain of darkness she could not penetrate, and she herself was part of it. She remembered Richard as if she were sitting in the darkness calling him to her. She suddenly longed to see him. She took writing paper from her bag, and wrote him a letter. Once she began to write she could tell him nothing but the news and that she longed to have him at her side right now. There was nothing else to say, and she noticed what a small piece of paper she needed to express herself. Declarations of loyalty, that's all her letters had been until now. At that moment her only desire was to see Richard, feel his closeness, and know that someone who loved her still stood at her side on the face of the earth.

She wrote a brief note to Dora with the news, and one to Mrs Hughes. She stopped short of writing to Bess Morris, then thought of writing to Mrs Evans in Blaen Ddôl, and asking her to tell Bess Morris's family. She had done all this, and her journey seemed scarcely to have begun. It would be eleven o'clock by the time she reached Bangor, and she did not know if she would reach home that night. She longed for her journey to be over. She wasn't afraid to look pain in the face this time. She was part of it, and she knew it was only with her family she could face the pain and grieve. She knew they would all feel it differently, but that each one would know that a link in the chain had been broken. The train stopped at every little station, and shook every time she tried to sleep. As the journey went on the grief grew sharper, and sharpest of all was disappointment. She had imagined the chateau where Bobi had spent his happy weeks of recuperation, and these last two weeks she had tried to picture the fever hospital where they had sent him. Now, in the train, she saw it clearly, a grey building with no trees around it, no flowers bordering the paths, only concrete everywhere. She tried to imagine how Bobi had felt at the sight of such a building. Did he despair, or did hope survive, with only the thought of coming home to lift his spirits? Was he conscious enough to realise his wish would never be granted? Did he face the last shadows knowing this? As she reached that place, her imagination failed, and she began to weep again quietly.

She arrived in Bangor her body almost too stiff to stand on her feet. She was amazed to see her brother Huw waiting there for her. She had not for a moment expected anyone to meet her, but if she had she would have expected Roland. But of course, Huw and her father had been able to get home from Liverpool hours before her.

'Griffith Morris's brake is here to take us home,' was his greeting.

'That's good. It can't be slower than the train,' she said.

Neither spoke of the event that had made the brake necessary.

'You must be hungry.'

'No, Mrs Beddoe made me some sandwiches, but I couldn't eat them. How are Mam and Dad?'

'They are surprisingly well on the surface, but they must keep going for Roland's sake.'

'Why? Is he worse?'

'He had a fainting fit this morning. It was he who told us the news. I'd say it was a fit rather than passing out, going on Mam's description.'

'And she was alone in the house with him?'

'She ran at once to fetch a neighbour, and Roland regained consciousness.'

'Oh, heavens,' said Ann more to herself than her brother. And for a moment Roland's problem took the place of the other pain.

She sat in the brake opposite Huw, the shawl her mother had

given her brother about her shoulders. His face was like a carved head opposite her under the dark blue starry sky, sobered. For a long while they said nothing to each other, only watched the vague details of trees and fields, the houses in the villages through which they passed. The horses trotted on, the regular beat of their hooves on the road the only sound to be heard in the silence of the night. There were people still awake in the houses, as they could tell from the light that showed faintly here and there in a window through dark curtains or blue stained glass. The driver sat on the high seat in front, the nape of his neck nodding in rhythm with the trotting of the horses. To Ann the whole journey seemed like something out of Thomas Hardy, and although it was so familiar to her, tonight it was like driving through a ghost land. They reached town as the clock was striking midnight. There was no one abroad but the odd policeman; the last one she saw stared at them as if he had seen a ghost. Bobi might have been fast asleep at home tonight, Ann thought, but she refused to think ahead, and she did not look at the street where she had taken him out to supper that night for a treat. Half an hour more and they'd be home. For the rest of her life she would remember the details of that journey, Huw's pale face, the dimly lit windows, cats crossing the road with their eyes shining for a second in the reflection of the lamps of the brake, the driver's neck, the sound of the horse's hooves.

The light in her house was not weak. Ann did not hurry in. She dawdled along behind the fence before reaching the light of the kitchen where the three others were sitting by the fire. There was an expression of shocked fear on all three faces, and Roland was white as chalk. They wept to see Ann.

'There you are,' said her mother, 'Ann has come, we'll feel better now.'

'Yes we will,' said Roland, and he wiped his tears away.

There was food on the table, and her mother hurried to pour boiling water into the teapot.

'There's a bit of haddock in the small oven,' she said, 'we must try to eat.'

The five of them sat round the table and ate in silence. Ann lifted her head once or twice, and caught a tear in the corner of her father's eye, and her mother's face looked as if she had suffered a long illness. But for a moment something like peace came to her heart. She was home, and she knew that the thoughts of every one of them were with the one who was not there.

18

Cattle, pigs and hens cannot wait for grief. They have to be fed, and next morning everyone was up early to work. Ann and Roland were in the house, and the others were in the byre. Ann cleared away the ashes, blackleaded the grate and tidied the hearth, and Roland cut bread in the dairy ready to bring to the table once Ann had finished. Their minds full of one thought, their bodies moved automatically performing their tasks from long habit. Ann washed her hands and prepared breakfast, remembering as she did so that she used to do the same things ten years ago in her schooldays, each child having a task to do every morning. Her job was preparing breakfast, and Roland's job was to keep the kindling box full of heather to light the fire next day. Bobi's job was to help Ann to carry the dishes to the table, a cup and saucer at a time.

'Pity I can't have this every day in Ynys-y-Grug,' remarked Ann looking at the plate of bread-and-butter, the butter gleaming on the slices of bread.

'Is the food bad?'

'Awful, especially butter and bacon and the things I like best. You don't need anything else with this bread and butter.'

'No,' said Roland dreamily. 'It's been lovely here these past weeks, working out in the fields all day and coming in to good food like this. I've been in my element, and Mam was happy, having Bobi's cheerful letters and more cash in hand since Dad's working, and Dad enjoying himself too. And then something like this happens.'

'Yes, as if someone played a cruel trick on us.'

'What a pity Bobi could not have seen how good it is to be safe.'

'Well, young people never see it. They'd be old before their time if they saw it.'

'It hurts to realise I never had a chance to know him better these last years.'

'You couldn't help it. You were away.'

'I remember him as a little boy running after us, his legs too short to catch up with us, and Huw and I would hide so he wouldn't find us because he was too small to play with us, but he so wanted to play with the big boys. We were horrible to the poor little chap.'

'Children are horrible. I saw a lot of him when I was in Blaen Ddôl, and I'm so grateful for that now. He wasn't happy in that old shop.'

'Who could be happy in a shop? It's a real prison.'

'Yes,' said Ann smiling, 'but he fought one battle for his rights when that housekeeper gave them bad food. He was brave enough then.'

'Let's hope that courage was with him at the end.'

'Yes, especially when he had to move to that other old hospital.'

She went to the dairy pretending to fetch milk, but really to hide the fact that the burden in her heart was almost choking her. Talking to Roland about Bobi was like talking about somebody else, someone they knew but who had nothing to do with them, someone impersonal who was still alive. It was good to talk about him like that. She hoped Roland did not feel as she did. She had really known Bobi, and she had loved him, loved him as a baby learning to walk, loved him in the last years of his short life.

'I slept better last night,' said Roland, 'I no longer felt fear, the sort of fear that keeps you awake.'

'And me,' she said. She did not tell him how she had woken suddenly wondering why there was a pain in her heart. And when she remembered, she had plunged again into the misery she had felt before she slept.

The others returned, and they ate their breakfast of tea, bread-and-butter and marmalade in silence. Ann could taste her food today. The postman rang, and he brought a pile of letters. Her mother did not look at them.

'No need to fear bad news today,' she said, weeping as she turned her chair to the fire.

They were letters of condolence, mostly to Ann. Her parents' friends did not write letters, they called in. There was more comfort in those letters than Ann had thought possible. Yet, once the letters were read the comfort cooled, and she knew in her bones that the comfort had come from being the object of sympathy and the centre of attention. When she read them again the other feeling came.

When the men went out after breakfast Ann and her mother prepared dinner then sat down to talk. Her mother's feeling ranged from pity for Bobi to vengeful rage at those responsible for the war. 'The big men' she called them. Lloyd George took a beating. No-one in their house had a good word to say about him and his zeal for the war.

'Let Lloyd George and those big men send their own children,' she said.

'To be fair,' Ann replied, 'the sons of the big men have enlisted voluntarily.'

'But they don't care about their children like the poor. They haven't reared them, fed them at the breast, and there would be no war if it weren't for them. It's the poor who really suffer the depths of misery.'

Ann heard the words of John Morris Jones intoning in her ear, 'The weak must carry the candle.'

'But what's the use of talking,' said Mam, 'it won't bring my boy back.'

Then she was roused to fury.

'Do you know what that know-all in the school said?'

'No, I don't.'

'She came to see me the beginning of the week, knowing Bobi was seriously ill. 'It's all right for you,' she said, 'some people have lost their children.''

'The old busybody, what was she doing coming here?'

'That's what I asked her. She won't come again.'

'No, not if she has any kind of conscience.'

Her mother began to weep again.

'And I haven't been well,' she said.

'Oh, no, Mam. Oh, why?'

'Yes, an ulcer I think, and it's been bleeding.'

'Oh, Mam, didn't you send for the doctor?'

'No, it was better once it bled. That's the second time, and such pain before it broke both times.'

'Well indeed you must have the doctor.'

'He won't do me any good. He can't cure my pain.'

Ann looked serious. All this had happened without her knowing. Her mother spoke again.

'As long as I live I'll remember the smell of the hearth-rug. Every day after milking I'd come in and lie down on the hearth-rug to wait for the postman, just to do something to stop me going mad with waiting.'

It was Ann's turn to cry.

'It must have been terribly hard for you.'

'And your poor Dad.'

After dinner people began to call in. They came in ones and twos bringing sympathy and the customary little gift. Some brought only tears. They came like pilgrims to Bardsey, the holy island of Enlli, some who had never before been in the house. All brought sincere condolence. And Jane Davies, Guto's mother came too. For a moment Ann did not recognise her, and she realised she had never before seen her dressed up in her best clothes. She did not go out much. Her best clothes were old-fashioned. Her coat narrowed at the waist then flared out like a fan. Secured by a ribbon beneath her chin was a fur bow like a woolly-bear caterpillar curled up in a circle. On her head she wore a bonnet. Her skirt belonged to some indeterminate period of fashion. She sat in the armchair saying nothing for a long time, her mouth twisted like a child about to cry, a handkerchief in her hand. She did not remove her long gloves.

'I'd have come sooner,' she said, 'if only there were a tunnel from my house to yours.'

'I understand, Jane Davies. You have to face people on the way.'

'Yes, and they don't know what it's like, especially those whose children are still home.'

As she spoke she looked at the clock.

'Many's the time when I heard Bobi had been wounded I thought of coming. But I didn't. I didn't have the heart to dress up to come.'

If it weren't such a sad day Jane Davies's visit would have been funny, thought Ann. And yet the old lady was completely sincere. Guto was her grief.

Mrs Evans came from Blaen Ddôl, and she brought Bess Morris. The visit surprised Ann. She expected a letter, that's all. Such kindness made her forget all Mrs Evans's funny ways and the strange behaviour of Bess Morris when she had visited Blaen Ddôl in the early months of the war. She thought only how kind Mrs Evans had been to Bobi, and how Bess used to go for walks with her and had talked such cheerful good sense. This was a different Bess. Her face was thin and sad, but she looked Ann in the eyes, not avoiding her glance as she had last time they met. There was little chance to talk alone to her because the weather was not fine enough for them to go out over the fields. They all talked across each other, Mrs Evans praising Bobi. She had kept on writing to him.

'Is there a collection here?' asked Bess. 'I want to post a letter.'

'Yes, I'll come with you,' said Ann.

'It's not really important, but I want to talk to you.'

'It's good of you to come, Bess. I'll never forget the good times we had in Blaen Ddôl.'

'Yes. Everything's changed now. The world is going to hell fast. I thought the war would have made us more serious.'

'I'm sure all who have suffered have been sobered,' said Ann.

'Maybe, but some people want the war to go on because they're making money out of it. They're making a fortune from the high price of things like butter.'

'That's true, but it's not worth bothering about. They are beneath contempt today, and so they will be tomorrow. It's better to think only of the young men. They're not in it for the money. It's a fine thing to remember them.'

'No-one will remember them either, once the war is over. It's an evil world.'

'Not completely, Bess. Bobi's heart was innocent, never mind

226

the world. I only care about what I knew of him. You are not bad either or you wouldn't have come to see us.'

It did not seem to touch Bess. She looked down without speaking. She offered Ann no sympathy, though she must have felt something. Hers was a strange sickness.

19

She could just see the back of Roland's head disappearing up the steps as her train puffed out of the station. He did not turn to wave. No doubt he was hiding his feelings, and they'd had a sensible talk at the door of the train. They hatched a plot to get the doctor to visit their mother without her knowing: the excuse was simple, that the war authorities had sent him to examine Roland. Ann wrote to the doctor to explain the problem and to ask for his co-operation.

Her long journey began once again. She wished she could fall asleep and wake up in Ynys-y-Grug. The moment of family parting was not as bad as she had dreaded, perhaps because they were all anxious not to upset Roland. Her father and Huw would be leaving next day. Huw had not shed a tear, but had gone about looking stunned as he had in the brake a few nights ago. Her father seemed afraid to be alone, clinging like a leech to Huw and Roland, or talking as he hugged the fire, a look of yearning in his eyes when he wasn't speaking. It was her mother whose feelings poured out most fiercely, except when Roland was about. Ann thought it better for her to express her anger against the War Office, and against the chapel people who had not once written to Bobi in his sickness. The chapel had no minister. It was in such matters that Mr Hughes Blaen Ddôl had been so good.

Her thoughts turned to Mrs Hughes. Ann had half-expected to see her. Her letter had only arrived just before her departure, and it was quite unlike the other letters of condolence. She sympathised, yet she did not sympathise. She wrote of the inadequacy of words. 'I thought of coming to see you,' she said, 'but I knew I'd be no use to you with all those people there. And even if we had some time to ourselves I couldn't do much to help. You alone know what this bereavement means to you. I know you loved your brother, but love draws a ring around a person that excludes all others, and what right have I to break the circle and try to understand your feelings. Any more than people understood how I felt when I lost Dan. I doubt even Richard – and I know you love him too, in a different way – could understand or console you now. The only comfort I can offer is to say that you alone can help yourself through it, and the struggle will be hard. So many things will bring back the pain, you won't be able to believe he is really dead, and every time you remember there will be another pang of loss. And for you there will be the added pain of thinking of him dying in the war far from home. All I can say is you must bear it, you must get through it. I can't say if God's arms truly support us. I know some people believe that. I'm inclined to believe we must lift ourselves up, and that God gives us the strength indirectly to do it. That's God's gift. You are young, and the fact that your parents are going through a greater grief than yours should help you to comfort them, and that will bring comfort to you too. I know by now you must think I care nothing about you. I do feel, but it's so hard to help you. It's easy enough to string sweet words together, tender, sympathetic. But the older you get the more you read self-indulgence in letters of condolence, not deliberate selfishness, but the writers often let slip a word that betrays what a formality condolence is.'

A strange letter, thought Ann, but the more she thought about it the more it made sense. This was her first grief, the first gap in the family. The road was dark and unknown. Her friend spoke from experience. The people of Blaen Ddôl had never understood her. 'An impetuous, unwise woman,' they said, 'quite unsuitable to be the minister's wife.' If impetuosity were a short-cut to intuitive understanding, then Mrs Hughes was wise indeed. Others had written glibly of 'the help of the Lord in a time of adversity', and it sounded more like cliché than the voice of experience.

Letters from the children of Blaen Ddôl and Ynys-y-Grug gave her far more satisfaction. Most wrote simply that they were very sorry to hear the news, and that was all. One girl from Blaen Ddôl said that she was thinking about her, and an older boy from Ynys-y-Grug told her about his brother who had also been killed in the war, and how he could no longer remember him as grownup and a soldier, only as the schoolboy who shared his bed, and how cold his feet always were in winter.

Thinking of experience, and words learned by rote, Ann remembered a talk she'd had with Bess Morris when they were out walking one evening in Blaen Ddôl. Bess, good Churchwoman as she was, explained how the experience of those who wrote the Book of Common Prayer became the experience of the congregation. It was a new thought to Ann, and she could not wholly agree with her. The truth dawned on Ann now after reading Mrs Hughes's letter, her words certainly not learnt parrot-fashion from others. Perhaps that night Bess was expressing other people's ideas and not her own. That did not undermine the truth of it, but it might explain why Bess had not written to her since the outbreak of war, and it might explain her strange attitude. She set herself the problem of trying to analyse her friend's mind. She didn't want to be unkind to her. She could not feel as warmly for her as she felt for Mrs Hughes or Dora. She recalled how uncomfortable Bess had been with her colleagues at Blaen Ddôl school, but then she'd had good cause. She worked hard, never sparing herself, and was impatient with those who failed to do likewise. She had no brothers to be sent to the war. With as much energy as she put into school, so they said, she worked without rest on the committee of the comforts fund. She was bitter to see how others failed to work as hard. She was bitter that some people made money out of the war. But in the midst of this industry she had not a word of pity to spare. Disillusion had hardened her heart. Mrs Hughes had lost all patience with her. Surely there must be a cause of Bess Morris's strange attitude. To help pass the journey Ann wrote a letter to Mrs Hughes about Bess Morris, more as a mental exercise than anything else. Ann could not understand her friend well enough to sympathise with her either.

She finished the letter. The train stopped, and people got out, slamming the doors. Other people boarded the train standing in the corridor a moment to look through the glass before entering, their shadows darkening the compartment. In the stations the sound of chattering came in. Silence followed, and the shaking of the train as it blew steam into the air and started on its way again.

Ann closed her eyes and daydreamed. She was returning from a visit home to see Bobi, who had just come home. Joy overwhelmed her grateful heart. Next, Bobi was on the mend, and once he was fitted with an artificial leg he would find work. She would work her heart out to save money to give him a good start. The dream ended there, for she saw only monotony ahead for Bobi, his adventures over. She could not dream his future. There was joy only in dreaming him alive. She began to brood upon what his life might have been had he lived. She could not see any future for him. Was it enough merely to be alive? Wasn't it better to die while still anticipating life, than to exist joylessly, alive just for the sake of it?

Her thoughts brooded on darkness and pity. As Ynys-y-Grug drew closer, she considered her own immediate future. Tomorrow she must go to school and face the children and her colleagues. Neither children nor teachers would be as they had been a week ago. Death stood between them and made them strangers. She would find it hard to begin a conversation, to know what to say. She missed the warmth of home. For three days, three long days, she had been at home and although they had not talked much, together they had focused all their thoughts on Bobi. They had been like children playing at holding hands in a circle, turning round and round. The links of that circle would be broken one by one as he stood in the centre with their thoughts turning to him, wherever they happened to be.

Strange how little she'd thought of Richard these past days. It was too soon to expect a letter from him. He'd hardly had time to hear the news. Her conscience began to trouble her that she had shut him from her mind at a time when she should have held him close. She silenced her conscience. She didn't need his help. Mrs Hughes's letter had been right – he wouldn't understand. In a flash other thoughts interceded. She had drawn the curtains of her mind against him deliberately so that she would not need his help. He was at the front and in danger, lonely, friendless and homesick. He tended the wounded, men just like Bobi, and surely did his best for them. Men like him had treated Bobi kindly, and Roland too. Within the family she could afford to be wrapped up in herself. Even grief could be selfish, she thought. But somehow, despite these thoughts, she could not bring herself to write and tell Richard how she felt.

20

'Take heart, and try to eat,' said Richard.

They sat in a tea-shop in Aberdociau. Richard had been given unexpected leave from France and had come straight to Ynys-y-Grug. It was too late to stop him coming, even if she had wanted to. It was a dark Saturday in November, and they were sitting in a secluded corner eating haddock in white sauce with toast.

'I am. I'm enjoying it,' she said looking down at her plate.

'You don't look well.'

She lifted her eyes and looked over Richard's shoulder at a mirror on the wall. She was thinner, paler, there were hollows in her cheeks and her face seemed longer, the roundness gone, the chin sharp. She looked at her love's face then at her own, and she took his hand. When his telegram came it had shaken her out of her fastidious state of mind. She felt a surge of excitement she had not known before even in the dawn of her love. An excitement that took her breath away, as if she were meeting a stranger, a suffocating excitement as if she had run a hard race, and someone at the finishing line grasped her to prevent her falling.

'Ann, I'm so sorry. I couldn't help you in my letter. Words are useless at times like this. I can't get inside your heart. But do you feel any better now we're together?'

'I know you care, Richard, and Bobi would be glad we're together. But I can't stop myself dreaming the impossible, that he's sitting there beside you enjoying a meal with us. I walk the streets of Ynys-y-Grug talking to him, telling him about all the things I would like to do for him, the things he's never had that

I'd like to give him. Then I wake up and remember that now he'll never be able to enjoy the sort of things I'll have, and have had, for that matter.'

'I understand that very well. That's how I felt when I lost Mam. Yearning became dreams. She wouldn't die. She'd get better, and I would do everything for her. I'd take toast to her room on a tray and she'd smile gratefully. I can't tell you what it was like to see another woman in her place by the fire, my uncle sitting on the settle, his head in his hand, staring at the fire. I know he was thinking of my mother in his own way. Then the housekeeper would say, 'Off to bed, Richard.' 'Yes, you'd better go, my boy,' my uncle would add gently. So I went to bed and hid under the blankets to cry.'

'It must have been terrible for you, and you only a lad.'

'I remember in spring I always expected to see her coming through the gap with the cattle, wearing an apron and a little shawl round her neck, standing back to let the cows go ahead through the gap. I could never pass through that gap without thinking about her and how after she died I used to hope she would come. I can't forget that dream.'

A tear fell on her plate.

'Yes, you grieving, and only a child, and Bobi only a child dying. I keep thinking of him, so innocent and facing death without his family near. That's what really hurts. What if he knew he'd never come home, after living since he was wounded just for that moment?'

'Don't think about it, Ann. Bobi wasn't as immature as you think.'

'He was a child again in his illness.'

'Possibly, but you know, you can never tell what's in someone's mind as they face – when they're in that condition. I have watched many men die, some lose consciousness hours before they go, others are conscious to the end and glad to go. All we know is that their suffering is over now. We're trying to imagine something we haven't experienced.'

'But you can understand how I can't stop thinking about it, knowing that Bobi had time to think over his mistakes. I agree with Mam, I wish he'd been killed instantly, his pain over in a second.'

'In a way, yes. But it's all over now. It's all one to him. It's you suffering, not him.'

That gave her a moment's comfort.

'It's cruel for my parents. After working hard all their lives, something like this happens to hurt them so badly. There's so little for them to look forward to.'

'Have you heard how your mother is?'

'Yes, I heard from the doctor. She's better. She has a stomach ulcer, and he's persuaded her to eat better.'

She returned to her obsession.

'I thought everything would be fine once Bobi came home. There was no sign of Roland going back, and Huw had failed the medical. So if only Bobi were home everything would be fine. I thought of nothing else.'

'You never thought of anything happening to me?'

'To be completely honest, Richard, no, I didn't. I somehow thought you'd be safe in the RAMC, and also, I can't explain, but from the very beginning, the moment Bobi enlisted, I knew he would never come back. I know it's silly, superstitious talk, but from the day I left college I've felt tremendously vulnerable about Bobi. I'll never forget his first communion, he was leaving childhood behind and I wanted to cry out loud. It's as if my sympathy failed to keep him safe, and sympathy, rather than fate, had driven him to his doom.'

Richard looked hurt.

'Ann, you can see I wasn't safe either. It's true that the shrapnel in my leg is nothing, but others like me have been killed.'

'I'm sorry, Richard, I don't know what's the matter with me. Recently Dora and I had a long talk, and in our opinion our whole lives are twisted. When I left college I was looking forward to a better life, not for me but for the family, and this has spoilt it forever. So it was natural for me to exclude everyone else.'

'Even me?'

She bowed her head.

'I know I'm wrapped up in myself, Richard, but I can't help it.'

'The worst thing for people like us is being forced to wait to marry. If we were married we'd have a family of our own. We can't grow up, leave our families and childhood behind. I know it's tougher for you, of course. The best thing we can do now is look forward to the future, if only to distract our minds from the present. Remember, a rigid mind drove Bess Morris to the state she's in now.'

'I don't know. She's become very strange.'

'According to you she's a girl who believes in helping others.'

'Yes.'

'And her only way to help with the war, since she had no-one in the army, was to help the soldiers, and as she discovered, not everyone shared her enthusiasm.'

'Yes, I suppose so.'

'The best thing she could have done was give up school and go nursing close to the Front. She could have given her energy to work like that, and felt the satisfaction people get from sacrificing their lives. She saw others doing so little, while she longed to do more.'

'Should I do the same, to keep my mind off myself and my family?'

'Oh, no. You don't know what to think of the war any more than I do, and you've already made your sacrifice. Bess Morris doesn't really love anybody, does she?'

'No, I don't think so. She is a placid girl who believes in doing her duty in all circumstances.'

Richard laughed.

'I seem to be trying to psychoanalyse you all and myself too. But dear Ann,' and he took her hand, 'I know one thing, only time will show you life is still worth living.'

'Yes, you've been through it. For me it's the first time. If I can only regain my sense of proportion you will fill my life once more. I feel shattered now. But Richard, it is so good to be with you.'

'It was worth coming home from France just to hear that. Hello! There's Dora,' said Richard looking towards the door.

Dora walked towards their table. Ann felt shy. It was the first time she had seen her friend since Bobi died. Dora had written her a warm letter of condolence, with no hint of animosity about their opposing views on the war. Now she looked Ann in the eyes and searched her face as if expecting to find her changed.

'I came here because I was bored alone in the house. I've only just arrived.'

'Stay and have a bite with us, Dora. We haven't finished.'

'No, we can start again,' said Richard happily.

Dora protested.

'No, you'll want to spend as much time as possible on your own.'

'There's no rush today. I've had a little accident and injured my leg in France, and I'm home for a while this time. Ann will get tired of me.'

He looked at Ann mischievously.

'What happened?'

'Well, I and another man got too close to the Front to carry a boy who'd been wounded, and a piece of shrapnel came out of the blue as I was crawling on my hands and knees.'

'What about the others?'

'Luckily only I was hit.'

'Did the boy recover?'

'Yes, or at least he's on the mend.'

Dora asked the same questions as Ann had asked the previous night.

'How is Harri?' Ann asked.

'Oh, he's in trouble again for attacking a sergeant. He's up in arms against everyone. In the beginning it was just the war he was against. Since changing his mind he's against everyone. The war, the English, the Welsh, the Germans, everybody.'

They all laughed, her words conjuring for Ann a perfect picture of the Harri she knew.

'A pity he couldn't do something to get himself sent home for good,' said Dora.

Richard fell silent, then broke the silence by turning the conversation to college days.

They all went to catch the same train, Dora getting out before them. Ann noticed that for all its cheerfulness Dora's face was becoming lined. There was an expression of yearning about her as she looked at Richard. She probably envied Ann.

'Harri had better watch out,' said Richard when Dora had gone. 'That's not the way to get home. The danger is he'll be killed by a British bullet.'

Ann shivered.

'That's Harri, always against everybody. He has a grudge against the world. I heard he came from an unhappy home, his father was violent to his mother. But why are we talking about other people tonight?'

He put his arm through hers. The intimacy of his touch warmed her heart, and for tonight at least she could forget her troubles. She was sad to leave him at the house, and to watch him turn away to walk to his own lodgings. She felt she would sleep tonight, and morning would come, Sunday morning, and she would see Richard again, earlier this time.

21

Ann discovered that eventually grief must settle down and life must go on. On the surface the waters appeared calm, the silt undisturbed. She had to teach the children and prepare them for their examinations. She worked harder than ever in order to forget and slumped exhausted in her chair as soon as she got home to her digs. Meagre rations did not help, but somehow she found the energy to go to evening meetings, and to mark the children's schoolwork. Miss Williams came to see her, and sometimes other teachers visited. Little changed in the staffroom at school, only one or two leaving to join the army. Some of the villagers later called to see her. They avoided mentioning the reason for their visit, speaking of other things rather than cause her pain. Neither did she speak of her grief. There was too much pain about in other people's lives. The fighting in France raged fiercely on, ships were mined at sea, and there were bombing raids over London and the East of England. She knew, in the roots of her being, that her grief was as deep as if nobody else in the world suffered, and though considering the suffering thousands did not diminish her own pain one jot, it kept her quiet about it in front of others. She was glad to hear the preacher say in chapel one Sunday morning that pain could not be multiplied, that one person's pain was as great as the pain of two hundred. These words were like a pat on the back, and they validated her own thoughts.

Richard's visit helped. They'd spent two quiet days, staying in her lodgings most of the time, talking over tea and supper. Little by little she could imagine him filling her life again, and for a moment she felt she was back in Blaen Ddôl and Richard on a visit from Bangor on his bicycle, one bright morning before the war darkened the world. It looked as if he would be spending some time in England because of his injured leg. He wrote regularly. He spent two days in Anglesey. Roland found work on a neighbouring farm and slept at home each night. Considering these matters Ann realised that those anxieties which had troubled her as the year opened had resolved themselves like vulgar fractions, except for one figure which would not go, would not fit any of the sums. It remained unresolved, refusing to submit to calculation.

Frequent letters arrived from Mrs Hughes, their frequency rather than their substance proof of her understanding, her implicit sympathy, as after Richard visited his old home she'd praised him lavishly if obliquely, compassion filtering through the words. Richard, she wrote, was so very concerned about Ann.

Then the depths were stirred by unexpected letters. The Mediterranean moved closer to Wales bringing details of Bobi's last days. Letters from the chaplain, the nurse who was with him when he died, letters from the boys who were with him on board ship on the voyage to Melita, a letter from a friend in the army wounded at the same time, who had been with him the whole time from Kinmel to the last hospital but one, and a letter from the nurse who had tended him in Salonika, and who had moved to London after he had been moved, and did not know he was dead. She asked after him, could he come to London some time, could she have his address so that should he ever find himself down her way she could visit him. Roland had sent all these letters on to Ann. All were proof of his popularity, but to Ann they were like letters in praise of a stranger, someone she did not know. The only thing she recognised was his endearing quality. The Bobi they described was somebody else. His young soldier friend described him best, in his boyish, almost childish letter, telling how they went everywhere together, and how, seeing Bobi moved to another hospital, he had cried his heart out. Bobi was a stranger in the photographs taken on board ship. Leaning on the arm of another soldier, his face long and marked by pain, his teeth looking as if they did not belong to him. The writer of that letter told how, as the weakest lad on board, he had been cared for by everyone, taken below deck to protect him from the enemy. He'd obviously been everyone's baby.

But these letters were sweet compared to the one from the nurse who was with him when he died. It was a cruel letter, wallowing in emotion, describing how Bobi prayed as he died, calling out his mother's name. From the moment she read this letter something like madness possessed her heart. She could have pulled her own hair out by the roots to think of Bobi driven into that narrow corner. She hoped Roland had not translated the letter for her mother. Before this her grief had been quiet, but now it burned and consumed her like a fire. She wrote at once to Richard. Just waiting for his reply was traumatic enough to drive her to prayer.

His answer came by return of post, and it was a comfort to her.

'I know her sort,' he wrote, 'I've seen plenty like her. Children of the well-off gone out as nurses, some of them seeing suffering for the first time in their lives, and all they can do is cry and make things worse with their false feelings, their melodramatic talk, as if they were acting in a play and the war gave them a chance to look pain in the eye. Were she herself in pain it would be a different story.'

A few days later the arrival of another letter and a parcel confirmed Richard's words. They came from the man in the next bed to Bobi when he died, a Welshman, according to his name, and he forwarded to Ann the letters and possessions that had been in Bobi's bedside cupboard. He'd read her address on one of the letters, and thought he would post everything to her instead of home. He'd heard so much about her from Bobi. He talked about the doctor, how good he had been, how he had moved Bobi's bed close to the door of his own room, how he had stayed with him through the night at the end. There was no word about a nurse, but he described how Bobi had fought to the end, and how more than once it seemed that he might defeat his illness. In the parcel, with the letters, were his comb and his toothbrush, and the red Army handkerchief, with traces of food on it. By now Ann felt ready to look at these personal things, though the pocket handkerchief was intimate with his last breath. She would burn it, rather than send it home.

The letters were from family and friends, many of them from her. If he had kept every one he had obviously not received all her letters, and she remembered him saying once how he waited and waited to hear from her, when all the time she had been writing to him two or three times a week, even when he could no longer answer them.

Among them was a letter written in a child-like hand from someone called Jennie who lived not far from their home. A little love letter clumsily written but full of longing. It was the only letter from her in the parcel, dated soon after Bobi had been sent overseas. Maybe he had destroyed other letters from the girl, or perhaps they were at the bottom of the sea like many of her own letters. The address did not suggest the girl was someone he'd met while he was stationed at Kinmel. Ann wondered who she was. Then she suddenly remembered how she and Bobi had gone to the eisteddfod meeting on Christmas night and how she had lost him among the crowd as they came out, and how he had arrived home later, breathless from running. The truth dawned on her. He had taken the girl home, forgetting his sister and everybody else. She had never known him do that before. She wanted to meet Jennie. Perhaps she too grieved and longed for him, and maybe they could meet and share their feelings. Without a second thought Ann wrote to ask her if they could meet and have tea together in town during the Christmas holidays.

At last came the reply, a cold, hard answer. She had not written again to Bobi when she heard he had been wounded. She did not see the point of continuing to write to Bobi, when he couldn't write back, and she had another boyfriend now. She was sorry to hear Bobi had died, but even had he come home she would not have seen him again.

The only thing that could be said for this letter was that Jennie had not been hypocritical enough to agree to a meeting. For Ann, not to meet her was reason for rejoicing. What it meant to Bobi waiting in vain to receive letters from Jennie, nobody would ever know. Before sending the parcel home she burnt the pocket handkerchief, and Jennie's letter to her brother.

She wrote at length to Richard, pouring out her heart, without thinking that it might cause him pain. Her imagination opened up the hospitals and the ships on the Mediterranean, visited every chaplain, nurse, friend, entered every room and opened every cupboard. She tried to enter Bobi's heart, and stopped herself in that place on the border of darkness and ignorance, that place where she must wait, imagining but never going in. Her head throbbed. Then there was Richard, alive, resilient. If she tried to discover his feelings, he could answer, the door would open revealing one who tried to understand and who loved her. Yet her mind followed Bobi, drawing a screen between her and Richard.

22

Ann's peace of mind was destroyed by the brooch. It arrived after all the other things, sent by a Welsh soldier who decided there was less risk of its being lost packed on its own than if it had been included with a letter. He had heard Bobi say he'd bought it to give his sister when he arrived home. He wanted to buy something for his mother too, something more fitting than a brooch, but he fell ill before he could do it. The brooch was oval, intricately worked in porcelain in a mosaic of flowers with blue petals and white centres, set so close together you couldn't get a needle between them. Not a petal was more than a twelfth of an inch across. It was not set in gold but held firm by its own intricate design.

It was yet another image of Bobi in that last month of his life. The brooch brought with it joy and pain and its beauty was not made of one or the other. Even had it been ugly it would have made her happy because it came from Bobi, not the Bobi who had denied her on the night of the chapel eisteddfod, and who had been so distant with her that Christmas, but dear Bobi who had treasured all that she gave him, every sixpenny piece, every meal, Bobi who thought of her in the distant parts of the world, so far from Wales. Now she wept that he had not been able to bring it home himself and watch her face light with pleasure. He obviously thought nothing of Jennie who had not written to him. It was Ann he remembered. She was glad to know that at least some of her postal orders must have reached him, since he must have had money to buy something like this. The more she looked at it the more she sorrowed. It was a symbol of hope, of loving thoughts, of looking forward to coming home. Gazing at it now, in its box, she saw the pattern of disappointment. She decided she could never wear it, but would cherish it in its box like a withered flower.

Every day she opened the box and gazed at the flower. The design was perfect, the porcelain so fine and bright. She wondered at the artist who could fit such tiny pieces together. She held it knowing Bobi's hands had held it too. And gazing at the intricacy of the pattern she remembered the platitudes preached in chapel, that the war was a part of God's design. She had accepted such statements without question, but now her whole nature cried out against them. She could not believe such cruelty to be part of God's design, and there were people all over the world suffering as she suffered now. Millions and millions of people expected their children to come home, and their hopes were dashed. It was impossible that God had planned it. Had He wished to purify the world through fire, He would have burnt those who caused the carnage and not the innocent. So if it was all the work of men, why had God not prevented it? Was He therefore a helpless God? There came no answer.

She wrote again to Richard, expecting no comfort. In his reply to her earlier letter he had tried and failed to help her. She needed someone to write to, to put her doubts into words even if she had no hope of satisfaction. Seeing them on paper seemed to crystallise them and made them look more reasonable. She was Counsel for the Prosecution, and God was the accused. The letter brought Richard to Ynys-y-Grug in person. She did not expect him, but was not surprised to see him. She felt no antipathy to him. Her bitterness was turned in another direction. Nor could she bring herself to speak a single tender word to Richard.

The weather was cold but they could not talk in the house, so they argued their way along the dark streets. He tried to persuade her to put such things out of her mind, to give up brooding on such matters, to let them go because in the end her questions were leading her nowhere.

'But I can't. It would be easier for me to say I don't exist on this earth. Since I do exist, I want to know why God treats human beings like this.'

'We'll never understand it, Ann. It's not our place to understand.'

'But we're taught God is all-powerful. So why doesn't He stop the war?'

'Did you read that article by Dr.—- in *Y Beirniad*?'

'No, I avoid reading anything about the war.'

'Well, Ann, in your present state of mind it would do you good to read it.'

'Why? What does he say?'

'In brief, that having given us free will God can't withdraw it, so humanity must take responsibility for human actions.'

'And allow us to destroy ourselves?'

'It's mankind's fault, not God's.'

'But surely God could prevent the suffering of the innocent?'

'There's no evidence He's ever done so, but there's plenty of evidence that He helps the innocent to endure bravely and behave like heroes.'

'That's no comfort to anybody.'

'Yes, it is, Ann. I don't think of the Lord as someone who keeps an eye on people and prevents the wicked harming the innocent.'

'You just said you don't understand anything, and now you are trying to understand.'

'Not with my mind, but with my faith. Have you ever thought what sort of world it would be if we understood it all completely?'

'Yes, very boring.'

'It wouldn't be worth living in. There would be no room for faith, and faith is important to me. It's easy to give half a crown here and a shilling there, but to believe is difficult.'

'Don't think, Richard, that I've stopped believing in God, but I don't trust Him any more. He's a friend who's let me down.'

'Trust will come back, Ann.'

'No, it won't,' she answered stubbornly.

'I don't know. I'd like to comfort you, but the way you are now I can't help you. I came down here thinking my presence might help, quite apart from what I'm trying to say.'

'I'm sorry Richard, but I can't change tonight.'

'We are young, Ann, inexperienced, and this great load is placed on our backs before we've had a chance to learn anything. Sitting at the bedside of some wounded soldier in France, I tried to think things through, though I could see no sense in so many young men suffering there. All I could see was that people like you and me must find our own happiness, and never depend on luck or on things outside ourselves.'

'But our families are more than luck or accident. They are part of us.'

'Yes, Ann, I know that, but the day must come, you know your Bible, when we must leave our families behind, and when we must decide that our love is enough to make us cleave together forsaking all others. It is cruel to say so.'

'Yes it is. But I know you're right.'

'And remember, Ann, you won't help your family if you go on like this.'

'I never speak a word about my feelings to them. I try to lift their spirits in my letters. I'm afraid I burden you.'

'No, it shows where you turn for comfort, even if I can't give it to you.'

He went home with her to her lodging house for supper. She went to her room to fetch the brooch to show it to him.

'Oh! I'm so glad to see it,' he said, 'I didn't like to ask.'

They stood under the light gazing at it, their heads leaning together, and he put his arm around her shoulders.

'It's wonderful, such a little thing. What a dear boy he was, and the thought behind it is beyond price, something to keep you close to him forever.'

'Yes, he was a dear boy.' And she could say it this time without tears choking her throat. Richard looked into her eyes.

'Oh Ann, I so wish I could take the sorrow from your eyes.'

They sat down to a supper of boiled eggs with toast and dripping.

'It's impossible to have anything better than this, Richard, and the dripping is miles better than butter. Mrs Beddoe boils a marrow bone and when the stock cools she skims the fat from the surface and puts it in with the Sunday roast, and that's how she makes this good dripping.'

'It's delicious, Ann bach, and to eat it here with you is very heaven. Do you feel better now?'

'I do. And it's good to be together, in spite of everything.'

'I love you so much, Ann. That's all I can say.'

23

Christmas came and Ann was home again. She sat with her mother by the fire after washing up the dinner dishes. Her father had gone to bed, and Huw and Roland were getting ready to go to the eisteddfod.

'Aren't you going, Ann?'

'No, I don't feel like it.'

'It was hard work making the boys go too, but someone should think about it.'

Ann agreed, but she just could not face it. Never before had they had a Christmas dinner like this one. The food was appetising enough, and there was plenty of it for once, but they had dined in silence, and when they did speak their words were as disconnected as telegrams. Dry talk, small talk, talk to hide what overwhelmed their minds. Far better, Ann thought, had they spoken openly, mingling the simple feast with their tears. Perhaps they feared to open the floodgates. She was glad when the meal was over, and sad that such delicious fare had been swallowed without pleasure.

The hearth was warm, fuel piled high, the grate gleaming, a new rug laid down the day before on top of the old one to give deeper comfort underfoot. Cooking aromas lingered about the oven, and in the old peat-well beside the fire clean clothes were airing. Her mother was better too, perhaps because grief was less dangerous than worry. But she was thin, and she ate very little.

'Well,' she said, 'the first Christmas without Bobi.'

There were no tears in her eyes or in her voice.

'We can do no more. Yesterday will never come back. But he's never out of my mind.'

'Nor mine,' said Ann.

'I can still see him in those hospitals as if he were a baby. It's as an innocent child I like to think of him, and maybe I should be thankful he was given a chance. He'd been able to hope, and he was looking forward to things, even if he never came home.'

Ann failed to understand her mother's attitude. The disappointment after hope had bewildered her. She wondered was her mother clinging to the last straw of comfort, a very doubtful comfort, in order to survive at all? There was something at the same time heartbreaking and consoling in the new things she had bought to cheer the house. The hearthrug, the teaset, the tablecloth. True, some things had been bought while they were still expecting Bobi to come home, and some after news of his death. Was this her mother's way of trying to shake herself out of grieving? She knew how much her mother loved things she could touch with her hands, dishes and fabrics, pats of butter and loaves of bread, and all her life she had linked such things with family happiness. Pretty china shone in the glass-fronted cupboard because she valued her home, and she valued home because she loved her family. Her spiritual life was earthy, thought Ann, not materialistic, but physical and earthy because through such things she gave happiness to those she loved.

'They say Bobi's better off where he is,' her mother said after a moment.

'They say so because they can't think of anything else to say,' said Ann.

'Yes, I know Bobi would have preferred to be home with us. He was so fond of his home, I don't know what possessed him to leave it.'

'Yes, it's hard to understand.'

'Your Dad and I have been talking about leaving this place, and finding a cottage without land to live in. Your father's spirit is broken, and he's so tired. He was exhausted when he got home last night.'

'Yes, he has aged.'

'But I'd hate to leave this house after all these years. If Bobi came home it's here he'd come looking for us and not to some strange house.'

Ann burst into tears. In her mother's words she found her excuse to let go the sorrows which had overwhelmed her heart since she saw Richard in Ynys-y-Grug. She had been happy enough in his company that night as they ate their supper and looked at the brooch together, and she had been comforted by his words and to see how much he loved her. But her heart had not responded to him. When he left she felt colder than a lump of ice. She knew she wasn't the sort of woman to stay frozen. She had been churned by powerful inner passions about one thing or another ever since the day she left college. She had never felt content except in Richard's company in the days before the war. She gazed and gazed at his face over the supper table that night in Ynys-y-Grug, seeing how much better he looked since he came home from France, and beyond his face she saw Bobi's wasted face like a shadow, long-suffering and innocent. The vision came back to her, and she found herself thinking that Richard had no right to be alive, and Bobi dead. She grew envious of his health and his escape from the perils of the war while Bobi . . . Such thoughts poisoned her, and broke her.

'There you are, you'll feel better now,' said Mam. 'We were locking up our feelings all through dinner. Let's have tea early, and maybe your father will wake up by then.'

Ann went out to prepare the tea. She fetched the new teaset. She placed the butter near the fire to soften. Her mother cut the bread, and put a loaf of bara brith on the table. The big black kettle was soon singing, its sound rising like nostalgia in the great fireplace as it had always done. Her father came down smiling to see the tea table.

'I feel much better now,' he said.

And neither of them asked him, 'better than when?'

They understood very well. This meal was different. Because the children had always gone out to the Chapel meeting on Christmas afternoon, it carried no memories. For a little while Ann could sweep away all envy and all bitterness, as she always wished to do but always failed when she took Holy Communion. Another feeling possessed her, a feeling of closeness to her father and mother, a feeling that the family would endure though it was no longer complete. She never wanted to leave this feeling of unity, and though she knew Richard was in Anglesey, she felt no desire to see him. To see him would bring home her bitterness. She would visit neighbours tonight, Jane Davies perhaps. She'd be glad of company, her first Christmas without Guto. Yet to stay home was like a healing syrup, bitter to taste, but sweet in its effect. Her mother had talked of leaving to live in a cottage, and maybe they would be settled in there by next Christmas, a house without hens, without a pig, without cows, without fields, without the fields they had walked for so many years. Everything would be different, and nothing would be left but the living and their memories of the old life. It turned her heart over. She would not go out tonight, she would visit Jane Davies tomorrow. If she went now the old lady would make her stay for supper, and she wanted to eat supper at home – early this time, not like other Christmas nights when they had all rushed home starving from the Chapel meeting. Sitting there at the tea table with her parents was like having a cold poultice on her brow when she had a sick headache, easing the pain a little.

She felt guilty about Richard now. She ought to meet him somewhere tomorrow, but she would not. This time she did not write to him to unburden her troubled mind. He was the problem now, and she could hardly write and tell him how jealous she felt that he was alive while Bobi was dead. Perhaps if she kept her distance these envious feelings would fade away. But what would come to take their place? Would other feelings replace her bitterness? She no longer laid the blame on God or felt anything for Him one way or the other, and the conversation in Ynys-y-Grug seemed no more than theology and as cold as Sunday School. Then she recalled what the woman in Anglesey had said, that Richard was hard. Had that foolish woman hit on the truth with her nonsense? She longed to see Mrs Hughes whom she had not met since Bobi's death, but not if Richard were there. She knew she was cruel, but took no pleasure in her cruelty. She existed, that's all, a cold lump, merciless. She longed to feel tenderness, but felt that there was only one river-bed where the waters of her heart could flow and that was towards her mother and father. She had an idea how they felt, but was not so sure she could be a soothing oil to them.

Before supper she went out for a walk. The night was dark and starry. There were few lights, but she knew at once where the town would be, and the prow of the Castle over the river. She knew roughly where Richard's house lay. What was he doing now? Reading by the fire, or talking with Mrs Hughes, talking about her perhaps. Perhaps he hated her. The thought hurt, till she saw how unreasonable that was. He had every right to hate her, if it came to it. A letter had arrived from him that very morning, friendly enough, but not warm. He was disappointed, he said, that nothing he could say had consoled her, and still more disappointed that she did not want to see him. He did not want to impose himself upon her, and he felt it best to keep away, in the hope that some light would break for her, if not from him then from some other source, and that one day she would be able to see things in their proper perspective. She wanted this too, and it was the one part of his letter which made her feel some of the old warmth towards him.

There was no sight nor sound of anyone on the road. They were all at the eisteddfod or home by the fire. The sky was so full of stars it made her giddy. The mountains of Snowdonia were one with the sky, the cart-track one with the bog. Nothing was distinct. Her eyes grew used to the darkness. The hedgerows sharpened. She turned back. The lights of Holyhead twinkled. There were men in peril on the sea, men fighting (perhaps not, for today hostilities might have been suspended), all far from home, some with the hope of fighting men, and some, like Bobi, without hope. As she turned in at the gate she caught a glimpse of the smooth flat stone where she used to sit when she was eight years old, with Bobi in his shawl in her arms. She could feel the silky skin of his face against her cheek and his soft hair tickling her eye. She hurried inside. The lamp with its gleaming glass shade shone on the table, supper was laid, Huw and Roland had come home early from the eisteddfod – too boring to stay to the end, they said – and just like in the old days, they were starving.

24

'This house is fine in summer, but it's like a sieve in the winter,' said Mrs Hughes, sliding the small mat with her foot closer to the door between the back kitchen and the best kitchen.

'It's very cosy with you,' said Ann, looking at the heavy curtains hanging on the middle door and on the front door.

'It's been a real blessing to me and the children anyway, and Richard has been so kind.'

It was the first time his name had been spoken between them since she arrived at her lover's home two hours ago, when he was already on his way back to camp. It was a cold day, the wind whipping along the road from the station. She thought of that day in summer when she and Richard had walked the same road when hope was real and alive. Today she had longed to reach her journey's end to talk to someone who would see it all from *her* point of view. When, the day after Christmas, her mother asked her if she intended seeing Richard, she'd said nothing, just that she didn't feel like it. Her mother's look had told her that she didn't accept such a bare explanation, as if she were excusing herself from no more than the Chapel Meeting. She knew what her mother was thinking, though she asked no more questions.

She, Mrs Hughes and the children were about to have supper, rice baked in the oven with melted cheese on top. The oil lamp shone on the white tablecloth, casting its pool of light as far as it could reach, then it ceased. The fire blazing in the grate and the heavy chenille curtains made the kitchen feel cosy. The children looked happy, growing fast, their faces filling out. Their mother was not as sturdy as she had been, and there was a dazed look about her. Her expression no longer changed from moment to moment, and since Ann arrived her voice had kept a level monotone. It was as if she had reached a state of being from which she could not wake. She gave Ann a small, formal smile. When she looked at her children her face brightened. Ann had never seen her like this in Blaen Ddôl. Nevertheless her table was as immaculate, her welcome as warm as ever.

When the children had gone to bed, Ann thought again of Blaen Ddôl and fireside talk. There was something special about a conversation with Mrs Hughes that Ann relished, and which could shake her from her despondence like sparks stirred from a dead fire. Not that tonight she could hope for more than a little understanding.

'What's gone wrong between you and Richard?' was the first question.

It wasn't what Ann expected and she was taken aback. It was a lawyer's question suggesting a rift. In Ann's mind there was no such thing as a rift between her and Richard.

'As far as I know nothing's gone wrong between him and me.'

'You didn't see him over Christmas, did you?'

'No, I couldn't.'

'I suppose you think I'm a busybody.'

Ann said nothing. She had not expected this.

'I haven't quarrelled with him, if that's what you're thinking.'

'A quarrel is not the worst thing that can happen between lovers. Coldness is worse.'

'Yes, and jealousy is worse still.'

Mrs Hughes looked startled and she coloured a little.

'Jealous? Jealous of whom?'

'Of Richard. Oh, I know I'll never make anyone understand how I feel. I've been through hell since Bobi died. Neither you nor anyone else understands how I felt about Bobi.'

'I know you were very fond of him.'

'Oh, it's more than that. He never had a chance, but what's the point of trying to explain? He lost more than his life, and in losing him we lost more than Bobi, and I can't help feeling it's so unfair that Richard is alive and Bobi is dead.'

'Ann, you're not saying you want Richard dead too?'

'No, I want both of them alive. But as one of them has gone I'd have more peace of mind if they were both dead.'

'I'm afraid I don't follow you, Ann. Doesn't Richard comfort you in your sorrow?'

'Nobody can, except those who grieve for Bobi with me. These days there's only comfort at home. We're all in the same boat.'

'Richard is terribly worried about you, that I do know, though he didn't say much. His silence probably spoke volumes.'

'Yes, I know he's doing his best to help. But it's cold comfort he talks, like Sunday School. The words sound cold and hard. It's all right for him to be brave about suffering. At least he's alive.'

Mrs Hughes raised her eyebrows.

'Would you like him to pour empty pity over you? Those are the hard people in my opinion.'

'There must be a middle way,' said Ann.

'Remember, Ann, it's not his grief. In the end we have to get on with our own grieving, that's my experience, and he had to go through it when he was only a child.'

'Yes I know, and now I can imagine what he must have suffered. But I wish he'd come down from his pulpit.'

'He's trying to get you to see reason.'

'Things like this don't belong to reason. Where's the reason in sending children away from home to get killed for something they don't understand at all.'

'You must look outside yourself, Ann. It's a great big world and there's plenty of suffering out there. There are thousands of lads like Bobi. Use your imagination and try to think about the others.'

'The world's not my responsibility. I know nothing about it and I don't care about it. My upbringing has taught me to love my home, every inch of it. Why did they send Bobi so far away to die?'

'Yes,' said Mrs Hughes, poking the fire, 'that's the sort of people we are, we Welsh. We're a narrow people, and our world is limited. That's what it was all about when you drank that glass of rum in the pub.'

'No,' replied Ann passionately, 'we are an ancient people, and history really matters to us. It's not at all like the glass of rum. People from the old nations can enjoy themselves. They like to sing and be in each other's company, and of course the pub. But we are forced to follow powerful nations all over the world instead of staying home and being happy.'

'I'm trying to cheer you up, Ann,' said Mrs Hughes more warmly this time, 'because you're looking awful, and wearing black makes you look even worse, and Richard looked terrible too at Christmas time. It would be so lovely to see you two become friends again. You don't hate Richard, do you Ann?'

'No. Hatred burns and there would be some hope that I might get over it. I feel worse than that. What's poisoning me is cold.'

'You're so far away I think I'd better leave you alone. I don't know if you're capable of sympathising with Richard. I'm absolutely sure you're the only one who can help him, and that he needs you more than anyone.'

'Oh,' said Ann, closing her eyes. 'Pity is a boat that carries you away then brings you home again. I have sympathised and sympathised, and for what? Only to find myself lying on my own bed of ice. I would love to feel for Richard, but he'd be no happier seeing me trying to feel if it doesn't come naturally. My feelings have to be real.'

Mrs Hughes rose to poke the fire, and raked beneath it.

'Look, I'm going to make us another cup of tea and some toast. We'll put the cups on the hearth and the bread on to toast.'

They waited for the kettle to boil without speaking a word. Mrs Hughes placed a chair next to Ann.

'I'm sure you think I'm very impertinent, Ann.'

'If I thought that I'd have stopped talking to you by now. It's good to be able to be so free with a friend. You never know, perhaps by talking like this I'll come to my senses. I don't need to be told I'm wrong. I just need to talk.'

'Yes, I think you're right. I've been quizzing you like a

lawyer trying to trip you up. Since I had a hint that things were not going well between you I've been longing to get you together again, because I know you, and because I've got to know Richard well enough to realise what a fine young man he is, and I think it would be a tragedy if you two split up. But I can see now that whatever one's character it makes no difference. If people don't want each other they should part. Richard is a lovely man though,' she added, as if she did not really believe what she had said.

'However perfect he is, I can't feel close to him tonight,' said Ann. 'The dead lie between us.'

'Well,' said Mrs Hughes, 'in time the dead grow further away from us. It is a cruel fact, but it's true. Remember, Ann, you can banish yourself so far that no-one will want you.'

In bed Ann turned their conversation over and over in her mind. Mrs Hughes lay beside her, and close by in her small bed her daughter slept peacefully. Ann was afraid to turn over in case she woke one of them. Occasionally there came a sound they had grown used to, the sound of an air-ship taking off from Cefn Du bound for some destination. Her mind led her all round the world, returning always to one place, the place where Bobi was buried. She was lying in bed in her lover's house, the place that had once been his childhood paradise. She had no right to be here. She was trespassing in a place which for him was full of memories, and as a trespasser the only value was what she could derive from here. She had come for what she could get, friendship, advice, sympathy. She was selfish, and her selfishness excluded all reason. Beside her lay a woman who had lost the man she'd loved and who had loved her, a woman who must go on living and bring up two children on the pension of a minister's widow, yet she was grateful for a cold house to live in. The universe was full of unfathomable mysteries. Would the dawn ever come? Would she, after all, spend the summer here with Richard, in this house, and feel again that she could not live without him? At that moment she was certain it would take a miracle to make it happen.

25

One cold Sunday morning Ann sat daydreaming before a roaring fire in her lodging house in Ynys-y-Grug. She had just finished writing letters. She hadn't gone to chapel. After yesterday's icy wind she still could not hear properly, and the same wind blew today, a bitter, sunless east wind that swirled black dust from the road in small clouds which came to rest in the corners of the doors. She was grateful there was no shortage of coal in Ynys-y-Grug. The fire radiated heat into the heart of the room, a fire that was beautiful to see, fierce red beneath and the small coal piled up like glowing gems.

She would have to shake herself out of it and go to Sunday School this afternoon. Her mind returned to yesterday, not a unique moment in her life, but part of its dispiriting routine. Dora had come, and they'd climbed the slopes on the far side of the valley and over the summits into the next valley. Both felt the need to walk, though only crazy people would have gone on such a walk on a day like that. Both were restless to be moving, rather than be still, though for different reasons, it's true. Both had something on their minds, and preferred to walk and talk rather than sit and talk, because walking meant they need not give too much away. They could keep their secrets if they did not have to look each other in the eye.

They walked in the teeth of the wind, and it pierced their clothes and blew dust into their eyes. Sometimes they turned their backs on it to stop it burning the skin of their faces. Once they lay down on the ground where they found a brief moment of shelter from it. Then they set off again along the open, unhedged road. They burst out laughing as they admitted what fools they were, the road and the mountain theirs alone. At last they reached a village, a mere four terraced rows of identical houses, and on one house a sign that said teas were served there. It seemed miraculous, because there was nothing else in the village to attract a visitor. Yet there was one person in that village with enough faith that a traveller would wander down out of the gloom, someone drawn perhaps to the solitude of the mountains. They went in and asked for tea.

'Of course,' said the friendly woman, 'but there's no fire in the parlour, so you'll have to come into the kitchen.'

'That's fine,' they said.

Three colliers were sitting by the kitchen fire, unwashed from the pit. Seeing the visitors they rose and went out. The woman made the tea while they warmed themselves at the fire. However, it was impossible for them to talk over their tea while she was fussing about them chatting, so they were soon on their way again, much warmer now. As they went out through the door they noticed the three men squatting on their haunches in the open while they were drinking their tea, and they laughed about it for a while as they went on their way.

To Ann, looking back on it today, there was something callous in the thought that they had walked the lonely hills and had tea while there was so much trouble in the world. They could not hear each other very well on the road home, and Dora had done most of the talking. Harri had left the army, registered once more as a conscientious objector, and was awaiting a tribunal. Dora felt happier, she said, that Harri had done exactly what she hoped he would do, and without any influence from her. She talked on, her voice mingling with the wind. She talked about evil, and about how happy she was that Harri had returned to his old beliefs. Ann was silent, thinking all the time only of Bobi. But when Dora remarked that she was surprised Ann had not changed her opinion now she'd lost a brother, she burst out.

'None of it will bring Bobi back, that's what I think about all the time, and my opinion on the war can make no difference one way or another.'

'I'd have thought the fact that the war took your brother would have turned you against it.'

'That could never make up for what's happened.'

'But it might help prevent another war.'

'Never while there are men on the face of the earth.'

Well, that's it, Ann thought, if it comforted Dora, let her find solace in it. But Ann was not so sure if it was Harri's stand for his principles or his safe haven from the dangers of war that had made her friend happy. It would be all too easy to make oneself believe they were one and the same thing.

Had Dora said that to work for one's convictions helped to forget grief, she would have believed her. That would be her salvation. It would give life a purpose. Her life was without purpose, in school, in chapel, in the village. She had no driving faith, only the need to pass time, trailing her memories behind her. It was a road without direction, a road without end, not a road to stroll along. Even yesterday afternoon with Dora had not been a stroll, just a walk along a length of the same monotonous road. She could remember a time when such a walk in the hills would have satisfied her soul as a mother giving breast to a baby in the middle of churning butter. She remembered how often she had seen that happen when Bobi was a baby, and how he would stop sucking to laugh in his mother's face, and beat her breast with his hand.

She was absorbed in these thoughts when there came a tap on the window, and Miss Williams stood holding a letter in her hand. Ann went to open the door. She had not looked in the letter-box today. She was not expecting a letter, and was surprised to see the envelope from Richard.

'Come by the fire and warm yourself.'

'You didn't go to chapel this morning.'

'No.' And Ann told her the story of the previous day's walk.

'I can well believe it. I know that place very well. Emily Bronte could have set her novel there. I suppose you wouldn't care to come out for a walk with me this afternoon?'

'I was thinking of going to Sunday School, but I don't feel like leaving the fire.'

'Yours is a better fire than mine.'

'Look, Miss Williams,' said Ann, 'come and have tea with me, and we can take a ten-minute walk first. Mrs Beddoe has bought me a cupboard to keep my dishes and food in, so it'll be no trouble.'

'Are you sure? That would be lovely. And we could have a talk.'

Ann was in no haste to open Richard's letter. She already owed him a reply. They still wrote to each other, infrequently on her part; she could not bring herself to finish with him completely. She had intended writing to him this evening to tell him about Harri, and other things. On the previous day she had noticed a slight difference in her feelings after months of being emotionally frozen. During that walk she had felt a small glimmer of longing for Richard's company. Dora's chatter had been so opinionated. Richard's conversation would have been more hesitant and more in tune with her own. She felt a little gleam of desire for Richard himself, even if she were to say nothing at all to him.

She opened his letter casually. It was only a brief note. He too had gone out walking on his own the previous day, away from the camp and into the countryside, and early in the afternoon he'd reached a little village, rather like the village they had found together near Shrewsbury. He had gone into a pub and asked for tea. He was so cold he ordered a large glass of rum to warm himself before he had his tea.

'I've finished my tea,' he said, 'and I have to write to you, Ann. I can't stop myself. The cold weather, the rum and a good tea have brought you back to me, you as you were in the pub in Blaen Ddôl that night, laughing out loud and saying how good life was. We little knew that night what lay ahead for us, and we lived for the moment looking neither ahead nor behind us. That is how I like to remember you, and I will treasure those moments and keep them with me. I would like to take you back to that time again. I know nothing can ever be the same, and the sorrows of these past few years must stand between us and those light-hearted days, and at least for me that is all the more reason why we should be together, taking what happiness we can, together, not apart.'

She let the letter slip from her hand. No wonder she had longed for his company the previous day. And then there began to flow through her, like a gentle stream, an awakening emotion, and at that moment she would have given the world for Richard's presence. She wanted him more than anyone in the world. This was the miracle, a sudden, unexpected, overwhelming surge of feeling. She could not explain it. It was there, that's all.

From the kitchen came sweet smells of dinner cooking, and Mrs Beddoe came in with the tablecloth and cutlery. Ann decided against going to Sunday School. She would for once neglect the dull road of duty, and she looked forward to Miss Williams's company for tea. She knew when to avoid talking about the war. And then, tonight, she would write to Richard, and would pour out her heart. The news about Harri would be no more than an excuse to tell him how much better a man he, Richard, was.

26

The peace which overcame her was a mystery to Ann. It came like a gentle shower of rain, its effect as refreshing, even though it was in no hurry. Instead of regretting that she had invited Miss Williams to tea, she was looking forward to it, as though it was a part of the blessing from the shower of rain. She was in no hurry to write her letter to Richard. Indeed, maybe it was better if she didn't.

She did not go to Sunday School. She sat before the fire and basked in her feelings without trying to discover whence they had come, accepting them as thirsty lips accept a drink of cold water. She sat drinking till her thirst was quenched.

She enjoyed seeing Miss Williams and listening to her talk. She was wearing the same coat and skirt that she had worn when they both went to London, and a white *Luvisca* blouse with a collar which showed her throat. She enjoyed the tea, she enjoyed the talk, and for once Ann did not feel jealous of her air of success or the aura of well-being which surrounded her. Her gentility and tone of voice were soothing to Ann's spirits, a voice which was rather monotone like her mother's, yet without the effect of a monotonous voice because everything she said was interesting. Today Miss Williams's attitude to the War did not raise Ann's hackles as it usually did, an attitude which took war to be as natural as washing and as necessary. Today she spoke of the women who worked for the War. She had a little fun at their expense, women who thought they could win the war just by wearing a uniform. The subject was not one which gave Ann any particular pleasure, but it more than helped to pass the time. It was a connection between her and the world outside her grief. It was entertaining, and proof that Miss Williams enjoyed coming to tea with her even though she was quiet. As she looked at her Ann decided she must wear something other than the black satin blouse she was used to wearing with her black coat and skirt, though it was a pretty blouse. It did not show up her dark hair. As if she could read her mind Miss Williams spoke.

'You should wear a white blouse, Ann. That's a lovely blouse, but it makes you look so pale and so melancholy.'

'That's just what I was thinking, though it has matched my feelings till now.'

'Your hair is so black, and you change with the clothes you wear. White suits you.'

'Yes. That's what Richard says.'

She was happy to have spoken his name.

'How is he?'

'He is well. He is in this country at the moment,' and she added with pleasure, 'luckily.'

'I do hope he won't have to go overseas again. You've had quite enough.'

'I hope so too,' she said with feeling.

'You're looking happier today.'

'Yes, I'm feeling better.'

But she did not tell Miss Williams the reason for this change. Indeed, her friend knew nothing of the coolness which had been between her and Richard.

They went to the evening service together. Ann listened, but she could not remember hearing a word of it. Yet she could not miss chapel tonight. The service seemed to act as an accompaniment to the gratitude which poured through her heart. She felt no need to rush away and on the way out she lingered a moment in the porch. At that moment she felt a longing to write to Richard, and at once it came over her like the longing to race home from chapel on Sunday nights to a tasty supper, and suddenly she thought of Roland and her mother at home, and Roland no doubt running home from chapel at this very moment, just like her.

Writing to Richard was not so easy after all. It was up to her to apologise, and yet, it seemed to her, she could not have changed how she felt. This could not be a letter full of news, like her recent letters. Harri's doings were news enough, but she knew Richard would not be very interested in him. Her mind returned to yesterday and to Dora. She had shown little interest in Dora's problems or sympathised with her about Harri. It was difficult to know what her friend's feelings really were. Did she worry that Harri changed with the wind, or was she proud that he had come round to her feelings about the war. She seemed happy. But perhaps she would have felt happy either way because it was Harri she wanted and nobody else, so it did not matter to her what he did or how many times he changed his mind. She had not stood by Richard like that, though he had been so unflinching all the way. It was she who was more like Harri, yet not like Harri either. A cloud had passed over the sun of her love. The sun was still there, she'd had enough proof of that since this morning. The cloud too was there, but it was moving. It could easily float back again, no doubt.

Her conscience once more began to trouble her about Bess Morris. She had done nothing to try and understand her distress. She recalled their friendship in Blaen Ddôl, their walks and talks, their shared feelings about school. She should have written to her more often. She could have overlooked her opinions and just remembered their friendship. There was always something to come between people, and they could not look beyond it to take the broader view rather than concentrate on a little quarrel.

Then she considered her own life. It only took a few minutes because it was so short. It was like a quiet meadow. It was not without its troubles and its confrontations, but these had passed by without leaving scars, things soon forgotten in the kindly breeze that blew over her now like the spirit of good will which held kith and kin together. Today she saw that the meadow was in two parts, and to pass between them she must cross the deep dividing ditch. Richard was on the far side, and Mrs Hughes and Dora and Bess Morris, though quite close to the nearer bank of the ditch. Tonight something told her that Richard would belong mostly to that other side, and that he would grow more important. For him the sheltered part of the meadow was very small, and the ditch scarred the early part of his life. If she could find the strength she would make that far side of the meadow more sheltering for him in every way. She saw now that Bobi belonged to her but not to Richard, that he had never belonged to him and never would. To her Bobi would be a treasure like the brooch in its box, something to look at still, but less often as life went on.

She thought about writing all this to Richard and trying to explain the feelings that caused her behaviour. Then second thoughts. That would be self-righteous. They had both tried to do too much analysing instead of trusting to instinct. The inexplicable could not be explained.

So she wrote a short note saying only that she had a great longing to see him. She went to bed and slept peacefully. She woke next day feeling just as she had when she posted her letter.

A telegram arrived. 'Bless you. Letter to follow.'

The letter was more than a balm to her spirit. It was the key to a new life. It was full of fresh energy and excitement as he wrote of a new beginning. And arrangements to meet somewhere half way between them no matter how cold the weather.

They were lucky to find a cafe in a village in the heart of the countryside, quite deserted that day because it was so cold. They ordered dinner and tea, and let the two meals almost run into each other with nothing but a walk in between to warm their feet. Ann could always talk better over a meal, but this time the happiness in Richard's face brought a lump to her throat as she thought of how she had withheld this joy from him for so long.

'You know, Ann, all I want is to look at your face today. I'll never forget Tuesday morning when I had your letter.'

'I'm not going to try and explain anything to you, Richard. I can't.'

'There's no need. I've tried to understand, and I can see it's impossible. Bobi was your treasure, loaned to me briefly through you . . .'

'You have been long-suffering.'

'Not a second too long, but it wasn't patience. It was something more, something which held us together, the same thing which holds your family together, though different.'

'Yes. I can see that now, but I have been most unkind to you . . .'

'It belongs very closely to love. No, Ann, I think all the more of you because of it, because it shows how you feel things to the quick. Had you been able to dismiss Bobi's death lightly, I would not have thought much of you.'

'That's such a comfort, because I know there are those who would call it something else, they'd call it selfishness.'

'There's a place for selfishness in some things. There's another way of looking at it, Ann. You and I belong to Wales, Wales has no politics of its own, only the politics of another nation. So we don't know why we are fighting this war. Of course there are many Welsh people who think England is our country, and they see things as the English do. The Irish knew why they were fighting, and I suppose the families of those who died did not think their sacrifice was in vain. Your grief would not have been so terrible if Bobi had died for Wales. Don't you think so, Ann?'

'Yes, I believe so,' said Ann, her voice trembling. 'There would be less disillusion, and maybe he would have fought better, facing up to the enemy rather than fleeing from a boring life for the sake of adventure.'

'Forgive me, Ann, if I've hurt you talking bluntly like that, but it's better to accept Bobi's death than avoid it. It's the way to rid yourself of dread.'

'I'm sure you're right. I've been longing for something I can never have back, and not thinking of the future.'

'One must yearn. It's natural. But Bobi will always be a child to you, and you will grow old, I hope. Perhaps, had Bobi grown older, he would not have meant so much to you. That's no consolation, of course. It was his life, and he would have enjoyed it.'

'Yes, he would,' she said thoughtfully, 'and maybe some selfish Jennie would have got hold of him. But he too might have enjoyed giving in to selfishness.'

'Well,' he said, 'we can never know, and we can't tell what the dead have missed. There are hard times ahead of us yet. The war has cost so much, and someone will have to pay for it. The future won't be all honey. But Ann I think you and I will find happiness yet, and together. I have seen many things since the war began, and if there's one thing I've realised it is that the world is very big and full of people who are different from us, their patterns and standards are different. I don't say we are better, but I believe some things will be quite changed when it's over. There'll be a break with the past, people will leave their homes and will not look back. Home will no longer mean anything to them. Knowing this makes me all the keener to hold on to the old ways, and to cling to home.'

'Oh, Richard, it is good to hear you say that.'

'I long for a home of my own, Ann. I've been without one since I was a boy, and I can't think of anyone but you to make a home with me, and the sooner the better.'

She saw a new life opening before her, the new life which once came to her father and mother, the new life which would come to Dora, and to her brothers no doubt. She could think of no-one but Richard to accompany her on such an adventure. She said nothing.

He continued, 'You were never meant to spend your whole life teaching children, or to shut yourself off from the world. That is what I was afraid would happen to you, turning your back on all pleasure and doing things that were alien to your nature, sacrificing your life on the altar of duty. I know very well how you can enjoy yourself. Laughter will come back, Ann, mingled with other things, but it will come, and you'll promise me now that we can marry soon, won't you? There's one bit of good news. I heard this week that I don't have to go back to the battle. I couldn't run fast enough with this limp. I will probably never have to go overseas again. So promise, Ann?'

'Promise,' she said, without looking into his eyes.

This time parting was difficult for both of them. Already they were in the second part of their lives. Their life had been one bright morning, Ann thought, and its beauty had protected them, but whether from tumultuous thunderstorms or the cloudless heat of the sun that came with the second part of their lives, she would ensure they sheltered each other. And it was in that spirit that she returned to Ynys-y-Grug, her feelings strong enough now to face the future.